Select praise for the novels of Viola Shipman

"A beautifully written story about second chances. Fans of women's fiction won't be able to put this down."

—*Publishers Weekly* on *The Secret of Snow*

"Viola Shipman knows relationships. *The Clover Girls* will sometimes make you smile and other times cry, but like a true friendship, it is a novel you will forever savor and treasure."

—**Mary Alice Monroe,** *New York Times* **bestselling author**

"Viola Shipman has written a love song to long-lost friends, an ode to the summers that define us and the people who make us who we are. The minute I finished *The Clover Girls*, I ordered copies for all my friends. It's that good."

—**Kristy Woodson Harvey,** *New York Times* **bestselling author**

"Reading Viola Shipman's novels is like talking with your best friend and wanting never to hang up the phone. *The Clover Girls* is [Shipman's] most beautiful novel yet, and [the] most important."

—**Nancy Thayer,** *New York Times* **bestselling author**

"Oh, the joy! *The Clover Girls* may be [Shipman's] best yet, taking readers on a heartwarming trip down memory lane… Ideal for summer… A redemptive tale, celebrating the power of friendship while focusing on what matters most. Perfect for the beach!"

—*New York Journal of Books*

"Every now and then a new voice in fiction arrives to completely charm, entertain and remind us what matters. Viola Shipman is that voice and *The Summer Cottage* is that absolutely irresistible and necessary novel… [It] brings us the astounding importance of home and underscores the importance of a loving family and of having a generous heart. Grab a glass of sweet tea and enjoy!"

—**Dorothea Benton Frank,** *New York Times* **bestselling author**

"Shipman's evocative novel is a love letter to Michigan summers, past and present, and to the value of lifelong friendships. A blissful summer read sure to please the author's many fans, and fans of writers like Elin Hilderbrand or Kristin Hannah."

—*Library Journal* on *The Heirloom Garden*

VIOLA SHIPMAN

a
wish
for
winter

GRAYDON
HOUSE

GRAYDON
HOUSE®

ISBN-13: 978-1-525-80484-7

Recycling programs
for this product may
not exist in your area.

A Wish for Winter
Copyright © 2022 by Viola Shipman

A Sugarplum Christmas
Copyright © 2022 by Viola Shipman

Graydon House
22 Adelaide St. West, 41st Floor
Toronto, Ontario M5H 4E3, Canada
www.GraydonHouseBooks.com
www.BookClubbish.com

Printed in U.S.A.

A winter wish for my readers:

May your darkest days always be filled with light

May your home always be filled with family and love

May your holidays always be filled with memories new and old

May your coldest days be filled with warmth

May a great book always be sitting near a roaring fire

And may you always remember how unique, beautiful and loved you are.

Thank you for your continued love and support!

a wish for winter

1st PRIZE
PETOSKEY ELEMENTARY SCHOOL
CHRISTMAS POETRY CONTEST

"The Single Kringle"
By Susan Norcross
4th Grade

My parents and grandparents told me
One day I would know
Because I'll meet a man whose beard
Would be white as snow.

His eyes would twinkle,
And his laugh would boom,
He'd make me feel like
The only gift in the room.

He will love me for me
Be generous and kind
And always let me
Read my books and speak my mind.

He may not have reindeer
Nor live at the North Pole
But he'll be filled with love
And have a good soul.

They said to love myself first
But to know a puzzle can still miss a piece
That hints at a picture
But never is complete.

They told me to believe
Especially in December
For that is the time
We celebrate and remember.

We light trees and bake cookies
Buy gifts for sister and brother
But the only gift that matters
Is the gift of each other.

That's the beauty of Christmas
And magic of St. Nick
We must remain as hopeful as kids
So our hearts don't become bricks.

Santa Claus is pure love
But he, too, once was single
He knew he was blessed
When he found his Mrs. Kringle.

I'll know the exact moment, too,
Because my heart will glisten like the bay
Bells will ring
And I'll hear Santa's sleigh.

People say Santa isn't real
But he was a man named St. Nicholas
To think otherwise
Is purely ridiculous.

We must believe in angels
Because faith is no game
There is purpose beyond us
Otherwise life is a shame.

How does one make
A wish come true?
By believing in others
But also believing in you.

So, until my day comes
I'll remain happy and bright
And I will believe in my Kringle
With all of my might.

prologue

Every family has a holiday tradition.

Some families bake sugar cookies and cut them out in the shapes of bells and reindeer, icing them a mile high and decorating them with colored candies and glittery sprinkles.

Other families decorate their trees with heirloom ornaments, telling the stories of where each Shiny Brite originated. Some drench their entire house and yard with lights à la Clark Griswold, while others go caroling or head to midnight mass on Christmas Eve.

The Norcross family dressed as Mr. and Mrs. Claus.

Starting the day after Thanksgiving, my parents and grandparents became—and I mean this quite literally—the Clauses.

23andMe may have said our family came from somewhere in Europe, but we knew better. We came from the North Pole.

Our blood was made of eggnog, our souls shone as bright as foil wrapping paper and our hearts were filled with Christmas spirit.

In fact, one of my ancestors—my great-great-grandfather—was known as Captain Santa. He operated a three-masted schooner—the sails lit by oil lamps made to look like holiday lights, the masts festooned with garland, the boat a floating forest—that famously sank during the holidays. It had been weighted down by a load of Northern Michigan evergreens bound for Chicago. His nickname had been bestowed on him by Chicago's newspapers for his generosity in giving the trees to families in need.

The foundation of my family tree has also been hope.

We were so Santa that my grandfather and father had been bestowed the name Nicholas. We were so Kringle that the very first time my mother and grandmother met the loves of their lives both men were dressed as Santa.

They may not have known what they looked like underneath the hat and beard, but they could see his good soul clearly.

My parents and grandparents rotated December days dressing as Mr. and Mrs. Claus, one set going from school to school and hotel to hotel while the other managed our bookstore. I was always the cheery elf in candy cane–striped stockings, a curled cap and a green dress with peppermint buttons, holding a tiny plastic hammer.

I would watch children from all over Northern Michigan crawl upon my dad and grampa's laps and whisper what they'd like for Christmas.

Every holiday, my family would gather to watch *Miracle on 34th Street*. It was our tradition.

And every night the week before Christmas, when a Claus would tuck me into bed, he or she would whisper, "There's a Single Kringle out there just waiting for you. It's destiny in our family. And one day you will find your Santa, and every day for the rest of your life—no matter the day of the year—will be as magical as Christmas day."

And then a Claus would ask, "What is your Christmas wish, Susan?"

I would prattle off a list of toys or dresses, never realizing until too late none of those wishes really mattered.

Today, as an adult, I shut my eyes every night the week leading up to Christmas and before I go to bed silently ask myself, *What is your Christmas wish, Susan?*

And I whisper to myself, "All I wish is for Christmas to be the way it used to."

chapter 1

This is *not* my Christmas wish.

"You drive a Smart car?"

"I do. Fits into any parking spot in Chicago. Come on. Get in."

I bend and contort, banging my head as I enter. I'm a tall girl, so getting into a car this small is like trying to break down a refrigerator box and stuff it into a recycling container. Moreover, I'm squeezed into a brand-new dress that Holly sent me from Chicago. It's very short, holiday gold and a touch too low-cut for my usual standards.

You gotta show the girls while you have a chance, Holly told me.

This is my best friend Holly's holiday wish.

Every year, I grant Holly one wish: she asks me to participate with her in Chicago's famed Santa Run in hopes that I will find a man dressed as Kris Kringle just like my mother and grandmother. Every year is an epic failure. So much so that I have recently sworn off dating. But since this is our fortieth Christmas on earth, Holly begged for an extra wish, which I reluctantly granted: a date with Cletus Bothwhistle.

Holly worked with Cletus on a social media launch in Chicago, and he was the trademark attorney. She said he loved the holidays, had family in nearby Gaylord, Michigan, about forty-five minutes due south and inland of Petoskey. His sister had recently had a baby, and Cletus was a doting new uncle. Holly told my grandparents this tidbit, and they all saw this as a sign of a good, caring man. Not to mention, Cletus was sporting a Santa cap in a Christmas party picture that Holly sent to seal the deal. Between the good-willed—albeit constant—prodding of Holly and my grandparents, I simply gave up. Overwhelmed with the bookstore at the holidays, my willpower was shot.

"I've never met anyone who lives in a pink house," Cletus says staring at my old Victorian.

"It's historic," I say. "Always been pink. Locals call it The Pink Lady."

"Looks like a Barbie Dreamhouse." Cletus leans into the door. "You're my Barbie, and I'm your dream."

I should not have had him pick me up at my house. I usually have my blind dates pick me up at the bookstore. It just seems safer. My grandparents and staff can suss them out first, let me know if there needs to be a "bookstore emergency." It's a number one rule of mine. Never let them know where you live.

"You in?" Cletus asks.

He shuts the door before I can even respond, and when I reach for my seat belt, I realize my hair is caught in the car door. I open it as he walks around the other side, and I free

my long blonde hair—which I've just spent an hour curling—
as he gets in on the other side.

His car door slams.

Well, *slam* would be a generous term. It sounds like the top
on a new bottle of ketchup just popped.

"Surprise!"

I turn toward Cletus.

At some point between shutting the door on my hair and
walking around the car, he's put on a Santa hat. I stare at
him, realizing now that his pictures on Facebook were obviously old.

Really old.

I remember now that he was wearing a Nehru collar in the
photo Holly sent me.

It's not that he's a troll or anything, it's just that he looks
closer to sixty than forty, he doesn't look to be an avid exer-
ciser and it's been years since Holly has seen him in person.

Stop it, Susan, I think. *Give him a chance. You never give anyone a chance anymore.*

"Everyone in town says you're the lady who's going to
marry a Santa! Ho ho ho! Here I am!"

"My reputation precedes me," I say.

"So, tell me about Susan Norcross," he says as he drives.

"Well, I am a just-turned forty-year-old bookstore owner
who loves books, authors and reading. I'm an avid runner.
And as you mentioned, I am famous—no, strike that—*infamous* around my hometown of Petoskey, Michigan, for being
the woman whose mother and grandmother both married
men who the first time they met happened to be dressed as
Santa Claus. I think everyone, including Holly, wants lightning to strike thrice."

"I once got hit by lightning," he says. "On the golf course.

I used to caddy during the summers in Gaylord. Everyone says that's why I'm extra bright."

I laugh, assuming he's kidding.

"I'm not kidding," he says.

For some reason, when Cletus is not talking, he is sucking air through his teeth, as if he just ate a pound of ground pepper and is trying to clean them.

I just want to be struck by lightning right now.

"I can't believe I'm on a date with the Single Kringle," he says.

"You can call me Susan," I say with a laugh. "It's easier."

"Susan it is," he says, continuing to free something from his teeth.

"Why don't we turn on some holiday music?" I suggest.

"Great idea!"

"Where are we going?" I ask.

"Oh, it's a surprise," he says, his voice chipper. "Can't give away the ending."

My heart lifts. As a bookstore owner, I love readers who don't walk in and jump to the end of a book.

"I agree," I say.

He heads the car toward Traverse City. The tiny car is buffeted around as we hit the road by the bay. Gale-force winds rock us back and forth, and I grip the passenger side of the car as we occasionally fishtail on the snowy road.

You cannot have a small car in Michigan in the winter. Yes, you can drive a convertible around for a few months in the summer, but a small car can't handle the nonstop pummeling of Michigan's winter weather. It's the equivalent of taking a syringe to Lake Michigan and trying to drain all the water out of it.

It just ain't gonna get the job done.

I chitchat to distract myself, peppering him—pardon the

pun——with lots of questions as I do readers who come into my bookstore.

Finally, Cletus pulls into the parking of the restaurant chain, That's A Mice Pizza.

"Is there something wrong with your car?" I ask. *This can't be our destination.*

"Surprise!"

"Surprise what?"

"We're here! I wanted to do something unexpected for our first date."

That's A Mice Pizza is a pizza parlor-arcade for children. That's actually being generous. It's an amusement park that serves cardboard cheese.

We're greeted by a costumed mouse who ushers us to the front.

"We have reservations," Cletus says excitedly. "Two for Bothwhistle."

A girl in bad goth makeup looks at me and says, "Wow, you look really nice."

I cock my head at her compliment, my first tonight. "Thank you so much."

"But your dress is probably going to get dirty or, like, ruined," she says. "I mean…"

She stops and points a black fingernail into the restaurant. It's chaos.

Children are running around screaming, bashing each other over the head with rubber bats and stuffed animals, chucking ice at one another and sneezing as if sneezing were just invented.

I emit a single, tiny, mournful squeak, but Cletus says to the girl, "And we had a bag of tokens, too." He looks at me. "I can't give these to you, though, until dinner's over."

We are seated smack-dab in the middle of four kids' parties. Two are birthday parties, one is a Christmas party and one Hanukkah party. It's like being seated in the eye of a hurricane. I take a seat in a plastic chair, and I instantly feel sets of eyes on me and my dress. I take the napkin off the table and drape it over my cleavage.

"I'm a sloppy eater," I say to Cletus.

Cletus orders two pizzas with "the works," and he tells me all the games he's going to play when we're done.

When the pizza arrives, the server grates some cheese on top at Cletus's request. When he begins to leave the table, Cletus says, "No, my man, make it rain."

The server begins to grate cheese until both pizzas are nicely covered. When he starts to leave again, Cletus says, "Your arm's gonna hurt by the time you're done."

The pizzas begin to disappear under a cloud of too-orange cheese.

"Sir, I gotta stop," the kid says. "I got a cramp the size of Detroit."

Cletus quickly downs a piece of pizza and starts on the second.

"Hi?"

I look up, and a little girl is standing before me holding a red balloon. "Is it your birthday, too?" she asks sweetly.

I nod and smile because I don't want her to be scarred in the future when she recalls the vacant look in my eyes. She hands me the balloon.

"Thank you, sweetheart."

When Cletus excuses himself to go to the bathroom, I pick up my cell and text Holly.

I'm at It's A Mice Pizza.

Three dots float and then—

What? The kids' place?

Yes, I type. I'm wearing your dress. I feel naked in here. And he just ate so much cheese, I'm worried he has an obstruction.

NO! I'm so sorry. But he was wearing a Santa hat!

He still is. How long has it been since you saw him in person?

A few years. He doesn't look like his pictures?

His yearbook photo was tin type.

I'm SO sorry. I keep saying that, don't I? Maybe he's a really nice guy. Give it a shot! Please. For me! You do this every time.

No, YOU do this every time. More later. Pray for me.

After dinner, a server brings out a cake covered in candles and decorated with an iced Santa cap. Words are written in cursive beneath it that read "Am I the One, Single Kringle?"

His brazenness—after just knowing each other for less than an hour—shakes me.

"Cletus, this is way too much," I say. "I'm a bit taken aback."

"Just make a wish," Cletus says, "and blow out the candles. Please. For me."

I shut my eyes and blow.

I wish this date were over.

"Our date has only begun!" Cletus declares.

He leads me to the arcade and hands me a bag of gold tokens. I love to play games with my family and friends, but shooting hoops and whacking moles in a dress and high heels is not my idea of a great first—or any—date.

But I am, to pardon another pun, game. My life has been

rooted in hope. I'm always game. Even if a little boy has just wiped his hands on the bottom of my dress.

I feel as if I've just about made it to the finish line, when I hear over the intercom, "Susan Norcross! Please make your way to the animatronic stage!"

I look at Cletus. "What is going on?"

"Can't spoil the surprise."

We walk over to a dark stage. It's a tiny, low-slung stage, actually, a Halloween mini Snickers version of a kids' stage where children might perform karaoke or a costumed mouse would sing Happy Birthday and dance.

"What is going on?"

"I planned this all for you," he says. "Get up there."

"Cletus," I say. "Please stop. The cake, this place, now this. I'm overwhelmed."

"I went to a lot of effort," he says.

I head up the steps and stand on the dark stage. Suddenly, the lights pop on, and animatronic mice—which I didn't notice in the shadows—spring to life. Mariah Carey's "All I Want for Christmas Is You" begins to play.

Two costumed mice jump from the wings, place a Santa cap on my head, take my arms and begin to kick.

As the music swells, a crowd begins to take seats in the folding chairs before the stage. Suddenly, I feel just like I'm in a cartoon version of *Mean Girls* when they sing "Jingle Bell Rock" in the high school Christmas talent contest.

Over the music, I hear a little boy yell, "Mommy, why is that old woman on stage trying to dance with the Nice Mice?"

I start to laugh, because children don't lie and play games. They're honest. They say exactly what they're thinking. I usually do as well. But when I'm on a date and a Santa hat is involved, I believe—despite all the pain of my past—that a miracle can happen.

I step off the stage. "I'm ready to call it a night," I say to Cletus. "I'm tired. Long drive. Long week."

Despite everything, Cletus hints at a second date on the drive home.

"You know," I start, "I really don't know much about you. What do you like to read?" I ask. "Who are some of your favorite authors?"

"Oh, I hate to read," he says. "Total waste of time."

My head silently explodes. "I don't understand."

"I'm much too busy to read," Cletus says. "What can a book teach me that I already don't know."

I don't intend to, but I shout, "Everything!"

He looks over at me.

"You sure are passionate about this."

"I own a bookstore!"

"Yes, and I'm an attorney, but I don't watch *Law and Order* all the time."

The world around me spins. Or perhaps it's just the car in the wind.

"Books expand our minds. They change our perspectives on the world. They allow us to escape, to hope, to dream, to mourn, to walk in someone else's shoes." I look at Cletus. "They save lives."

"Last book I read was in college. Anyway, do I seem like the type of guy who needs to read?"

"Yes!"

"Well, okay, then. I'll let you pick out a book for me, and I'll give it a shot."

"Drop me at my bookstore, please."

"I thought you were tired."

"I am," I say.

When he pulls up to Sleigh By the Bay, I ask him to wait. His smile expands with happiness.

I rush into the store, and my grandparents—still dressed as Santa and Mrs. Claus—bellow "HO! HO! HO!" That's when they see my expression and say, "No, no, no."

"Oh, yes," I say. "Just wait."

I rush through into the fiction section. "Where are you?" I ask, scanning the shelves. "Here you are!"

I rush back outside and hand Cletus a book. He looks at the cover.

"*A Confederacy of Dunces*?" he asks. "I don't understand."

"Read it," I say. "Trust me."

"Can I call you?" he asks.

"Yes," I say. "With your credit card number to pay for this. Have a good night."

My grandparents are waiting at the door. Instead of giving them the blow by blow, I simply say, "He doesn't read."

They nod their heads in understanding.

My family may be destined to meet the loves of our lives dressed as Santa, but the loves of our lives must be readers.

My grandma's eyes glance at the clock on the wall. It's *8:15 p.m.*

"Long night," she comments.

"Join the club."

"How many families had their pictures taken with you to-night?" I ask.

"Lost count at forty," my grampa says.

"The store had a great night," my grandma adds. "Sold lots of books and lots of holiday gifts."

"Well, that's good news," I say. "And we do it all again to-morrow."

"Want a Manhattan?" my grampa asks.

"No, thanks. Not with what I just had to eat."

They look at me. You've never seen Santa and Mrs. Claus look so concerned.

"I'll be okay, but I think I'm going to head home and have an Emergen-C cocktail instead." I look around for other employees. "Where's Noah?"

"He had a date, too," my grandma says, before taking off her little Claus glasses, widening her eyes and adding, "*Online*."

"'Tis the season," I say. "You okay to lock up?"

"Same lock since we bought this place," my grampa says. He looks at me. "What? I've only had one Manhattan."

My grandma shoots him a look.

"Okay, two. But I've been nice this year." He booms a big belly laugh, and my grandma giggles, too. Then she gives him the sweetest kiss I've ever seen.

My heart pings.

"See you tomorrow," I say. "I think I'll walk home. Can I borrow your jacket, Santa?"

Grampa takes off his big velvet jacket and drapes it around my shoulders.

"Fresh air will do you good," he says, giving me a kiss on the cheek.

I grab the door, the bell jingling, and before I walk out, my grandma says, "He just wasn't the right Santa, Susan."

Don't say it, Grandma.

"Always remember that faith is believing in things when common sense tells you not to!" she calls.

I head out into the dark.

On my way home, strolling in the snow past Petoskey's pretty shops all lit up on this December night, I think the last really good date I had was in fifth grade, the year after I'd won the poetry contest, a year after my parents died.

I stop for a moment in the cold, willing myself not to cry after this interminable evening.

Kyle Trimble asked me to McDonald's. My grandparents were busy with the store, so my mom's longtime friend Rita sat in a booth on the other side of the restaurant and watched as Kyle walked into McDonald's wearing a Santa cap, bought me a Happy Meal and gave me a mood ring for Christmas. When I put it on, it immediately turned dark blue, meaning I was happy.

For the first time since I lost everything.

"I like you, Susan," he said plainly. "I know it's gotta be hard right now. But, if you'll let me, I'll be your Single Kringle." He stopped, looked down and fidgeted with a French fry. "Maybe forever."

And then Kyle stood up, took my hand and asked me to dance, right in the middle of McDonald's. As we slow danced, customers walked around us and the entire world faded away. It was just the two of us.

When I look up, I realize I'm home.

That memory now seems as old and historic as The Pink Lady, which is drenched in lights and looks so delighted to see me. I'm happy someone is waiting for me, and I rush inside and immediately feel safe.

I put on my pajamas, start a fire, grab a big fluffy blanket, make an Emergen-C and lay down on the couch. I flick on the TV, head to Netflix and search for the holiday movie I always watch after a bad Santa date, the movie my family has always watched starting post-Thanksgiving.

"Ah," I sigh, sipping my fizzy cocktail.

I talk to *Miracle on 34th Street* as it plays.

"You have no idea what it's like to be named after you, Susan," I say to young Natalie Wood's character. "There is so much pressure."

Though I was named for her, I am in many ways the opposite of the little girl in the movie. I was a little girl raised to believe in Santa and the miracles of Christmas.

Over time, tragedy, grief and life itself have drained me of those wonders.

I watch this movie, though, because somewhere, deep inside, as the fictitious Susan Walker finally says, "I believe, I believe, I believe."

I still watch it as an adult because as Kris Kringle says, "Christmas isn't just a day. It's a frame of mind."

My eyes wander to a wall filled with family photos. In one, I am sitting on Santa's lap, staring at him, my eyes filled with wonder. Mrs. Claus is standing behind us, her gloved hands framing her tilted head.

My heart shatters.

I am now forty, the same age as my mom was...

I turn back to the TV.

Even at forty, I still watch *Miracle on 34th Street* because, as Fred Gailey and my grandma always say, "Faith is believing in things when common sense tells you not to."

chapter 2

"You look just like my wife!"

I glance up and scan the sea of Santas.

Everyone looks the same: Kris Kringle in ASICS running shoes.

I'm standing in a throng of mostly drunken revelers-slash-runners—all bedecked in holiday-themed costumes—waiting for Chicago's famous 10K Santa Run to begin. Many of the twenty- and thirtysomething men are dressed only in Speedos, a tradition in the run, despite the fact that it is spitting snow and the windchill is lower than most of their body fat percentages. But they've worked hard to show off their egg-nog-free abs and thighs that have never met a snickerdoodle.

However, most runners are dressed as Santa, not only to honor the run's theme but also to avoid hypothermia.

"Over here!"

I turn, and Santa is waving at me. I glance around. At least, I think he's waving at me.

This particular Santa is better dressed than the lot, and—believe me—I know my Santa suits. In fact, his costume looks vintage, handmade. The jacket is a rich, dark red velvet, and the white fur trim is not used sparingly: it runs the length and circumference of his jacket, rings his wrists and even outlines the top of his black boots. His gloves are white, and not dingy, and his black belt—even from a distance—looks like real leather, not shiny plastic.

He's wearing a red velvet cap that falls perfectly over his white hair. His pink lips are curled in a genuinely happy smile behind his long, curly beard. And, unlike so many of the surrounding Santas, I can tell that his bowl full of jelly is all stuffing because…

"That Santa has the best legs I've seen all day!"

My BFF, Holly.

"He's hot!" she continues.

Santa is wearing very short running shorts, and his thighs look like they're carved from marble.

Then I see my image reflected back from the granny glasses perched on the end of my nose.

"I'm not hot," I say. "I'm dressed as Mrs. Claus."

"That's why he's hitting on you," Holly says. "He can see what's underneath all that."

"He's Santa," I say, "not Superman."

I already know what's underneath, and it's not the perfected image of what men prefer these days. I am still blessedly, thankfully, girlishly youthful looking for a woman of forty. I thank the long Michigan winters and years inside a bookstore for keeping my skin largely untarnished by the sun, despite my love of running outdoors. I am alabaster in the summer, a bit ghostly in the winter. I have long, blond hair which I usually keep twisted in a bun or a high pony. Petoskey peeps say I look like my mom, and bookstore shoppers always tend to point a finger toward a popular memoir we carry by Broadway star and TV actress Sutton Foster that features her face on the cover. Both are huge compliments. But when most people compliment me, it's usually a backhanded one: *Man, you look great for your age.*

I always wonder what that means. Who sets the standards? I never walk up to a man and say, "Man, you look great for your age." I usually just gawk at his too-young girlfriend.

"Well, you are a superwoman," Holly says, knocking me from my thoughts. "Smart, beautiful, sweet, well-read, well traveled…"

"Well used," I say. "I'm like that great scarf you find at Goodwill for a dollar."

"Stop it!" Holly laughs.

"This is my last Santa Run ever," I say. "This is your final wish. I've knocked both off for you in the last few days. I'm done."

"Uh-huh," she says, rolling her big eyes.

I look at my friend. Holly is what you would call innocently sexy, the thing most men love. She's Daphne from *Bridgerton*. She's breathtakingly beautiful, but it doesn't come off as threatening to men or women. She's forty, but no one says she looks good for her age because everyone thinks she's twenty-seven.

I point my gloved finger up and down her body, and I continue. "And how do you know he wasn't waving at you? I mean, look at you."

Holly is dressed as a sexy elf. It's not a stretch from her naughty nurse costume at Halloween, or her cute Cupid at Valentine's. Holly has always dressed like a Real Housewife at a theme party. Now she gets paid for it. Not only does she handle the website and social media for Sleigh By the Bay, but this is all part of her bigger lifestyle brand, Have A Holly Jolly. She just substitutes the particular holiday depending on the time of the year, and then "teaches" her 1.2 million followers how to decorate their homes, paint their faces, style their homes and hair and, essentially, pay her for doing what she's done her whole life: Be perfect without really trying. Me—and my bookstore—are always her guinea pigs.

She tried to dress me as a hot leprechaun—in full green body paint—for St. Patrick's Day last March, and everyone asked me if I had the stomach flu. In honor of today's run and our family tradition, Holly suggested I pull one of my grandmother's countless Mrs. Claus costumes from the bookstore closet. I look very maiden aunt compared to Holly's hotness.

Not that I'm the least bit jealous, mind you. Holly is so sweet, she's basically like divinity candy come to life: spun sugar.

We met in college. She was my freshman roommate, and I hated her that first day. She arrived early, took the bed with the better mattress and the desk by the window overlooking the quad, and had already been rushed by the best sorority on campus. By that night, she had me laughing harder than anyone had in my life. By the end of the week, we were inseparable. We thought we would both be married by now, with big families. Instead, we're forty, still single and still doing stupid things like the Santa Run. We also thought we would conquer the publishing world. Instead, I now own and run my family's bookstore, and Holly runs her online empire. Sometimes, I think she got a lot closer to the finish line than I did.

"Wave back!" Holly says, elbowing me in the side.

"Ouch." I wave.

Santa waves back immediately, and Holly screeches, "Told you!"

"You look just like my wife!" Santa repeats.

I laugh and continue waving like an idiot.

"Are you Christmas?" he yells.

I shake my head and then lift my hands, not understanding his question.

"Because I want to merry you."

I groan audibly and immediately turn away. Same line, different Santa.

I've already heard them all today:

Shouldn't you be on top of the tree, Angel?

Hi! Santa said you wished for me. Good choice.

I didn't think I was a snowman, but you just made my heart melt.

"Please make it stop," I say to Holly. "How drunk and desperate are these guys to hit on women dressed as a kindly grandmother?"

We are lined up on Halstead, in a neighborhood of shops and bars, and I wonder how she talked me into doing this yet again. I can endure the cold, but I can't endure the searing pain of enduring horrible holiday pickup lines from drunken randos dressed in Christmas costumes. I've heard them my whole life, from college to the bookstore.

They say your tongue is the strongest muscle in your body. Wanna fight?

That's how a fraternity guy once asked me out.

"There's something wrong with my cell phone," a summer resorter in Petoskey asked me as I picked up my morning latte.

"Oh, no," I said.

"Yeah, it doesn't have your number in it."

And who could forget these gems from working at the bookstore.

Are you reading Fahrenheit 451? *Because, dang girl, you're smokin'.*

Boy, you must be a library book, because I can't stop checking you out.

If you were a book, I'd need glasses, because you'd definitely be fine print.

I look around for a way to escape, but I'm packed into the street alongside thousands of runners tighter than a can of sardines.

"At least he's a bit sweeter and more original than the other Santas," Holly says in her always optimistic tone. "And it's not like I haven't used a cheesy line or two on some hot Santas today."

"No, you use them to ward off weird Santas," I say. "What was the one you just used at the bar?"

"Why is Christmas just like another day at the office?" Holly says with a laugh. "A woman does all the work, and the fat guy in the suit gets all the credit."

"Last Santa Run ever!" I say to her. "Why do I even try anymore? Lightning doesn't strike twice, much less three times. In the winter."

"Oh, Susan."

"I think you just want me to find love like this so you can have a post that goes viral."

"Stop it. Now you're just being snippy. I didn't dress you like the Grinch. I asked you to come here and dressed you like Mrs. Claus because your family has such a crazy holiday history at finding love. I mean, think of your parents and grandparents."

An errant snowflake lands on my lash and melts, mimicking a tear.

"It's so much easier to stay at home and get these terrible come-on lines online," I say. "You can just block these creeps without ever seeing them. And be warm. If I had a dime for every cheeseball line I've received in my life, I'd be a very rich Mrs. Claus."

"AH-hhemmm."

Holly clears her throat dramatically and skews her eyes to the left. I turn. Hot Santa is standing before me.

"Sorry," he says. "I thought I was being clever. Obviously not." He extends his hand. "Hi, I'm Santa. But you already knew that."

I stand motionless. Holly jabs me again. I extend my hand.

"Mrs. Claus," I reply. "And I only work a few days a year. I negotiated a very good deal."

"I kind of guessed that already," he says. "You must have a great boss. Mrs. Claus seems a touch formal, though. Should I call you Gertrude? Or are you new-school Jessica?"

My heart stops. "Excuse me?"

"Sorry," he says. "My bad again, I guess. I just sort of love everything about Christmas."

"No," I say, trying to catch my breath. "I get it. Mrs. Claus was the creation of James Rees in his 1849 book *Mysteries of City Life*. Rees was the first to name Mrs. Claus as well, calling her Gertrude in his stories, although pop culture has given her the name Jessica.

"Because of the…" I begin, before Santa says at the same time with me, "modern-day, stop-motion holiday special, *Santa Claus Is Comin' to Town*."

We laugh.

Holly is staring at us, open-mouthed.

"Mrs. Claus is introduced as a schoolteacher in the cartoon," I explain to her. "It's the first time anyone tried to explain how Kris Kringle ended up meeting and marrying Mrs. Claus."

"That's so weird that you both know that," Holly says. "We elves don't really get much information besides what the two of you decide to tell us. The *North Pole Times* isn't exactly stocked with news. I just try to stick to the four main food groups—candy, candy canes, candy corn and syrup." Holly extends her hand to Santa. "I'm an elf. That was a line from *Elf*. See how using a line works? It's supposed to be sweet, not creepy."

"This is my best friend, Holly," I say.

"It's nice to meet you, Buddy," Santa says.

"Back at'cha, Kris."

Santa looks at me. For the first time I notice his eyes are the color of the sky behind him: not just blue, but the hue of a snow sky.

As if on cue, it begins to snow in earnest.

"I dialed this up to impress you," Santa says.

I smile and then blush in the cold. My cheeks feel on fire.

"You're getting better, Santa," Holly says with a dramatic wink of a fake glitter lash. "Smile! I want to take an elfie."

She pulls her phone from the fanny pack cinched around her waist, which looks like a brightly colored peppermint candy. Santa slides his gloved hand around my waist, and my heart hitches. Holly takes the photo, and Santa's hand trails slowly around my back. My breath catches in my throat. I release it in a big puff that floats in front of my face.

"That's a keeper!" Holly says, reviewing the shot in her screen.

In the near distance, bells ring, signaling the race is about to start.

"I'm going to get a few more before the race starts," Holly says. "Be back in a sec."

Santa keeps his arm around my waist. He is taller than me, a rare thing considering my height of nearly five-feet-eleven-inches. He turns me a few degrees until I'm facing him, and his eyes fix on the Christmas pin I'm wearing on the fur lapel of my Mrs. Claus coat.

"That's so beautiful," he says. "It looks like it has a history. Was it your mother's?"

My heart balloons.

How would he know that?

I touch the pin. It's a red-and-green bejeweled angel, blowing a golden trumpet. I can picture my mother standing in church singing "Hark! The Herald Angels Sing." I can picture my mother being greeted into heaven by a fleet of angels trumpeting her arrival.

My mother is my guardian angel.

"Thank you," I say. "It does have a history." I hesitate. "It was my mother's, the one she wore on her Mrs. Claus costume every year."

"Was?" he asks, his voice low. "I'm so sorry."

"Thanks."

"It's strange, but I feel like we already know each other," Santa says. "And that's not a line. It's like we have some sort of connection, a history, just like with your pin."

It sounds like another cheesy line, but he's right: this man seems as familiar as a favorite blanket. Suddenly, a sleigh filled with waving Santas pulled by a team of runners parts the crowd. The crowd buzzes.

"Runners, take your marks!" a voice echoes.

"What's your name?" Santa asks me.

I open my mouth to answer, but before I can reply a big bell chimes to start the race, echoing in the cold air. A crush of people surges forward, and Santa is swept away.

"Meet me at O'Malley's!" I hear him exclaim as he is carried out of sight.

Holly returns in the St. Nick of time, grabs my hand, and we run next to one another until the crowd of runners thins, and we have the street to ourselves.

"What just happened?" she says, her eyes wide. "I knew it! This is your miracle on 34th Street!"

"You mean, on Halstead Street?"

"Everything has led up to this moment," she gushes. "Every snowflake, every kiss, every bad line, every Cletus, every bad date, every Christmas alone! Santa's been waiting, just like he was for your mom and grandma."

"You're getting *way* ahead of yourself," I say, my words coming out in short spurts as we run.

"Just wait!" Holly says. She looks at me and starts to laugh. "How can you even run in that? We didn't think of that."

My costume is very heavy, the Mrs. Claus wig is hot, my glasses bounce up and down my nose, and my slick-soled boots feel as if they might just slide from beneath me at any moment.

"Am I running?" I ask.

Holly laughs even harder.

But I know the answer already.

I've run 5Ks, 10Ks and marathons. I'm a very good runner. I've been running my whole life.

Santa's line echoes in my head: *I just sort of love everything about Christmas.*

I smile inside.

If my life were a book, it would be *A Christmas Carol*.

If my life were a movie, it would be *Miracle on 34th Street*, right down to being named after the little girl played by Natalie Wood.

Unlike her, though, I was raised to believe in fairy tales. I was taught to believe in Santa. I was raised on hope and Christmas miracles.

Until Death came to visit, jaws bared as if the taste of grief were so delicious he had to eat my entire family. That's when I learned that Santa's just a guy in a rental costume, Christmas comes just one day a year, *A Christmas Carol* is all about ghosts, and fairy tales are written for children who've yet to be hurt by life.

Holly grabs my hand, knocking me from my thoughts.

"Stop it!" she says. "I know where that mind of yours just went. Don't self-sabotage. Be in the moment!"

I nod, and we run—as best we can in our costumes—until we cross the finish line. We fight the throng of people congregated outside of O'Malley's, Holly's good looks and my padded behind gaining us entrance and access to the bar.

"Two shots of tequila!" Holly shouts into the air, and— Holly being Holly—two shots appear.

"To Santa!" she cries.

We down our shots and then angle our bodies toward the front door of O'Malley's.

We watch Santas come and go all afternoon, each one who approaches bringing as much hope and excitement as the real guy sliding down your chimney. I hold on to hope until the light fades and the snow intensifies. As the hours—and shots— continue, I begin to remove my glasses, my wig, my gloves.

"I'm so sorry," Holly says. "It's going to be all right, I promise. Let's just put today behind us."

When we finally head out into the cold and the dark, I am instantly sobered. Mrs. Claus has become Susan again. The holiday fantasy is over before it even began.

We hop on the L, and the world flies by, a twirl of Christmas lights.

The train stops, and a drunken man in a dingy Santa cap and spotty beard holding on to a half-empty whiskey bottle hops onboard.

"Ho! Ho! Ho!" he bellows to the passengers.

I shake my head. Holly leans over and asks in a slurred voice, "How about him?"

I consider the man for much too long. Holly stares at me.

"What?" I shrug. "Maybe he's a fixer-upper."

"A real Santa is like a good man," Holly says. "He never needs fixing." She stops. "Or a stint in rehab."

And I laugh because it feels good to laugh.

Holly puts her head on my shoulder. "Santa's waiting for you, you know? He's waiting for all of us Single Kringles. We just have to believe, right?"

Her voice sounds so sad and yet so, so hopeful. I can feel my heart deflate like a ruined soufflé.

I nod and give her a kiss on top of the head.

"Right," I say with as much conviction as I can muster although I know in my heart I'm done trying to find *the one* since I've gone oh for two with Holly's wish list this year, oh for dating-the-past-forty-years.

My head bobs, my eyelids grow heavy, and my chin brushes the fur collar of my costume. The L changes tracks, and I open my eyes with a start.

My mother's angel is staring at me, its little cheeks puffed. I swear I can see it turn its head to me and whisper, "You just have to believe again, Susan."

"It's still so hard without you, Mom," I whisper back.

chapter 3

The snow begins to pick up in earnest when I reach Cadillac. The storm gains muscle the farther north I drive, going from pretty, dancing dust to a frozen powerhouse. The snow clogs my wipers and freezes in thin sheets on my windshield. I crank up the heat and turn the defroster to high.

My headlights can no longer penetrate the snow, and I slow to a crawl, trying to decipher the center line of the road. I have driven in snow my entire life, but the moment I turned forty, God's gift to me was night blindness.

I kick myself for spending the next morning in Chicago nursing my post-race hangover and swilling coffee at a Starbucks while Holly posted about their new holiday lattes and cups.

I scream as the driver of a semi lays on his horn. I jerk my steering wheel to the right, the car fishtailing in the snow.

For a long few seconds, I am floating in a snow globe. My hands are steady on the wheel, and I say a prayer until the road appears again. As soon as I realize my car is not only still on the road but also going in the right direction, I begin to shake.

I click off the audiobook I've been listening to from Desiree Delmonico, a famed romance author we will be hosting at Sleigh By the Bay this month. Her novels sell like hotcakes despite all being roughly the same: naughty riffs on a different holiday with covers featuring hot, male shirtless models. Desiree made the cover model of her new book famous, too, because she's dating him, even though she's well into her seventies. Her latest novel, *Jingle My Bells*, features her boyfriend—of course—wearing a Santa hat and carrying a sack of what I can only guess is filled with containers of protein powder, baby oil and an unsigned prenuptial agreement.

Another semi passes me, and I grip the wheel, my knuckles white.

I click on the radio, and I immediately laugh. A Pure Michigan commercial touting the beauty of winter plays.

I laugh again thinking of the Pure Michigan parody ads that are sent to me all year long. One in the summer jokes about how local drivers accidentally hit resorters walking the streets eating fudge and must hide the bodies, while one of the winter ads jokes about Michigan drivers sliding into a ditch or falling on ice and giving a cheery thumbs-up.

Nothing says winter like a purple bruise on your backside. That's the beauty of… Pure Michigan.

Mariah Carey's "All I Want for Christmas Is You" comes on, and I realize this is another Pure Michigan tradition. Pop radio stations all over Michigan switch to holiday music the day after Halloween and play it continuously until New Year's Day.

Despite the song's fun dance beat, the lyrics hit a bit close after my Santa Run debacle and family history.

"Pure Michigan," I say to myself.

And then, as if the DJ is trying to torture me, he follows up Mariah with Bing Crosby crooning "I'll Be Home for Christmas," and then—to rub it in—"Same Old Lang Syne" by Dan Fogelberg.

"Thank you very much," I say sarcastically.

But when Wham!'s "Last Christmas" comes on, I have to pull to the side of the road and put on my blinkers.

DECEMBER 1992

"Last Christmas" begins to play, and I stifle a happy scream. I can feel my body wanting to jump up and down like a pogo stick, but I sink my feet into the ground and smile.

"Why, yes, Kyle, I would love to dance with you."

I put my hands around his waist, and we begin to slow dance. The gym decorations look like the weather outside: snowflakes fall from the ceiling and dance in the twinkling lights. Kyle leans in, and I shut my eyes.

"What are you doing, Susan?"

I open my eyes. I am dancing with air in my pink bedroom.

"Get out!" I yell at my dad. He is dressed as Santa.

"What are you wearing?"

I turn slightly, and I catch my reflection in the mirror. I saved all my money from working at the bookstore to buy this dress: a beautiful short trumpet gown with metallic stripes of holiday red, black and gold, a black velvet bow at the waist and fluted bottom with sheer red taffeta jutting out at the edge.

"I bought this for the Christmas formal, remember?"

I can't help myself. I twirl in the mirror, and the skirt flares.

My mom appears in the doorway dressed as Mrs. Claus. "What's with all the commotion?" she asks.

"You don't remember, do you?" I ask, my voice barely audible above Wham!

My mom and dad look at each other.

"You don't," I say. "Tonight's my first Christmas formal. Fourth grade. It's kind of a big deal."

My mom takes a step forward very carefully, as if she's walking through a minefield.

"But, honey, the Stafford's Perry Hotel's Christmas party is tonight," she says gingerly. "The entire town will be there. The entire town is expecting us to be there."

For my whole life, I—like the entire town of Petoskey—have stood in the shadow of the gorgeous, historic hotel holding court on the corner of Bay and Lewis Streets, overlooking Little Traverse Bay like a grande dame. It's been the place where VIPs, literati—even Hemingway—have stayed. It's the place that has had a hold on my family's Christmases forever.

"Everyone will want their picture with their favorite elf," my father adds just as gingerly. "It's the million-dollar shot."

The million-dollar shot.

The breathtaking vistas from the hotel—literally from all of Petoskey—have made the area famous for its Million Dollar Sunset. For once in my life, I don't want to see the reflection of the sunset on water, I don't want to be captured as a Christmas cartoon character in someone's keepsake photo, I don't want to be Mr. and Mrs. Claus's kid, I just want to be a kid.

"I'm not going, and you can't make me!" I cry. "It's my first formal!"

I don't want to burst into tears and ruin the touch of makeup I'm secretly wearing, but I do. I blubber and wail. My mother sweeps me up into the folds of her arms and holds me until I stop and her velvety jacket is damp.

"You should go," she says. "You're right, we forgot. You

know how busy we are this time of year. I'm so sorry, honey. Please forgive us."

I look up at my mom. She wipes my eyes with her gloved finger.

"Thank you."

I look at her again.

"Do you have any idea what it's like to be the daughter and granddaughter of the most loved man and woman in town?" I ask. "No, in the world?"

"Do you have any idea what it's like to love a little girl more than any other in the entire world?" she asks. "You are, and will forever be, the greatest gift Mr. and Mrs. Claus ever received."

We load into the car, and my father clicks on the radio to a holiday station. We listen to holiday music as he drives, and, as if on cue, "Last Christmas" begins to play as we pull in front of the gym. My heart leaps, imagining Kyle asking me to dance. Maybe even one day asking me on a date.

My parents drop me off at the school and, as they drive away, the strains of the song hang in the cold air, mingling with the snow. I hear the crunch of their tires over the snow, and then there is silence, the quiet only found in the midst of a Northern Michigan snow.

My parents' headlights disappear into the dark, and I turn to walk into the gym.

And as if irony had saved all of its irony just for me, it would be my parents' last Christmas, too.

Another semi flies by, laying on its horn, and I jump.

I am still on the side of the road, defroster roaring, radio blaring "Last Christmas."

Timing.

In life and literature, it really all comes down to timing, don't you think?

What makes a great book?

Interesting characters. Intriguing story line. Wonderful setting. An author's ability to make the universal seem deeply personal.

But pacing—timing—is perhaps what either makes or breaks a book.

I read countless books a year, often two or three a week. It's integral to my job. But how often do I lose interest in even the most well written of books, be they fiction or nonfiction?

More often than not. There's just something that doesn't capture and keep my interest.

And I rest that solely on timing.

The chapters don't flow quite right. The plot is as dense as a fruitcake. The dialogue is stilted. Writing is hard, hard work. But the hardest of work, I know, comes after the writing is done. I've heard countless authors say to an aspiring writer in the audience who proudly announces he or she has completed a first draft, "Congratulations! You have about fifty more to write!"

That's what makes the timing right. It's not luck. It's hard work.

Perhaps my personal life has been doomed by my love of literature. I've had too many memorable characters live and die in my own memoir. I've believed in luck. And then I've put in the hard work. And, still, the timing has been off my whole life.

My parents and grandparents met because of timing. My grandma wandered into the Stafford for the annual Christmas party and met my grandfather, dressed as Santa. My mom met my dad at a fraternity party.

But timing isn't always magical.

What if I had gone with my parents to the Stafford that night? They wouldn't have had to cross town from dropping me off at the school and run into a drunk driver.

What if the winds had not come up that day on Lake Michigan? My great-great-grandfather would not only have delivered a ship of trees to families in Chicago, but Captain Santa would have had another Christmas with his family.

What if that semi driver that just plowed past me had looked down at an incoming text or reached over to take a swig of his coffee?

Timing.

Which is what has me so emotional this year in particular.

I am forty. I lost my mother when she was forty. And my mind, heart and soul are consumed with these milestone anniversaries and all the things my mother achieved by forty—finding true love, having children—that I have yet to accomplish. It's like this lake effect snow, overshadowing all the good things I do have in my life. I know it's sunny just a few miles away, but I'm overwhelmed by the clouds.

And I can't help but wonder how much time I actually have left. If the average life expectancy of a woman in the US is seventy-nine, my life is half over.

I can't help but think that it's too late for me to have children, a yearning I buried deep in my internal snowbank years ago.

I can't help but realize that there will be no one in my family—no spouse, no kids—to take over the bookstore, to keep our community and Christmas legacy alive.

I try not to dwell on something bad happening to me this year, but I can't help it. And I can't help but wonder if my time for love has passed already, like summer in Michigan.

Perhaps I'm meant to live my life through books. Perhaps that's why publishers admire my judgment, my gut on when the timing is right for a book and author to soar. Perhaps as my grandma Betty still says, "If if's and but's were candy and nuts, oh, what a Merry Christmas it would be."

My phone rings, and I jump.

The car's display reads Incoming call Holly.

"He fell!" she's yelling before I even have a chance to say hello.

"Who fell? Are you okay? What are you talking about?"

"Your Santa!" Holly says. "He fell. *That's* why he didn't come to O'Malley's."

"How do you know all this?"

"There's an article in the *Tribune* about the Santa Run," Holly says. I can hear the paper rustling. Holly still gets a real paper because she's friends with me, and I give her a subscription—along with about a dozen books—for her birthday every year to keep her grounded in the world outside social media and technology. "Listen to this." The paper rustles again. "'A record 25,000 runners participated in this year's Santa Run, and—with the inclement weather and slippery roads—a record number of reported injuries.'"

"I'm sitting on the side of the road in a snowstorm," I say. "I'm not really tracking what you're saying."

"Your Santa was one of the injuries. I just know it. In fact, I texted a friend at the *Tribune* to find out the names of those who were injured, but she didn't have them. And she said if they did, they couldn't share them. So I texted a friend of mine who helps do the social media for the race. She said they didn't have the names of the injured either, *but*..." Holly says this very dramatically "...she did send me the race link that has all the runners' names and ages."

"Wow, great work, Agatha Christie," I say. "So we have a one in 25,000 chance to find the guy who stood me up? Sounds like a great plan."

"Listen, I know in my heart he didn't stand you up. I just know it. I think he got hurt somehow during the run. Or there was an emergency. Something happened. He didn't stand you up. He didn't show because he couldn't."

I take a deep breath. The air in the car is hot and dry.

"I appreciate your optimism," I say, "but the timing's not right."

There is silence.

"The timing's never right for you because you always put a period in your life where an ellipsis should go."

"Look at you," I say. "Quite the wordsmith. You should take my job."

"It's Christmas, Susan. I know this time of year is both so wonderful and so hard for you and your family. I also know this year is filled with huge anniversaries, both happy and sad. But your parents would want you to be happy. You know that."

"I *am* happy. I don't need a man to complete or fulfill me. And neither do you. We're all duped by the faux joy of Christmas, a Hallmark mentality to fall in love, and TikTok desire to be perfect. None of it is true."

I continue despite the fact Holly's silence is telling me otherwise.

"You know why Christmas books are so popular? Because our holidays suck. We all have this desire to make our lives seem more beautiful and more magical than they really are. Most of us are lonely. Most of us are sad. Most of us have lost someone who means the world to us. Most of us just want to fill that void, and a book with a great title, a pretty cover, a Ho ho ho and a happy ending stuffs that gnawing hole in our soul, just like a half dozen snickerdoodles, a cup of hot chocolate and a gallon of eggnog."

Holly doesn't reply for nearly a minute. I don't hang up because I can hear her breathing. And then she says very softly, "It's not about needing a man to fulfill either of us. And it's not just about believing in happy endings. It's about finding someone who completes us, someone who wants us to be our best selves, someone who will love us and be there for us no matter what. Like you do for me." Holly stops and clears her throat. When she speaks again, her voice is quivering. "It's about the love we deserve, Susan. And you *deserve* to be loved. And there's nothing fake about wanting or needing that. So forgive me for being your best friend who only wants the best for you and will fight like hell to make that happen." She hesitates. "And, by the way, I love all the Christmas books you send me. And I love Hallmark movies. And I love making people feel festive and happy this time of year because I know so many of us need—just for one hot moment—not to feel sad. And, by the way, I do believe in happy endings. Our books are not written yet, Susan."

My heart hiccups. I think of my parents and grandparents. I think of the poem I wrote so long ago.

And, despite trying to stop myself, I think of the Santa I just met, the one who got away.

It's not about believing in happy endings. It's about the love we deserve, Susan. And you deserve to be loved.

I open my mouth to respond, but Holly hangs up.

She's always had impeccable timing.

chapter 4

My family's bookstore, Sleigh By the Bay, is perched atop a hill in downtown Petoskey's historic Gaslight District. We share a miniscule parking lot with the coffee shop next door to us—a place that has essentially leeched my IRA dry due to my love of and need for caffeine and sugar—but I'm not allowed to park here.

Want to talk about the perfect way to raise the blood pressure of any store owner or politician in the Bay?

Parking.

It's tight in the winter, and a literal doomsday scenario in the summer. I've seen locals and resorters nearly come to fisticuffs over who spotted an open parking spot first.

All of Sleigh By the Bay's staff park in a dirt lot behind the movie theater kitty-corner from the bookstore so our custom-

ers can use the limited spaces. Even on a winter Monday, the
lot is packed. Today, since I have a delivery and my motiva-
tion is at nil without coffee in my system yet, I park in a fire
zone in front of the store praying I don't get a ticket.

It is snowing lightly. I turn to gaze at Little Traverse Bay.
The Bay is Lake Michigan's fourth largest bay, behind Green
Bay, Grand Traverse Bay and Bay de Noc. It is packed in the
summer with sailboats, motorboats and swimmers, but I've
always believed it truly comes to life in the winter. There is
nothing—not one thing—to obscure its beauty, and it stretches
from shore to horizon, shimmering in the snow, thrilled to
be on its own winter vacation.

Memories flood my mind. I can picture my mom teaching
me to ice skate when the bay was frozen over completely. I remember my dad building sand castles with me. On this milestone year, my life's birthday and anniversary cake is covered
in flickering candles and moments from the past.

Why—when you try to push something out of your mind—
does it only become more firmly entrenched? The good and
the bad? Like when you watch a horror movie before bed,
and you promise yourself you won't think about the creepy
killer once it's over? Or, now when I eat pizza, I only see
cheese and Cletus?

Or, with it snowing lightly as it is right now, why do I remember the brief encounter with a man who stood me up?
I can still feel his hand on my back, his eyes, the way he felt
like…

I look at the bay and the bookstore.

He felt like home.

Why do I miss that missed connection?

"Because you're a glutton for punishment," I mutter as I
get out of the car.

I pop the trunk and pull out a handcart. I then stack ten

boxes onto it, shut the trunk and give the cart a pull with a grandiose grunt.

If there's one thing you need to know about a bookstore owner, it's that we are pack mules. Everyone has this notion we sit around in nubby sweaters sipping tea and reading, or hosting famous authors at champagne-drenched dinners, but we're mostly manual labor.

We haul, stack, box, unbox, ship, pack, unpack, lug, carry and then do it all over again the next day. We have strong minds, great imaginations and bad backs.

Today's haul is the latest novel from literary lion Phillip Strauss. Strauss was a wunderkind in publishing a decade ago, with a novel written as though from a privileged little girl's perspective about "raising" her own parents in Beverly Hills and trying to make them better people. It was an instant *New York Times* bestseller, shortlisted for the Booker and Pulitzer, and the media and readers expected the author to have the heart of his protagonist. Phillip has anything but. He showed up very drunk for our sold-out event for two hundred, read for five minutes, refused to answer questions or sign books, and then told the handler from his publishing house—a very young, junior publicity assistant fresh out of Smith—to get him, and I quote, "out of this Hemingway hellhole ASAP."

I worked hard to kill his career. His next two books bombed.

But now he's back with a new novel—one his new publisher reportedly paid a million dollars for—as well as a "new" image.

A kinder, gentler jackass.

Bookselling—like publishing—is a very small circle. Everyone knows everyone, we all run on the same track, and we talk. A lot. I've heard rumblings that Phillip is still the same when not in public, but his new publisher begged me to give him another chance after his recent flops. We agreed on a luncheon event tomorrow. I can help make or break this book. Phillip and his publisher need my indie sales for the bestseller lists as well as to bolster and round out their numbers for the *Times* list. I am not one who is great at giving someone second chances. You should get it right the first time—*right, Cletus?*—be a decent person from the moment you open your mouth to speak to a stranger.

I look up at the bookstore. My heart rises.

My parents didn't get a second chance.

I glance back at the bay.

And I never got an apology from the man who...

I grunt lugging the cart toward the door.

I've been granted a few hundred hard covers of Phillip's latest, *Must Be Nice*, whose "laydown" date is tomorrow. In publishing, new books are released every Tuesday. Books that are expecting a strong and immediate demand from a publisher— think Kristin Hannah or James Patterson—are given firm laydown dates, meaning no one can see them or buy them in a bookstore in advance of that moment. It builds anticipation.

Phillip's new novel is a sweeping, family saga told from the perspectives of three generations of women who achieve great success but must play by the changing rules and expectations of society over the last hundred years. It's also a heavy wink and nod to Phillip's own past.

It's well written but dense. And the female perspectives still feel very male-driven. I also hated the fact that Phillip's novel is classified as "literature" while a female author whose work I greatly admire and whose new book which just published and I adored was classified as "contemporary women's fiction." It's downright gross. And yet that's another thing we bookstore owners battle: We must market the work to our readers, but we also must work hard not to diminish work by out-of-date categorization.

I pull the door open. A whoosh of warm air greets me. I hold the door with my rear and yank the cart inside. Noah and Leah come rushing over to help me.

"How was…" Noah starts.

"Don't ask," I reply.

"Diva, I know it's only Monday, but you're talking to me like Christina Applegate's agent after she turned down the starring role in *Legally Blonde* that went to Reese. I will not stand for that." He folds his arms dramatically.

"I'm sorry," I start. "Is…?"

Leah nods and points upstairs. She mouths, *Rita's already here.*

Rita Preston. My Monday mainstay. My mom's friend turned my literary support system and weekly nuisance. Rita buys hundreds of dollars' worth of books a week, but the purchase price is a piece of my soul every Monday morning.

"Is there any coffee?"

"This ain't *Mad Men*, and I ain't, Joan, oh-kay?" Noah says. He unfolds his arms very dramatically and puts them on his hips.

I laugh. I know Noah's "attitude" is a way to obscure all of his deep-seated insecurities, ones from childhood that have never disappeared.

Noah and Leah are known as my "Ah-Team," coined, of course, by Noah, who is fluent in obscure Hollywood facts, film and TV as well as Oscar Wilde and Dorothy Parker. Noah considers himself to be the Mr. T of the team, with Leah as the more polished George Peppard.

I hired Noah right out of college. He started for me the Monday after he graduated from the University of Michigan. It was his idea. I've known him since he was a boy, since he used to spend entire evenings and weekends in our bookstore.

Noah came here to read, but he also came here to hide. Sleigh
By the Bay was his refuge. He may be "fierce" and proudly
out today, and he may joke that he knew he was gay in the
womb, but he was a frightened, lost little boy who needed
the love, support and encouragement his family had trouble
providing. My grandma and grampa used to talk with him
when he'd come in. At first, they suggested books for him
to read—The Hardy Boys, then Nancy Drew, *Where the Red
Fern Grows* before he became obsessed with Erma Bombeck
(yes, you heard me)—then they gave him the chair in their
office and allowed him to shut the door and read. Eventually,
they invited him to read to kids, and Noah began not only to
emerge but to become the beautiful butterfly God intended.

"It's okay to be smart. It's okay to be different. Our unique-
ness is all we have that sets us apart in this world. Promise us
you'll never lose that just to fit in," I heard my grandparents
tell him.

"I promise," he finally said.

When I asked Noah why he wanted to work here—knowing, as a U-M grad he could land a job anywhere and for sig-
nificantly more money—he said simply, "Books save lives.
They saved mine. I can't imagine a more worthwhile career."
He looked at me. "But you're gonna have to help pay down
my student loans, diva."

He is now our nonfiction buyer and special events manager. Leah is our accounts supervisor, accountant and children's book buyer. Leah ran a successful CPA firm with her
husband in Chicago. They had four children, and summered
in Petoskey in a beautiful Victorian with a wraparound porch
that overlooked the water. The home literally glowed in the
light reflected off the bay. She named it MoonGlow. She came
into the bookstore nearly every day when she was on vacation
to buy books for herself or her kids. When their last child left

for college, her husband left her for a twenty-two-year-old assistant in their office. She got divorced and left Chicago, retaining a stake in the business, getting half the estate as well as the cottage here. She came in one fall day to buy books, and I asked if she was on vacation. She told me her life story over coffee.

"I began to believe I was a cliché," she told me. "Husband leaves fifty-year-old empty-nester for young assistant. I mean, come on, right? But you know what I never realized? He's the cliché. So many authors write books about my life because it's happened to them, and it will always happen. It happens every day despite the fact I did everything right."

Leah came in the next week, saying she couldn't sleep, that the moon's reflection off the water was so bright, it kept her awake. She hadn't realized that until then. So she bought a book about the moon. When she returned a few days later, she told me, "The moon doesn't produce its own light. Moonlight is actually sunlight that shines on the moon and bounces off." I looked at her, not understanding. "Women are moonlight. We reflect the light of those we love—our husbands, our children, our families, our friends. I think it's time I'm the sunlight. Hire me."

I did that day.

It would be a mammoth understatement to say I've surrounded myself with an eclectic team. I hear loud footsteps upstairs, like a marching band is blowing through the fiction section.

Leah points again and mouths, *Your grandparents are here, too.*

"How can they have more energy than me?" I ask. "I'm forty and exhausted. They're in their eighties and still energetic."

"I've had it wrong this whole time," Noah says in a deadpan voice. "I thought you were in your eighties, and they were forty."

"Ha ha," I say. "Well, this is making for a wonderful start to the week. Your old humor. New Phillip Strauss. New Desiree Delmonico. I have to move my old car, and I need fresh coffee. I'll be back in a few minutes."

"Hey, diva."

I turn.

"Bring me one, too," Noah says. "A triple vanilla latte. Oat milk. No whip for these hips."

"This ain't *Mad Men*, and I ain't Joan," I say.

"I've taught you way too well," Noah says. He snaps his fingers up and down my body, grabs the cart, turns on his heel and says as he wheels it away, "Rita's waiting. Don't make her wait."

I open the front door of Petoskey Scones. Fred Jr. begins to make my coffee—a skim, triple shot caramel white mocha—as soon as he sees me.

"How was the Windy City?" he asks.

As the heated air hits my skin, my mind flits back to my missed connection, the hot Santa who got on his sleigh and rode away without so much as a Ho! Ho! Ho! A shiver slides down my spine, and I feel cold again, inside and out.

Since the book of my life is an ironic tale, Fred Jr. looks exactly like Fred, the jock, from Scooby-Doo. Noah, of course, pointed this out to me, and now I can never get the image out of my mind. Fred Jr.'s wearing a Santa hat, and I think of this weekend.

"Cold," I finally reply.

"Well," he says, handing me my latte, "this should warm you up."

"And a cinnamon scone, too, thanks."

Fred is a personal trainer at the local gym in the afternoon and evening. He invited me to do P90X and CrossFit, but guys in their twenties forget that women in their forties don't enjoy turning tractor tires over with their bare hands. We already spend enough time reshaping the world while also warding off its unachievable expectations.

All without scraping our nail polish.

Petoskey Scones makes the most incredible baked goods. Sarah, the owner, comes in at dawn to bake. We often see each other while the sun is still asleep, along with the entire town. The store's name is a riff off the famed Petoskey Stone, Michigan's official state stone, a rare beauty that draws rock hunters from all over the world to our shores to seek the elusive prehistoric fossil. The Petoskey stone is actually ancient coral, and the stone consists of tightly packed, six-sided corallites, the skeletons of once-living coral polyps. When the stone is wet, it is easier to find, and vacationers spend their days walking inches at a time along the beach to gather them.

Fred hands me my scone.

"Thank you," I say. "Have a nice day."

I start to head out the front door but stop, remembering.

"Oh, Fred, I forgot—I also need a triple vanilla latte with oat milk and no whip."

"For Noah?" he asks.

I cock my head. "Yes? How did you know?"

"I try to remember every customer's favorite," he says. "And it's kind of hard not to remember Noah."

I swear his cheeks blush as he says this. He hands me the coffee, and I again head out the door and step onto Lake Street. I can't avoid Rita—or my grandparents—forever.

And yet, I do. I decide to go for a quick stroll around the block.

I forget just how quant my beautiful little hometown is until I get a moment to be still and actually look.

I love winter in Petoskey. I have my resort town back again.

I can walk right in and get a coffee. I can chat with customers. I can get a seat at a restaurant without a three-week wait.

Downtown Petoskey has been a shopping area for more than a hundred years. It bursts with independent shops, boutiques, galleries and restaurants, and was named one of the Best Small Towns in America by *Smithsonian Magazine*. The downtown sits on angled, sloping streets, akin to a miniature, snow globe version of San Francisco, and they're lined with historic gaslights. At Christmas, fresh pine wreaths are placed on the lights, or the poles are wrapped in greenery, all with white lights and big, red bows.

I kick the snow with my boot, and I feel like a kid again. I sip my coffee and crunch down the street. There is nothing like Petoskey. It feels exhilarating to live in a wondrous little town whose independent streak matches not only my own but that of most locals.

Picturesque Petoskey was named for the Ottawa Indian Chief Pe-to-se-ga. The loose translation of Petosegay is "rising sun." I think of Leah and smile.

If you own and run a bookstore, you have to know the history of the town. And the state. And, well, pretty much everything without acting like you know too much. Books on the history of a resort town as well as coffee table books filled with stunning photographs of the area are ever popular.

For our area, lumber was its lifeline for many decades, thanks to access to Lake Michigan that allowed Great Lakes freighters to ferry lumber to ports all over the Midwest. The area's lumber was instrumental in helping rebuild Chicago after the Great Fire. The area began to become a summer resort destination starting in the late 1800s when rail lines brought urbanites looking to escape the heat of cities like Detroit, Indianapolis, Chicago and Cincinnati. Steamships then began to bring passengers from ports across the Great Lakes for a reasonable rate. Once here, visitors could walk, bike, stagecoach or carriage anywhere.

Not much has changed, I think, looking around. *Even the buildings.*

Grandpa Shorter's Gifts is iconic, NorthGoods showcases amazing local artisans and American Spoon truly makes the finest fruit preserves in the world with our Michigan fruit.

One of my favorite stores in town—and the world—is Symons General Store. It is akin to an old-fashioned apothecary, candy store, deli, grocery and restaurant all rolled into one. Symons features a candy counter with all my childhood favorites, a wine selection to rival any city, handmade sandwiches and, down an alley behind the general store and thriving under the street, is Chandler's, one of Michigan's finest eateries. Ironically, Symons was built in 1879 from brick, a first, used to safeguard against the destruction fires caused in other Michigan lumber towns, like Saugatuck. In fact, the Stafford's Perry Hotel was Petoskey's first brick hotel. At the turn of the century, the Perry was advertised as the only fireproof hotel in town and is the only original resort hotel still operating in Petoskey.

People just want to feel safe in this world.

Which is the reason many people buy books. To escape from their troubles. To fade into another world, if even for a little while.

I stop. Sleigh By the Bay greets me like a warm hug on this winter's day. Sleigh is a five-thousand-square foot, two-story general bookstore that brings to mind an inviting cottage. The exterior is brick, but the windows are framed with ornate, forest green casings, the trim painted in shiny gold. A bright red awning, with fresh pine boughs, hangs over the entrance reading *Sleigh By the Bay Booksellers* in gold lettering.

The roofline of this building is unlike any other in town,

as it was designed to mimic a wave off the bay. Over time, however, people began to think it resembled a sleigh. As a result, the former hardware store began to place a mammoth sleigh atop the roof at Christmastime as a way to excite holiday shoppers. The sleigh became a beloved site in town, and the hardware store kept it atop the building permanently. It seemed as if my grandparents were destined to buy the building. Who knew the name they gave it would stick forever and become so iconic?

Two red window boxes stand under the windows, and are festooned in fresh pine boughs and filled with red Shiny Brite ornaments and curly gold ting ting branches. Snow has dusted the pine as if a photo shoot for *Midwest Living* is about to take place.

The decor is the handiwork of Noah, but the window displays are all me and my grandparents. One window advertises the upcoming event with Desiree Delmonico. A huge poster of her book cover under a sign that reads "Christmas Is Going to Be Hot This Year!" is surrounded by stacks of her latest holiday book.

The other window—as it has since my grandparents bought this former hardware store some fifty years ago and turned it into a bookstore—has featured a "throne" for Mr. and Mrs. Claus every December. The high-back chair is upholstered in bright red, tufted velvet with ornate gold legs and sits at an angle on an heirloom rug of soft red and gold. A Christmas tree—decorated in multicolored lights, tinsel and book ornaments sent to us by beloved authors over the years—stands near the front. Every night in December, Santa and Mrs. Claus read to children, help families shop and then take photos. Even in the height of summer, we throw a huge "Christmas in July" party so that resorters can see my grandparents and take their holiday photos. Our longstanding customers would have it no other way.

"Santa needs a vacation, too!" my grampa tells kids when they ask why he's not at the North Pole. "But he never takes a vacation from you! Ho! Ho! Ho!"

But the adults love it just as much or more than their children. They remember doing the same when they were their kids' ages.

A gust of wind rushes up the hill from the bay, and I shiver.

How much longer can this tradition continue? I think.

I tug open the red Victorian door with my free hand.

I take a deep breath and inhale the scent of books.

I'm home.

The bookstore is all knotty pine paneling. The second floor—as you walk in off Lake Street—features our fiction, nonfiction, travel sections, and magazines and newspapers, while the ground floor features our children's section, with a fireplace, cozy reading nook, book club meeting room and our offices.

"Ho! Ho! Ho!"

The bell on the door hasn't even stopped jingling. Santa's laugh booms through the bookstore.

"How-how-how was your weekend in the city?"

"Don't ask," Noah says, then turns to me and demands, "Where's my coffee."

I hand it to him.

"Made with love!"

He takes a sip.

"Made with ice. It's cold, diva."

"Maybe your demeanor is making it that way."

"Touché!"

He returns to shelving books onto our "Featured in Our Newsletter!" display.

"Hi, Grampa!"

My life is defined by Santas. But this one's always been there for me. He's never stood me up.

"It was okay."

He hugs me with all his might, managing—even at his age—to lift me off the ground.

"Okay is not okay," he says.

He puts me down and holds me at arm's length.

My grandfather—Nicholas Norcross—is no faux Santa. He's the real deal. He looks exactly like Edmund Gwenn, the actor who won the Oscar for playing Kris Kringle in *Miracle on 34th Street*. And he sounds exactly like Burl Ives, who narrated the *Rudolph the Red-Nosed Reindeer* TV special. In fact, his beard is real, his hair is white, his laugh booms, his eyes twinkle, but it's what's on the inside that truly makes him Kris Kringle: his heart is pure, his soul is good, and he radiates kindness, joy and empathy.

He *is* Santa.

My grampa has remained the epitome of goodness despite losing a son and a daughter-in-law and trading in his golden years to raise his granddaughter and not only gift her a bookstore but continue to help manage it. I would not be here without my grandparents.

"Let's just say I'm not convinced there's a Single Kringle out there for me," I say.

"No!" he bellows, placing a Santa-gloved hand over my mouth. My grandparents are pretty much in costume through December 24/7 as much, I've come to believe, for themselves as the customers. "Shut your eyes."

"Grampa…" I start.

"Shut your eyes."

I do as instructed. He grabs my hands.

"My parents and grandparents told me, one day I would know," he begins.

"Grampa," I object again. "Not my silly poem again."

He continues undeterred.

"Because I'll meet a man whose beard, would be white as snow."

He gives my hands a gentle shake, and I join him. We recite together:

"His eyes would twinkle, and his laugh would boom, he'd make me feel like, the only gift in the room. He will love me for me, be generous and kind, and always let me read my books and speak my mind. He may not have reindeer, nor live at the North Pole, but he'll be filled with love, and have a good soul."

As I say the words to the poem I wrote decades ago, I'm amazed at how this man can remember each and every line, despite the fact that at least once a week he leaves the bookstore coffeepot on until the entire place smells like burning tires and the fire department shows.

We finish, I open my eyes and my grampa's blue eyes are sparkling.

"You wrote that poem for a reason. Because you believed. Children believe in magic. We lose that when life and loss come to call. But we can't stop hoping and believing, can we? If we did, there would be no reason for Christmas." He clears his throat. "We all know how difficult this year is for you, Susan... for all of us. It seems like yesterday still." He stops again. "But try to focus on the happy and not dwell on the sad."

"Grampa—" I start.

"Susan!" He emphasizes my name dramatically. "Remember why your parents named you that."

My heart swells, but then I hear Noah call, "To curse her with a name that would forever repel men on Tinder?"

My grandfather shakes his head. He has no idea what Noah is saying half the time. "Tinder?" he asks.

"Never mind," I say.

"It's an online dating app, Mr. Norcross," Noah says.

"Get her on that immediately," Grampa says.

Noah gets the giggles, which my grampa catches, and laughter ricochets across the bookstore.

"Bookstores are meant to be quiet," I say. "Where's Grandma?"

"Charming Rita," Noah says. "You can't avoid her forever."

I swill my coffee and follow Noah down the stairs to the reading nook by the fireplace.

"As the Bangles used to sing, it's just another manic Monday," Noah says. He looks at me and whispers, "Your safe word today is *Bette Davis*."

Noah gives me and Leah safe words to utilize in stressful situations. I have never asked, for my own sanity, how this bizarre ritual began in his own life, but I must admit it's saved all of us here at one time or another. There's nothing like hearing me yell, "Lana Turner!" or hearing Leah say, "Danny Partridge!" when we're at our wit's end with a difficult customer or author.

"Good morning, Grandma! Morning, Rita!"

My voice comes out too high, like a songbird that's being placed into a girdle.

"Hi, sweetheart," Grandma says, standing. She gives me a big hug in her Mrs. Claus outfit. "How was your weekend in Chicago?"

"Don't ask!" Noah bellows from the checkout counter.

"Let's just say dressing like you for the Santa Run didn't end with a medal."

My grandma chuckles. "How's Holly? When is she coming to see us again?"

"Soon," I say. "She says hi."

My grandma skews her eyes behind the tiny glasses perched on the end of her nose.

"Well," she says, clapping her gloved hands together. "I'll let you two chat. I have to get going anyway. Papers to serve!"

"Grandma, really?" I ask. "Don't you think—"

She stops me cold. "The extra cash still helps keep this place afloat in the winter, and the pursuit makes my blood flow. Good for the health of me and the store. It's a win-win."

My octogenarian grandmother, Betty Norcross, is not simply a bookstore owner, but she's also a part-time process server. Who serves papers while dressed as Mrs. Claus.

"Who is it today, Grandma?"

"Loose lips sink ships," she says with a wink. "Don't worry, though. It's not you."

"Got the sleigh warmed up, Santa?" she calls.

My grampa appears.

He was an attorney and my grandmother a paralegal when they bought this place. Their business background and legal acumen were actually a wonderful foundation for being bookstore owners. When the store fell on hard times, my grandma became a process server. She might be the most loved—and feared—woman in the county. I mean, who wouldn't open a door, or take a package, from Mrs. Claus?

She has more stories than this store has novels.

"Rudolph's ready to go!" my grampa calls. "Ho! Ho! Ho!"

I watch them head out the store. Noah slaps my grandma on the behind and says, "Someone's still doing Pilates, am I right, Betty?"

"It's a pillow," she laughs.

I don't work in a bookstore. I work in an asylum.

And now I have to go one-on-one with *A Man Called Ove* disguised as a kindly older woman with a wash-and-set perm and Northern Reflections sweater featuring a happy, glittered cardinal on a snowy branch.

"How was your weekend, Rita?" I ask, taking off my coat and tossing it over the chair across from her.

I squeeze my soul to exude excitement and empathy.

I already know the answer.

"Awful," she says. "Two more dead. I had to pay my respects, of course." She takes a sip of her coffee from one of the mugs we sell that, ironically, states, "That's What I Do: I Read Books & Know Things!"

Rita knows everything.

About everyone.

"Remember Mrs. Demmings? That lovely woman who came in here and only bought books about Michigan?"

"I do," I say. "She hasn't been in for a while."

"That's because she had a stroke a few months back," Rita says.

"Oh, no."

"That's the funeral I attended on Saturday, remember?"

"I was out of town," I say. "Slipped my mind. I'm so sorry. How was it?"

"Poorly attended." She looks around the store, leans in and whispers, "Probably because that daughter of hers turned her little orchard into that abomination of a winery. I mean, who drinks wine at eleven in the morning?"

I do, I want to say. *In fact, I just did this weekend.*

I shrug.

"And that poor, poor Della Adams," Rita continues. "Lost her fourth husband. She has the worst luck. But I was there for her."

Rita reaches out and touches my hand.

She looks me in the eye, and I can feel my heart twinge.

"You're always there, Rita."

"Thank you, Susan."

Rita was one of my mother's best friends growing up, albeit long distance. They met at summer camp; Rita was born and raised in Petoskey, and my mom in Columbus, Ohio. The two bunked in the same cabin, Pinewood, and helped put on all the camp plays and musicals. I've heard all the stories, from my mom and from the entire town. The most shocking part of Rita's memoir? She used to be the wild child in town. She dated all the rich resort boys as a teenager. My mom used to spend summers with Rita and her family in Petoskey, working at a local resort. Both ended up being loyal to their home turf: Rita went to Michigan to study acting while my mom went to Ohio State to study acting and business. They were going to move to New York City and become Broadway stars together. But after my mom met my dad at a college party, largely thanks to Rita, and Rita's father was diagnosed with cancer her last month in college, the two BFFs moved back to Petoskey. The two best friends were finally reunited in the same town, destined to be together forever. Forever summer. Forever friends. And yet, time and life—as they are wont to do—changed and separated them. Rita never married or had children.

When my parents were killed, Rita felt it was her obligation to become my surrogate mom. She baked casseroles and cleaned the house. She helped pay bills, she opened the bookstore for my grandparents, she took me to school activities.

Even though I sometimes find it hard to be around Rita, I don't dislike her at all. I just hate looking in her eyes, because I can see myself—my past and my future—reflected. Rita has been defined by grief. She's still grieving for her father and her best friend. It's like we're both reading books that have no end. We are unable to write a new chapter.

"Well," Rita says. "Shall we get started?"

Rita puts down her coffee on the round table in front of the fireplace. She picks up her readers along with the weekly local paper, which comes out every Monday. She puts on her glasses, opens the paper—flicking it exactly five times—and smooths it on her lap. She turns the pages, licking her fingers every time she does. I have no idea why she doesn't head directly to the obituary section, but this is all part of the ritual.

"Oh, no!" Rita says. "Dr. Jenkins died."

She acts surprised, but I know she already knows this.

"I thought he retired early and moved to Florida in the early 2000s."

"He did," Rita says, scanning the paper. "But they're having a memorial in town." She looks at me. "This one's going to be tough." Rita flicks the paper in her lap and looks at me.

"Does it mention if he has grandchildren or great-grandchildren?" I ask.

"Two greats," Rita says.

"I'll be right back."

I beeline to the children's section across from the fireplace. I return a few seconds later. "Voilà!" I say.

Rita looks at the bright cover of the kid's book entitled *M Is for Mitten*.

She cocks her head.

"It's about Michigan, part of the Discover America State by State series," I say, opening the book, which is filled with colorful illustrations. "Kids can fly on the back of a robin to the Mackinac Bridge, head to Detroit to drink Vernors and then to Battle Creek to eat Kellogg's cereal, or go back in history to paddle through our state's lakes and bays in a birch bark canoe with Native Americans. It will be a way for his youngest family members to understand why he loved this state and area so much. It will be a way they can stay connected to their history."

Rita takes the book and thumbs through it. "Perfect! As always, Susan. Bravo."

"Thank you."

"Next!" Rita says, placing the book on the table next to her coffee. "Agnes Weaver."

After my parents died, my grandparents said that Rita started coming in Sleigh By the Bay every Monday when the store opened to buy a local paper and scan the obits. That tradition has continued. Now it's me who picks out the perfect book for her to take to the funeral or wake as a gift. And if no one in town has passed, I bring Rita the Traverse City paper or Detroit Free-Press, and she will pick out a person, I'll pick out a book, and we will send a book to the funeral home for the living spouse, children or relative. It's a rather morbid ritual I realize, but a necessary one, and an act I understand completely.

Rita needs to stay connected to me and to her past. She needs to feel in charge of a world that is too often filled with more mystery, gut-wrenching loss and unexplainable curveballs than a Gillian Flynn novel.

Mostly, Rita—just like me—is seeking to find an answer in a book that will never have closure.

"Weren't Mrs. Weaver and her son big birders?" I ask.

"Oh, yes, you're right. They were!"

I return with a book and hand it to Rita. She looks at me.

"*H Is for Hawk* is a memoir of the author's year spent training a northern goshawk in the wake of her father's unexpected death," I say. "It's really a book about the grieving process. I thought it might help and be just right."

The edges of Rita's lips actually turn up.

"Onto the next one," Rita says. "Oh, poor Judge Wilson. Only seventy-eight."

chapter 5

"The house smells so good!"

"It should," I say to my grandma as I take her coat. "It's your stew recipe."

"And The Pink Lady looks great," Grampa adds, "especially this time of year."

"Yeah, she still dresses up nicely for the holidays, doesn't she?"

My old home defines the quirk and character of Northern Michigan's cottage culture. She's a century-old, two-story Victorian featuring a wraparound porch, scalloped shingles at the top, and trim, trim and more trim, all in white. A white arrow hangs from the top gable pointing directly toward the lake. But her signature feature is her color: a pale pink with a deep pink roof.

The Pink Lady.

I bought her painted pink, and—much to local preservationists' relief—have kept it that way. I cannot imagine changing her true colors as she is a true lady—a Victorian classic, much like Elizabeth Gaskill—and I'm proud to be her steward for this time in her, and my, life.

It was the first home since my parents' that actually felt like mine. I loved—and still love—my grandparents' house, but it never was *my* home. Though my grandparents never conveyed this and would be mortified to know I felt this way, I did—especially as a teenage girl—feel like an interloper, the piece of new furniture in the vintage room that never quite fit in. I understand now this was my grief talking, but The Pink Lady is the closest replica of what I grew up in, with its own history and charm, and the place I knew could house all of my mother's heirlooms that had been in storage for so many decades: Her china cabinet, four-poster bed, hook rugs and Jenny Lind chairs.

I had a small housewarming party the first week in this house, where I made malts, barbecued burgers and watched—in honor of my Pink Lady—*Grease*. That's where it all started, how my best friends and I came to call ourselves the Pink Ladies. When they came to help me unpack and settle into my new home, and we started watching *Grease*, we all looked around, pointing at one another. We decided that Holly was Marty Maraschino—most attractive of the Pink Ladies. Leah, always a friend to all, was Frenchy; Noah—even though he was still in college at the time and working summers at the store—was Rizzo; and I was Sandy, still destined to meet the love of her life.

I glance up at my old house. She's been my lifeline and savior. In the summer, hydrangeas bloom in breathtaking blue and pretty pink all around the sweeping porch, patriotic bun-ting billowing over the rails and birdhouses hooked up high. Adirondack chairs line the front porch, and white camp lights are strung over the deck in the backyard. In the winter, pine boughs are hung over the railings, white lights highlight every angle, votive candles line the sidewalk, inflatables of Santa and Rudolph take the place of the Adirondack chairs, and a giant, pink bow is tied to the arrow.

"It's cold tonight," my grandma says. "You're letting all the heat out."

I close the front door, my grandparents kick off their snowy boots and I hang their coats.

My grampa sniffs the air, following the scent of the stew, like a bloodhound on the trail. He heads into the kitchen and lifts the lid on the pot.

"You have to work for your dinner first," I say.

My grampa grunts and places the lid back on the pot. "Then Santa deserves a Manhattan. He never takes a day off."

I laugh and make my father's favorite cocktail. I pour a glass of a hearty Pinot Noir for me and Grandma.

"This'll warm me up from the inside out," she says. "Cheers to another Christmas."

We all clink glasses and head to the living room.

A ten-foot-tall Christmas tree stands in the living room. Balsam fir has always been our family's favorite tree. Not only does it have soft, dark green needles and strong branches to hold our beloved ornaments but it also has an aromatic evergreen scent that fills the house with Christmas spirit.

My grampa groans. "I forgot how many boxes of ornaments there are."

"Grumpy Santa," my grandma says. "Sip your Manhattan."

It's almost odd to see my grandparents out of costume. I am so used to seeing them as Mr. and Mrs. Claus, that it's always shocking to see them simply as Nicholas and Betty Norcross this time of year.

My grandma and grampa make for a very striking couple. They were Woodward-Newman gorgeous in their youth, and I believe time has only made them even more beautiful. Today, my grandma might resemble a slightly older Jean Smart. She is polished and pretty. Grandma keeps her white hair shoulder length and softly curled. She got tired of the hassle—and heat—of wearing wigs, especially since she has to "stuff" her costume, so she adopted a hairstyle that could serve double duty as Mrs. Norcross and Mrs. Claus. Grandma attends her Silver Sneakers exercise class three times a week, and she walks nearly every other day, spring through fall, on the Little Traverse Wheelway, where I run nearly every day—even in the winter—and train for my races. The Wheelway is a twenty-six-mile, rail-to-trail bike path and paved trail which starts in Charlevoix and ends in Harbor Springs, running smack-dab through Petoskey and along the bay. It features some of the most stunning views in Michigan.

Out of his Santa costume, people say Grampa looks like the actor Charles Durning. He has a round, affable face, silver hair that he sweeps back with a bit of gel, a big bubble of a nose and rosy cheeks. As my grandma jokes, *Your grandfather does not need to stuff his costume.*

But my grampa is sturdy. He's the type of man who can hold chubby triplets in his arms without any effort and smile for the camera, or hoist a box of books on each shoulder and walk across the store.

In other words, he is St. Nick.

I open the first box of decorations. Each box and bin is carefully marked: Great-grandma's Tree Skirt, Grandma's Shiny Brites, Travel Ornaments. We each take an ornament and hang it on the branch, my grampa going high to decorate the top of the tree. Eventually, we come to the last boxes, marked in my mother's looping cursive, *My Christmas Ornaments*.

I open it slowly. Inside are her beloved ornaments, many of which she purchased in little Michigan gift shops when I was by her side: beautiful butterflies, fragile flowers and countless vintage Santa ornaments, many of which feature the year she bought them.

I retrieve an ornament—an ornate Christopher Radko Mrs. Claus—from its little box. Inside is the original gift tag in my childish script that reads:

To: Mom
From: Susan
Merry Christmas, 1991!

My grandma smiles, and I lift the ornament to the lights on the tree. My hand trembles ever so slightly. My grandma puts her arm around me.

"It looks so much like her when she would get all dolled up in her costume, doesn't it?"

The mouth on the ornament is open, an O, as if she's singing, or—like my mom—telling a story.

"Marilyn never knew a comma or period in her life, did she?" my grampa asks with a booming laugh. "Remember how your father would just walk into another room when she was in the middle of a story without any end and yell, 'Land the plane, Marilyn!'"

The two of them roll in laughter.

I nod. If I open my mouth, I will start crying. Even so many years later, it feels especially raw this year.

"How do you do it?" I finally ask. "Rather, how have you always done it? To just speak about them so freely? Every year,

I open these ornaments, and my heart just wants to shatter no matter how much time has passed."

"So does mine, Susan," Grandma says softly. "But what good does it do if we don't remember their lives? What happens if we don't honor their memories, especially this time of year? Everything just fades into oblivion. And that's not right."

"I would give my own life to bring your parents back," Grampa says. "I wished every day for years it would have been me. But none of us can undo time. None of us can go back in time. We can—and should—only move forward. It's the only thing that honors our lives and their memories."

"But what if..." I start.

"If if's and but's were candy and nuts, oh, what a Merry Christmas it would be," my grandma says. "We can't live the rest of our lives wondering what if. We can't live small simply to minimize the pain, because the world needs our strength and resilience. Just look at Rita. She stopped living the moment grief overtook her life." My grandma looks at the tree, and then back at me. "I grieve every single day. I grieve every holiday season. I grieve for my babies. I grieve for the state of the world. But you can't leave your heart in a box forever like these ornaments, unopened, unwilling to be touched. That's why I have to celebrate the lives of a son and daughter-in-law who gave us the greatest Christmas gift in the world. You."

I lean into her arms, and she holds me.

"You're going to make it through this holiday and this year, okay?" she says. "Actually, you're going to shine. I just know it."

My grampa takes a sip of his Manhattan and sits on the sofa. He touches a schooner ornament, and it floats back and forth as if it's sailing on rocky seas.

"No one's life is lived in vain if their memory is celebrated," he says. "Just look at my grandfather, Captain Santa. Trees still wash up on shore to this day, a century later, that people swear are from that boat. Legend says the lake never gives up her dead, and the Christmas tree ship was no exception. No bodies were ever recovered. But his legacy of kindness and goodwill lives on to this day. Years after my grandfather died, they found his wallet, made of waterproof oilskin, still watertight, the contents undamaged. They returned the wallet to my grandmother, and we all went to see it. Inside was a picture of the two of them, on the bow of the boat, as fresh as the day it was taken. 'A little piece of him came home to me,' she said, 'but he'll always live inside of me because he made my life better. That's what love is.'"

My grampa turns his gaze on me. "And you know the name of the fishing boat that recovered Captain Santa's wallet?"

"*The Reindeer*," I say in unison with him.

He smiles and continues. "That's right. My grandma's buried right next to his headstone. Her tombstone is a simple stone with an evergreen etched in it. The last time I visited, I was greeted with the overwhelming scent of pine, as real as this tree before me right now. In fact, the whole cemetery smelled like Christmas. I like to believe that my grandfather did make it home to be with my grandma." He focuses on me again. "I need to believe that we'll all be reunited again. I need to continue that legacy of providing kindness to complete strangers. That's how I go on. That's why it's an honor to be Santa."

We hang the Mrs. Claus ornament front and center, finish decorating and then have our stew in front of the tree. Later, I walk my grandparents to their car and then sit by the tree with my phone in my hand, waiting for them to call to say they've made it to their knotty-pine cottage by the bay ten minutes away. When I know they're home safe and sound, I head up the narrow staircase to the second floor.

Everyone is charmed by the Pink Lady's tiny turret. The room is round and has an old ornate fireplace that I've switched to gas, burnished woodwork and tall, narrow windows with what Realtors here call a "seasonal view," meaning you can see the bay when all the leaves are off the trees in town. I've made it into a guest room, because everyone wants to stay in here. They love its quirk as well as the fact they can sit in the window seat and read, or drink coffee and watch summer tourists bike, jog or walk their dogs.

Down the hall is a room I keep locked. I call it my office, and people don't question it. But it's actually a spare bedroom I decorate for the holidays all on my own.

If my public life were a book, Sleigh By the Bay would be the cover. It's how people see me. It defines me. It's a picture of what I like readers to see, and how I want them to buy into my character. My home would be the first chapter. It sells readers on my story. I decorate for the holidays, for instance, because I love Christmas. But I also want to portray an image and storyline so people believe that I believe in happy endings.

But I keep a room all to myself. In a book, this room might be what an author would term as her "little darling."

"Kill your darlings" is one of the most common pieces of advice given by authors to aspiring writers. It's when an author must rid a work of an unnecessary passage, character or story-line—often one that the author loves, thus, a "darling"—for the overall sake of the work. It's often attributed to William Faulkner, but its literary roots go all the way back to English writer Sir Arthur Quiller-Couch who more brutally stated, *"Murder your darlings."*

I have a few darlings I've tried hard in my life to rid myself of, but I have yet to convince myself my overall life would be better without them.

I open the door, click on the light and step inside. A small desk sits below the window, and there's a twin bed against one wall. Bookcases filled with my mother's and father's favorite books line another.

I open the tiny closet and pull out two bins stacked atop one another and drag them over to the bed. I pull free a Charlie Brown tree—a replica of the sad little bent tree from the Christmas cartoon special, right down to the single red ornament that weighed it down—and place it on a nightstand. It's a tree my mom bought me for my bedroom when I was little. I wrap the base in its little blue Linus blanket and surround it with Charlie Brown, Snoopy, Lucy, Linus and Sally figurines. On the other nightstand, I stack my favorite childhood Christmas books, including *How the Grinch Stole Christmas* by Dr. Seuss.

I retrieve the other bin and open it. The scents—like those of the balsam fir in my living room and the evergreen at the cemetery in my grandfather's memory—overwhelm me. I pull out two pillows and place them vertically on the bed as if they were people laying down for a nap. I retrieve two Santa caps and place them on the tops of the pillows.

And then I pull each into my arms and inhale.

Old Spice and Shalimar.

My father's favorite cologne and my mother's favorite perfume are still fragrant on their pillows and velvet caps that I've kept hidden and all to myself for so many years.

I hold them forever, place them back on the bed and lay down with my parents.

This room is akin to lighting a candle at church or visiting the Wailing Wall and sliding a note into the rocks. It is sacred to me.

I shut my eyes, say a prayer and then cast my eyes upward. On the wall over the headboard is my poem from fourth grade, "The Single Kringle." It is housed in a red frame, and the first prize medal I won for writing and reciting it in elementary school hangs beside it.

I look at the words, upside down, and think that is exactly how my life has been since my parents' deaths.

To the outside world, Susan is good.

In here, surrounded by the darlings she cannot surrender, she is alone.

And yet... I can still recite the poem I wrote so long ago.

People say Santa isn't real
But he was a man named St. Nicholas
To think otherwise
Is purely ridiculous.

We must believe
Because faith is no game
There is purpose beyond us
Otherwise life is a shame.

How does one make
A wish come true?
By believing in others
But also believing in you.

So, until my day comes
I'll remain happy and bright
And I will believe in my Kringle
With all of my might.

I must believe. I must remember. I must remain happy and bright with all my might.

Why?

I sit up and reach for the framed poem. It is heavy, heavier than I remember, heavier than anyone would ever know.

I remove it from the wall.

The poem is a ruse.

I set the frame on the bed and remove the panel on the back to reveal a virtual mini safe beneath the glass.

To reveal the reason behind my childhood words and fading belief.

"Merry Christmas, Mom and Dad."

Many people keep their loved ones' ashes in urns on mantels or vases beside their bed. My grandparents have what I secretly call a "death shelf" dedicated to my parents: framed photos of them from all stages of their lives sit on a specially made shelf in their den surrounding a beautiful urn that resembles, fittingly, a book. My grandparents like to gaze upon it as they read or watch TV in front of the fire.

"It feels like they're with us."

I've never told them that it sort of creeps me out. When I try to watch TV with them, my eyes focus on the book. If I nod off and wake to see my parents in pictures, my dazed disappointment is almost too much to bear. So I keep some of my parents' ashes in the place I know is closest to my heart, the words I wrote in tribute to them and their undying love so long ago.

I've told most people that I scattered my parents' ashes on the bay Christmas Day decades ago, but I'm a wonderful little white liar, and I can scatter my half-truths softly into the air like winter's first snowflakes. I've kept people—pardon the pun—at bay for so long by telling them what they want to hear.

Yes, I'm seeing someone.

Yes, the holidays are hard, but I focus on how much I was loved.

You know men these days. No one wants to commit.

Online dating is so hard. I wish I could meet someone like my parents and grandparents did.

I've had horrible dates—*Hello, Cletus!*—and heartbreaking disappointments—*Hello, mysterious Santa!*—that have made me swear off men, but—many moons ago—I've also had a few wonderful dates. I've gone on first dates where I've felt a real connection, second dates that led to a kiss, and third, fourth and fifth dates that could actually make me see a future. And, oh, how that terrified me. Waving goodbye in the morning to a husband and child, watching them pull out of the driveway and then wondering every second of every hour of every day if they would be okay and return home to me.

People often say you hit forty, and you stop giving a damn. You stop caring about what other people think.

That's not entirely true.

It's that when you hit forty, you start looking at the finish line of your life, and you see there aren't that many people in front of you. And when I hit forty, the age my mother passed away—without having achieved the things she had, like love and children—well, it wants to stop me cold in my tracks even more quickly than a blizzard blowing off the bay.

Such milestones and markers either bring great clarity or great confusion.

It's brought both to me. I know what I want, what I need, what I deserve, but I'm too paralyzed to make that happen. And so you learn to be content with who you are and what you have.

You become content with the reality of being alone, because it's less terrifying than having it all and losing it all over again.

"What do you wish for Christmas this year?" I ask the ashes.

The wind whistles around the Pink Lady's old gables.

"Me, too," I whisper. "Me, too."

I close the frame and place it back on the wall with a little kiss.

Over at the bookshelf, I scan the titles, running my fingers over the spines of the books, before I see one that makes total sense. Every Christmas, I pick out a new book—one that I think will make the perfect gift—for a dead stranger.

You see, Rita may have been the one who started this tradition long ago.

But I think I was the one who perfected it.

chapter 6

"Merry Christmas, Jordan."

I grab a chair perched uninvitingly against a back wall and scooch it next to his bed.

"How have you been?"

The ventilator exhales.

"It's time for our annual holiday visits again. Can you believe a year has passed since I saw you last Christmas? Time flies, doesn't it?"

The heart monitor beeps.

"My parents are missing another holiday season," I say. "I turned forty this year." I stop. "My mom's last birthday was forty."

The word *forty* echoes in the sterile room.

Two cardinals light upon a branch outside his window.

They're here. My parents are here right now.

"I brought a book I hope you'll like this year," I say. "It's a classic. I was going through my parents' favorites, and this caught my eye. It just seemed perfect this year."

I hold up the book.

"*The Polar Express.*"

I look at Jordan.

"Did you ever read it?"

Silence.

"Well, it's about a boy who's skeptical about the existence of Santa Claus. He is lying on his bed, waiting to see if his disbelief in magic will be proven. He doesn't believe in things he can't see. At five minutes to midnight, he spots a train, The Polar Express, waiting on his doorstep, bound for the North Pole. After some hesitation, he finally boards the train in his pajamas and is sent on a journey of friendship, courage and belief. He reaches the North Pole…" I stop. "I don't want to give away the ending. I have so many readers who come into the bookstore and read the ending of a book. I'm still shocked by that. The ending of anything must be a journey of discovery. Shall we get started?"

I being to read the first pages.

After a few minutes, I stop and look at Jordan.

"So, do you think God is a pantser or a plotter?"

Silence.

"It's a question I've been wrestling with for a very long time now."

More silence.

"Yeah, me neither."

Are you a pantser or a plotter? is a question most every author receives from a reader while on tour. Being a pantser as an author means that you write by the seat of your pants, letting the characters take you on their journey. An author may not know, day to day, where the story is headed, or even what the ending will be. A plotter meticulously plans and outlines their stories before they begin writing. Some authors may write a hundred pages or so for a novel before they even type the first word. Many approach the process of writing like screenwriters do a script, laying plots and subplots out on the walls around them so they can see how it unfolds.

"I can often tell if an author is a plotter or a panster during the first few minutes we meet," I continue. "But God's got me fooled. He's a mystery. Do you think all of this was planned, or do you think it just happened accidentally?"

Silence.

"Tell me, Jordan!" I suddenly yell. "Tell me you're sorry!"

My voice booming back to me in the room startles me, and I start to cry.

I hear a squeak. I wipe my eyes and turn.

A kindly looking woman in tennis shoes, scrubs and dark bags under her eyes is peeking into the room.

"Hello, there," she says.

"Hi," I say.

"I thought I heard someone in here," she says. "It's so nice to see Jordan has a visitor. You know the last of his family passed last year? His mom sure doted on him, but the rest of the family never visited. I'm just glad he has a friend."

Friend?

"He used to come into my bookstore," I say. "I read to him every Christmas."

"What a sweet thing to do," she says, clapping her hands together. "My goodness, you're like a real-life Santa, spreading joy to strangers."

I can only nod. When she leaves, I stand and hold up the book.

"So how do you think it's going to end?"

I look directly into Jordan's unresponsive face.

"I can't give away the ending."

chapter 7

"If Holly FaceTimes, don't pick up," I say rushing into Sleigh By the Bay the next day. "She's called twenty times." I set my phone down. "I'm waiting for Phillip's publicist to call. Only pick up if it's him. It'll be a 212 New York area code, okay?"

My staff stares at me. I continue without a breath.

"He's supposed to arrive at 11:30 for the noon luncheon at the Perry. A rush of customers is coming at ten to pick up the new releases—remember, most of them are either autographed or have personalized bookplates for each customer—and I want to make sure everything is perfect for the event. I sold most of the tickets to this to the Bay Book Club, and you know what perfectionists they are."

"Take a breath, diva," Noah says, hands on his hips. "Right now, you're spewing as much minutiae as the rider in Mariah

Carey's Las Vegas residency contract." He looks at me. "We got you, boo."

I literally take two steps when I hear, "Hi, Holly! She's right here."

I turn and glare at Noah. He's got Holly on FaceTime. "Girlfriends call for a reason," he says, shrugging his shoulders. "If a BFF calls more than twice, it's either an emergency, a bad date, an even worse haircut or they just eloped. Am I right, diva?"

Holly laughs.

"Hi, Holly!" Leah waves at the screen.

I walk over.

"You look beautiful, Marty Maraschino," Noah continues. "What's your secret?"

"The magic elixirs you send me," Holly says. "You could open your own shop in Chicago."

"I know, right? Maybe 'Noah Knows,' or wait! 'Noah's Ark.' I could bundle two things together, like an eye cream and wrinkle reducer."

"I love it!"

I step behind the counter and lean into the video call. "I hate to break up this girls' weekend, but I am overwhelmed. What's the urgent matter? Split ends?"

"Meow," Holly starts. "And with this holiday hair? Never."

Holly has her hair sculpted into an actual wreath atop her head.

"Did you swallow a Michaels store?" I ask.

"It's a rope twist crown braid that I decorated with green ribbon, holly leaves, red bows and little Christmas balls! It's already gotten a half million views."

"Congrats," I say. "I have a luncheon for a hundred in a few hours, and new books for waiting customers."

"Well, I'll make this quick since you haven't returned my calls in nearly two weeks since the Santa Run."

"I told you I'm done with all that. I'm fine being single." I think of my poem.

"See, you just said 'fine,' not 'happy' being single, or even 'content,'" Holly says. "Fine is only good if it's china. We're going to find that Santa Claus who was hitting on you."

"What?"

The simultaneous gasp from Noah and Leah echoes in the bookstore.

"Do tell," Leah says.

"She didn't tell you?" Holly asks. "A very handsome man…"

"He was dressed as Santa," I interject. "And I was dressed as Mrs. Claus in one of my grandma's costumes. He might have looked like a werewolf underneath his costume."

"Anyway," Holly continues, undaunted, "they had a connection. You could feel it in the air. He didn't just hit on Susan, he liked her and then asked her to meet him at a bar after the race."

"He didn't show."

"Because he fell on the ice," Holly adds quickly. "I'm convinced of it."

"Says Angela Lansbury."

"Stop it!" Noah cries. "This is like watching a live version of *What Ever Happened to Baby Jane?* Just cut to the chase."

Holly raises an eyebrow. "Soooo… I have the list of every runner who participated in the run. Of the 25,000 runners, about 12,000 were men. Of those, half were repeat runners who knew O'Malley's Bar from previous years. Of those roughly six thousand eligible men, half were in the age range of thirty-five to fifty, which I'm guessing—by the shape of your Santa's legs and the fine lines around his eyes—he had to be."

"This is insane," I say.

"So we're down to about three thousand men, who I plan to stalk on social media to see if they're married, if they posted photos from the run on social media. Speaking of which!" Holly claps her hands together. "I posted that photo I took of you with Hot Santa on my social media accounts. With my huge following, it just seemed like the perfect place to start. Maybe one of my followers will recognize him. Or maybe he's already one of my followers."

"You are the Chicago Kardarshian, diva!" Noah says.

"If if's and but's were candy and nuts, oh, what a Merry Christmas it would be," I mutter.

"Bah humbug," Noah says, sticking his tongue out at me.

"I'm coming up next week for your Desiree Delmonico event, and we're going to start there."

"My life finally has purpose!" Noah cheers.

"I'm in, too!" Leah adds.

"You're single, Noah," I say. "And so are you, Leah. You both need to focus on finding your own Claus."

"You're way more fun," Leah says. "I need a holiday project. Each of us can take about 750 guys and compile a list. Maybe we get down to a couple of hundred we can send a Facebook message to or something like that."

"Yes!" Holly says.

"I'm hanging up," I say.

Holly opens her mouth to continue talking, and I hit End. Noah and Leah are staring at me.

"Enough crazy talk for today," I say. "The guy was hitting on me with a bunch of bad come-on lines."

"'Can I take a picture of you, so I can show Santa exactly what I want for Christmas?'" Noah says.

I look at him.

"What?" he continues. "I've used a few of those lines before, too. It doesn't mean someone's a bad person. It just means that he's nervous to talk to someone he likes." Noah hesitates. "He's nervous to show the world who he is for fear he'll be rejected like he has been his whole life." He pauses again. "Or maybe someone is simply afraid to take a risk anymore for fear *she'll* lose somebody again."

He looks at me and then busily begins to organize the new books that had arrived on Tuesday.

"I'm so far behind now," I say, walking away. Then I stop and turn. "I hear you. Thank you."

As I head upstairs, I can hear Noah and Leah giggle. The words "Sexy Santa" float in the air.

"Were you calling me?" my grampa asks, walking in the door.

The two burst into laughter.

"I feel like I'm on the coast of Italy."

Kathleen, Phillip's publicist, is standing at one of the large windows in The H.O. Rose Room overlooking Little Traverse Bay. She is wearing the typical New York publicist's ensemble: black pants, black turtleneck, black coat, black hair. "Save for the snow."

"You know, this area is the reason bay windows were invented," I say.

"Really?" Kathleen takes a big step back and clamps her hand over her heart. "I never knew that."

"I'm just teasing," I say. "It was one of my father's favorite jokes."

She laughs. "You got me. Is he coming today?"

I look out the windows facing the bay. In the far distance, nearly on the horizon, an icebreaker—Christmas red—slowly churns through the frigid waters, making a safe pathway for other boats and ships.

"He passed away when I was young, along with my mom."

"Oh, my gosh, Susan. I'm so sorry. I didn't know. May I ask how it happened?"

My eyes remain on the boat. "A drunk driver," I say. "They were on their way here, actually, dressed as Mr. and Mrs. Claus, for the town's big Christmas party. They were carrying on the tradition of my grampa and grandma."

"Like you're doing with the store," Kathleen says. She puts her hand on my back. "I can't imagine."

There is a very long silence.

"May I say something?" she finally asks. "Something personal?"

I turn to look at her. "Of course."

"You are so, so strong, Susan. To go through all of that, to come out the other side the incredibly smart and savvy woman you are, to continue the legacy of Sleigh By the Bay and to give Phillip a second chance is something few of us could do. It's a testament to the foundation and love your grandparents gave you and to the fact that you want to make the world a better place."

My eyes flit back to the icebreaker before it disappears, a red Santa cap just floating away, and I cannot help but think that Kathleen's words are like that ship, knocking down chunks of a frozen wall I've built over the years to protect myself.

Second chances. Jordan. Holly. Phillip. My Hot Santa.

Maybe all that ice has inhibited passage into my heart.

"Thank you," I finally say. "That means more than you'll ever know."

"Ladies."

We turn.

"Phillip," Kathleen says.

If you were to call a casting agent looking for an actor to play an East Coast literary novelist, they would send you Phillip Strauss. He resembles Jeremy Irons, back in the day, with his piercing eyes and longer hair—gray at the temples—that falls just-so. He wears brow line tortoise eyeglasses—a term I learned from Holly—a more modern version of the 1950s glasses my grampa wore when he was younger. His eyes do not look distorted behind them, and I wonder if they're merely an accessory.

"Welcome to the Perry Hotel," I say. "And huge congratulations on *Must Be Nice*."

"Thank you, Susan," he says. "This is just lovely. These views are simply breathtaking."

"This hotel was built in 1899 and is the only one of Petoskey's gorgeous turn-of-the-century hotels still in existence," I say. "In 1916 Ernest Hemingway hiked and camped his way to Northern Michigan from his home in Illinois with a friend. When he arrived in Petoskey, Hemingway stayed right here at the Perry Hotel. He paid seventy-five cents for his room before heading to the family cottage, Windemere, at Walloon Lake."

"You're a fount of knowledge," Phillip says. "A walking map of Michigan."

I hold up my hand, and Phillip flinches.

"I'm not going to slap you," I say.

"You have every right after my last visit."

Second chances. Maybe he has changed.

"We use our hand as a map in Michigan. It's shaped like a mitten. See?" I point to the tip of my middle finger. "You're here. Hemingway's summer home was on Walloon Lake, a glacial-formed lake that is one of Michigan's most majestic inland lakes. It empties into Lake Michigan. Walloon Lake is right down here." I point again on my hand.

"Fascinating," he says.

There's something I now realize about the way he says *fascinating* that gives me pause. It comes out as "fashinating," a bit slurry. I look closely at Phillip. His eyes are a bit bloodshot behind his glasses, and he smells like he had a hard night—or morning—and has put on loads of cologne to cover the alcohol.

"Born and raised here."

"There's something to be said for roots and staying put, especially in such a quirky little town. It's so rare these days." He looks at me and smiles. "You're practically a dinosaur."

Dinoshaur.

I know I should take this as a compliment but, considering our past experience, it feels a little like a dig.

"I hope you had a good night's sleep?"

"I did," he says. "We got in late from Chicago. Two stops there yesterday and a load of media appearances, thanks to Kathleen. Publisher is saying presales and first week's sales are very strong, especially at the big-box stores."

"Well, we have a wonderful event planned today. Our Bay Book Club are our special guests, and they loved your first novel…"

Phillip gives me a look, and Kathleen shifts on her feet. Their reactions silently say, *That was two books ago, thank you very much.*

"…they're literary readers, and I will get them to buy your book not only for their January discussion but also for holiday gifts. I'm hoping for sales of over a hundred books this afternoon."

"Wonderful," Phillip says.

Men and women begin to file into the Rose Room, chatting and perusing the long table of books set up by the entrance that Leah is managing.

"We should meet and greet," I say.

I walk Phillip over to meet Dee Whitcroft, the head of the book club and head of pretty much every charity event in Northern Michigan. Her family owns a massive swath of prime lakeshore property that's been sold over the years—as the region has become a vacation mecca—to real estate and

commercial developers. Her home on the lake is built to resemble a ship. It sits on a bluff and as you approach looks as if
the home is floating atop the water.

"Is that a Birkin bag?" Phillip asks Dee.

"You have an exquisite eye, Mr. Strauss."

"I have an appreciation of the finer things," he says. "Great
literature is like great fashion. Works of art."

The two take some champagne and continue chatting. I
slip over next to Leah.

"Is that…" she starts.

"Yes, it's the Holy Grail of purses," I say, finishing her
thought. "Holly posted about it once. She said it was worth
more than my house."

"I thought she said it was worth way more than your house."

"Thank you, Leah."

"Sorry. That didn't come out right. But this event is. If
he schmoozes Mrs. Whitcroft enough, she'll buy a thousand
copies and give them away at her charity events. Win-win
for all of us."

Tuxedoed waitstaff circulates amongst the guests as silently
as ghosts, serving champagne and light hors d'oeuvres. After
fifteen minutes or so, we take our seats. I sit on one side of
our round table with a group of women who have been customers of the store since my grandparents first bought it. Phillip sits across from me, next to Dee. A luncheon of planked
whitefish—a Michigan specialty in which the locally caught
fish is cooked and served on a cedar plank alongside garlic
mashed potatoes and vegetables—is served along with wine.
I notice that, in less than ten minutes, Phillip's wineglass is
empty and he's motioning for a refill. When I see him slam
that and gesture for another, I stand in a rush—rattling my
silverware across my plate in order to introduce him earlier

than expected in hopes he might not slur his speech or start singing "Sweet Caroline."

"It is my great honor," I start, the microphone producing a blast of shrill feedback, "to welcome *New York Times* bestselling author Phillip Strauss here today to talk about his latest novel, *Must Be Nice*, which is earning rave reviews. And we are more than honored that Phillip has made Sleigh By the Bay a part of his launch week's tour. It's the highest compliment to us as a community of readers. Thank you, Phillip."

I continue, reading Phillip's bio and a summary of the novel. Then I stop for a moment. I always love to make a book and an author as personal as humanly possible for readers in order to make them fall in love with the person behind the book, and goodness knows Phillip needs that love from me.

"Phillip and I were talking about Ernest Hemingway earlier today, and how he stayed at the Perry and summered at Walloon with his family, but did you know, Phillip, that in a December just like this some 103 years ago, Hemingway wore an Italian cape and uniform while addressing the Ladies Aid Society about his World War I experiences, and during the event he met the Connable family, who connected him with an editor from the *Toronto Star* newspaper. This interaction in Michigan started his career as a European correspondent with the paper. Michigan may be known as the Mitten, but I think the analogy goes deeper than that. We are always willing to reach out a hand to others, from those in need to those we admire. With that in mind, let's put our hands together for Phillip Strauss."

I lead a round of applause.

"Phillip?" I call for him to take the podium at the front of the room.

He makes his way toward me, wineglass and papers in hand, in a way that can only be described as a bird flying in a hurricane. I return to my seat. Phillip plops down his wine on the podium, grabs it for support and then begins to laugh like a madman.

How much of a head start has he had today?

"You come to a place like this, especially in the winter, and it's no wonder Hemingway drank so much, is it? Am I right?"

There is shocked silence, followed by a smattering of nervous giggles.

"Susan was very loquacious in her introduction. One might think Hemingway was actually here with his latest book. He's not. I am." Phillip laughs.

What is he doing?

"The reality is I wrote a masterpiece on the level of some of Hemingway's greatest novels, and Susan is hosting me because she was forced to host me."

Why is he doing this?

He takes a gulp of his wine.

"Isn't that right, Susan?"

All heads turn toward me. I search to find Kathleen. She is on her phone in the lobby. I motion for her.

"Susan?"

"I'm hosting you," I say, my heart pulsing in my temples, "because I believe in supporting authors and bringing a diverse group of voices and books to Northern Michigan."

Phillip laughs again and grabs a piece of paper from the stack on his podium. He flaps it in the air. "Like Desiree Delmonico?" he asks with a dismissive grunt. "I'm preceding the Queen of Steam? Is that one of the 'diverse' group of voices you're bringing to your readers?"

The world around me dissolves. As a bookseller, I've been involved in countless confrontations, from rude customers to angry authors to bats in the store. I can handle anything. But the one thing I cannot tolerate is a mean drunk.

"Different readers have different tastes," I hear myself saying. "Many simply want—and need—an escape from this world, and a book can take them anywhere in their minds. Who are you to say what is a better, or a more literary, book than another? Who are you to decide what authors deserve attention and what authors do not? Who are you to demean what book someone chooses to read? The common denominator is that our community reads, and that's a glorious common denominator, don't you think?"

One clap turns into two, and soon the room is echoing with applause and cheers. I turn. Even Dee Whitcroft is standing.

Phillip lurches off the podium and storms across the room. I follow.

"What the hell just happened?" Kathleen asks, catching up with us in the lobby.

"He hasn't changed," I say.

"Neither have you." Phillip pivots to face me. "I know you tried to kill my career. I thought I'd return the favor."

"You pathetic drunk," I say.

"Okay, enough," Kathleen says, stepping between us. "Can we just call it a day?"

Phillip pulls keys from his pocket. "I need some fresh air," he says.

At first, I think he is going back to his room to change and go for a walk, but I look more closely and see the keys are for a rental car. I race forward and pull the keys from his hands.

"What are you doing?"

"How dare you!" I suddenly yell. "You should be ashamed!"

"For what?" he says, red-faced.

"For caring so little about anyone but yourself! You may be an ass, but I won't let you kill yourself or anyone in our community." I glare at him. "Even an ass deserves to live. I pray you get clarity."

He storms out, footsteps slowly fading as he heads down the staircase, and the lobby falls eerily quiet save for the buzz in the Rose Room.

"I'm so deeply sorry," Kathleen says. "What can I do to make this up to you?"

"Don't represent him?" I offer, lifting my shoulders.

"'A man without ethics is a wild beast loosed upon this world,'" Kathleen says.

I look at her.

"Albert Camus," she explains. "I signed a contract, and there is an ethics clause in it. He's breaking that clause, and I plan to speak with his publisher about his actions as soon as we're done talking. Know this cannot and will not be tolerated. He will not treat another bookstore like this."

Kathleen continues. "I know that's not enough, but I promise I will not let him act like this again. Publishing, as you know, is a small circle. And believe me, I can and will quietly get the word out about him until all of publishing is playing the telephone tag like we did as kids, and Phillip's image is forever tarnished."

"You would do that?"

"I'm a publicist. I can do anything. And this doesn't require an ounce of spin," Kathleen says. "I can spin Phillip's books, life and career, but I can't spin his soul. None of us can hire a publicist to spin our own lives. We don't need to anyway. We do a good enough job of that all on our own, don't we?"

"Thank you."

"Can I get real with you?"

"You're not already?"

Kathleen laughs. "I can apologize for Phillip until I'm blue in the face, but you're never going to get an apology from him." She looks at me for the longest time until I shift on my feet. "And I have a feeling from the way you reacted to him that's not really the apology you're seeking."

"It isn't," I say.

"This is totally none of my business, but have you ever spoken with a grief counselor?"

"I did for much of my childhood," I say, "and well into my thirties, but, as you might know, grief is a tricky thing. It's like the ice on our bay. Despite being aware of it and doing everything possible to clear it away, you still have no idea how thick it's gotten and how dangerous it is until it's too late."

"You're a strong, brave woman," Kathleen says. "Thank you for having the courage to stand up to him. Thank you for having the courage to stop him from driving. Thank you for being you."

The emotions of the day hit me, and I hug Kathleen tightly.

"It's hard to be me," I say.

"It's hard to be anyone these days."

I laugh.

"What do you wish for Christmas?" Kathleen asks, releasing me. "I owe you."

All I wish for Christmas is the way it used to be, I think.

"To sell about a hundred books other than Phillip's so I can break even today," I say instead. "That would be a Christmas miracle."

"Well, then, I'm your Christmas miracle worker," Kathleen says. "I have an author whose debut is going to be a Reese Witherspoon book club pick in January. Nobody's supposed to know yet, but it's our little secret, right? We can get those preorders before anybody else. Let's go."

We head into the Rose Room, and Kathleen beelines for the podium.

As she begins to speak to the room, another boat—red as Santa's cap—floats on the bay, knocking away the ice yet again.

chapter 8

As if on cue, "Ice Ice Baby" by Vanilla Ice plays in my ears.

If there was a problem, yo, I'll solve it…

Oh, I'll solve it, all right, I think to myself.

I pick up my running pace as the song reverberates in my ears.

Ice, ice, baby…

Thank you, irony. My life should be an O. Henry story.

There are patches of ice on Little Traverse Wheelway, and—after the week I've had—the last thing I need is a fall. But things are improving, at least weatherwise. We've had two surprise days in the forties, a virtual heat wave here by winter standards, and I've already seen countless Michiganders come into the store wearing shorts and flip-flops.

I watch the path, but I can't help but look out at the view. Even after years of running this same path, it is still breathtaking in its magnitude: the bay shimmers in the sun, the ice making the water resemble a giant, deep blue cocktail.

Sometimes I lie to myself when I run. Well, *lie* is perhaps too strong a word. I *fool* myself. I tell myself—when my body is tired, my mind weary—if I go one more mile, I can stop, knowing full well I won't. It's a trick that both runners and authors utilize: one more step, one more word, one more mile, one more page. Running and writing are cumulative. You do not see the progress at first, and then a mile becomes five, and a page turns into a chapter, and you push yourself to limits you never dreamed you could achieve.

Both are endurance miracles really, feats of the body and imagination. I can do only one. But I admire the other. It's why I run. It's why I do what I do. Because somewhere, deep inside, I still believe in miracles, that this long, often punishing journey will have a miraculous finish line.

The segment of the path I am currently running, between Petoskey's Bayfront Park to Petoskey State Park, follows closely the path of the original Little Traverse Wheelway that stretched from Petoskey to Harbor Springs in the late 1800s. In fact, I run directly underneath a gate over the trail at the east end of Bayfront Park that proclaims "No Teaming or Driving." This sign replicates the original gate that stood at nearly the same spot. It is a reminder of a time when people were prohibited from riding horses or horse-drawn carriages on the trail.

The sign, along with the lack of people on the path, does make me feel as if I've gone back in time. Those of us who live and work full-time in resort communities often don't get to play in, or fully appreciate, the places others flock to on vacation. But in the winter, we tend to get a piece of the place we love back.

I scan the bay. It's just iced over like a beautiful cake.

From April through October, the Wheelway is clogged with bikers, joggers and Rollerbladers. I joke, only half-heartedly, that my neck is perpetually kinked spring through fall from the constant calls of "On your left!" as exercisers pass me on the path.

I chug along the Wheelway that hugs a huge bluff rising over Little Traverse Bay. This section is called Resorts Bluff and considered a crown jewel of the path's crown for a reason: the views make even the most ardent of exercisers slow and take in the expanse.

I pass a fishing pond left over from an old limestone quarry, just steps away from the bay, where the exposed shoreline is the perfect place to pluck Petoskey stones. Salmon-colored sidewalks, shoveled clean of the snow, signal my entry into the historic Bay View neighborhood, dominated by Victorian homes much larger and much older than mine. Bay View has long been a summer getaway for prominent Michigan families. I follow the trail for another mile and a half, passing a trail entrance to Petoskey State Park. I head down the trail and am greeted by sweeping sand dunes. In the summer, this swimming beach is jammed to the gills. Today, it is all mine.

At least for a few minutes until I meet my grandma.

I stop and lift my face to the sun. I remove my earbuds. The chilly wind off the water dries my sweat. The sound of the waves stills my heart. I open my eyes.

Why did I choose to remain in a town where my parents were killed? Where I am constantly surrounded by ghosts?

Because this is home.

I have walked these same paths and strolled these same beaches with my parents and grandparents my entire life. My grandma found her first Petoskey stone as a girl right over there. My mom used to paint sunsets on this beach. My dad would fish, and my grampa told me about his very first kiss on this beach.

There is a map in my heart that is shaped like a mitten, and it always leads me home.

And I know in my heart I yearn for someone to see what I still see here.

Family.

"Susan!"

I hear my name carried on the wind, and I turn. Grandma and Grampa are standing way down the beach, motioning for me to join them.

I take off, jogging along the shoreline, dancing this way and that like a piping plover to avoid the waves.

"Grampa's walking?" I ask, catching my breath. "Hell has officially frozen over."

He rubs his belly. "Santa's gotta stay in shape, too. He's got a big day coming up." My grampa laughs. "And nothing's completely frozen over yet. Beautiful December day, isn't it?"

I nod.

"How was your run, sweetheart?" my grandma asks.

"Great," I say. "Why'd you call me all the way down here? Trailhead's up there."

"That's why. Look!"

My grandma points, and I follow her index finger.

On a large swath of beach, where the sand is hard, stands a sculpture garden.

To be more accurate, a sculpture garden created by Mother Nature.

"Wow!" is the only word I can muster.

Hundreds of shapes—some a few feet high—dot the shoreline. This happens on rare occasions during early winter on the beaches of Michigan. Frozen, sculpted sand along the lake emerge when strong winds erode the frozen sand.

The end result feels as if you've wandered into someone's pottery studio and are perusing half-finished works of art.

I take a few steps closer and study the shapes.

A number of them resemble the vintage turned wood Christmas ornaments my mom and grandma collected.

"Oh, my gosh," I say. "Look at that. Someone's already been out here. They drew a figure eight around those two ornaments."

My grampa laughs.

"What's so funny?"

"It's not a figure eight," he says, "it's an infinity sign."

I look again.

"Listen," he continues. "Sssshhhh."

A gust of wind whips off the water and encircles two sand ballerinas. The wind picks up the sand, and the ladies look as if they are dancing in the sunshine. I move my eyes down the figures, and the wind is creating an infinity sign around them.

"We know how hard this holiday season is for you," my grandma says. "We just wanted to remind you of how beautiful it is, too. You work so hard, you rarely take time to enjoy what's around you anymore. Sometimes, we have to remind ourselves to stop and look around."

My grampa gestures to the shapes in front of us.

"Not to get all preachy on you, but we just wanted you to see the beauty of what can be created when we allow the wind to wash over us and allow our true selves to emerge," he says. "I believe God is telling us that when we still our minds and bodies, when we believe in something greater than simply what we see that surrounds us, then the image of what was originally intended will finally be born.

"Infinity," my grampa continues. "God's understanding has no limit. It's infinite. We are all connected."

I look at my grandfather. His faith has carried him this far after so much loss.

He looks at me and then scans the horizon. "I believe I will see your mother and father again, or I would not be able to go on with such joy and determination. Our lives are a continuum. Death is not the end, it's the beginning. We are living in infinity, but we refuse to see it that way."

My grampa takes a seat on a stool made of sand. He pats similar ones next to him, and me and my grandma join him.

"People forget that the legend of Santa Claus began with a Christian monk named Nicholas. He was born around 280 AD in what is now known as Turkey. Nicholas was from a very wealthy family, but he gave away all the money he had to help the poor and sick," my grampa says. "Legend says he once saved three sisters who were going to be sold as slaves by providing them with a dowry so they could be married. As a result, Santa Claus became a phonetic holiday version of St. Nick."

He continues. "The name 'Kris Kringle' dates back to the German *Kristkindl*, meaning 'Christ Child.' During the Protestant Reformation in the 1500s, Martin Luther wanted to discourage the figure of St. Nicholas, as he believed praying to any saint was against Scripture. Luther and his followers introduced the idea that the *Christkind* would secretly come on Christmas Eve to bring presents to all the good children. *Christkind* was modified to Kris Kringle. Although the first documented use of that name dates back centuries, do you know where many believe the name became entrenched in our society?"

I shake my head.

"*Miracle on 34th Street*," my grandma says. "The name of the lead character who believes he's Santa Claus. Americans began to adopt the idea that Santa's real name was Kris Kringle, believing it was connected to St. Nicholas and not German for *Christ Child*. It's the reason your parents named you Susan. You are part of the continuum. You are our infinity."

I stare at my grandparents, shaking my head. I open my mouth, but my grandfather cuts me off before I can utter a word.

"Books, Susan," he says with his signature Santa laugh. "That's how we booksellers know so much."

"And the occasional Christmas and Hallmark movie," my grandma adds. "Where would we be without *White Christmas*, *It's A Wonderful Life*, *Elf* and *Christmas Vacation*?"

"And don't forget *Die Hard*," my grampa says. He continues. "Family should be infinite, too, Susan. We're not perfect. Far from it. No family is. But, done right, family provides a foundation for being your best self. Too few get this start in life."

"Too few are given unconditional love like I've been blessed to be shown my whole life," my grandma says. "Why do you think I married your grandfather?"

"You better say because I was handsome."

"Well, that part is true," she says, "but, mostly, you were just a good person, like my father and mother. You all taught me the meaning of unconditional love. It sounds so simple, but it's so, so hard—to love *unconditionally*. What does that mean? That you love without any conditions. You don't set rules for how, when and why you love. So many grow up believing they are not deserving of great love, and that their love must come with conditions. It's okay if he treats me poorly if he tells me he loves me. It's okay if I make less than other workers if I still have a job. It's okay if he yells at me if he apologizes when he's done. If we're not demonstrated unconditional love growing up we have zero concept of what it means."

Without warning, I start blubbering. It's quite a show, a

real Desiree Delmonico scene. My grandparents walk over to me and pat my shoulders.

"Too many of us are scarred by our families," my grandma says. "What can we as parents and grandparents get right in this life? No, what should we get right in this life? To demonstrate and teach our children and grandchildren unconditional love."

"Susan," my grampa says, "your grandma and I just don't want you to get consumed by your grief again. We're here, like we've always been, if and when you need us." He smiles. "That's all. Sermon over."

I stand and turn. "I wouldn't be here today without you."

We hug as one.

"Since it seems this walk has turned into an impromptu therapy session," my grandma says with a wink, "I just want to say one last thing."

"Do I need to brace myself?"

"After the Phillip Strauss drama," my grandma continues, "I'm just concerned that you're not the Susan we once knew."

I begin to lie, but I stop. I have lied to this woman. I don't want to anymore. "I'm happy, I really am. I'm just not..." I stop, searching for the right word "...complete."

"Well," my grampa says, "Noah told us about the mysterious Santa in Chicago. And I know you've had your share of dates..."

"Share?" I laugh. "I've dated every eligible man in Petoskey. Or scared them off."

"Are you seeing anyone?"

I think of Jordan. More irony.

"No."

"When was the last time you went on a real date?" my grandma asks.

"You remember, right? The Cletus debacle."

"Let me just say this," my grandma continues. "Men are intimidated by smart women. And when you're pretty, too…"

I start to protest.

"Uh-huh, not on my watch," she continues. "You think you aren't, but you are. You're a natural beauty. I think you and Holly both scare men off, and I also think that's a good thing because you both need to meet strong, smart men who not only love you unconditionally but also who respect you, who not only complete you but want you to be the best people you can be."

"But you must be best friends and make a real team, right, Mrs. Claus?" my grampa asks. "To be completely transparent, Susan, I think you have this ill-conceived notion that our relationship, like your parents' relationship, was as magical and simple as a sleigh ride around the world. It wasn't. We all need to take a leap of faith. Sixty years of marriage just doesn't happen without a lot of hard work, compromise, mistakes and faith."

"I wasn't looking for a man dressed as Santa, nor was your mother," my grandma says. "Neither of us were even looking for someone. But when they appeared, we had to put our hearts on the line. We had to take a risk. And after all the grief you've experienced in this life, I can only imagine how scary that must be for you. But if you want a Christmas miracle, Susan, you still gotta believe in Santa."

"Sorry to bring you all the way out here to pull an Oprah moment on you, but we just want you to focus on how many people love you. We just want you to love *you* that much."

"I do," I say. I stop. "Most of the time."

"Well, we better get back to the store," my grandma says. "Take some time for yourself. Remember, we greet the kids at 5:30 and then we have the event at the local library."

"I'll be there well before then," I say. "Thank you."

I watch my grandparents head up the beach, slowly growing smaller until they become one with the mist off the water. I sit down again on one of the sandy stools that has been formed directly on the shoreline, just feet from the water's edge. I stare out at the bay. The shoreline curves in a sweeping arc, mimicking the infinity symbol before me. I lift my face to the sun and close my eyes. I think of my parents and grandparents when they first met. Two young women meeting two young men dressed in Santa suits. The absurdity of the universe makes me laugh out loud.

Over my laughter, the waves call and crash, louder and louder. It takes me a moment to come out of my thoughts and realize that something sounds as if it's washed ashore. I open my eyes, and I jump up with a start.

The top part of a pine tree—drenched, yet green, fragrant and freshly cut—sits at my feet.

At first, I laugh anew, but then my laughter turns to tears.

As crazy as it sounds, I cannot help but think this tree was sent as a sign from Captain Santa himself, or perhaps from my parents, or even the depths of Lake Michigan, as a reminder and wake-up call that I am here—right here, this Christmas—for a reason.

"Infinity," I say to the pine, touching its wet needles.

chapter 9

I stand outside Sleigh By the Bay later that day and watch the happy scene in my front window.

A big sign on the front door reads: SANTA IS IN THE HO-HO-HOUSE!

A tiny paper plate clock that I made in grade school—red dots with the numbers written on them marking the time, popsicle sticks as the hands for the time—hangs underneath that sign stating: HERE UNTIL 6:30 P.M.

Every December night from 5:30–6:30 p.m. might be the happiest of happy hours in Northern Michigan. In fact, one of the local restaurants owners once asked if they could put a pop-up bar and food truck outside because we received more winter foot traffic than any other place in town, even the Alpine Ski Shop.

I take a step back and can't help but smile. A cold front has moved in from our Canadian neighbors this afternoon bringing sharply colder temperatures and a gentle snowfall. People are already lined up out the door waiting to get their children's picture taken with Santa. They also sip hot chocolate, snack on iced sugar cookies Mrs. Claus makes and shop for Christmas gifts, but I know why they're really here.

The memories.

Mrs. Claus takes the tiny hand of a little boy in a red bow tie and white shirt and leads him toward Santa. The boy is built like a fireplug, and he doesn't walk as much as he waddles and toddles. He stops on a dime and stares in awe at the world around him: the tree, the gifts, the big chair and even bigger man. The boy points, and I can see him mouth, *Santa?*

My grandma nods and Grampa sweeps the boy into his arms with a hearty laugh.

Santa rocks the boy gently on his lap, and then I can see him ask his name. The boy looks toward his parents—so young and happy with their shiny, unlined faces—in need of assistance.

Through the window, I can hear the mother say, "You know your name! It's the same as Santa's. Nicholas!"

"Ho! Ho! Ho!" Santa says. "The perfect name!"

The boy giggles.

Santa looks at him, and I know his next question by heart: "What would you like for Christmas, Nicholas?"

Santa leans his ear toward the boy's mouth—because it must remain a secret between child and Santa only—and Nicholas whispers what must be an expansive list by the length of his message.

Santa nods and gives the boy a kiss on top of the head. Then he turns and smiles for the camera.

The parents take a million shots.

My eyes scan the bookshelves behind the scene in the window.

When I watch children sit on Santa's lap every Christmas in my bookstore, I'm always reminded of the fine line between life and literature and childhood and adulthood.

When is the exact moment when we stop believing in miracles?

And why are we more willing to embrace happy endings in books but not in life?

I don't remember the first time I sat in Santa's lap, but I have a photo of me—just like the one this family took, like the ones all families have—hanging in my office. I am staring in wonder at a bearded man in a red suit whose joyous laugh and twinkling eyes have captured my attention. I cannot remember that moment any longer, but I can still recall the feeling.

Who is this strange, joyous creature who can make all my dreams come true?

I did not know Santa was my father, or that Mrs. Claus was my mom, but I know I understood, even as a child, that this man loved me and only wanted the best for me.

My breath catches in my throat and, for a moment, the scene turns misty before me.

"Susan?"

I turn.

"Hi, Michelle," I say.

"Are you okay?" she asks.

"Yes. Just reminiscing."

"This must be such a hard time of year for you, especially this year..." Michelle hesitates. "The whole forty thing."

Michelle's husband is standing in line with their four children. I went to high school with her and John. They come every year to get a family photo with Santa. Their oldest daughter is now fourteen. Her life has been so incredibly, beautifully normal.

I wave at her family. They wave back, and my heart pangs.

"It's certainly more emotional than usual," I say. "My mind and heart have been playing a few tricks on me lately."

"Well, your grandparents are Petoskey's miracles," she says, nodding toward the window. "Everyone in town wants this act to continue forever."

"Me, too," I say.

I want to correct Michelle, but I don't.

This is not an act for my grandparents. It is a continuum of their belief in life and in the goodness of life. If it's anyone who is acting, it's me. And to live, to truly live and embrace the miracle of the season and a happy ending, I must risk my heart, I must believe, but, mostly, I must forgive.

Myself and others.

"Hey, I hate to be nosy, but I'm going to be," Michelle says with a laugh. "Are you seeing anyone? I heard through the grapevine that you've had a few clunkers recently."

"I have."

"And that some mystery Santa in Chicago disappeared before you could meet?"

"Word travels fast around here," I say.

"You know the Petoskey pipeline, and I follow your friend Holly on social media. I guess none of her followers have identified him yet." Michelle shrugs. "Listen, I have a friend who's moving full-time to Traverse City. He owns his own business, a tech company that he's moving from Detroit because he wants to live where he vacations. I thought perhaps you might like to meet. He's a great guy."

"Can I think about it?" I say. "As you know, Holly is trying to set me up with about three thousand men. And I mean that literally."

Michelle laughs. "Well, if your dance card slows, call me. And just call me, Susan. I miss hanging out."

"I will. I promise."

We hug, and she heads back to her family.

I head into the store just in time to hear a baby scream.

My grandma sweeps the child from her husband's lap and coos. The baby finally stops with a few red-faced gasps and is then placed back in Santa's arms for a photo.

Now her parents have a wonderful story to tell and pass down forever about Christmas.

Infinity.

Michelle's family—the girls in matching green velvet dresses and the boys in ties with dancing snowflakes—pose for a photo.

I watch Michelle wrap her arms around her children, and my heart twinges.

"Call me," Michelle says again on her way out, her arms filled with books. "Don't keep yourself a secret, Susan."

"I will," I say. "And I won't."

"Now, where were we?"

I hold up the book and show Jordan an illustration from *The Polar Express.*

I begin to read.

Images from the book suddenly combine with my own memories, from tonight and long ago.

My mother used to read to Jordan in the bookstore. Though he was older than me, I remember him being such a bright, happy kid when I was little. Then he just sort of disappeared from the world.

I used to want to get on the Polar Express, but I didn't want it to take me to the North Pole. I wanted it to take me far, far from home, to a place where Santa and Christmas didn't exist.

Instead, I ran here every holiday season, avoiding Jordan's mother, seeking—no, *deserving*—an apology from Jordan.

And, I'm sorry for thinking this, God, but I came here to

pray for you to take him. I wanted him removed from this earth, just like he so callously removed my parents.

I believed it was the only way I could go on.

And yet, here I sit, Christmas after Christmas, reading to a man who will never move, much less open his mouth to apologize. He will die here, alone.

His final memory will forever be his worst.

I can choose to forge new ones, better ones.

And I'm beginning to understand that without my memories—even the very worst ones—without my pain, my loss, my grief, my humanity, the steps that have taken me to where I am right now, I would not be who I am.

None of us would.

I look at my watch. It is late, and yet I continue reading.

"Seeing is believing, but sometimes the most real things in the world are the things we can't see."

I stop and blink away surprise tears.

I think of all those children getting their picture taken with Santa. I think of Michelle, and the girl I used to be.

Don't be a secret, Susan.

I scooch my chair closer to the bed.

"Do you mind if I hold your hand, Jordan?"

chapter 10

I rush inside Sleigh By the Bay, my arms filled with poinsettias, to a long table set up by the fireplace. I begin to arrange the holiday flowers next to the paperwhites.

I always go all out for Desiree Delmonico. My parents and I loved and championed her work long before she was a perennial *New York Times* bestseller and had a nonstop run of hit Netflix series. Unlike Phillip Strauss, Desiree has never forgotten and always repays our early belief in her with great events and oodles of kindness.

She may be as kooky as Blitzen at a reindeer happy hour, but she also still makes a lot of lonely readers believe in love.

Desiree loves red and white flowers for her Christmas launches. She also loves to sip rosé as she speaks and signs, a bottle of which I have chilling on the table, as well as to nibble on Christmas M&M's, which I have poured into a large glass bowl.

"I'm here!"

Holly rushes through the door.

"For real?" I ask, looking at her outfit.

She is dressed as a sexy Rudolph, complete with adorable baby antlers popping forth from her hair, which is curled and pulled into a high pony, big doe eye makeup, and, of course, a red nose. She is wearing a formfitting red sweater that reads Team Rudolph.

"I'm livestreaming this event, girl. You're gonna sell out before she's done speaking! Get ready for the online orders!" She points at her feet. "You missed all this, by the way."

I look down. She is, quite literally, wearing reindeer feet. They're actually the most adorable shoes I've ever seen, adorned with a T-strap featuring appliques of happy reindeer faces, a sweet red satin bow and a green glitter heel.

"Right?" she answers for me. "I made them! Already sold out. Just like I'm going to do for you."

"Diva! Those shoes!"

Noah comes rushing over to greet Holly, arms open wide.

"Back at'cha!"

The two rock back and forth. As they do, I notice Noah has a faux reindeer tail attached to his backside.

"Obviously, you two reindeer have been in cahoots."

He shakes his tail, and his body jingles. I groan.

"*Jingle My Bells*!" Noah says.

"It's all for Desiree," Holly adds.

"Right," I say. "Are you sure it's not all for the hot Santa on the cover who's coming?"

They throw their hands over their mouths in mock surprise.

"Do we have time to get a coffee before this starts?" Holly

asks. "I need a little pick-me-up. The traffic getting out of Chicago was horrible."

"I'll finish up," Leah says, walking over and hugging Holly. "I can't go from coffee to wine that quickly anymore."

We head out the front door to Petoskey Scones. As we wait in line, Holly eyes the baristas.

"That guy is hot," she says.

"That's Fred," Noah says. "Actually Fred Jr. He's a trainer. And works here, obviously."

"Go on," Holly says with a laugh.

"Okay, I will," I say, emphasizing every word. "He's in his twenties."

"And I *look* like I'm in my twenties," Holly says. "And he's wearing a Santa hat!"

Holly nudges me with her pointy elbow.

"Ouch," I say. "And diapers. No go."

"I told Susan a long time ago that I think he looks just like Fred from Scooby-Doo," Noah says.

"Oh, my gosh! He does."

Holly walks up to place her order. "I'll take a nonfat, no-whip gingerbread latte with an extra shot." She leans over, putting her arms on the counter, and blinks dramatically. "This little reindeer is very thirsty." She winks. "And apologies for my nose. It always turns red when I talk to a cute guy."

The tall, muscular-chested Fred's face flushes, even in the warm shop.

"So," Holly continues, "what Scooby Snacks do you recommend?"

"I don't really eat carbs," he says, "but we're known for our scones. It's the name of our shop."

"Pick something out just for me."

"Okay, ma'am."

I can see Holly's soul leave her body when Fred calls her "ma'am."

Holly and I check out and head to a table.

"He called me *ma'am*," she says. "Did he just have cataract surgery?"

She looks at her scone and then her receipt.

"Oh, my gosh! He gave me a prune scone! How old does he think I am?"

Noah walks up to the table. "My latte was on the house," he says. "Isn't that sweet?"

Holly's eyes widen. She looks at me.

"What did he say?"

Noah takes a sip of his coffee and cocks his head. "He said it was a Christmas gift for always being so nice when I come into the store."

Holly looks at Noah and then his mug. "He drew a flying reindeer on top of your coffee! He made you latte art! He put my latte in a to-go cup! He's gay!"

People have turned and are now staring at our table.

"No, he's not, diva," Noah says. "He's shy. I've seen him on dates with women."

"My gaydar is *never* wrong," Holly says.

"Your straight radar is," I say under my breath.

"I heard that," Holly says, giving me the eye. "He's fake dating. We all do it. I mean, Susan's been fake dating her whole life."

"Ha ha," I say.

Holly continues. "He's too hot not to have a girlfriend. Trust me."

"Just eat your prunes, ma'am," I say.

"I'm not saying I'm buying a word of what you're saying," Noah says, "but why would a guy like that..." Noah hesitates, and his always chipper voice drops to a low hum "...be interested in a guy like me? We're total opposites." He stops again. "People think dating in the straight world is easy. Try being gay." His voice quivers. "No one wants someone like me. No one's ever wanted someone like me."

My heart cracks.

"Everyone wants someone like you, Noah."

I reach out and take his hand.

"You're a sweet, smart, sensitive, funny, nurturing guy who doesn't focus solely on looks."

"I wouldn't go that far," he says.

Holly laughs.

"Thank you, Susan," Noah says. "I just want someone who…"

He glances toward the coffee counter.

"…believes. In me. In us. In all the good in the world. In Christmas."

"Me, too," Holly says.

"Me, three," I finish.

The lower level of the bookstore is jammed with over a hundred fans listening to Desiree Delmonico with rapt attention.

She reads:

"Gigi waited until the last family had taken a picture with Santa. As he stood, Gigi asked, 'Do you have time for one more photo?'

'I thought—' Santa started.

'But without your costume,' Gigi said, removing his beard and his glasses. She took off his Santa cap and placed it on her head. 'We all wear costumes, but you and I don't need any of that. All we need is each other. All we need to remember is the spirit of Christmas. You're the only gift I need. You're the only gift I ever needed.'

He swept Gigi off her feet. Gigi closed her eyes, and he kissed her deeply.

When she opened her eyes, the crowd in the mall was applauding.

And then the two walked out together, knowing that although there was no sleigh waiting or a retreat to the North Pole, they had rediscovered not only the magic of one another but also the magic of Christmas."

Desiree removes her red-framed glasses and smiles at the applause that follows. "Thank you very much for coming. I can't tell you how much it means to see all of your smiling faces every holiday season. Does anyone have questions?"

Fifty hands pop up. I already know the question: *Are you dating the shirtless Santa sitting beside you that graces this year's book cover?*

I shout out a question to delay the inevitable. "Can you talk a bit about what Christmas means to you?"

"Wonderful question, Susan." Desiree stands. She has old-school Jackie Collins glamour with loads of makeup and huge hair. She is wearing a glamorous, fitted tuxedo jacket in red with green lapels, a gold Christmas tree pin with rubies as the ornaments and a mega diamond on top.

"I grew up very poor in the Ozarks," she says. "My grandmother was a seamstress who made all of my clothes. She saved coins in a crock in her garage so I could go to college. Her sacrifices changed my life. And yet, she and my grandfather were the richest, happiest people I've ever known. I will never forget the way they looked at one another, or the way they reached for each other's hands when they watched the sunset, or the way they fed fresh strawberries to one another seated in the garden. They not only modeled the way true love should be, they modeled the way a relationship should grow over time."

Desiree looks at me with the slightest of smiles and continues. "One of the first big Christmas presents I remember receiving was an aqua blue Selectric typewriter, from my grandparents. It's what inspired me to start writing. About love. I still have that typewriter on a shelf in my office, and I look at it every day and feel as if my grandparents are still with me. That's what Christmas means to me."

I think of my poem and my parents, and a tear springs to my eye. My grandma puts her hand on my back.

"Are you dating the shirtless Santa sitting beside you?" Holly asks.

My eyes widen. I look at Holly, who shrugs and whispers, "Someone had to ask, right?"

Desiree laughs. "The eternal question. Luka, why don't you answer?"

"His name's Luka," Holly whispers to me. "Hers is Desiree. Just like one of her books. Of course."

Luka doesn't stand as much as he overtakes the room. If The Rock and Jason Momoa were fused and injected with a touch of Ryan Gosling, Luka would be the scientific result. He's wearing slim-fitting tuxedo pants, a black tux jacket with red lapels, no shirt and a Santa cap. He doesn't just look like the book cover—a giant poster board of which sits beside him—he looks better than the book cover.

"I prefer not to discuss my personal life," Luka says in a voice like thunder with an accent I cannot place. "I will say, however, that I have never met a more talented or beautiful woman in my life." He turns and takes Desiree's hand. "She is my greatest gift this year."

The crowd applauds wildly.

"Desiree will be signing at the table with the flowers," I say, "and Luka will be posing for photos."

An hour later, we've sold out of books, and we have online orders for another two hundred. Suffice it to say, it's been a very, very good day at Sleigh By the Bay.

When the crowd finally thins, I tell Desiree and Luka that we have reservations at Chandler's at seven.

"Why don't you meet us there after you have a chance to rest and relax."

The two head off to the Perry to change. A few minutes after they leave, my grampa shows up to take Santa photos for the families already lining up outside and run the store until closing.

"Ho-Ho-Holly!" he booms. "How's my favorite girl?"

"Hey!" I say.

Holly races over and hugs him with all her might.

"Why don't you be in the pictures with us tonight?" Grandma asks. "Your outfit is too adorable!"

"I'll make Manhattans after to celebrate!" Grampa says.

"And I'll make dinner!" my grandma adds. "Roast chicken with all the fixings!"

Holly turns and gives me a sheepish look.

I know that Holly uses her oven to store shoes. I joke that her DoorDash deliveryman is in her will.

"It's okay," I say. "I can see you salivating. Why don't you have dinner with them after they close the bookstore, and we'll go to Chandler's, okay?"

Noah's head whips back and forth between us.

"You can go with Holly," I say with a laugh. "I know you two are connected at the hip."

"Thank you!" Noah says. "It's so much easier to talk about you when you're not around. And I'm not sure how much of a conversationalist Luka is going to be."

"And he's going to be wearing a shirt, too," Holly says with a sigh.

"It's a win-win," I say. "I'll actually save a lot of money in my expense account, considering the way you two eat and drink when you know it's free. Leah, you still want to come with me, right?"

"I do," she says. "I have so many questions for Desiree. Thank you."

As Leah breaks down the tables and returns the lower level of the store back to normal, I head to the office to double-check the online orders and gather the hundreds of bookplates that I will need Desiree to personalize and autograph so I can stick them in books tomorrow and get them in the mail.

I stop and look at all the literary plaques lining the walls that I have been gifted over the years by friends and authors.

One is a quote from Dr. Seuss: "The more that you read, the more things you will know. The more that you learn, the more places you'll go."

The next, from Margaret Mitchell, was given to me by Desiree as a not-so-subtle joke: "In a weak moment, I have written a book." That plaque features a glorious photo of her, hands fluttering over her typewriter like a hummingbird, her face looking both bemused and forlorn.

The next is the classic Emerson quote: "Do not go where the path may lead, go instead where there is no path and leave a trail."

Another plaque, given to me by the late, great Southern author Dorothea Benton Frank, is a quote from Dorothy Parker that reads, "If you have any young friends who aspire to become writers, the second greatest favor you can give them is to present them with copies of *The Elements of Style*. The first greatest, of course, is to shoot them now, while they're happy."

And, finally, there is a quote from Erma Bombeck that my father gave my mother shortly after they were married: "Great dreams...never even get out of the box. It takes an uncommon amount of guts to put your dreams on the line, to hold

them up and say to the world, 'How good or how bad am I?'
That's where courage comes in."

Dreams. Courage. Places to go.

Outside my office, I can hear my grandparents cackling
with Holly and Noah.

"What!" I hear Noah yell. "How did I not know this?"

I stick my head out of the doorframe.

"I can hear you! Spill the beans."

"I was just saying that maybe Luka, since he's wearing a
Santa hat, could be your Single Kringle," Holly says.

"And then we mentioned your childhood poem," my
grandma adds with a sheepish grin.

"Which I never knew about!" Noah yells. "Now I understand *everything*. How could I work here this long and have
you keep such a secret from me? I feel very, very duped, diva."

"First, come down a notch, Bette Davis," I say. "I guess
I thought you knew..." I stop myself. I don't want to lie or
make excuses. "Actually, I guess I never talked about it spe-
cifically because I didn't want any more attention brought to
it. It's like this *Game of Thrones* holiday legend hanging over
my head. Will I find my true love awaiting me wearing a
Santa hat? When you say it out loud, it just sounds so silly. I'm
forty years old, and I wrote that poem when I was just a little
girl. I've dated enough bad Santas to know perhaps I'm better off alone. Or, maybe I've had it wrong all these years, and
I should be looking for a cute Cupid, or loving Leprechaun."

"You remember St. Patrick's Day, right?" Holly asks. "Every
potential Leprechaun thought you had eaten a bad bowl of
clam chowder."

"The point is," my grandma says, "you wrote that poem
when you still truly believed. After your parents died, you lost
faith. We all understand why." My grandma gestures with her
arms. "But all of this—love, friendship, literature, life—is too

grand and too planned to simply be happenstance. We miss it all if we don't have faith."

My grampa steps toward me. "Let's be honest here. Your grandma and I don't have a lot of time left on this earth, Susan. The only thing we want is for you to be happy."

"I am happy."

"Then we'll let this all go," Grampa says. "All this Single Kringle silliness ends today. Deal?"

My eyes actually pop from my head. I look at my grandma. Her eyes match mine. "Really?" I ask.

"Yes," he says. "I just have one question for you?"

"Okay."

"If you could only have one Christmas gift for the rest of your life, what would it be?" my grampa asks.

Tears spring to my eyes. "That you and Grandma would live forever."

"We can't, honey," he says, gently. "And we won't. At some point, we'll be reunited with your parents." My grampa takes my hand. "You are a strong, smart, sensitive, funny, wonderful woman, and I have no doubts the rest of your life is going to be amazing. But I'm not convinced it will be completely fulfilled unless you forgive yourself for a tragic accident and learn to believe in miracles again."

For the first time, I see him, not as Santa, or as my grampa, or as others see him in our tiny town, but as a real, flesh-and-blood man who's had lost hopes and dreams, who's laughed and cried, who's suffered just the same as I have.

He continues. "I actually think the one gift you want for Christmas—and out of life—is what your grandma and I have and what your parents had."

My cheeks quiver. I cannot make them stop.

"True love. You want someone, as you wrote in your poem so long ago, who makes you feel like the only gift in the room.

That's all any of us want, Susan. And it's okay to verbalize that, even if it scares the heck out of you and you think it may never come true. You have to utter it into existence, otherwise it remains only a wish."

My grandma grabs my other hand. "We must believe because faith is not a game..." she starts. My grampa joins her. "There is purpose beyond us, otherwise life is a shame. So, until my day comes, I'll remain happy and bright, and I will believe in my Kringle with all of my might."

I hold them with all my might.

"I'm not crying, you are!" Noah says, rushing over with Holly to join us in a big group hug.

chapter 11

Turns out, Luka is an incredible conversationalist.

Even in a shirt.

In one of the most shocking twists since *Gone Girl*, Luka majored in business and comparative literature at NYU and now runs the modeling agency that provides the men on Desiree's covers.

"I modeled to help pay my way through college," he explains.

"I hired him for my Cowboy Christmas covers back in the day," Desiree says. "Nobody remembers that anymore. Luka was handsome, while so many other models were pretty. You ever meet a pretty cowboy?"

Leah and I laugh.

"I never met an ugly one either," Leah says.

Luka smiles at her quip.

"I continued modeling," Luka says, "and then I bought a share of the agency. After a few years, I bought it outright with Desiree's help. We provide all the models for her covers…" Luka hesitates and then winks "…and for her tours."

"But I thought—" Leah starts.

"That we were dating?" Desiree laughs. "Honey, I'm a good writer and a great businesswoman, but I am not a cradle robber."

"You had me fooled," I say, "even after all these years."

"It's part of my brand," Desiree says. She whisks her glass of rosé directly from the waiter's hands and takes a healthy sip. "All of this is part of my brand, what I wear, what I drink, how I look. Let's be real—I'm a writer. I sit around much of the day writing in sweats and a coffee-stained robe. I mean, I scare UPS drivers when I'm out of my makeup."

I laugh.

Desiree continues. "I'm a romance writer. Readers buy my books because they love to believe in love, but they also want to believe that there are women out there in the world who are in passionate relationships, wearing beautiful dresses and going to dinner in Greece rather than sitting on their couch eating Ben & Jerry's and watching *90 Day Fiancé*. I give them that fantasy." She looks at Luka. "*He* gives them that fantasy."

"Wow," I say.

"And do you want to know what I do most nights?" Desiree asks. "I sit in my pj's on my couch eating Ben & Jerry's watching *90 Day Fiancé*. I write about love because I'm not good at it. I have beautiful men come with me on tour because it takes the pressure off an introvert who hates public speaking. I give readers what they want to see. But I still go home alone after all of this is over."

"Have you ever been in love?" I ask.

Desiree picks up her glass and studies the wine. "I don't know."

We all wait expectantly for her to continue.

"Isn't that the saddest thing in the world to say?" she asks. "It's even sadder to realize. My grandparents were my world. They modeled true love and marriage to me. I never found what they had. The older I get I wonder if I had unrealistic expectations. I believe I probably idealized their relationship, and it was never as perfect as I believed. And now the older I am, I create suspicions as to why men might be interested in a woman my age. Money? Fame?"

The waiter arrives, and we order dinner—four specials of the halibut with parmesan risotto, shiitake mushrooms, herbs and arugula—in the purest of pure Michigan restaurants: fine food, great wine and white tablecloths set against knotty pine walls dotted with beautiful watercolors and oils of the lake.

Desiree sips her wine.

"Is it hard to write romance?" Leah asks. "Critics tend to assume it's easier than other genres."

Desiree cackles. "Do they now? Critics who have never written a book in their lives?" She eyes the busy bar and looks at Leah. "You already know some of my back story, but you may not know it all. In my thirties, I was real estate agent Trudy Williams. I had a lot of downtime during my open houses. Let's just say I didn't get the best listings. I would read book after book and think, 'I can do this.' So I started to take my old typewriter to listings, and that's how I began writing."

She continues. "I sent about a hundred pages of the novel I was working on to LuAnn Roth…"

"The Southern novelist?" Leah says. "I've always loved her books."

"Me, too," Desiree says. "She hosts a workshop for aspiring writers every year, and I was so honored to be accepted. There were a half dozen writers who went to Savannah, and LuAnn greeted us the very first minute with, 'All of your work is terrible.' I nearly died. When it was my turn, she took me to her patio outside. It was brick, and all these live oaks were lit and dripping with Spanish moss, just like in her books. It was an out-of-body experience. She looked at me and said my writing was good, but I had no voice. And then she gave me an assignment. LuAnn told me to write about the one thing that had always scared me, the one thing I even feared admitting to myself. And she gave me thirty minutes."

"What did you do?" I ask.

"I wrote, and for the first time in my life, I didn't think about how I should write, or what I should write, I just wrote, and my voice sprang to life."

"Do you mind if I ask what your greatest fear was?" Leah asks.

"Dying alone," Desiree says. "And nothing has changed. It's just that now I have a voice for that fear. My books are my partners. I breathe life into them, and they breathe life into me. I am never alone." She looks at Leah. "What is yours?"

Leah blushes.

"We're all friends here," Desiree says.

"That I will only be seen as an ex-wife and a mother," she says quietly. "I will never be seen as the woman I am."

Without warning, Luka reaches out and touches her arm. "I see you," he says.

Leah looks at him, stunned, and then at me. I smile.

"Thank you," Leah finally manages to say. "What about you, Luka?"

"My greatest fear is that I will never find true love," he says. "Women treat me as a sex object, and men treat me like I'm an idiot. I'm just a guy who's worked hard his whole life to be successful."

Our dinners arrive, and we chat about Desiree's newest

work, what's next and how difficult it is for authors to stay on top in this business.

As Leah and Luka chat, Desiree catches my eye and asks, "What about you, Susan? You never got a chance to answer the question. I think that was by design."

"You writers never miss a thing," I say. I begin to speak, but my breath hitches in my throat. "I think I'd have to show you my greatest fear."

Desiree looks at her watch. "I'm buzzed, it's only 8:30, and I'm always down to help a girlfriend."

"This is my greatest fear."

Desiree looks at Jordan. She scans the room, blinking in time with the beep of the heart monitor.

"I don't understand."

"I fear that I will be forever like him," I say, my voice barely audible. "I fear that I'll be trapped for eternity in a state of perpetual inertia. I fear that I will be trapped in a nightmare, forever alone with my shame."

I stop.

"I fear I already am."

Desiree turns her intense gaze upon me. She looks so out of place here, so majestic, so beautiful, so alive. And yet I feel—seeing her out of a bookstore or nice restaurant—that I am seeing her for the first time. I can see the makeup, hairspray and clothing are just a disguise and distraction—much like Noah's humor, Leah's careful analysis, Holly's outrageousness and my cautiousness with dating—to keep people from getting too close.

I look out Jordan's window that faces the parking lot. A snowplow driver makes his way through the lot, pushing piles of white, the beeps from his truck matching those in the room. Within seconds, a wall is formed.

I tell Desiree the story about how my parents were killed, and how it continues to haunt me. I fill her in on this milestone year and anniversary in my life.

"I knew about your parents, but I just didn't know how it happened. I never asked. Shame on me."

Desiree pulls a chair from the back of the room next to one in front of Jordan's bed, takes a seat and pats the empty one.

"No, shame on me. I've come here every Christmas for the last few decades. I prayed for him to die, and then I prayed for him to wake up miraculously."

"Why?" Desiree asks.

"So he would apologize."

I let out a shuddering sigh.

"Oh, dear Susan."

Desiree puts her hand on my arm.

"I wish I could rewrite your life story, but I can't. I can only do that in fiction. I want you to hear something, okay? You can't—and shouldn't—excise the awful stuff in your life. It makes you who you are."

"Not this, though. I can't help but feel I killed my parents."

"You were a girl. It was a terrible accident. You had nothing to do with this." She grabs my hand. "You had *nothing* to do with this, Susan."

Maybe it's because Desiree is a semi-stranger, maybe it's because she's strong, maybe it's because her strength reminds me of my mother and grandmother, but I lean my head onto her shoulder and weep.

"I can kill all the darlings I want in my books, leave out the parts I don't like or need or want, but we can't do that in life," she soothes. "I want you to listen to me. I know in my soul—as a writer and a human—if this man could wake up and apologize, I guarantee you he would. If he could take back that night, that last drink, that reach for his keys, I know in my soul he would gladly give up his own life to return your parents. Perhaps this is God's punishment, Susan. But I don't think so. I prefer to look at this as God's teaching."

"How?"

"I believe in life we're forced to confront our grief or succumb to it," Desiree says. "I was forced to confront mine after my grandparents' deaths. I nearly succumbed. But I believe in the ripple effect of kindness in this world. Just look at the impact LuAnn Roth had on my life in just two short days. We can either magnify the pain we feel and choose to make that our ripple to inflict hurt on others, or we can learn from the pain we've experienced and choose to magnify goodness to help others."

Desiree rubs my back. "When I take off this wig, I'm little, ol' Trudy Williams from the Ozarks, who sleeps alone in her bed every night. But when I put it on, I'm a force of nature whose ripple effect as a writer is escapism, hope and love. What's yours going to be?"

I lift my head and dry my eyes with the back of my hand. I shrug like a little kid.

"Jordan's not the one who needs to apologize, Susan."

I look at her.

"You do," Desiree continues. "To yourself. For your guilt at what happened. Look at Jordan, Susan."

I take a deep breath.

"Really look at him."

I do.

"You're the only one remaining with a brain and a conscience. You're the one who has legs that function, a heart that aches, a voice that still works. You can either run, or you can forgive yourself. And him. You have to."

"And what if I can't?"

"Then you'll be as trapped as he is forever."

chapter 12

We know every word to every song by heart now.

We go together like rama lama lama ka dinga da dinga dong

I look around the room at my Pink Ladies dancing in my Pink Lady.

We do go together.

The third weekend of December, after Desiree's event and our staff party, the "girls" join me at my house for our Christmas party.

Our annual holiday sleepover never changes. I make snowman pancakes to kick off the morning; Holly makes mimosas; Leah bakes her family's beloved cinnamon rolls with cream cheese frosting; Noah bakes his mom's cranberry-orange muffins and then goes on our latte run.

We gorge and start watching the following movies, always in this order and always in our pajamas: *Elf*, *Christmas Vacation* and *Miracle on 34th Street*. Then we shower, Holly and Noah do our makeup, we get dressed up as our *Grease* characters, we order pizza, drink wine, exchange our Secret Santa gifts and then we watch *Grease*—singing and dancing our particular numbers.

As we do every year, we buy each other books for our Secret Santa.

Yes, as bookstore folk, we read constantly. But, as bookstore folk, we always read within the genre we buy for, and usually only books months in advance of their publication. As a result, I only read fiction, Noah only reads nonfiction, Leah only reads children's books, and Holly only reads the summaries we send her so she can post our recommendations and bookseller picks on social media and our website.

"I wonder what it is?" Noah asks with a laugh, shaking the package.

He opens it.

"No!" he says. "An autographed copy of *The Lost Library*. How'd you get this?"

"A publishing friend owed me a favor," I say, thinking of Kathleen.

"What's it about?" Holly asks.

"It's a novel about a lonely boy in the future, where books no longer exist, and he discovers a hidden library." Noah looks at me. "It sold for a million dollars, and it's not coming out for a year. It's a heavily guarded secret." Noah looks at me. "Susan. Thank you."

Noah gifts Holly a coffee table book that is a tutorial on the hottest new makeup trends, and Holly gifts Leah travel books about Greece, Spain and Italy, the three places she wants most to visit before sixty.

I look around and hold out my hands. "Gee, thanks for the love."

The three of them look sheepishly at me and then began nodding and pecking the air at one another like The Drinking Bird I had on my desk when I was little.

"Spill it," I say.

Holly stands and pulls out a wrapped present from underneath the cushion.

"What is going on?"

She holds it out. The package is quite large, almost the size and thickness of the scrapbooks my grandma has stacked on her wooden coffee table.

I unwrap it, tossing paper this way and that, like an excited child.

"What in the world?" I ask.

It is, indeed, a scrapbook. Embossed on the black leather cover in bright red lettering are the words *The Single Kringle*.

I open the scrapbook.

A copy of my fourth grade poem—in my childish cursive—is enclosed in a plastic sleeve.

"What in the world?" is the only thing I can manage to repeat like a crazed parrot.

I turn the page.

There is the photo Holly took with me and the hot Santa surrounded by stickers of hearts and falling snow, a reindeer-led sleigh flying over a city that looks like Chicago.

"You all really seem like scrapbookers," I say.

I turn the page to a printout of what looks to be a Facebook page profile of a handsome man wearing a Santa costume.

I turn the page.

There is another, and another, another. In fact, there is an entire scrapbook filled with mysterious men all in holiday attire.

My eyes bulge. "Someone's been busy," I say, glaring at Holly.

"We've all been busy," Leah says.

"Let me explain, please," Holly says. She walks over to the rocker I'm sitting in. She slides in next to me, and the chair rocks wildly back and forth, just like my mind is doing. "I had mentioned that I might do a little research..."

"A little research? This is like *CSI: North Pole!*" I say.

"Actually, we all did a little research," Noah adds. "Holly gave us the names of all the men who fit the criteria of the guy who hit on you at the Santa Run. Age range, lives in Chicago, works out or is a runner."

"And I received a ton of emails from followers who thought they might know who this guy is based on appearance and the fact that they knew someone who ran the race in a Santa costume. We spent a lot of time narrowing the list down," Holly says. "A lot!"

"Really?" I ask. "You know this is insane, right? I mean, you all are aware you're off your..." I push back, and Holly and I go swinging "...rockers."

"We do," Holly says. "And we weren't even going to give this to you, but after having dinner with your grandparents..."

"I knew I smelled a Christmas rat," I say.

"...they said if we didn't push you, they were worried— after your last disaster—that you might never take a chance again," she continues.

"But they just told me my perfect guy might not be dressed as Santa!" I say.

"He has to be!" Noah yelps. "I just know it has to be! That's your happy ending!"

"Look at me, Susan," Holly says.

My mind whirs back to Desiree, who uttered the same words. I look at Holly.

"I'm worried you might never take a chance again, too, now that you've hit forty. I know you, better than I know myself. You can say you're fine on your own, you can say you're happy, but I can feel in my soul that you had a connection with this mystery man. I know this is Crazy Christmas with capital *K*s, but I also know that I don't want you to look back on your life in twenty years and be filled with a single regret."

"Why do we watch *Miracle on 34th Street* every single year?" Noah asks.

"Because faith is believing in things when common sense tells you not to," the three of them say in unison.

"You've taught us too well," Leah says with a wink.

"Maybe it's silly to believe in these movies any longer. Maybe it's silly to watch Hallmark and read books with happy endings," I say.

"We all deserve love," Noah says.

"We all deserve a happy ending," Leah adds.

"What do you want, Susan?" Holly asks.

"More wine?"

"Be honest," she presses.

I glance at the pictures of my parents and grandparents.

"I don't know if I need anybody—" I start.

Everyone groans.

"*But*, if I did find someone, I'd want our relationship to be like my parents' and grandparents'. It's not perfect, it's not always easy, but a relationship where someone supports my dreams like my grandparents did with each other when they made a leap of faith to open Sleigh By the Bay. I want a relationship where someone finishes my sentences like my parents did, or to look in his eyes and know exactly what he's thinking and feeling. I want someone who's my best friend, like my grandparents are to each other." I look at my Pink Ladies. "What do you want?"

"Danny Zuko," the three say with a laugh.

I look at them and then flip through the pages of the scrapbook. Man after man in Santa caps, beards and red velvet coats look back at me.

I want to believe, I do, but I don't know if I can handle another bad date, another cheesy line, another awkward conversation.

I shut the scrapbook. *Be honest, Susan*, I think to myself. *You actually don't know if you can handle any more hurt in your life. Another loss. What if you fell in love and…*

"Can't we just watch *Grease*?" I ask. "We've gone off script."

Leah fills our glasses with wine.

When each of our characters has a big number, we must stand and sing. The wine flows, especially for me, since I have so many numbers as Sandy.

When Noah sings "Look at Me, I'm Sandra Dee," we all gather around him on the floor as if he were Rizzo. Although we are just mimicking make-believe characters in a movie, my heart drops when he sings:

Watch it, hey, I'm Doris Day, I was not brought up that way

I watch Noah place a blond wig on his head, pretending to be Sandy.

How was I brought up?

To believe in Santa, as Susan does in *Miracle on 34th Street*.

To believe in love and herself, as Sandy does in *Grease*.

To believe, as Noah just said, in things when common sense tells you not to.

When the song finishes, I return to my rocker and can picture myself in twenty years—long after my grandparents are gone, perhaps even when my friends have moved on in their lives and we no longer share traditions like this—rocking alone.

I awake with a start, my neck cramping and head thumping.

My mouth feels like the Sahara. My eyelashes are clumped with too much mascara.

The tree lights are still plugged in, and I glance around the room. My Pink Ladies now resemble an old oil painting of women in repose. Wigs and wineglasses are scattered everywhere, and I reconsider my thought: the room resembles Moulin Rouge.

My phone continues to vibrate somewhere on my body. It's the reason I'm awake.

I feel the constant trill, and I fish around until I find my phone stuffed in an empty bag of holiday Hershey's Kisses underneath my rump. My lap is filled with tiny bits of foil.

I squint at my cell.

1,343 notifications.

I sit up too quickly, and the rocker catapults me back and forth, making my stomach lurch.

I click on my Facebook account.

My last personal post was a few days ago, a photo of me at Chandler's with Desiree, Luka and Leah.

I scroll. There are so many new posts in which I'm tagged, my previous photo doesn't even appear no matter how quickly my finger scrolls. I go to Instagram. My IG is flooded with comments. Twitter is atwitter, both on my personal and professional feed. I click back to Facebook.

I begin to read the posts.

Is this you?

I'm the hot Santa!

I'm your Miracle on 34th Street!

I click on the link accompanying each post. A photo of me and the hot Santa appears along with this:

COULD YOU BE THIS
WOMAN'S SINGLE KRINGLE?

On December 2, Susan Norcross—a Michigan bookstore owner and avid runner—participated in Chicago's famed Santa Run…dressed as Mrs. Claus! At the start of the race, the man pictured in this Santa Claus costume (with very nice reindeer legs!) yelled a corny pickup line at Susan, before approaching her and discussing something very specific. When the race began, the two drifted apart like the snowflakes that cold day. As Santa disappeared, he yelled for Susan to meet him at a specific bar. But Santa never showed. Susan's friends and family believe it was fate the two were destined to meet. Why? Susan's mother and grandmother both met their future husbands at the holidays when the men were dressed—you guessed it!—as Santa. Please help us find him! If you feel you are the missing Santa—or know who it is—you must include the pickup line you used, what the two of you discussed, and the bar where you were supposed to meet. What happened to you, Santa? Where did you run after the Santa Run?
X's & O's & Ho-Ho-Ho's!

When I stop reading, I realize my mouth hasn't just fallen open, my entire jaw has come unhinged. My phone—and mind–continue to trill.

I also realize my Christmas scrapbook was just a ruse. The Pink Ladies had already hatched their plot to set me up.

"Wake up!" I yell.

The three, likely still a little drunk, jerk upright with a start. I hold up my cell.

"What have you naughty, naughty elves been up to?"

chapter 13

JANUARY

January is known in publishing as "New Year, New You!"

After gorging their way through the holiday season—one often filled with too much food and feuding with family—readers want to kick off their year with a new, healthy, positive mindset.

"Do you need help?"

I glare at Noah and Leah, who are hovering around me like nervous ghosts while I decorate the front windows.

"I think you've done enough, thank you very much."

They scoot away.

I am hanging a huge banner that reads: SLEIGH THIS YEAR! NEW BOOKS FOR THE NEW YOU!

Huge stars dangle with falling snowflakes over a slew of self-improvement and self-help books arranged in the window: diet books, celebrity exercise books, books on travel, finance, home improvement, finding a new career, renewing a marriage, becoming a better parent and—of course—dating.

I move off the stepladder and look out the window at the frozen world. My heart seems to match the iciness and frigidity of the polar vortex that has descended upon Northern Michigan. The land is hard. Frost has created a beautifully intricate design around the edges of the old glass.

It has, pardon the pun, been a very frosty holiday season since The Single Kringle post went viral. The only noise in the store apart from customers has been the classical music playing to offset the uncomfortable quiet. Christmas with my grandparents was subdued, to say the least. In fact, I powered off my phone over ten days ago, after everything blew up. I told Holly—since she created this blizzard of holiday insanity—to deal with the endless emails from Santas all across the world as well as the maelstrom of media inquiries. Every newspaper reporter, radio deejay, podcaster and TV host from Idaho to Poughkeepsie wanted to speak with the lonely lady looking for love. And Holly obliged until I finally went radio silent. I have yet to speak of it again with anyone. In fact, this morning is the first day I've had the courage to turn on my phone.

I know part of my anger is pride coupled with embarrassment: now, the entire world not only knows I'm single but that I'm also seeking a man.

Dressed as Santa.

And I know the media coverage will only make it seem even odder.

And yet...

As I've had a chance to think about it and cool down a bit, I know in my heart that my friends had the best of intentions at heart.

I also know, deep down in my heart, I want to find my Hot Santa, too.

Should they maybe have asked me first? Yes!

I think part of me is angered by the fact that those I love seem to believe that I need a man to make me happy and fulfilled. I do not.

And yet…

I step into the window and look out at Petoskey in January. I am frozen. In time. In life. Even worse, my heart is frozen.

But putting my soul online for the world to see is the equivalent of watching a train wreck episode of *The Bachelor*. Do you know how many crazy stalkers slid into my DMs dressed as Santa before I turned off my phone?

It's beyond unnerving, especially to realize they can all google me and find where I work.

Secretive Susan is the one who's on display. I have nowhere to hide.

Especially since…

My mind whirs, thinking of the Monday paper I set out for Rita, and all the newspapers that arrived at dawn.

After my post went viral on social media, news and entertainment outlets immediately began to contact me. As in, hours after I woke up in my rocker with my tongue glued to the roof of my mouth.

The first was the *Chicago Tribune*, which caught me totally off guard. I babbled about my parents and grandparents, before Holly grabbed the phone and began talking about love, the holidays and the bookstore.

"It's all about branding," she said to me while I was still in shock.

That was followed by WGN, TMZ, *Extra* and *ET*. By noon, Holly had me at Sleigh By the Bay in full makeup and a Santa cap doing interviews.

"Sell those books," Holly kept saying.

But I knew she wanted me to sell myself.

I began to implode when even the local papers got wind of the story, and the community seemed to rally behind finding the lonely bookseller a Christmas miracle. I received endless calls and texts from mothers, brothers, sisters and friends, all of whom had friends with brothers whose cousins might have been at the run. The lampposts all over downtown were covered in posters with my face—as if I were a lost dog—alongside a big question mark, as if I were the Riddler from Batman.

All of this dredged up memories of my mom and dad, especially when the local media asked me for pictures of them as Santa and Mrs. Claus, and I learned that Noah and Holly were in on the Santa dating experiment, too. The headline and article read:

THE SEARCH FOR THE SINGLE KRINGLE
Petoskey Native Susan Norcross Seeks Mystery Man Dressed as Santa Who Could Be "The One"

Susan Norcross's mother and grandmother met their future husbands while they were dressed as Santa. They fell in love before they even knew what he looked like. Susan was even named after the little girl in *Miracle on 34th Street*. Now, her friends and family believe it's her turn.

After meeting a man dressed as Santa Claus in Chicago (pictured below), Susan says she felt "an instant connection." But he disappeared without a trace. Her friends and family are asking for your help in finding her "Single Kringle."

And two of her employees say they are willing to help their boss and friend out by riding in the dating sleigh with her.

I'm what one might term an extroverted introvert. My best friends are books. My heroes are authors. I love my friends, I love going out, I love my store and my community, but my energy comes from words. I prefer to lose myself in the worlds that others create, rather than creating a new one of my own.

It's not my grandparents' fault. If anything, they deserve all the credit in the world for refusing to keep me in a bubble. They pushed me out of the nest. I would not be who—or where—I am without that. But, I've always been more comfortable alone. I've always been more comfortable reading about romance and love in Desiree's novels than I have seeking it out on my own.

And I know why.

Everyone does.

When you lose those you love at such a seminal age, scar tissue develops around your soul, and it emits tendrils that grow so quietly and yet so quickly from all your internal sorrow and tears that you don't even notice until your entire heart is encapsulated. You realize it only when you take a step, reach out a hand, touch another, are kissed and your instinct is to withdraw, not because you don't yearn to be loved and caressed but because you are too scared of weeding your soul only to be hurt yet again.

Ah, the irony in life, love and literature.

So I do what I did so many years ago when I lost my parents, I did the things my friends and grandparents feared: I turned off the world. It was easier to do it as a kid, before technology. I used to wear a ball cap and a big coat, nose buried in a book, to keep people at bay.

Now I've stopped checking social media. I hid at home waiting for the holidays and the Santa madness to end.

I retreated.

Again.

I turn, my back toward the glass, and begin arranging stacks of a new celebrity diet cookbook from a chef who—on her show—famously only uses butter, lard and sugar. I open the book to a recipe for red velvet cake and glance at the ingredients below the mouthwatering photo: it calls for butter, lard and sugar. Confused, I turn back to the opening page and read the chef's note to readers. It states: "This is a diet cookbook because you're only supposed to eat half the recommended serving. Good luck!"

I laugh. Probably the most realistic diet cookbook I've ever seen. I'll sell a ton of these.

A knock on the glass makes me turn.

A little girl in a pink puffy coat and even pinker scarf is waving at me. I wave back. She releases her mother's hand, walks up close to the window and blows on the glass. In the steam, she draws a big heart. She blows again. This time, she draws a flower over the heart. The girl giggles, takes her mother's hand and skips off.

For a moment, it lingers on the window, a silhouette of hope. And then, slowly, it fades before my eyes. Condensation trickles from the petals to the fading heart.

Tendrils.

I hear the bell jingle on the front door. I look up, and Rita is arriving for our Monday meeting.

"Paper ready?" she asks. "Tellie Mae tells me she's been busy!"

Tellie Mae owns the local funeral home. Tellie Mae tells everyone that most infirmed people wait to make it until January before they die so they can see their families at the holidays one last time.

I glance at the heart and flower. They have disappeared.

"Coming?" Rita calls as she makes her way downstairs.

I take a deep breath and follow her. I watch her take a seat by the fireplace and then pop the local paper over, wetting her finger and turning to the obits.

"I'm so sorry, Rita," I say. "I forgot I have another appointment this morning."

"You can't!" she protests.

"Unfortunately, I do. But NOAH—" I yell this so he will hear "—would be happy to assist you today."

I walk toward the counter.

"Diva," he whispers. "You can't."

"I can," I say. "Payback."

Noah slaps himself—rather hard actually—and yells with faux chipperness, "Good morning, Rita! How have you been?"

"Not good, not good," she says.

The duo disappear toward the fireplace.

The back door on the lower level opens—the one used mostly by staff and for deliveries—and my grandparents come inside, a whoosh of frigid air following them. I don't look at them. Although we spent Christmas together, this was a particularly icy one. I refused to talk about what they'd conspired to do. I simply turned up the holiday tunes and baked with my grandma, singing louder when she'd try to apologize or talk about it. We opened gifts quickly, stuffed ourselves, and I went home and fell asleep.

"And I thought it was cold outside," my grampa remarks.

My grandma tucks her scarf and mittens into her coat pockets and hangs her heavy coat on the rack in the office. She walks out, looks at me, waiting for me to say something. When I don't, she says, "Can we talk?"

"You sound like Joan Rivers," I say. "And, no, we can't. I need some fresh air."

"I'm so sorry, Susan," she says, her voice cracking. "You wouldn't say a word over the holidays. Enough's enough. I know we overstepped our boundaries. We were just trying to help. We all love you so much. We just want you to be happy."

"I am happy!"

"Sure seems like it," I can hear Noah call.

"It was all my idea," my grampa says.

"What?" I yelp.

He walks toward me. "It really was. I just want you to have the companionship I know you want and deserve. Your grandma and I aren't going to be around forever. We want you to have someone in your life. I was being selfish. If you want to blame someone, blame me."

I grab my coat.

I know I'm being as immature as a teenager, I know there are better ways to handle things, but having my past exposed so openly right now just makes me want to do what I did when I was little and couldn't deal with the pain or scrutiny: disappear.

"Blame me, Susan!" my grampa calls as I head outside.

The tone of his voice shatters my heart, but I blame it on the cold. I get in my car, crank the heat and drive to the shoreline.

January and February are long months in Michigan. The days are often cloud-filled and dark, and night falls in the early afternoon. My grampa used to always say it took a certain type of person to weather winter in Northern Michigan. Yes, one had to love the snow and cold, the dry skin, a running red nose and the warmth of a wood fire, and, yes, one had to be hearty of soul, but—more than anything—one had to be ever patient and hopeful.

Spring is just around the corner, and those who live in Northern Michigan must wait longer than almost anyone else for it to arrive, he still says. *But when it does! Well, I believe we appreciate it more than others because we've been so patient.*

On the rare days when the weather turns so cold and yet so

sunny, there is an isolated spot on the bay—where the shore-line arcs into a narrow point—my grampa used to take me.

I pull off the main road and down a long driveway hugged by pines heavy with snow. The Chapmans live here. They come every July and August to the old family cottage as well as at Christmas. I knew the driveway would be plowed.

There are wonderful and not-so-wonderful aspects of being a local in a resort town. Everyone knows your business, personal and professional. You can't escape the public glare. You can't walk down the street more than a few seconds without being stopped by someone who knows you, or by someone whose mom or grandma knows you. Everyone in town would give you the shirt off their backs. You can get a seat in a restaurant even if it's full.

And, maybe most importantly, you know who's in town and who's not, so—perhaps—you know when it's okay to use their private beach on a beautiful day in June when the public one is packed, have an October beach bonfire, or—like today—sneak in to see a winter phenomenon.

I pull in front of the old cottage and smile. It's an original Petoskey cabin, a tiny, cramped knotty-pine two-story with a soaring fireplace made of lake stones pulled directly from the bay some hundred years ago. The region has become over-run by new money. People buy the old cottages for the land on the lake and tear them down without a second thought or care about their history.

I get out of my car. The old cottage's roof bows under the heavy snow, and, to me, it resembles an old man smiling.

I think of my grampa and what he said as I left. *Blame me, Susan!*

The old, meandering stairs leading to the water have not been shoveled. I grab the rail—made from old tree branches—and carefully navigate my way here and there, stepping carefully as I go. The stairs end where the edge of the woods meets the beach, and I'm spit directly into a big drift. I high step my way until I am on the frozen sand.

And then I see it.

Blue ice.

This is the name Michigan natives have given to the towering chunks of ice that pile up along the shoreline in brilliant blue hues.

A local photographer and author paired up to publish a gorgeous coffee table book entitled *Michigan Blue* with photos of this winter spectacle. I invited them to speak at the store. The author, also a professor at the University of Michigan, said our blue ice was comparable to the formation of glaciers in that the snow on top of the ice compresses and squeezes out all the air bubbles, thus increasing its density. As a result of this process, ice absorbs colors, which culminates in chunks of blue ice.

On a bright, cold day like this, when the light hits the shoreline, the blues are breathtaking and otherworldly.

I asked my grampa when I was little if I could drink the entire lake.

"Why?" he asked.

"Because it looks like a giant blue raspberry Mr. Misty from Dairy Queen," I said.

"Don't ever look at the world any other way than that," he told me. "Magical."

I grab my cell—thankful for no reception here on the lakeshore—and take photos of my blue Michigan. I stop and scan the undeveloped horizon, taking a mental picture just for myself, and then begin the long climb back up the steep stairs.

I return to my car and turn on the radio. The holiday music continues, undeterred, in Michigan, even though the holidays are over.

I shake my head. "Last Christmas" by Wham! begins to play.

As soon as I hit the main road, my phone begins to trill. I knew I shouldn't have turned it on.

That's when I see I have about a half dozen voice mails from Holly.

Uh-huh, I think. *You can't just apologize and get back in my good graces that easily.*

I hit the last voice mail she left, and it begins to play in my car.

"Where have you been?"

Her voice is high, nearly unrecognizable. "I've been trying to get ahold of you." She stops and begins to cry uncontrollably. My heart rises into my throat.

I jerk my car to the side of the road.

"It's your grampa. He had a heart attack."

chapter 14

My grandma and I are seated in a waiting room outside the emergency room. Ambulances wail outside, people wail inside.

I am holding Grandma's hand. Her head, formerly bowed in prayer, is now bobbing from exhaustion. Her eyes pop open when a nurse rushes by, or a wheelchair tire squeaks. For that brief second, she doesn't understand where she is, and there is a moment of calm on her face. But then she looks around the room in a panic, suddenly aware of what is happening, and she cries anew, before once again bowing her head to pray and falling asleep.

For a control freak, there is no worse place to be than a hospital.

You have no control over time. You have no control over what is happening. You have no control over the outcome.

I want to do something, and yet all I can do is sit here.

I remember the scene in Larry McMurtry's book *Terms of Endearment* when the mother, played by Shirley MacLaine in the movie, begs the nursing staff to give her daughter a shot because she cannot bear to see her in pain any longer.

I cannot bear to see those I love in pain. I watch her wake again with a start and then slip away, and my heart shatters in a million pieces. When my grandma falls asleep again, I let go of her hand slowly, finger by finger, and, as if led by a sign, head to the chapel.

It is tiny. There are four pews underneath a stained glass window of a cross surrounded by peace doves and trillium, elegant three-petal white blossoms that seem to float from dense green leaves resembling tiny hostas. Locals consider them a harbinger of spring, but I always considered them a harbinger of hope, the first sign that winter was over and beauty was about to be reborn across the state.

A tiny smile crosses my face.

Hope.

Will my grandfather see another spring? Another trillium? Another day?

We too often take the beautiful routine of our daily lives and the people we love for granted until tragedy strikes out of the blue, a lightning strike on an otherwise sunny day.

I shut my eyes, lower my head and pray.

I hear a whoosh of the chapel door opening and then soft footsteps. I turn.

Holly is standing in the aisle.

"I got here as fast as I could," she says. "I'm so sorry."

She slides in the booth and holds me, and then we both pray.

I look up and down the hospital corridor. When the coast is clear, I give the vending machine a good kick.

"Boy, I guess you really want those Funyuns," Holly says. I kick it again.

"I'm guessing that's probably meant for me," she adds. I smile. "Here, let me give it a shot." Holly doesn't lift her foot, instead she jabs a hip into the machine—as if she's a maniacal hula dancer—and the Funyuns pop free.

"It's all in the hips," she says.

We take a seat in the hallway. My grandma is now surrounded not only by Leah and Noah but also a rotation of old friends, including Rita. Another beauty of small town life: people show up in force when you need them.

I eat a Funyun—they still taste the same as they did when I was little, like a faux onion ring—and then I place one on my left ring finger.

"Did you do this when you were little?" I ask.

Holly looks at me. She is not dressed up as anyone or anything today. There is no theme. Her face is free of makeup, her hair in a messy ponytail, and she is wearing a Bears hoodie. She looks just like the girl I met in college.

"Wear my food?" she asks.

I hold my Funyun finger out and examine it. "I used to pretend I was married, just like my mom and grandma. What happened to me?"

"Almost all little girls mimic their moms and pretend they're married," Holly says. "It's natural."

"But that's all it's ever been for me," I say. "Pretend."

"Susan, you have carved out an incredible life. You have a successful small business that is both your career and passion. You are loved by family and friends. You're smart, funny and well traveled. None of that is pretend." Holly grabs the Funyun off my finger and eats it. "Gross."

I smile.

Holly continues. "What's pretend is the pressure women

like us place on ourselves to be perfect in society's eyes. We *must* have a husband. We *must* have a family. But what we must do first is be happy and fulfilled, or those around us won't. We don't need a man to do that."

"I know that," I say. "I do. But when I look at my grandparents, and how they've been there for each other through thick and thin, and what my mom had at my age, part of me wants that." I look at Holly. "And I don't think I want to grow old alone. I'd love to share my life with someone."

"You have me," she says. "You'll always have me."

"I know," I say. "But life happens. What if you fall in love? Move away? What if Noah and Leah fall in love? What happens when…"

"Don't say it!" Holly says. "It's like talking about an illness and showing it on your body. It makes it real."

"Do you ever feel like a failure for not being married at our age?"

"Sometimes. There's a lot of societal pressure still on women of a certain age who aren't married. It's an unfair stigma, as if something is wrong with us." Holly looks down the hall. "But I love being single. I love my career."

"I do, too," I say. "I think, for me, the loss of my parents at such an early age made me feel like I should be alone, that perhaps my family's 'bad luck' might rub off on someone else. I also think, for a long time, I couldn't have survived the loss of someone else I loved in my life. This year, my grampa, everything has sort of coalesced to make me ask myself if I've ever really given anyone a chance." I look at Holly. "I just can't imagine losing my grandparents and being all alone."

She grabs my hand and continues. "You will never be alone," Holly says. "I promise you."

I put my head on her shoulder and cry until the shoulder of her gray hoodie turns dark.

"Susan Norcross?"

I look up. A nurse is standing before me in scrubs.

"Your grandmother is looking for you," she says. "Dr. Straube is with her right now."

The steady beep of the heart monitor matches the one in Jordan's room.

My grandfather is sedated and out cold following the anesthesia. He is sleeping with his head elevated and tilted to one side.

"How's our Santa doing?" a nurse says, checking his vitals.

He looks nothing like Santa right now. His skin is ashen, his cheeks sunken, his white hair standing on end, his mouth open but unable to emit a booming laugh.

The only twinkling light is on the monitor.

"He's a lucky one," Jackie, the nurse, says.

Jackie is—*what?*—in her midtwenties now, I think. She used to come into the store as a girl all the time, and she comes every Christmas now to get a picture with her husband and baby girl.

My grandfather suffered only a minor heart attack, a miracle considering he had a 98 percent blockage in his left anterior descending artery. A one hundred percent blockage is called the "widow maker."

"And you are a miracle worker, Mrs. Claus," Jackie says, walking over to rub my grandma's shoulders. "You called 9-1-1 so quickly, I hear."

"Wasn't me," my grandma says. "Leah got him to chew and swallow an aspirin before he lost consciousness, and then Noah performed CPR. I have a wonderful family."

The room starts to feel claustrophobic. I can see my grampa's face as I was storming out of the bookstore. I can hear his voice clear as a bell.

Your grandma and I aren't going to be around forever. We want you to have someone in your life. I was being selfish. If you want to blame someone, blame me. Blame me, Susan!

I rush out of the room.

"You did this to him," I say to myself, my face in my hands. "Blame yourself."

"You didn't do this."

I move my hands.

My grandma is looking at me.

"I'm so sorry, Grandma. I'm so, so sorry."

She pulls me into her embrace. "I know you are, honey," she says. "But it's not your fault. He's old. Too many Manhattans and snickerdoodles and not enough exercise. I should have acted sooner. I noticed he was getting so winded over the holidays.

"He's going to be okay," she continues. "Nothing a couple of stents won't solve right now."

She looks at me, her voice hitting the words "right now" hard. They hang in the air.

My grandma is telling me he won't live forever. She is telling me none of us will. But I know she is also telling me to appreciate these moments in life even more.

"I think your grampa's heart has always been a bit too full of love and a bit too full of sadness," she says. "That's why it finally needed a little extra help."

She takes my face and holds it in her tiny hands.

"You know what they've always said about Santa, don't you?" Grandma whispers. "People are mistaken thinking Santa comes down the chimney. He really enters through our hearts."

chapter 15

Jed Freely, one of my grandparents' oldest friends—a country man if I've ever known one, a farmer I've never seen out of a pair of Carhartt coveralls—walks into my grampa's hospital room, gives him the sweetest peck on top of the head and then places a Santa cap on his noggin. "You get better now, buddy, you hear me. We need you."

I can see his cheeks quiver as he struggles with his emotions. He takes my grandma's hand for a second, nods at me and leaves the room. It takes all my willpower not to weep.

My grampa is still asleep following surgery.

Word spreads fast in a small town. It's like a childhood game of "telephone." My cell is exploding with worried friends and customers. Rita has left and is coordinating the home front for my grandparents, organizing and freezing all the casserole deliveries, making sure the driveway and sidewalk are shoveled, checking in at the store. She texts me every few hours for an update.

I cannot take the quiet, the interminable beeping. I've been told my grampa should be just fine after rehab, but it's the not knowing for sure until I see him wake up that is so unsettling. His room feels like Jordan's, so I ask my grandma, "Tell me the story of how you and Grampa met."

She takes a sip of her coffee and cocks her head at me. I've heard the story a million times. Everyone in town has heard it. The greeter at Walmart can even tell the tale. But I need the silence filled, I need the static in my head to still for a moment, so I ask.

My grandmother nods.

"It's a beauty, you know," she says with a wink.

BETTY
DECEMBER 1951

"It wasn't even supposed to snow!"

I stared out my window.

"My dress!" I yelled. "My shoes!"

I spun and looked at myself in the bedroom mirror. The frame was white and painted with pink and blue butterflies. My bangs were the perfect length, and it had taken me an hour to get the curl just right on the ends of my shoulder-length blond hair.

My taffeta dress was Christmas green—as green as the Petoskey pines outside my bedroom window. And it was wide! My mother had worked for weeks to make its circumference as big as the bay, adding endless layers of crinoline.

But I worried most about my shoes, which had been dyed to match my dress.

"It's going to be okay," my mother said.

"Dyed shoes are not waterproof, Mother!"

I willed back tears, so as not to ruin my makeup.

My mother stood in the door, fidgeting with a tray of snacks she was taking to my brother and his friends. Bowls of Ruffles potato chips and M&Ms were perched next to a platter of hot dogs stacked high. Boys could care less about dances, only their stomachs.

I looked in the mirror again.

There was only one boy I cared about, though.

"It's going to be okay," my mother said again. "I'll get your father."

My father appeared in the door. "I'll put an umbrella over your head and carry your shoes. You'll need to wear your snow boots."

"Into the dance?" I yelled.

"No, Betty, to the car, so your shoes won't get ruined." He looked at me and folded his arms. "It's *supposed* to snow in December in Michigan. You can't stop it."

I checked my appearance one last time, did a twirl in the mirror, kicked off my shoes and handed them to my father. He waited for me to head down the stairs where my mom was waiting. I posed for a hundred photos.

"Your first Christmas formal at the Perry Hotel," my mother beamed. "My, how time flies. I just can't understand why that Francis Calloway wouldn't pick you up."

"Be cool, Mom," I said. "All the dreamboats go to the dance together. But Frank told me to meet him there. It's a date."

My mother shook her head. I could read her mind: *That doesn't sound like a date to me.*

The snow picked up in earnest on the way to the dance. The roads were thick with white, and I could even feel my dad's '51 Chevy Deluxe Tin Woody—a tank if there ever was one—slip and slide in the snow.

My father pulled in front of the Perry Hotel and into a long line of cars.

"Here are the rules," my father said. "No back seat bingo…"

"Daddy!" I cried, mortified.

"I mean it, young lady. You may be eighteen, but that doesn't mean you're a woman."

My passenger door suddenly flung open, and all my friends began to scream.

"Betty!"

I swung my legs out, pulled off my boots, slipped on my heels and stepped out of the car.

"One more thing, young lady!" he called.

I turned.

"Don't call me to pick you up in the middle of *Red Skelton*, got it?"

I shut the door, and the screaming started anew.

We raced up the steps into the hotel and then entered the grand lobby.

I stopped and turned in a circle.

The lobby smelled of fresh pine. Trees in white lights were scattered throughout the grand space, the chandeliers were flocked in garland and I had never seen so many poinsettias in my life.

Finally, the girls turned to look at one another, and we began jumping up and down, our hoops bouncing, the taffeta floating. The senior girls and boys at Petoskey High had held their Christmas formal here every year, and it was the most anticipated dance of our high school career. We had been planning for this night for four years and had helped pick out each other's dresses, but seeing it all in person finally made it real.

"Christmas formal!" they squealed. "'51 may be fun, but '52 is gonna be true!"

We raced to the ladies' room to check our makeup and hair

and then into the lobby full throttle, holding hands, not slowing until we reached the entrance of the Rose Room. There we slowed and sashayed inside as if we were Audrey Hepburn.

A band was set up by the windows in front of the bay, and the singer was crooning, "Too Young." He looked just like Nat King Cole and as if he were floating on the water.

Tammy Babcock nudged me with her elbow. I followed her gaze across the parquet floor, over the red carpet and to the corner of the room, where a group of boys were standing by the punch bowl.

Frank Calloway, even more handsome and mysterious than Marlon Brando in *A Streetcar Named Desire*, leaned against the wall in his tuxedo and skinny bow tie as if he owned the place. His blond hair was slicked back, and his perfect jaw was set with the slightest of smiles.

Frank was the captain of our basketball team, the son of the town's doctor, the student body president, the golden boy of Petoskey. The joke in school was that Michigan sunsets were jealous of Frank because he received more attention.

And he asked *me* to meet him at the dance.

My heart skipped a beat.

"Go talk to him!" Tammy said.

Tammy was not subtle. She was head cheerleader, and even when she whispered, her voice boomed as if she were standing in front of a crowd on a football sideline.

"He asked me to meet him," I said. "Shouldn't he come to me? It's not appropriate."

"It's 1951, Betty. It's a new day, so stop acting like Doris Day."

My friends all nodded in agreement. I took a deep breath, smoothed my dress and began to walk. As I did, I could feel myself floating, just like the singer over the bay. I looked down at my shoes, steadying myself so as not to trip, and moved across the carpet. My green dress set against the red filled me with Christmas spirit. It filled me with hope.

Frank was not only going to be my Christmas gift but be mine forever. I just knew it. I would be the queen of Petoskey, the wife of a doctor, the girl who reeled in the biggest fish in the bay.

When I finally saw the legs of the long table in my periphery, I looked up.

Frank was still leaning against the wall. I took a step and opened my mouth to say his name when Lynda Lou Wilcox appeared out of nowhere in a dress much too short for a formal dance.

What was she doing here? The most popular girl of last year's graduating class shouldn't be at a stupid high school dance on her college break.

I stopped. It was all a blur: Lynda Lou touched Frank's arm and laughed. He ducked his head. The singer began to croon, *"Be My Love"* by Mario Lanza. Lynda Lou looked toward the dance floor, batted her lashes and touched Frank's arm again. I watched in slow motion as he extended his hand. She took it. They walked right past me, as if I were a ghost, and began to slow dance. The last thing I saw before I ran from the Rose Room was Lynda Lou putting her head on Frank's shoulder.

My friends rushed into the lobby to console me. As if on cue, the song switched to "Jezebel."

As they hugged me, I believed Frank would follow me, apologize, explain that he was only trying to make me jealous, but he never came.

"Go," I told them. "Go have fun. I'm not going to ruin your formal."

One by one, they drifted back inside. Song by song, I could see boys approach them and ask them to dance.

I heard a boom of laughter. I turned, and a costumed Santa

was making his way into the lobby. He stopped, knocked snow off his boots and then from his shoulders. He took a spin around the room, admiring each and every tree as if it were the first he'd ever seen, and then took a seat in an ornate chair positioned in the far corner of the mammoth room.

For a moment, the room was filled with only the music that spilled from the band in the Rose Room and a few people milling in and out of the hotel. But in the blink of an eye, the lobby was filled with children and families, a line stretching through the lobby and down the stairs that led to the hotel's front entrance.

I pivoted on the large couch on which I was seated and watched the scene.

Child after child approached, wide-eyed in wonder. Santa lifted them upon his lap as if they were light as snowflakes, asked their names and then whispered into their ears, "What do you wish for Christmas?"

For some reason, I couldn't avert my eyes because of his: they literally twinkled.

Not from the lights off the tree, or the flashbulbs used by the hotel photographer, but from some inner light.

How could such an old man still express such glee?

I thought of how consumed I had been with this formal—my dress, my hair, Frank—and not with all the things I usually loved about Christmas: cutting down a tree from our woods, drenching it in tinsel, decorating cookies with my stupid brother, watching holiday movies with my parents.

And the one thing about Christmas in which I no longer believed—Santa Claus himself—had given me a sliver of hope on an awful night.

I watched the holiday spectacle until my friends came to check on me. They all had a boy on their arms now, but I waved them away.

"Don't be sad," Tammy said reassuringly. "Frank will come back to you."

I looked at my friend. "I'm not sad," I said. "I'm grateful."

Tammy looked at me and shrugged, and then she screamed when "Come On-a My House" began to play, and she and the others raced back into the Rose Room to dance with their new beaus.

I glanced at the clock over the staircase. I still had time to phone my father before *Red Skelton* started. I stood, then sat again, kicking off my heels and rubbing my feet, before heading barefoot to the phone in the lobby to call my father.

On my way, I noticed Santa waving. I looked around the lobby, searching for a child who had perhaps wandered in at the last moment, but when I looked back at him, I realized he was waving at me.

"Ho! Ho! Ho!"

"Hi," I said.

"Don't you know my name, miss?"

"Of course I do," I said. My face flushed. I felt like a fool for saying it out loud. I lowered my voice and glanced around the lobby. "Santa."

"Yes!" his voice boomed. "And what is your name?"

I rolled my eyes.

"You shouldn't roll your eyes at Santa. I'm here to help. What's your name?"

"Betty."

"What a pretty name!" he said. "Beautiful name for a beautiful girl. May I ask you another question, Betty?"

I nodded.

"Why do you look so sad?"

I glanced toward the Rose Room.

"A boy," I sighed. "I thought he liked me." I looked at Santa. "He didn't, as it turns out."

"His loss, then," Santa said. "What's his name?"

"Frank," I said. "Francis Calloway."

Santa nodded his head, and the tip of his cap bounced.

"Yes, I know Francis," Santa said. "He'll be getting a lump of coal this year."

I giggled.

"It's true!" Santa continued. "Do you know why I give coal to those who've been naughty? It's convenient! When I travel down the chimney to leave gifts, I come across lots and lots of coal. I place it in stockings for those who haven't been so nice. And I hear Francis is never nice. You on the other hand…you're always nice."

"Not always," I said.

"Well, the best of us know when we're not at our best. The worst do not. Now, what would you like for Christmas, Betty?"

My heart fluttered. I hadn't been asked this question since I was a tiny girl who sat upon Santa's lap. It felt so real then, before I started making lists and leaving them for parents.

What did I want for Christmas?

I knew it wasn't another pretty dress, a University of Michigan sweatshirt where I was going to college, or even tickets to see The Andrews Sisters.

"I want a copy of *From Here to Eternity* by James Jones," I said quickly.

"We have a reader!" Santa said. "I love to read, too!" And then he looked into my eyes and said, "But what do you really want, Betty?"

I looked around the lobby at the trees, garland, poinsettias and light.

I knew what I wanted.

"Whisper your wish to me, Betty, so it will come true," Santa said.

I leaned in until my mouth was so close to his ear that his beard tickled my face.

"All I want for Christmas is the way it used to be."

I leaned away from Santa. For the longest time, he was as still as the snowfall outside the Perry.

"That's the most beautiful Christmas wish I've ever heard, Betty," he said. "And always remember if you forever have the heart of a child, then Christmas—no matter the heartache we endure in life—will remain the way it was because we will always carry the two greatest gifts in life. Memories and hope."

Santa stood, took off his cap and glasses, and removed his white hair and beard.

"Nicholas Norcross?" I asked, my eyes bulging.

He nodded.

"I thought you were an old man," I laughed. "What are you doing here?"

"I'm on Christmas break from Michigan State," he said. "I work part-time at the old hardware store to earn money when I'm back home. You know the shop with the sleigh on the roof? Mr. Vanderwall is the town Santa. He does it every Christmas to promote the hardware store for holiday shopping. His truck got stuck in a drift outside of town when he was making a delivery, and he asked me to fill in for him tonight. You know, I've always dreamed of doing it."

"Why?"

"Reminds me of the way things used to be."

And that's when I remembered.

"I'm so sorry about your father," I said. "I know what a shock it was to your family. My father really admired him. Said he was the only honest attorney he'd ever known."

Nicholas laughed. "Now that is a compliment." He stopped. "I miss him. It's hard. Especially this time of year. This brought me some much-needed joy."

He continued, "It's like I was given permission to be a kid again, permission to have fun and to hand out joy. We rarely get that feeling as adults. What a gift it is to bring joy into people's lives when I now understand the sadness that lies beneath."

Nicholas lifted his Santa cap. "Not only was I named after St. Nick, but my grampa was Captain Santa."

"*The* Captain Santa?" I asked. "My father swears he finds a pine tree washed ashore every Christmas."

Nicholas smiled.

"Well, I'm sorry for all your loss," I said.

"We all experience loss. It's how we handle it which defines us."

I actually saw Nicholas for the first time that day. Not as the gawky, smart kid, or the lumpy lineman who protected the quarterback in high school, but as a good, kind man.

I didn't just see him either. I saw his soul. The light in his eyes.

The band in the Rose Room began to play "Blue Christmas."

"Would you like to dance?"

"Here?"

He nodded, took my hands, placed his Santa cap atop my head, and we swayed in the lobby as the snow fell around us outside.

"Not so blue anymore, is it?" he whispered into my ear.

We danced the night away, one song melding into another, before we left together.

"Francis gave you a ride home?" my mother asked when I walked in the front door. "And at such a decent hour? I was wrong about him."

"It wasn't Francis," I said, rushing over to give her a kiss on the cheek. "And you weren't wrong, Mom."

"Who gave you a ride, then?" my father asked.

"Santa!" I said. I pointed at my cap. "See!"

I stooped and kissed my dad on top of the head. He looked at my mother and then called, as I raced up the stairs, "Have you been drinking, young lady?"

I stood for the longest time in my dress, watching it snow outside my bedroom window. It looked and felt so different than it had hours earlier.

"It's going to be a white Christmas this year," I whispered to myself. "Just the way it used to be when I was a kid. Or maybe a blue Christmas!"

And then I went to bed and dreamed of my St. Nick.

"You know that feeling when you see someone out of context?" my grandma asks, staring at her husband in the Santa cap still on his head. "Maybe it's a little boy getting his first T-ball hit and he's so excited he doesn't know which way to run, and you no longer see him as your baby anymore? Or maybe it's when you turn to leave your granddaughter in her college dorm room, and you realize she's all grown up now? You see them for the first time in a completely new way? That's how I was with your grampa that night."

I reach for her hand.

She continues. "It's like when that top hat is placed on Frosty the Snowman's head, and he immediately comes to life. Your grampa was—and still is—like that when he puts on that silly Santa cap."

"I love that story."

My grandma and I yelp at the same time.

"Nicholas!"

"Grampa!"

We rush to his side, and my grandma rains his head with kisses.

"I'm so, so sorry, Grampa," I say. "I would never blame you. I love you."

His eyes flutter, and I see what my grandma saw so long ago.

"Love you both," he says in a barely audible whisper. "Boy, that anesthesia is stronger than a Manhattan."

I buzz the nurse.

"Now you understand," my grandma says. "It was his eyes, sweetheart. I could see right into his soul, like a child does when he looks at Santa. And do you know what I saw? Kindness. That's all any of us wish for, isn't it?"

The nurse comes in and begins to check his vitals.

"Mr. Norcross?" she asks.

"Ho! Ho! Ho!" he says.

"Yes," she says. "Santa's got a lot of holiday spirit left in him."

I lay my head into my grandfather's shoulder. He leans his head toward me until the tip of the Santa cap falls across my face.

chapter 16

"How long have you been coming here?"

In the quiet of Jordan's room, my grandma's voice sounds even sadder echoing back to me.

"Quite a few years," I say. "I only come in December."

I feel a mix of utter relief and complete discomfort at the discovery of my long-held secret. But, after what happened with my grampa, I couldn't hold this back any longer.

My grandma takes a seat in a chair and looks at Jordan's frozen face.

"I thought he died years ago," she says. "Truly, I did. Why didn't you tell me, Susan?"

She turns to look at me. I shrug.

"I don't know." I stop. "I do know. I was scared. I thought

you wouldn't understand. I thought you would be mad. It became my little secret. Just the two of us."

My grandma nods. "His mother was the kindest woman.
And he was such a precious little boy. I don't know if you'll
remember, but he used to come into the store and use his
paper route money to buy books. He even used to read to you
sometimes when you were a girl."

My heart aches at the irony of the distant memory.

"But secrets keep us frozen in time," Grandma says. "And it
wasn't just the two of you whose lives were changed forever.
Your grandfather and I lost our son and daughter-in-law. Jordan's parents lost their son, his sister lost a brother, the family
lost its hopes, dreams and any chance of a normal life again
in this town." She pats the chair next to her, and I take a seat.

"Why are you putting yourself through this?" she continues. "Over and over and over?"

"I wanted an apology."

"Oh, Susan."

"I wanted him to wake up and tell me he was sorry for ru-
ining my life. I wanted him to take responsibility. I wanted
him to say he was sorry for not allowing me to be able to open
my heart to anyone again because I knew they were just going
to die and leave me alone again."

"Oh, Susan," my grandma repeats. "And you read to him?"
she asks.

I gesture toward the book that still sits on the table by his
bed—*The Polar Express*—the one I never finished.

"That was one of your parents' favorites," she says. "They
sold it like crazy at the holidays. Can I see it?"

I retrieve the book and give it to my grandma. She flips
through the pages, a small smile on her face and, without
warning, begins to read to Jordan. I shut my eyes and lis-

ten to my grandma read, one of my favorite things from my childhood.

"'The thing about trains,'" my grandma reads in the conductor's voice. "'It doesn't matter where they're going. What matters is deciding to get on.'"

She stops and looks at me.

"You have to decide to get on the train again, Susan. We only have a short ride here on earth."

My grandma stands, takes Jordan's lifeless hand in hers, leans down and whispers, "I forgive you, dear boy."

She stands and looks at me again.

"Your turn."

Tears spring to my eyes. I lean down and whisper into Jordan's ear, "I forgive you, too."

Grandma rubs my shoulder and smiles.

"Now, there's only one person left you need to forgive."

chapter 17

"What are we doing here?" I look at my grandma.

"My turn to share a secret," she says cryptically.

After leaving Jordan, I pull my car into a snow-cleared spot at Bayfront Park, stopping when the bumper nestles against a two-foot-high drift.

We pull on our mittens and scarves, and my grandmother reaches into the floorboard to retrieve two pairs of earmuffs.

"You're gonna need these," she says, handing me one.

We head toward the Petoskey break wall, and I see a tent set up on the icy bay.

"It's early this year," I say.

"It's icier and colder this year," she says. "But the timing is perfect."

I already know what we're headed to see.

I haven't been here since…

We walk out on a cleared dock about eight hundred feet offshore.

An underwater crucifix, white as a ghost, shimmers under the bay through a hole in the ice.

My grandma grabs my mittened hand and squeezes it, hard.

An eleven-foot-tall cross, with a five-and-a-half-foot figure of Jesus Christ nailed to it, lies at the bay's bottom, illuminated by lights. Lake fish and flora swirl around the crucifix, glowing in the white light.

"You know the story, right?" Grandma asks.

"Bits and pieces," I say. "It's been so long since I've been here." I look at my grandmother. "I never returned after Mom and Dad died."

Grandma walks to the edge and stoops over the hole in the ice. When she speaks, her breath comes out in big puffs and lingers around her head like thought bubbles in a cartoon.

"The crucifix came to Petoskey in 1962, albeit in an odd way. A grieving mother and father from Michigan's Thumb had the crucifix built in Italy in memory of their teenage son, who was killed in a tragic accident, but it was broken during shipping, the family rejected it, and the cross made its way to Little Traverse Bay where it was sold in an insurance sale to a dive club," Grandma says. "They bought it to honor a diver who drowned, and it was placed here during a huge town event."

My grandmother stands, her gaze still fixed upon the crucifix, and continues. "In the '80s, the crucifix was lifted from the water and repaired. It was secured to a new base that was built in the Petoskey marina and then replaced in the bay. A winter viewing of the crucifix was proposed, lights were added under the water, and a hole was cut in the ice. Today, people from all over Michigan and the world come to view the crucifix in winter, not only to memorialize all those who have perished at sea but also to remind them that even in the depths of their own grief, there is hope."

My grandma walks over to me.

"Our family has had too much grief in our lives," she says. "Your parents, Captain Santa, Jordan. But I come here every winter with your grampa to think of that family who lost their son so long ago, and from all of their pain arose a glorious tribute to remind us that we truly never die. We may all try to bury our pain below the surface, but when we allow our light to shine, we can change the world."

"What didn't you ever tell me?" I ask.

"We all have secrets, don't we, Susan?" she says with a wink. "Did my eye move? I think it's frozen."

I laugh and put my arm around my grandma's waist. She is warm.

"We all continue to suffer in ways big and small from what happened so many years ago," Grandma says, her voice muffled in the wind. She looks out over the bay and then down at the water. "This helps me put it all in perspective. This helps light the dark days of winter."

I walk over to the hole in the ice and look into the murky depths below.

Dark to light.

I stare at the crucifix and then study the life that still churns all around it.

"Grandma!" I suddenly call. "Look!"

Nestled against the base of the shrine are a carpet of pine trees.

"Do you think...?" I start.

My grandma smiles. "I do," she says.

"Captain Santa still working his magic," I say.

"Your grampa actually started that," my grandma says.

I look back at her. "What?"

"To honor his grandfather and as a way to protect the statue's base and provide a home for fish," she says. "It was his idea, long ago. Every December, before the bay freezes over, the city dumps Christmas trees here."

"How did I not know that?" I ask.

"It's amazing how connected we all are if we're just willing to extend a hand."

I extend my hand.

"Would you join me in a prayer?" I ask.

My grandma takes my hand and bows her head. I shut my eyes.

When I open them, light spills from the darkness below, and the icy bay glows.

chapter 18

"Did you bring me a Manhattan?"

My grampa is sitting up in bed when we return. Noah and Leah are visiting.

"It's water and green tea for you," Noah says. He stands and picks up a cup off the tray and holds out the straw to my grampa. "And maybe a touch of Ensure."

"Yum," Grampa says with a groan. He takes a sip and pretends to gag at the taste. "Santa prefers eggnog with a little something extra."

My grandma walks over and pats his stomach. "Santa's already got a little something extra. You're getting healthy this year," she says. She removes his Santa cap, gives him a big smooch on the noggin and replaces his hat. "What are we going to do with you, you old coot?"

It finally dawns on me that my entire team is here in the hospital.

"Who's running the store?" I ask.

"Holly," Leah says. "She hasn't left."

"Where's she staying?"

"With me," Noah finally says, eyes down. "She didn't want to bother you. She knows how overwhelmed you are."

My heart drops. I sigh. "I'm so sorry," I say. "To everyone. I just felt a bit like I woke up and I was being pushed into a corner trying to confront some things I haven't wanted to."

"Nobody puts baby in a corner," Noah says.

I smile.

"I just felt a bit like a feral cat with all the attention. I do appreciate all of your love and concern, I just didn't know how to handle it."

Noah nods. "Don't worry. Holly and I have been Laverne and Shirley. I even sewed big N and H letters on our sweaters." He looks at me and opens his coat. "See, I'm not kidding."

My grampa laughs and shakes his head. I think he considers Noah to be a combination of the grandson he never had and a magical unicorn. Then he begins to cough.

"I think it's time for a rest," my grandma says. "Lots of company and excitement today."

"Wanna get some lunch?" Leah asks.

I nod.

"We'll meet you in the cafeteria in a bit," she says.

They leave, and my grandma and I take a seat in the chair by his bed.

"My girls," my grampa says, looking at us.

"I'm so sorry, Grampa. I don't know if I could have lived with myself if something had happened to you. I feel so awful for everything that happened." I shake my head. "I know I overreacted to the whole Single Kringle thing. I'm sorry.

About everything. I sound like a broken record. It's true what I just said—I did sort of feel like a feral cat who suddenly is confronted by a group of well-meaning rescuers pushing companionship when she's used to sort of doing it all on her own. The idea of…something new…can be scary."

"I understand," he says. "And it's not your fault, honey. My ticker just got a little sicker for a bit. On the mend now."

I stand, take a seat on the mattress beside him and take his hand in mine.

"I just need you to know that you didn't do anything wrong. You did everything right." My grampa is staring at me. "You took me in and raised me not as your granddaughter but as your own daughter. You didn't act all weird, as if Mom and Dad never existed. You kept their memory alive. You talked about them with happiness and not tears. You didn't keep me in a bubble, you pushed me out of my comfort zone so I'd have a normal life just like any other kid. You believed in me enough to hand me your dream, the reins to Sleigh By the Bay. I love you more than anything."

"Oh, Susan," he says. "I know that. I've never doubted that. And I love you more than anything in this world, too. Do you know why we opened Sleigh By the Bay?"

"You loved books? You wanted to be your own boss?"

"Because books are just like Christmas. They're gifts that bring joy, allow us to see the world in a new way, and something you never want to end," my grampa says. A tiny smile crawls across his face. "What a gift it is to bring joy into people's lives every day of the year. That's what you do for us."

"I need to have as much faith in myself as you've always had in me," I say.

Grampa gives my hand a little shake. "It doesn't take a Santa cap to make yourself magical," he says. "It just takes a little faith."

Forgiveness.

Darkness.

Light.

Hope.

All separated by just a few letters but a world of faith.

"I promise I'll give your whacky Single Kringle idea a shot," I say. "Just a few dates. I'll have faith in you and me."

I hear a resounding whoop echo in the hallway.

"You didn't go to lunch, did you?" I call.

Noah races back into the room, followed closely by Leah.

"Can I call Holly with the news?" Noah asks. "And can I finally dress you up like Sandy at the end of *Grease*? You could at least do with a bit more eye makeup and a red lip. And no to your puffy coats and the athletic wear you think looks appropriate in public. Ooh! Let's do leather. And get you in a pump. Can I cut your hair?"

"Yes, you can tell Holly," I say. "And no you can't put me in leather pants or cut my hair."

Leah walks up to me and puts her hand on my back.

"We've all been talking, too," she says.

"We?"

"Me, Holly and Noah. And we have decided to have more faith in ourselves, too. I need to get back out there as well. So we promise that we're putting ourselves out there again so you won't have to go through this alone."

I cock my head. "Meaning?"

"We're going to date, too. Noah and I are going to be Single Kringles, too."

I suddenly remember the article in the Petoskey paper. "The Three Stooges," I say. "This has disaster written all over it." They laugh. "And, I cannot believe I have to go back on social media."

"Everything is changing so quickly," my grampa says.

"Kids can now track my progress around the world with the NORAD Santa Tracker. It's a new world."

"And now they'll be able to track our dating lives," I say with a sigh. "What a gift to the world."

"Santa's on vacation until next year," he says. "All eyes are on Susan."

"It's gonna be a long winter," I say.

chapter 19

FEBRUARY

Our staff meeting has turned into an episode of *The Dating Game*.

I used to watch this show in reruns when I was a teenager. I would sneak downstairs to my grandparents' basement to pretend to study and read, but bad TV would always win. Many times, I would watch the show—as I do now when I watch *The Bachelor*, or HGTV's *House Hunters*—and scream at the screen, *None of them! Don't pick any of them!*

That's what I'm silently yelling right now.

Our discussion about new books, upcoming events, online promotions and our e-newsletter got sidetracked when we began discussing Valentine's Day books and window displays.

Noah has designed and handcrafted a gorgeous, retro-inspired design for the window. He has created two-foot-high hearts from pink and red construction paper and absolutely drenched them in glitter so they resemble giant SweeTarts. Inside each, he has written messages, just like the ones you would find inscribed on the candy: Be Mine! Luv You! Hug Me! XOXO! True Love!

The banners for the windows read:

YOU'RE BOOKED FOR VALENTINE'S!

And:

YOU CAN'T SPELL NOVEL WITHOUT LOVE!

But Noah's pièce de résistance is a handmade mailbox—big and pink—just like the ones I made in grade school for Valentine's. On the side it reads *Cupid stops here!* and the flag is a red construction paper exclamation point finished with a heart on the bottom.

My mind somersaults back in time to when I was a girl. I can remember, as clearly as the sun is shining today, the hours I'd spend creating my Valentine's Day mailboxes with my mom's help and then walking around the classroom personally delivering old-fashioned cards to each classmate like a kiddie postman.

My heart would catch when a boy I liked would stop and place a card in my box. When everyone was seated, I would open my decorated shoebox as quickly as I could to read my mail. Even as a girl, I tried to decipher the meaning of the card I was given, the way the cartoon Cupid looked, the words on the card and the messages written by the boys.

As the days following Valentine's passed, so would the notes.

Do you like me?

Yes/No.

Circle one.

A trail of glitter on the bookstore floor shimmers in the light, and I suddenly remember a grade school Valentine from a boy I've kept forever.

Love!

Everyone loves love. They love to talk about it, giggle about it, dream about it, believe in it, but what is love?

It's ethereal and mysterious. It's life-affirming and soul-crushing.

It's the reason we exist.

We love our friends. We love our pets. We love our parents. We love our spouses. We love our children and grandchildren.

We can teach our children about love. We can fill their lives with love. But we cannot prepare them for love.

Because it must start within.

"Hello? Earth to Susan?"

I shake my head and look at Holly. She was here to go over the updates to the website and how to incentivize sales during what can be the brutal winter months when locals are worn down by the cold and resorters are months away from returning to town, but she's turned into my personal Bob Eubanks.

"We've narrowed it down to three potential Santas," she says.

"Is this the most productive thing to be discussing right now in the midst of a staff meeting?" I ask.

"YES!" Holly, Leah, Noah and my grandmother yell at the same time.

I give my grandma the evil eye, and she says, "Well, it is. And you promised your grampa."

"You don't play fair at all," I say.

"So," Holly continues, "out of the thousands of online responses and from all the media attention, three men answered all the questions correctly we placed in our ad. Moreover, they resemble—in size, stature and complexion—the photo I took of your mystery man. Finally, they all said they talked to a woman dressed as Mrs. Claus before the race. So, I have a very good feeling that one of them is your secret Santa."

My mind spins again.

This time, I am standing in the crowd at the Santa Run, talking with the mysterious St. Nick.

I can see his eyes, the color of a snow sky.

I can feel his presence, as familiar as my favorite blanket.

I also remember that there were a lot of runners dressed as Santa and Mrs. Claus. *A lot.*

And then I remember the one thing that we discussed that Holly did not witness, the one thing that was not in the required dating "criteria," the one thing that will let me know if he's the one or not: my mother's angel pin.

"Okay, where did you go?" Holly asks. "I can read your mind. You have nothing to worry about: The four of us spent a lot of time researching their histories, so we don't throw you into a *Tinder Swindler* situation. On the surface, they seem like nice guys with good jobs, friends, family and hobbies."

"And they all read," Leah adds.

"Books?" I ask. "Or do you mean that literally? As in they *can* read?"

"Ha ha," Holly says, handing her cell to me. "The first Santa we've picked out for you is a thirty-eight-year-old financial planner named Jamie Martin from Chicago. He's a big runner, he has a dog, and he loves good food and wine."

"It sounds like I'm going on a date with a stock character from a Hallmark movie."

"And wouldn't that be nice?" Leah asks.

"When is all this going down?"

"Valentine's Day," Holly says.

"Valentine's Day?" I practically yell. "Are you kidding me? How much additional pressure can you add to this insane experiment?"

"It's a test," Holly says, "to see if he's romantic. Maybe he'll bring you roses."

"He's coming here?"

"Yes," she says. "We felt you'd be more comfortable on your home turf."

"I'm not a basketball team."

"Anyway, he's planning the whole thing," Holly continues. "And I think it's important we have the date on a holiday. They're important to you personally and professionally." She hesitates and looks at her coconspirators. "In fact, all of your dates are going to be held around a holiday—Valentine's, St. Patrick's Day and Easter."

"Easter? That's just weird. You want me to go to Easter egg hunting with bachelor number three? Or have the first Santa turn into Cupid?"

"Trust me," Holly says. "I know what I'm doing."

I nearly spit out my water. "And what about the rest of my Pink Ladies? When are you going to start dating?"

"We've been talking about that," Leah says. "In fact, each of us is going to shadow you on the date."

This time, I choke on my water. "This sounds like witness protection."

"Noah and I are actually going to ask someone out and be on a date while you are, so you aren't going through this alone."

"What about you, Holly?"

"I'm coordinating all of this," she says with a shrug.

"Like Dr. Evil?" I ask.

"Like a friend who loves you," Holly says. "If I meet someone in the process, so be it."

"I don't know what to say?"

"How about 'thank you,'" my grandma says.

She gives me a look that slaps me back into reality.

"Thank you," I say. "Now, can we get back to business?"

When we finish our meeting, my grandma admires Noah's decorations. "You know when I was young, we used to call those candies with little sayings *conversation hearts*. We'd hand them out to boys we liked in order to engage a conversation since boys were so shy." She looks at me. "Remember, you have to be willing to get on the train."

When everyone leaves, I stare at a conversation heart that reads TEXT ME!

It is a new age of technology, and yet—foundationally— nothing has changed in the game of love.

I touch the glittering letters on the heart.

I did text you.

Many years ago, after a series of bad dates, when I was home alone at the holidays, feeling lonely and stressed after a long week of work, when I was well into my second glass of wine—*okay, third*—I found my childhood boyfriend, Kyle Trimble, on Facebook.

I hadn't thought about him for decades, but I had earlier that evening discovered the mood ring he'd given me at Christmas squirreled away in a little box inside a red container filled with a Valentine's card he'd made for me along with some fragile holiday decorations and some of my mother's costume Christmas jewelry.

I stalked him for a couple of hours, flicking through hundreds of photos, stopping on the shirtless ones of him on vacation, or working out, discovering he was now a doctor living in Chicago and that he had been married young and divorced, no children. Then—after another sip and with my heart in my throat—I sent him a short message and a photo of the mood ring.

Was at a Petoskey party, and someone mentioned your name, I typed, in my wondrous white lie way. Got home and was curious to see how you were doing. Hope all is well. P.S. Look what I found!

I woke up the next morning with not only a pounding

headache but also a message from Kyle. I mentally kicked my-self for reaching out to him and then, with a dramatic sigh, opened it.

Hi, stranger! Can't believe my first "girlfriend" kept the best gift I've ever gotten anyone. LOL! You were my first date. Man, those were the days. So many memories. We were so young. We went through a lot together at an early age, didn't we?

My heart lifted. I could still hear his voice. He helped me with my grief so much, even though I don't think he real-ized it at the time. He made me feel normal again, and that's all a child wants.

I continued to read.

Hoping to get back to Petoskey this summer with my girlfriend. Chicago gets too hot and crowded. Barely get a day off from my rotation at the hospital. So much pressure. I feel like I could be doing more with my life and skills. I applied to Médecins Sans Frontières—Doctors Without Borders—but it's tough to be accepted. Even thinking of getting off social media. Too much negativity.

"How perfect is this guy?" I yelled out loud. "Really? You could be doing more with your life? I drink alone. And if I went off social media, I wouldn't have anyone to drunk text. I could solve global warming."

Miss you & hope all is well! Kyle

I don't know why, but I could feel my heart shatter just a touch, like when you catch the edge of a teacup on the counter. Would be good to see you and meet her, I wrote. LMK!

I had put my cell down when I heard it trill.

Hey, does that mood ring still work? he wrote.

I slipped it on my finger. The stone began to change color.

It does!

What color is it?

I looked at my finger.

The mood ring immediately turned dark blue, the same color it had when Kyle gave it to me at McDonald's.

Dark blue! I wrote. It means happy!

My finger hovered over the send button.

And then I erased the message.

chapter 20

Simone is yelling at me.

I change the incline on my treadmill to *hill*, crank up the speed two notches, and the terrain on my screen suddenly changes from California coastline to the streets of San Francisco. I had been jogging on the beach by the Pacific Ocean. I could hear the waves and the seagulls. I could feel the warm breeze and sand under my feet.

But my virtual instructor had sensed me slowing and challenged me to do more.

"You can do it!" Simone yells.

I am now running up a nightmarish hill that resembles a mammoth cobra. It snakes this way and that, and the higher I traverse, the longer it seems.

"Faster!" Simone admonishes me. "Faster!"

It is much too cold—and much too dangerous—for me to run outside. February is a winter bully in Michigan: It taunts you endlessly, hammering you as soon as you leave your home, whistling in your ear, getting in your head, wearing you down until you finally break.

I relented a few years ago and bought a state-of-the-art treadmill and bike, so that I could bring the exercise bullying inside.

"You're slowing down! Pick up the pace!"

Simone looks like an anime Barbie. Her blond hair is pulled back into a perfect ponytail that bounces back and forth between each toned shoulder. She is sporting a pink shimmer on her lips and can wear a cropped pink athletic top that shows off her tanned midriff because she doesn't have an ounce of fat that shifts when she springs around on the balls of her feet. Her sweat is melting gold.

A mirror on the wall in my basement turned home gym shows only a part of me running: hips to neck.

I did not often see women like me featured on the covers of fitness or fashion magazines growing up. I have always been a bit too tall, a bit too gangly, the girl told by the school photographers to stand in the back row and slouch or take a seat in the tiny chair in the front row so the rest of the class would seem in proportion. Not to mention the fact I felt guilty wearing heels so as not to make my dates feel "uncomfortable." I bought so many pairs of flats, I could have joined the high school ski team.

I train my eyes on the size of the new hill in front of me.

I wonder if the Pink Ladies checked the height of my dates, I think. *How awkward would it be to stand a head taller than them, or if they feel compelled to haul a box out and hop onto it for a photograph.* I think back to the Santa Run. *He was taller than me.*

"Don't stop," Simone yells.

Do stop, Susan, I think. *Stop self-sabotaging.*

Years of being called "giraffe" and asked *How's the weather up there?* have taken root. How many times have I walked into a restaurant or coffee shop to meet a first date and watched him control his reaction until he can't take it and inquires, *Now, how tall are you?*

It's taken me forty years to realize it's not my fault. I am proud of how I am and how I look.

I trudge up the hill, my eyes focused on Simone.

How unfair is it that fitness magazines rarely featured a woman like Leah, a woman in her early fifties who has raised a family and is healthy, happy but not the size zero so admired in society? When we go to the beach I've watched her worry about stretchmarks and cellulite—the beauty marks of a wonderful life—and her discomfort that people will look at and judge her is so palpable that I can feel it in the air.

I can't wait for winter, she has said. *So I can cover up again.*

And what about Noah? He had little to no representation in the small town where he grew up. Confused and scared, he lost himself in books at an early age, quietly searching for someone like him, someone to give him hope, someone to prove that he should not only be proud of who he was but also worthy of being loved.

I glance at myself in the mirror again.

The expectations society places on those who do not fit within its preconceived standards of beauty or acceptance, those who cannot float throughout the world as easily as Simone is traversing these hills, doom us from an early age.

That's why publishing is so exciting these days. The number of diverse voices and underrepresented authors writing uniquely personal stories that have never been published before feels like a sea change.

My incline finally ends, and I finish my run by the ocean.

Sea change.

Can a sea change happen in my life?

And the lives of my friends?

Or are our stories already written?

Simone thanks me for my energy, and I thank her for my already aching back.

The treadmill slows.

The world is changing. I must keep pace.

Simone waves goodbye to me as I grab a towel and step off the treadmill.

I head upstairs to my kitchen, chug a glass of water and then pour another, which I take into the living room. It is awash in red.

I go immediately from Christmas lights to Valentine's lights, stringing red lights across my mantel and outside across my porch railing. I place heart-shaped lamps on tables and decorate a Valentine's tree in my window.

I've heard from many a newcomer to town who believed my old Victorian was a brothel when they first arrived.

I've even had a few random knocks on my door from drunken strangers and even more surprised looks on their faces when I answer it in a robe and facial mask carrying a book.

I do not like the dark of February, and I must light my world in any way I can. I hate sitting at home at four in the afternoon on a Sunday in the pitch black.

The light makes me feel happier, as if...

I'm not alone.

I start a fire and stand in front of it, thinking about the first Yule logs and why they were started.

We yearned to not only warm our homes but also fill them with light.

That flame, quite literally, ignited our love of holiday lights, which united our need for light in winter with our faith.

Our need for light in dark times.

My fireplace is an original wood burner. I have wood cut and stacked in my garage, and I carry it inside and stack it in my firewood rack. Yes, this is not as convenient as a gas fireplace, but I love the smell of a real fire. I even love the process of starting one. There is a feeling of accomplishment when the flicker bursts into a flame, when the living room becomes toasty and warm.

And it fills my Pink Lady with a glorious glow.

I pull a blanket around me and sit in my favorite rocker in front of the fire for a minute, drinking my water and staring into the light. I remember, as if it were yesterday, sitting in this same rocker—my dad's favorite chair, which I've reupholstered in Pendleton camp blanket fabric—staring into the fire and writing the following lines to my childhood poem:

So, until my day comes
I'll remain happy and bright
And I will believe in my Kringle
With all of my might.

Light.
Bright.
Love.
Might.
Hope.
Faith.

I watch the flames change colors before my eyes, blue then red.

I set my water down, pull the blanket around me even tighter, and I fall asleep and dream I'm wearing a magical mood ring whose stone is made of fire, and it changes color with every beat of my heart.

I don't know how it got on my finger, and I cannot remove it. And yet, it's so beautiful that I can't help but touch it, over and over again.

Each time I do, I get burned.

chapter 21

My eyes are on fire.

And I'm no longer dreaming.

The Meryl Streep of publishing has returned not only with her latest Valentine's romance, *Stupid Cupid*, but also with her flaming hot matchmaker in tow.

Luka is shirtless, his torso flecked in gold, and he's dressed in a white Greek god romper that wraps over a muscled shoulder that rises like Mount Olympus. He is sporting a rope belt with dangling hearts, a pair of golden wrist cuffs and Greek sandals, and a golden quiver of arrows is strapped to his back.

I may loathe and wax philosophical about the unfair expectations society places on women's beauty, but I'm not sorry about thinking this: *Cupid is hot.*

"Holy Son of Eros, Batman!" Noah yells.

Desiree Delmonico—dressed in a red, flowing, sexy, Old Hollywood chiffon gown with feathers that I swear was once lingerie—laughs.

"Who wants to be shot by Cupid's arrow?" Desiree asks the crowd who has packed into Sleigh By the Bay—despite the frigid temperatures—to see this spectacle. "I guarantee love with every arrow and book you buy!"

Noah nearly knocks a woman unconscious throwing his arm into the air.

We are sold out of our supply of two hundred books in under an hour and have online orders for fifty more. As the store clears, I pour Desiree a glass of rosé and bring her a stack of bookplates to personalize and sign.

"Thank you for keeping us going in the winter," I say.

"Thank you for helping to keep me going in the winter of my career," she says.

"Winter?" I laugh.

"Four books a year is a lot of work. I never have a day off. I miss sleeping in on a Saturday, or blowing off a Friday. Every day I must meet a personal and professional deadline. It's totally rewarding and utterly exhausting."

"I understand completely."

"How's your grandfather doing, by the way?" Desiree asks. "I hope he got the flowers I sent."

"He did, and he's doing very well. Back at home and nearly ready to return to the store."

"Well, he's amazing," she says as she signs her name with a red Sharpie. "As are you."

"While he was in the hospital…" I hesitate "…I took my grandma to meet Jordan."

Her heavily mascaraed eyes widen. "Do tell."

"Let's just say there was a lot of forgiveness."

"But not total forgiveness?"

I don't answer.

Desiree returns to signing her heart-shaped bookplates and then stops and touches the steamy cover of her book, a shirt-less Luka piercing a woman's heart with a golden arrow. "So how's *your* love life?" Desiree asks.

I look back at my staff checking out customers.

"You've heard."

"The whole world has heard, Susan. In fact, I think you may have inspired my next holiday romance, *The Single Kringle*. It's perfect."

A slight twinge of jealousy quivers through my own heart, and I guess I'm not good at hiding my reaction because Desiree immediately adds, "It's your life and idea, of course. Maybe we collaborate in the future?"

"If I survive."

I fill Desiree in on the three men who've been selected to go out with me.

"Are you going into this with an open heart and open mind?" she asks.

Her question pierces my soul.

"Promise me you will."

I look away.

"Look, Susan, I can write romance on the page, but I can't write it for myself," Desiree says. "I've been closed off and alone for way too long. And I'm happy and content in life, but a part of me late at night when I'm all alone wonders, 'What if?' I've been successful because I've turned societal expecta-tions on its ear through my books. The men are the sex ob-jects, and the women are smart, successful and in charge, never desperate. But the appeal is that every single character—deep down—is open to love, no matter how much life has hurt them." Desiree's butterfly lashes cast a shadow on her cheeks. "My heart's had a Closed sign on it for way too long. One day, you wake up, and it's frozen as solid as the bay outside these windows. That doesn't mean it can't thaw, it just means it takes longer and longer to do because so many layers get built up over time."

"I promise," I say.

Desiree nods and winks.

I then tell her my Pink Ladies are putting their hearts on the line as well.

"Who's first in line?" she asks.

"You know what? I have absolutely no idea. They have been keeping it such a secret."

I watch Leah check out customers while Noah wraps their books in pink tissue paper and Holly posts video to our website and social media channels.

"I think I know," Desiree says.

My jaw drops. "You do? Who? Spill the beans."

Desiree gestures toward the back of the bookstore.

I watch as Luka pulls an arrow with a heart-shaped tip from the quiver, inserts it into his magical bow and arcs it into the air. I follow its trajectory.

The arrow hits Leah directly in the heart and then bounces onto the counter.

"You missed me!" Noah yells.

As if in a trance, Leah moves from behind the counter and walks toward Luka.

"What is happening?"

I meant to think this, but I say it out loud instead.

Desiree laughs, hard.

"They've been texting and calling one another since my holiday signing event," she says. "Seems they stayed for dessert and drinks at Chandler's after we left, and really hit it off."

Luka and Leah?

It's the equivalent of Pete Davidson dating Kim Kardashian.

No, nix that.

It's like a soccer mom and Zac Efron.

Or me with Luka?

What am I missing?

I jump.

Desiree has slapped a heart-shaped bookplate on my red sweater. I tilt my head to read what it says.

OPEN YOURS!

"It's your own conversation heart," Desiree says. "Have one with yourself."

I watch Leah and Luka stare into one another's eyes. She puts a hand on his bicep, and he whispers something in her ear. Leah laughs.

From across the store, I hear Noah start to sing the old '80s song, "Poison Arrow."

I can't help but join in when he reaches the chorus:

Bow to the target, blame Cupid, Cupid.
You think you're smart, stupid, stupid.

chapter 22

Reese Witherspoon may have a glam squad, but I have a "gram" squad.

My grandma and grampa are seated in my bedroom watching the spectacle while Holly—dressed as the Queen of Hearts not only for a Facebook Live Valentine's Day party she is hosting but also to read to kids at a special event at Sleigh By the Bay—helps get me ready for my first Single Kringle date. Noah is assisting Leah for her date with Luka.

"I just pray that Noah doesn't decide to give Leah a sleeping pill and show up for her date in a wig," Holly says.

My grampa starts laughing, which makes Holly start laughing so hard that her arm shakes, and the eyeliner she is holding travels up and across my forehead.

"I'm so sorry," she says. "It feels good to laugh."

Holly grabs a tissue and begins to wipe my face. "I feel like I started this whole mess from the moment I made you talk to the Santa at the Santa Run. I feel like…" Holly stops wiping and looks me in the eye "… I've pushed you way too far."

"We've," my grampa calls from the bedroom. "*We've* pushed you too far."

"Maybe it's for a reason," I say. "Maybe you're pushing me out of my comfort zone. Maybe I need to be pushed out of my comfort zone again, especially this year."

I think of what Desiree said to me. I picture Luka and Leah.

I mean if Leah can muster the courage to go out on a date with a human statue of *David* then I can take a chance, too.

"So," I continue. "Prep me again for my date tonight."

"Jamie is a thirty-eight-year-old financial planner from Chicago. He's a big runner, he has a dog, and he loves good food and wine," Holly says. "He's very handsome. You said he sounded like a Hallmark character, and he really does look like a Hallmark actor."

"How tall is he?"

"Tall enough to drive here."

She nods excitedly as if that's a sufficient answer.

"As I've said, Susan," she continues as if I'm a child, "based on the photo I took, he looks to be about the same size as the guy you met, so taller than you, which is a feat of nature."

"Ha ha."

She continues. "But I know photos can be deceiving, à la Cletus, and I didn't request his medical charts. And if he's shorter than you, or has green eyes, then you'll know he's not the real Santa, right?"

"Or if he shows up in a Smart car," my grampa calls. The two begin to laugh so hard that Holly falls into a fit of giggles.

"Ha ha again," I say. "Where was he born?"

"Okay, Susan. You need some things to talk about at dinner. You already know more about this guy than if some rando asked you out at a bar, right?" Holly says, squinting as she applies my makeup, her breath on my face. "And Leah is going to be at Chandler's, too, so it's like you have a friend and a bodyguard. Remember, if she goes to the bathroom, you're supposed to excuse yourself so you can check in with her, got it?"

I nod. "This is like a Desiree Delmonico novel."

"Except Leah's already got Cupid."

We look at each other and say at the same time, "How did that happen?"

"Because they're both good people at their core," my grandma calls. "Have you been paying attention to their conversations?"

I think back. I haven't. I've been so consumed in my own personal drama that I didn't pay attention to any chemistry they may have demonstrated or listened in on any conversation they have had.

"They have so much in common," Grandma continues. "I think it's wonderful that they really seem to see into each other's heart. And I love that an older woman is getting a younger man. He's an old soul, and she's a bright light. And, she's been helping him with his business, and he's been helping her work out."

"Sort of like us," I can hear my grampa say.

I can hear them talk and giggle in the next room, and my own heart wants to burst. Their whispers sound the same as my parents' did when I would stand at their bedroom door and listen to them talk about their day.

Although they were together all day long, there was no one else in the entire world they wanted to be with at night.

"Okay, you can look," Holly says.

I finally look into the mirror.

I look like myself, only better.

In the TV show *Younger*, my doppelgänger Sutton Foster cannot get a job in publishing in her forties after being out of the industry for so long raising her family, so she pretends to be in her twenties—by sporting youthful hair, makeup and clothing—and it works.

"I look..." I start, leaning in and touching my face and hair. "Younger."

"All smoke and mirrors," Holly teases.

"Hey!"

"It's the truth. You still got what the good Lord gave you, Cupid just added a little Valentine's Day glitter. Now, for the clothes!"

We head to my closet. It used to be a cramped space, considering people didn't have big wardrobes when this house was built in the late 1800s, but I pushed the bathroom and bedroom out to create much-needed room.

"You have to wear something red," Holly says.

She moves by me and into my closet quickly. Though my closet may be bigger, Holly's hoop skirt fills the space.

"Is there room for me?" I ask.

She repositions her hoop. I step inside, and her mammoth wig scratches my face.

Holly laughs.

"It's a holiday! Get in the holiday spirit!"

I think of my last date with Cletus. Holly can read my mind.

"At least you're meeting him at the restaurant. You can run if you want."

Holly begins handing me clothes that either I haven't worn in years or would only be appropriate if the temperature were seventy degrees warmer.

I hang them back up as quickly as she hands them to me.

"Let's compromise, okay?" Holly asks.

She hands me a flurry of dresses, and I hand them back.

"I will not compromise on pants," Holly says. "You have to show off those legs."

"It's freezing outside."

"Let me tell you something, missy. You're eating in a lovely restaurant that has heat. And you're not lying on your couch in sweats. You have to dress appropriately for a date."

I pluck a playing card from her wig.

"Card flip," I say. "If it lands face up with the queen showing, I'll wear what you choose. If it lands with the face down, dealer's choice. Okay?"

"Okay."

I flip the card into the air, and—for a second—it feels like an overtime coin toss in the Super Bowl. The card flits and floats, bounces off Holly's hoop, takes another turn into the air before, finally, landing.

"Heads!" Holly crows. She begins to dance in the closet. She reaches for a back rack and plucks a red bikini that I wore ages ago to a summer "Christmas in July" party she threw by the pool on her rooftop condo building in Chicago overlooking Lake Michigan. I'd never seen so many shirtless Santas.

"Just kidding," Holly says with a laugh.

After much searching, Holly finally settles on a fitted red sweater with flared sleeves, a plaid, wool skirt, black tights and a pair of pretty pink pumps.

"How about a beret?" Holly asks.

"I'm not Emily in Paris," I say. "I'm Susan in Petoskey."

She grabs my shoulders. "And that's amazing."

I head into the bedroom and do a twirl for my grandparents. They applaud their approval.

"You look beautiful," my grandma says.

"Are you ready to meet your first Santa?" Grampa asks.

"Meeting Santa on Valentine's Day," I say. "It's like meeting the Easter Bunny on the Fourth of July."

My grandparents stand and walk over to me.

"You can never predict when you'll fall in love," my grandmother says. "Or with whom. You just have to believe."

"In miracles, Susan," my grampa says. "We're living proof. So were your parents."

Time stops.

"This could be the night, just like it was for them," Grandma says. "When you least expect it."

MARILYN
OCTOBER 1977

"Our hair is taking over your entire dorm room."

My friend Rita laughed and added another giant roller to her hair.

"It can never be big enough," she said, touching one side of her feathered Farrah do. "These wings still have room to fly."

Rita turned and added another roller to my hair. She continued, "We have to look perfect. This is the biggest fraternity party of the year, Marilyn. I can't believe we got invited. And that my boring roommate went home this weekend."

"*You* got invited," I said. "I'm just a guest. And a hostile one at that."

Rita laughed. "I'm just glad your long weekend coincided with this party. Just don't wear anything with a buckeye on it. In fact, don't even mention that you go to Ohio State…"

"*The* Ohio State," I emphasized.

"…whatever," Rita dismissed. "If anyone on campus knew that a Michigan girl was best friends with an Ohio State girl, I'd be ostracized."

"Border war!" I cry.

"Well, just keep your mouth shut," Rita said. "Especially since this is sort of a border party."

"What is it again?" I asked.

"It's the annual Sigma Pi Around the World Party," Rita said. "Every room in the fraternity is decorated as a different country, each with its own special drink. Every brother spends so much time coming up with their theme, costume and drink."

"Meaning Everclear and Kool-Aid in a plastic cup," I said.

"This is Michigan, not Ohio State. We're a bit classier than that." Rita laughed. "*Not.*"

ABBA began to play.

"C'mon, dancing queen."

Rita grabbed my arm, and we began to dance around her tiny dorm room. She twirled me, and I spun until I fell atop the tiny bed on the far side of her room, toppling all the clothes I'd pulled from my suitcase and laid out carefully.

I stood and began pawing through my potential party outfits. I held one up.

"No!"

Another.

"No!" Rita repeated.

One more.

"No, Marilyn!"

Rita walked over and pulled the outfit from my hand.

"I know how much you loved the way Diane Keaton dressed in *Annie Hall*, but you can't go to a party looking like you just rummaged through your father's closet. This is the party of the year! You have to dress like it."

Rita walked over to her miniscule closet, shrugged off her robe and pulled on what she was wearing: a black jumpsuit with a halter top, flared legs and a teardrop shaped cutout on the stomach. She did a *Charlie's Angels* pose and blinked dramatically, her blue eyeshadow literally glowing in the dim dorm.

"Come here," she urged.

I walked reluctantly to her closet.

"So, we can go all punk if you want," she said. "Sometimes, I go to some of the edgier bars dressed like this and listen to bands."

Rita handed me a black leather jacket with heavy zippers covered in band pins, a yellow Ramones T-shirt, a short, pleated red plaid skirt drenched in safety pins, torn black fishnet stockings and black boots.

"There is no way I'm wearing this," I said. "I am so not punk."

Rita groaned. "Boring."

"What if I got too close to a magnet," I said. "You'd never see me again."

Rita laughed and turned her attention back to her closet.

"Perfect!" she yelled.

She pulled a gauzy gold, chiffon dress—a sort of Halston prairie dress—that draped over one shoulder, was fitted at the bodice and flowing at the bottom.

"Isn't this too dressy for a frat party?" I asked.

Rita crossed her arms. "Every girl on campus is going to be there. Do you want to stand out or not?"

I shook my head no.

"Try again," she said.

This time I nodded.

"Groovy," she said. "Now let's get dressed!"

I could hear KC and the Sunshine Band reverberating as we crossed the campus. As we drew closer, I could hear the din of the party. The three columns of the Sigma Pi house held a massive banner that read AROUND THE WORLD PARTY 1977! The columns and sign were illuminated, and the white three-story house glowed in the night. Through the windows on every floor, I could see people dancing and drinking, and it looked as though the house was alive.

There was just something old-fashioned, nostalgic and comforting about a college campus that I loved, no matter if it was a rival's or not.

I loved the way the autumn leaves danced across campus on a crisp fall evening.

I loved the smell of the library when I walked inside to study.

I loved the way the old wood floors creaked in the halls when I would walk to class.

I loved the warmth of the sun on my face as I studied in the quad.

But most of all, I loved books.

They contained a world of information, emotion, viewpoints all within a single cover.

There was a throng of people laughing in the yard, and we headed up the steps where a guy in a Hawaiian shirt was sitting on top of a keg.

"Tickets?"

Rita pulled them from the little purse she was carrying.

We started to walk inside when the fraternity brother put a hand on my shoulder.

"You—"

"I have a ticket," I said. "She just showed it to you."

"—look amazing," he finished. "You're a stone fox."

Rita pulled me inside the Sigma Pi house and said, "You just officially got hit on by a Michigan guy." She jumped up and down.

"Is that a good thing?"

"Ha ha," she laughed. "This calls for a drink!"

"Where do we start?" I asked.

The large meeting room downstairs—lined with composite

photos going back decades—was the main dance floor. KC and the Sunshine Band had morphed into "Car Wash," and—without warning—foam appeared out of nowhere.

"My hair!" Rita yelled, pulling me back toward the entry and up the stairs.

The second floor of the house was jammed with people, coming in and out of the different bedrooms, all of which were marked with a sign or a country's flag.

We stopped in Mexico and had a margarita, hopped over to Japan, which was serving sake, and then over to Italy, whose brothers were serving pizza, red wine and shots of limoncello.

Up the stairs we went again, like salmon fighting against those coming down in a drunken rush, visiting Ireland for Guinness and Hawaii for mai tai's.

When we finally reached the tiny room at the top of the house—a transformed attic where you had to stoop to walk until you reached the center—a sign reading THE NORTH POLE greeted us.

"Ho! Ho! Ho!"

A man dressed as Santa Claus was standing behind a make-shift bar.

"What would you ladies like for Christmas? I'm guessing a drink."

His laugh boomed throughout the room.

"What are you serving?" I asked.

Santa gestured with a white glove to a Sno-Kone machine stationed next to him.

"Where did you get that?"

"The North Pole, of course," he said with a laugh. Santa leaned toward me. "I work part-time in the commons. We used this to greet incoming freshmen this year. It was 90 degrees. Let's just say that I borrowed it for tonight."

I laughed as he scooped the shaved ice into paper funnels and then poured a red liquid over the top.

"Just like you had as a kid," Santa said, handing one to me and Rita. "Well, not quite."

"What's in this?" Rita asked.

"Holiday magic," he said.

"Come on," Rita said.

"Everclear and Kool-Aid," he said.

"I knew it!" I pointed at Rita and did a little dance. "Michigan isn't any classier than Ohio State. Every college party serves gasoline and Kool-Aid."

The room went silent. People turned, began to point at me and boo.

"Okay," Santa said. "No need to make a visitor to the North Pole feel badly. She'll get her lump of coal when we kick the Buckeyes' butts!"

The crowd went crazy.

"I had to do that," Santa said with a jolly wink. "Sorry. Only way to defuse the crowd. They're like children. Just give them a little candy to make them stop throwing a tantrum."

"Thank you," I said. "I guess."

"What's your name?" he asked.

"Marilyn," I said. "And this is my friend Rita. What's your name?"

"Nicholas."

"Seriously," I said, chomping on my snow cone. "What is it?"

"It's Nicholas, Nick for short. No, I mean, it really is. I was named after my father."

"St. Nick?" I asked.

"Sort of," he said. "My mom and dad own a bookstore in Petoskey, Michigan, called Sleigh By the Bay. They first met at a Christmas party when he was dressed as Santa. To this day, they both dress as Mr. and Mrs. Claus at the holidays and all over our little town. Where do you think I got this idea and costume?"

"Are you kidding me?" Rita was practically screaming, her eyes wide. "Nick? Nick Norcross? I didn't recognize you. Of course, you'd be Santa! It's Rita. Rita Hanselmann."

"Oh, my gosh. It's good to see you."

The two hugged.

"What's going on?"

"We went to high school together," Rita said. "Ran in different circles. I had no idea you were a Sigma Pi."

"We grew up in a small town and went to a big university," he said. Nick looks at Rita and then me. "Rita was very popular in high school. I worked a lot."

"His parents are the nicest people in town," Rita said. "Sleigh By the Bay is an institution. They dress up as Santa and Mrs. Claus every year. They really sum up Petoskey. You've been in the store before. Marilyn has spent a few summers with me and my family," she says to Nick. "We worked at the resort and caused a lot of trouble."

"*You* caused a lot of trouble," I said with a laugh.

"And, despite being from Ohio and Michigan, we are inseparable." Rita leaned in and whispered, "Although I'm way more fun."

"Well, this is a Christmas miracle," Nick said. "And my family loves Christmas." Nick pointed around the room. "And so do kids of all ages. Merry Christmas!"

The room responded in kind with a big cheers to Santa.

Rita called me over and whispered into my ear. "Nick's a really nice guy, but I don't want him going back to town and spreading rumors about how wild I am. So, is it okay if I leave you for a while? I trust him. And I sort of want to go back to Mexico. The guys were way hotter and not such jive turkeys.

Come find me when you head downstairs." She looked at me and then called to Nick. "Peace out!"

"Rita has been looking forward to this party all semester," I said to Nick as she left. "I can't believe you two know each other. What a small world. I think she believes she's going to meet the guy of her dreams tonight."

"Here?" Nick laughed, dishing out alcohol-fueled snow cones to partygoers. "Are you having fun, Marilyn?"

I looked at St. Nick. "I am, actually," I said. "I had no idea what to expect, but this is exceeding my expectations."

"Your cone's leaking," Santa said.

I looked down, and there were red stains on Rita's gold dress.

"She's going to kill me!" I said.

Nick came out from behind the bar with a funnel filled with ice. He handed me a white towel. "Here," he said.

I began to blot the melting ice, and, slowly, the red disappeared, but faint stains still remained.

"Thanks," I said, handing him back the towel. "I better go find Rita. I'd hate for her to wake up tomorrow a little hungover and bug out when she discovers I ruined her threads."

"Let's book it, then," Nick said.

"You can't leave your own party."

"I'm the president of the fraternity," he said. "I can do anything I want." He looked around at his room, which was thoroughly being trashed. "And, believe me, you'd be doing me a solid."

"Groovy," I said. "Let's roll."

"Everyone out," Nick said. "Now. North Pole is melting. Climate change. You heard it here first. Check back with me in forty years." He pointed at his Sno-Kone machine which was, in fact, leaking. "Time to go!"

He locked his room, and we followed the horde of revelers down the stairs. I finally found Rita in Mexico, where she was drinking tequila and dancing with a guy sporting a terrible mustache.

"I'll catch you on the flip side," I yelled at her. "Nick and I are going somewhere to talk."

"Have fun!" Rita slurred. "He's such a nice guy. Too nice for my tastes. I never found Santa to be my type."

"He's *dressed* as Santa, Rita," I said. I grabbed her. "And you're wearing beer goggles right now. Your guy can't even grow a real stache. Mine has a whole beard."

She laughed, and we hugged.

"If you're not back at the room by two, I'm sending out Rudolph to find you."

"Your nose will be red enough to do the job by then," I said.

Nick and I headed out the front door and strolled through campus.

"Hey, Santa!" people yelled as we passed. "Can I give you my Christmas list?"

"Have you been naughty or nice?" Nick called back.

"Naughty!" nearly every person yelled with a big laugh.

"I gotcha then!" he would reply.

We headed off campus and down the bustling street. He stopped in front of a small window front. I looked up.

"The Maize and Blue?" I asked.

"It's our local bookstore," he said. "My parents are friends with the owners. I work part-time here as well."

"Wow," I said. "You are a hard worker."

"My parents taught me that," he said. "C'mon. I think you'll love this place. And they serve wine."

The Maize and Blue was part bar, part bookstore. The front of the store was lined with shelves and filled with books, and it indeed felt like a maze: books were stacked in piles on the floor, and there was barely enough room for one person to pass through an aisle. Through the narrow aisles, a small bar glowed.

I stopped and began to peruse the books.

"So many books, so little time," I sighed. "I love to read. Just not enough time anymore between classes." I looked at Nick. "The library is my favorite place. Yes, I'm a dork."

"You're not a dork," he protested. "Books are my life, too."

He began to turn in circles, holding up copies of *Jaws*, *Watership Down* and *All the President's Men*.

"Just when I think our world is about to implode, I walk through here or my parents' bookstore and look at what the world is reading, and I have hope again." Nick's voice was hushed, his words softened and cushioned by all the books surrounding him. "Look at these books. Look at what they represent. They're not just books, they're a sea change disguised as a book. We are entertained, we fall in love, we escape to places we've never been, we discover something about ourselves, we discover awful things about our history, and through them, we are changed. We become better people."

My heart rose into my throat.

"Who *are* you?" I asked.

He laughed. "Just a college guy dressed as Santa."

We ducked through a bookshelf and headed to the bar.

"Didn't think I'd see you tonight, Santa," the young bartender said. She was sporting very high-waisted jeans and a side pony.

"Christmas came early," Nick said.

"Well, aren't you the lucky one," she said to me. "Nick's a sweetheart."

He ordered two glasses of wine.

"On the house," she said. "Especially since Mick and Sarah aren't here."

"And, Suzi," Nick said, "we have a minor problem." He pointed to the stains on my dress.

"Hold on," Suzi said, walking away. She returned a moment later with a white cloth. Suzi poured some club soda on it and walked from behind the bar. "Do you mind?"

I shook my head and extended my arm, and she began to blot the sleeve of my dress.

She grinned. "Club soda's essentially just water with carbon dioxide dissolved in it, along with some salts. The aeration works to lift stains and prevent them from permanently settling down into the fibers."

I did a hammy double take.

"I'm a biology major," Suzi said. "I get that look a lot."

I laughed.

"Never let appearances fool you," she said with a wink.

She walked back behind the bar and got another white cloth and dampened it with water. She handed that to me. "Now blot."

I did for a few seconds, and when I looked, the stains were nearly imperceptible.

"Thank you," I said, holding up my wine.

"You're welcome. Let me know if you two need anything else."

Nick lifted his glass.

"To the North Pole!" he said.

We clinked glasses. He began to take a sip but stopped.

"Darn beard," he said. "Gets in the way."

In slow motion, I watched Nick remove his costume.

The moment of truth, I thought. *The ultimate reveal. I have no idea what this guy really looks like.*

Nick took off his cap and placed it on the bar. He pulled off his white wig and then, in one fell swoop, his beard.

I nearly fell off my stool.

Do you know during a college football game—let's just say Michigan versus Ohio State, for instance—when the camera focuses on a student in the bleachers, an insane fan who's painted his body half blue and half gold, or half red and half gray, and is going absolutely crazy? A young man that just looks like the typical all-American Midwestern kid who is having the time of his life?

That's how Nick looked.

"You're not a total turkey," I said.

"You realize you just said that out loud," Nick said with a laugh.

"I'm sorry," I said. "I'm just in shock. It's a big change to go from Santa to this."

"Only matters what's on the inside, though, right? Cover of a book is only part of the story."

I nodded, lifted my glass and clinked his again.

We talked about our majors—him literature, me acting with a minor in business—and what we wanted to do with our lives. I wanted to move to New York and make it on Broadway with Rita, and Nick wanted to return home and help his parents expand their store.

Suzi kept refilling our wine, and I had no idea what time it was until I realized that the place was empty and Suzi had cleaned the bar.

Nick took my hand and led me toward the front door. As we cut through the shelves, a book caught my eye. I grabbed it.

"*The Grass Is Always Greener over the Septic Tank*," I said. "Oh, my mom adores Erma Bombeck. I haven't heard of this one."

"We received an early galley of it," he said.

"She's an Ohio gal, too. Dayton."

"Keep your voice down in Michigan," Nick laughed.

"She makes my mom laugh," I said. "And my mom deserves to laugh. She's worked so hard to send me to college."

"Take it," Nick said. "We have more. Consider it my gift to you, and your gift to your mom. Tell her that Erma bridged the border war. And tell her she raised a wonderful woman."

The fall full moon hung in the sky, and our walk home felt like it was happening at dawn rather than the middle of the night. When we returned to the dorm, Nick said, "I'd like to see you again."

"I'd like that, too."

"Maybe you can come visit Rita again this summer," he said. "Or maybe even drive up to Petoskey to see the holiday lights. We do Christmas up right."

"I bet you do," I said. "I'd love to see you again."

Nick leaned in and kissed me, and when I opened my eyes, the moon was reflecting in his eyes, almost as if he were illuminating his soul, only for me to see.

He placed the Santa cap he was holding on top of my head, and curled the top just so.

"So you'll remember me," he said. "And continue to believe in miracles."

I watched him walk all the way across campus until his body became a shadow and until his shadow disappeared.

I tried to sneak into Rita's room, but banged my knee, hard, on the end of her bed.

"Ow!" I said.

"Serves you right," Rita said. "I was starting to get worried about you. Did you have a good time?"

"Santa is real," I said.

"You're drunk," Rita said. "Go to sleep."

I slipped out of her dress and into bed, pulling the covers up to my chin.

"No, it's true," I whispered to myself, before falling asleep and dreaming of the snow sparkling under a winter moon and a sleigh filled with books.

★ ★ ★

I hug my grandparents, hard.

"What was that for?" my grandma asks.

"Respecting history," I say. "Loving books."

They look at me, confused.

"You better get going, or you'll be late," Holly says. "I don't want anything to go wrong."

I look at her and lift my eyebrows. "What could go wrong?"

She laughs, and we head out of my bedroom and toward the front door. I grab my coat, open the door and then stop.

"I forgot one thing," I say, rushing down the hall and then up the stairs, my pumps clip-clopping on the old, wood floor.

"What in the world?" I can hear my grandma say.

I look back to make sure no one is following me and then sneak into the guest room. I head to the closet, open a dresser drawer and grab my mother's angel pin.

I shut the door, turn and see my poem before me. One line seems written in bold, and it stares at me, challenging me.

We must believe in angels.

I slip the jewelry into my pocket to pin on myself later when I'm away from prying eyes.

My guardian angel, I think, touching it. *And my secret weapon.*

chapter 23

Luka and Leah are seated at a table across the restaurant. I arrive a bit early, at Noah's behest, to go over the game plan. He developed a list of signals—much like a third base coach in baseball—so that Leah and I could communicate on the QT should I need help, run into any trouble, wish to end the date abruptly, or continue it should Jamie be the cap that fits my Santa noggin.

Leave it to Noah, however, to go old-school with his signs.

If I tug on my ear, like comedian Carol Burnett used to do at the end of her monologue, it means I need Leah to come over to my table immediately and intervene.

If I break into a fit of faux giggles—like Mary Tyler Moore did during the funeral for Chuckles the Clown—and excuse myself to go to the bathroom, I need to talk to Leah in private.

If I pull a Lucille Ball and start performing kooky physical pantomime—a headache or stomach cramp—Leah will appear out of the blue, say she's a friend and offer to take me home.

And if I act all flirty—touching my hair or fluttering my hand over my heart à la Sarah Jessica Parker—then I'm good to go.

The problem is—despite all of this planning—the restaurant is very dim. I know it's supposed to be romantic, but I realize once I'm seated that I can barely even see Luka and Leah across the room. They're mere shadows.

And they say love is blind.

Thank you, night blindness at forty!

I am seated at an intimate table for two facing the entrance. At promptly 7 p.m., a shadow enters the restaurant. I watch as a body comes into view. It's a good body. A really good body. With a good face. Hallmark handsome. He's better than I imagined. Way better. And way better out of a Santa suit.

The hostess greets him, and he walks directly toward me.

Breathe, Susan.

"Susan?"

I stand.

"Yes."

"I'm Jamie Martin. It's so nice to meet you." He smiles. "Again."

He is holding a dozen roses.

First box is checked. He's a sweet romantic.

"These are for you. Happy Valentine's Day."

My face flushes.

"These are lovely," I say. "Thank you."

"Would you like me to hold these for you until dinner is over?" the hostess asks. "It's an intimate table."

"Yes, thank you," I say.

"I didn't know whether to bring you chocolates or flowers," Jamie says. "I thought since you were such a big runner, you'd prefer roses over sugar."

"Thank you," I say, "but that's why I run. So I can sweat out all the M&M's and See's chocolates I eat when I'm stressed."

He laughs. It's a good laugh, a real one from the gut, not a fake one to please me.

"That's why I run, too," he says.

My heart lifts. A mutual interest.

"How was your drive from Chicago?" I ask.

"Remarkably uneventful," he says. "You know how traffic can be leaving the city."

"Where are you staying tonight?" I ask. "You're not driving all the way back are you?"

"No," he says. "Holly suggested the Perry."

"She thinks of everything, doesn't she?" I say. "And so do you. This is my favorite restaurant."

The waiter approaches and tells us about the prix fixe menu for the evening. Jamie orders two glasses of champagne. When the waiter departs, there is silence.

"This isn't awkward at all, is it?" he asks.

This time, I laugh, and much of my tension seems to be released into the air.

Across the restaurant, I can see Leah stand.

Oh, no. She must have thought I was pulling either a Lucy or a Mary Tyler Moore.

I gesture wildly with my hands as Leah begins to move.

She stops and stares at me.

I'm sure, in this lighting, she can't tell if I'm doing a jig or hailing a cab.

Thanks, Noah.

"Are you okay?" Jamie asks.

Leah sits again. I breathe.

"Oh, me? Yes," I say. "I thought I saw someone I knew.

Couldn't tell because it's so dark in here." I reach for my cell. "Do you mind if I use my flashlight? I can't even read the menu."

Jamie smiles. "Thank goodness. I was just going to order the special and call it a night."

I turn on my flashlight, which I do not have trained on my menu. The light illuminates Jamie's face momentarily, and his blue eyes—the color of a snow sky—shine.

My heart races.

He is very handsome.

Hallmark handsome, I can hear Holly say in my head. Down to the perfect cleft in his chin. He is wearing a red turtleneck and dark jacket with dark jeans. His hair looks freshly gelled, and I picture him hurriedly getting ready after driving all afternoon.

The waiter brings our champagne, and Jamie lifts his glass. "To taking a risk," he says.

I clink his glass and take a sip of my champagne.

"This is sort of like *To Tell the Truth,*" I say. "The new *and* old version."

He nods. "Actually, this is sort of like *To Tell the Truth* meets The Masked Singer."

I laugh. "Even better."

We chitchat for a few minutes and order our dinner.

"You know an awful lot about me from Holly and all the media I would guess," I eventually say. "My life, my career, my dating life, my secrets…" I laugh.

He nods. "I do."

"So, tell me a little about yourself."

Jamie ducks his head. "Well, probably the best place to start—which will explain so much about me and why I'm here—is where I was born and raised."

"Where was that?" I ask.

"Santa Claus, Indiana."

"You're kidding me?"

"I am not," he says. "My great-grandfather was known as the Santa of Santa Claus, Indiana, as he was the postmaster famed for writing letters, at his own expense, to children who mailed their Christmas lists to the town, believing Santa lived there. The town really became famous when Robert Ripley of *Believe It or Not* featured the town's post office and my great-grandfather. After that, mail and tourists blanketed the town."

My eyes are wide. "We have so much in common," I say, and tell him about Captain Santa. "Tell me more. Can you tell I'm riveted?"

"The size of your eyes was a giveaway." Jamie grins. "Well, according to local legend, the founders originally wanted to name the town Santa Fe, but it was already taken, so on a cold Christmas Eve night, the townsfolk gathered in a small, log church to discuss a name, but there was no consensus."

The door of the restaurant opens, and a cold gust of wind dashes inside. Jamie smiles and continues.

"Well, that was perfect timing because that's just what happened in the church that night. A sudden gust of wind blew the door open, and the sound of sleigh bells echoed in the cold. Children ran to the door and shouted, 'Santa Claus!' The decision was made that night," Jamie says.

I think of my poem, of hearing bells when I meet my Kringle.

Jamie goes on. "It took off from there. The world's first themed attraction, Santa's Candy Castle—sponsored by the inventors of Baby Ruth and Butterfinger candy bars—was dedicated in 1935."

"Now you're talking," I say.

"And the same year, a twenty-two-foot Santa Claus statue— which is dedicated to the children of the world—and the Santa

Claus Park, which is now the location of the Santa Claus Museum & Village, were built," he says. "A decade later, Santa Claus Land, the first themed amusement park in the world, opened. Today, the town is home to many Christmas-themed businesses and attractions, and people flock to town for the Santa Claus Christmas Celebration the first three weekends in December. The town stays busy in the summer, too, when families can go horseback riding at Santa's Stables or take in a movie at the Holiday Drive-In."

"Do you get paid to advertise for the town?" I laugh.

"I'm actually on the town's chamber of commerce," he admits.

"And you know I have to ask this question," I start.

"Did I ever dress as Santa?" Jamie asks. "Besides at the Santa Run?"

"Yeah," I say. "It's kind of important."

"In high school, as a descendant of the famed postmaster, I sat in the post office in a Santa cap and personally wrote letters from Santa to children all over the world," Jamie says. "I'd stamp all the letters with the postmark, 'Merry Christmas! From Santa Claus, Indiana!'" Jamie looks directly into my eyes. "It's kind of important to me, too."

My heart is racing.

"But I think the biggest thing I want you to know about me is that I was talking to a woman dressed as Mrs. Claus at the Santa Run, and I felt an instant connection," Jamie says. "I hit on her with a terrible pickup line, and then—because I'm such a big reader—we talked about the history of Mrs. Claus. I asked her to meet me at O'Malley's, but I never made it because I had a work emergency."

Now my heart is racing even faster. I mean, roller-skating to the Backstreet Boys fast.

Jamie explains, "The Dow futures had the market poised

for a massive sell-off on Monday, and I had a number of clients frothing at the mouth to make changes to their portfolio the moment the market opened, so I had to go to work. I called the bar, but it was chaos."

"It was," I say.

"I never knew if you got the message."

"I think I finally did," I say.

He smiles and lifts his glass.

Our dinners come, and we talk like old friends about our favorite books, Chicago, running, the holidays and our families.

"Have you ever been married?" I ask.

He shakes his head. "No," he says. "I've been so focused on my career that I've never slowed down." Jamie places his fork on his plate. "I'm happy, and I'm content. I say that, and I feel like I'm convincing myself—and everyone around me—to believe it, but it's true. It's just that I don't want to wake up one day and be all alone. My life is full, but my heart is empty." Jamie hesitates. "If that makes a lick of sense."

His words hit me like a copy of *The Goldfinch* dropped from the roof.

"I feel much the same way," I say. "Thank you for being so open. That's often not been my strong suit."

"The Queen of Hearts often doesn't wear her heart on her puffy sleeve," Jamie says.

I duck my head and laugh.

"So true," I say. "Unless, of course, you're Holly."

For dessert, Jamie orders a slice of red velvet cake—topped with the thickest, richest cream cheese icing—and we share it.

I don't realize how long we've been chatting until I look around and notice that the restaurant is nearly empty, and Luka and Leah are approaching our table.

"Oh, my gosh, what are you two doing here?"

Leah has to stifle a laugh at my dramatic overreaction.

"Just finishing a beautiful dinner. What a lovely surprise to see you, Susan."

Luka looks as if he's just been handed the envelope at the Oscars announcing Best Actress, and he's deciding which performance should win.

"Jamie, this is Leah, she works with me at Sleigh By the Bay, and this is Luka," I say. "Her date."

Jamie stands and shakes their hands.

"You look so familiar," Jamie says to Luka.

"I get that a lot," Luka says.

As Jamie sits, Luka gives Leah and me a wink. I'm floored by how humble he is.

"Well," Leah says. "We'll let you two enjoy the rest of your dinner. It was so nice to meet you, Jamie."

"You, too," he says.

Before she heads out the door, Leah turns and gives me a big, corny thumbs-up. She mouths, *He's so cute!*

They exit, and another cold gust of wind scurries by.

Finally, when we are the last two in the restaurant, and the staff is wiping down tables and giving us the eye, we stand to leave. I retrieve my coat and roses on the way out of the restaurant, we head up the alley toward the street and stand in the bitter cold. It is a crystal clear night, the kind where the stars are so bright in the winter sky you can almost feel your soul crack like the branches on the frozen trees.

"My dad always said a February night this clear portended a big storm."

"We've had enough snow already, thank you very much," I say.

We both shift on our feet.

This is always what it comes down to on a first date. When you finally stop talking, and your subconscious begins to broadcast its own talk show.

Who will make the first move?
Will there be a first move?
Does he want to kiss me?
Does my breath smell like scallop risotto?
"Well," I start.

"I had a really wonderful evening," Jamie says. "I know this isn't a typical first date, but I'm kind of proud of that."

"Me, too."

In the cold, his eyes seem to twinkle even more.

I look into them and think of what my grandmother said. *I see kindness.*

Jamie leans in, as if he's moving in slow motion, and kisses me. At first, it is tenuous and soft, but I lean into him, and it grows in intensity, until I can feel my knees wobble. When we begin to pull back from one another, I realize we are stuck.

Literally.

We both look down at the same time to try and identify the issue, and we bang our heads.

"Ouch," we say at the same time.

It's then I see that my mother's angel pin I fastened to the lapel of my coat is hooked to a button on his coat. I'd been so enraptured in Jamie that I'd forgotten about my final clue. I use my fingers to loosen the pin and set us free.

"Talk about this not being a typical first date," I say.

He laughs. "What is that?"

I show him the pin.

"It's pretty," he says. "Where did you get it?"

It's as if the entire world has collapsed around me, and I am standing alone in the middle of the universe.

"Remember?" I ask, hoping against hope.

"I've never seen it before," he says, his brows raised, giving me a quizzical look.

I can almost feel my heart freeze standing here in the cold.

I can almost visualize the beautiful petals on the red roses turning black and curling.

It's not him. It's not the guy I met at the race. How could that be?

"Oh, right," I say. *Unflappable Susan.* "Duh. What was I thinking? It was my mother's," I say, "the one she wore on her Mrs. Claus costume every year."

"Oh, that is so sweet," Jamie says.

His words come out in a muffled voice that sounds exactly like Charlie Brown's teacher.

"Can I call you?" Jamie asks.

"Yes," I say, although my voice sounds hollow to me. "That would be nice."

"I'll go through you this time instead of Holly, if that's okay."

I smile.

"Preferable actually."

"Thank you, Susan. I couldn't think of a better way to spend Valentine's Day, and I can't wait until the next time. Have a wonderful week."

"Have a safe drive tomorrow. And thank you, Jamie."

"I'll text you."

He turns and walks toward the Perry, his body slowly disappearing into the shadows.

I scurry to my car to escape the cold and my thoughts, but I cannot drive home just yet. I don't want to be alone, and I don't want to deal with the endless texts from Holly, Leah, Noah and my grandparents that are waiting to be read.

I drive instead to a parking lot by the bay. I shut off my lights. Before me, the bay glows.

I know the crucifix is shimmering below the icy surface.

Maybe Jamie isn't the man I met at the Santa Run, but that's okay, right? Maybe he's the right one, just in a different cap. Maybe that man at the race led me to meet him.

I think of how my parents and grandparents met.

Totally random.

This fits the bill.

My window begins to fog up. I crack the window and listen.

I smile to myself.

In Northern Michigan, when it is completely still and you are all alone, you can hear the ice sing. It is a combination of the cold, the wind, the freezing and unfreezing, and the ice's constant movement and shifting.

My grampa says it's the voice of our ancestors trying to speak to us.

My grandma contends it's the voice of God.

For the longest time, the sound haunted me, reminding me of what I'd lost rather than what I had. And though the bay still sings the same song, it sounds different to me the older I get and the more time passes.

It's more comforting now than haunting.

I can hear the ice sing to me. I can even make out the lyrics.

Even in the depths of our own grief, there is always hope to light the dark days of winter.

I shut my eyes.

Believe, Susan, the bay calls. *Believe.*

chapter 24

"He was…"

I stop midsentence and look at Holly, Leah and Noah, searching not only for the right words but also the soft spot between truth and lie.

Not the right Santa?

Not the right Santa but maybe the right guy?

"Nice."

"Nice?" Holly groans.

We are seated the next morning at a table in the front window of Petoskey Scones, and her voice echoes off the frosty glass.

"Nice?" she repeats. Holly whacks the table, and the froth on top of our lattes streams over the edges, a mini coffee waterfall.

"You have a knack of bringing attention to us in this place," I say.

"The Queen of Hearts is quite the tart," Noah says, altering the lyrics to the famed children's poem.

Holly picks up her cell. "I have probably twenty texts from Jamie saying it was the best date of his life." She looks up from her phone, her eyes wide. I can still see a silhouette of a heart on her cheek. Holly is breathing intensely, making the ghostly heart look as if it's beating wildly. "He said there was a connection. Just like at the run."

I study the foam art atop my latte. It's a beautiful snowflake, as fragile as the ones falling outside.

I think of what Jamie said about a clear February sky portending a big storm. Our beloved, local meteorologist, Sonny Dunes, is predicting a foot of snow over the next twenty-four hours.

When my heart feels something, do I intentionally create a blizzard in order to bury my heart from any more pain?

Petoskey Scones and Sleigh By the Bay sit on a high hill that slopes toward Little Traverse Bay. In the distance, I see a red icebreaker—just like the one I saw a couple of months ago—cut through the ice. This entire area was created by massive glaciers. In fact, the north side of the Bay and the entire Petoskey business district are built on the Algonquin Terrace, a raised area overlooking the water.

How many years did it take for the terrain to shapeshift into what it is now?

How many years will it take my heart to unthaw and be inhabitable?

"There was," I finally say.

"Thank you!" Holly says.

"So," Noah says. "Spill the coffee beans, diva."

I tell them everything about the date, from his roses to our kiss, from the Santa Run to Santa Claus, Indiana.

But when I start to tell them about the pin and getting stuck together, the words get stuck in my throat. I look at Holly, who is seated on the edge of her seat, thrilled that she believes she has made a love connection.

And maybe she has. Maybe Jamie is the one. I don't know.

I just can't, at this moment, bring myself to say he wasn't the man I met at the Santa run. I know my friends and grandparents promised they wouldn't pressure me to meet someone like my parents did, and I know I have two more dates to go, but after what I went through with my grampa, I cannot stand to break anybody's heart right now.

And, to be completely honest, I actually thought he *was* the one. To mix a lot of unmixable analogies, I tripped right over Cupid and fell into Santa's sleigh hook, line and sinker.

"This coffee," I say. "Would you excuse me while I run to the little girl's room." I stand. "Leah, would you mind joining me?"

Holly's head jerks. "Are we twelve years old?"

"Just wanted some company," I say. "And I want to make sure we have Noah's hand signs down the next time around. It was dark in that restaurant, and my night vision is awful."

"Good idea!" Noah says. "Holly and I will gossip about you while you're gone."

I drag Leah into the bathroom and tell her what happened.

"And then we got stuck together. Literally," I say in a Shakespearian whisper. "I was wearing an angel pin on my coat that got stuck on one of his buttons."

I tell Leah about my mother's pin and what it means to me, and then I tell her about the moment Holly missed at the Santa Run when I told my mystery man about it and how he knew—before I said a word—that it was my mom's.

"So Jamie isn't *the one*?" Leah finally says, disappointed. "He actually met another Mrs. Claus, and you met a different Santa?"

"Nope and yep," I say. "But I liked him. And maybe he is the one. Just out of order."

"He *has* worn a Santa cap in his life," Leah reasons.

"Just not when I met him."

"And he has the perfect back story."

"I know, right?" I say. "Maybe I'm the one putting too much emphasis on *exactly* how my parents and grandparents met. Maybe their stories and maybe the guy I met at the Santa Run were meant to lead me to Jamie."

"It is a great story," Leah adds.

"How did you do it?" I ask Leah.

She cocks her head. "Do what?"

"How did you open your heart again?"

Leah sighs and looks out the curtained window at the snow falling.

"I didn't think about it," she says. "It's like jumping into a toboggan and sledding down that hill toward the bay. If you asked me to do it at my age, and I took a second to consider it, I wouldn't do it. I would be paralyzed with fear."

Leah continues. "I'm a woman of a certain age with a résumé that includes two grown children and a heart-shattering divorce. I put my husband first. I put my children first. I wouldn't change a thing because I love my kids more than anything else in this world." She hesitates. "And yet that still wasn't enough to complete me because I've never truly loved myself. I know that may sound selfish, especially for a mother to say, but it's true. In so many ways, I was all alone after my divorce, and I only had myself to rely on. Books saved my life. *You* all saved my life."

I take Leah's hand in mine. It is toasty warm even on this cold day.

"I realized I never really loved my husband," Leah says. "I thought I did because it was what was expected of me at that time. Get married, have a family, everything will be perfect. But it wasn't. It never was. And I never thought I'd find later-in-life love, especially with a guy like Luka, who could have any woman he wanted. Why would he pick a woman like me with stretchmarks on her stomach and her heart? I thought he was using me in some way. He told me to stop thinking like Desiree. It turns out he's just a nice guy with a beautiful body, and I was judging him as harshly as I judged myself. Is this just a fling? Maybe. Will I pass out cold when he finally makes the moves on me? Probably. But it feels nice to feel something again. Even if it means my heart will be shattered all over again. At least, it will be shattered on my own terms, because I took a risk."

Leah clenches my hand.

"You're a bookseller, Susan," she continues. "One of the best in America. You understand better than anyone else how many writers there are out there who start a book but never finish. How many times have you heard aspiring writers say, 'I can start a million books, but that middle part of the story is where everything gets complicated, so I gave up.' But, Susan, if you fight your way through that, stick with it—no matter how hard that middle part of the story is—then you can finally write the ending you dreamed. It's not always going to be a perfectly happy one, but it will be an ending, and there is nothing worse than not finishing a great book."

"Please don't tell anyone about this," I say, my voice a little shaky. "I don't want to hurt Holly or break Noah's or my grandparents' hearts. I just want to keep this our secret, and see where things go. Okay?"

"Okay."

There is a knock on the door, and Leah and I scream and then rush out, giggling like schoolgirls, and scurry back to the table. We take a seat, still giggling.

"Is everything okay over here?"

We look up, and Fred is standing at our table.

"I'm so sorry," I say. "We're louder than a table full of schoolgirls."

"Oh, it's no problem at all, Susan. Is everyone enjoying the coffee?"

We all nod and look at our lattes.

"How curious," Holly says. "We all got snowflakes on top of our lattes, and look, Noah, you got a heart."

Noah's face turns as red as a Valentine, and he nervously touches his curly dark hair.

"How's your latte, Noah?" Fred asks.

He ducks his head. The man with a quip and comeback for any situation is quiet as a church mouse.

Holly nudges Noah, hard, in the side.

"Answer your favorite barista," she says.

"It's great," he says quietly, unable to look Fred in the face. "Thank you."

"Diva," Holly adds. "You meant to say, 'Thank you, diva,' right?"

Noah's doe eyes implore Holly to stop.

"Well, if there's anything else you need, don't hesitate to ask."

I can feel Holly's leg take flight under the table. It makes a resounding, dull thud.

"Ow!" Noah says.

"Wasn't there something you wanted to ask Fred?" Holly says, her voice all innocent. "Remember, since we're all supporting Susan? Since it's public Petoskey news?"

If looks could kill, Holly would be a guest corpse on *CSI*.

Noah clears his throat. "I was wondering," he starts, his voice warbling. "I'm sorry. I—"

"I'd love to," Fred says.

Noah looks up. "What?"

"I'd love to go out with you," Fred says. "I've been waiting years for you to ask."

"But I thought…" Noah starts.

"I know," he says. "I'm just not as comfortable with myself yet as you are. But I'm trying, I promise."

The table is silent.

"Can I give you my number?" Fred asks.

Noah hands him his phone.

"Let me know if you'd like to meet for a cup of coffee," Fred says as he types. "I know a great place. And a great barista."

Fred hands the cell back to Noah. Just before he turns to leave, he places his hand on Noah's shoulder and gives it a gentle squeeze. In slow motion, I watch Noah's face morph from surprise to happiness. As Fred goes back to the counter, Noah touches his shoulder, and a smile comes over his face. Then he looks at me, and a tear pops into the corner of his eye. It takes every fiber of my soul not to cry.

I look out at the snow, the hill and the icebreaker on the bay.

Something, deep inside of me, melts just a bit when I look back at Noah.

"I can't wait for my next date," I say.

"Yes!" Holly yells.

Once more, the line of customers at Petoskey Scones turns and stares, but no one at our table cares that they are looking.

chapter 25

The windows in Sleigh By the Bay have been transformed from red to green.

Four-leaf clovers grow in green grass, and a rainbow starts in one window and ends in the other into a pot filled not with gold but books.

The first window reads: HAPPY ST. PATRICK'S DAY!

A banner in the second window declares: A GREAT FRIEND & A GREAT BOOK ARE LIKE 4-LEAF CLOVERS: HARD TO FIND & LUCKY TO HAVE!

It's a play on words from an old Irish saying.

I admire my handiwork. Typically, Noah handles the windows, especially if I'm overwhelmed, but I needed something to distract myself from all the dating pressure. I plan to head to Chicago for a work conference with Noah that will also

include a St. Patty's Day double date with the next Single
Kringle.

What could go wrong?

I think of another Irish saying that sums it up so perfectly:
*As you slide down the banister of life, may the splinters never point
in the wrong direction.*

The windows may be green, but the mid-March Michigan
sky is as gray as the landscape. The piles of snow that line the
streets are sad and slumped, their shoulders exhausted from
winter.

We still have a long way to go, I think.

I look at the window boxes that have been filled with flow-
ering cabbage and kale, a way to provide a pop of green toward
the end of winter. Just looking at something green causes my
heart to flutter in anticipation of warmer days.

*That is, if you can call mid-March the end of winter in Michigan.
Sometimes, it seems like the beginning.*

It often will snow until May. To me, snowdrops are the
first sign that spring is coming. They pop through the white
with such unabated hope as if to say, "Just hold on a little
while longer!"

The first happy daffodils are a tease like the faux warmth
that typically accompany them. One day, the wind will not feel
fatal, and you fool yourself into cracking the windows in your
home, and maybe even placing a chair on the deck or patio.

And then the snow returns, heavier, thicker than you even
remembered.

You think you've finally made it through winter when the
Crayola-hued tulips begin to pop. A kaleidoscope of color
lines picket fences and encircles trees, and it's so unexpected,
so breathtaking, that I skip—*actually skip!*—like a little girl.

But over the bay one afternoon you will see a bank of
clouds, dark and ominous. The waves will begin to whip, the

tulips will bend and winter will laugh, "I'm not done with you quite yet, my pretty!"

A northerly gust off the bay dances up the hillside, down Lake Street and numbs my ears. I place my mittens over my ears and do an Irish jig to warm my body.

The bell tinkles as Rita strolls in. I cross my arms to ward off the cold that penetrates every layer I'm wearing and stare at the windows.

"Love your windows!"

"Thank you," I say.

I have walked outside to admire my handiwork and to see if the windows will have the impact to pull passersby inside to shop that I desire.

"Puts me in the mood to read something about the Irish plague," she says.

Cheery, I think.

One of my favorite things about being a bookstore owner is that—as opposed to Rita—it keeps me connected to being a kid. It also keeps me connected to children, and—though I may never have kids of my own—that fills my soul. In addition, a part of me remains a child at heart, and the older I get, the more I realize how necessary that is not only to be happy but also remain optimistic.

Like schoolteachers and children, who are some of my best customers, I must embrace every holiday throughout the year: New Year's, Valentine's, St. Patrick's Day, Easter, Memorial Day, the Fourth of July, Labor Day, Halloween, Thanksgiving, Hanukkah, Eid, Holi and Diwali.

Even Mother's Day, Father's Day and Christmas, the most difficult holidays of the year for me.

I am forced to find the child within—no matter how much my heart may ache, no matter how much the memories sting—and celebrate the spirit of each holiday and each season.

I decorate with hearts, even though mine has been broken for so many years.

I dress up as the Easter Bunny and hand out chocolates in the store even though I'd like to hop over a big part of my history.

Sleigh By the Bay becomes a virtual haunted house at Halloween despite the fact I am often consumed by nightmares.

And doing this over the last few decades has allowed me to cling to a piece of childhood innocence, that part of us we too often lose as adults that makes us remember what matters most in life.

I walk to the window and pretend to pluck a construction paper four-leaf clover inside.

I'm going to need all the luck I can get.

"It's a fine day, lassy!"

I jump at the sound of an Irish voice. I turn, and a leprechaun is dancing before me.

Noah's face is painted green, and he's sporting a red beard, a green top hat and little Leprechaun suit with white leggings and black buckle shoes. He's holding a little black pot that is filled not with gold coins but with candy.

"What did the leprechaun say to the girl who saved a four-leaf clover in a book?"

I look at him and shrug.

"Don't press your luck."

"Why couldn't the leprechaun pay his bar tab on St. Paddy's Day?"

"Are we really doing this?" I sigh.

"Don't make me drop ye in a bog," he says. "Play along, lassy, or no candy for ye. Why couldn't the leprechaun pay his bar tab on St. Paddy's Day?"

"I don't know," I say.

"He was a little short!"

I don't mean to, but I laugh.

"What are the best sandwiches to serve at a St. Patrick's Day party?"

I actually stop and think about this riddle.

"Paddy melts!" I cry triumphantly.

Noah holds out his pot, and I pluck a chocolate that looks like a gold coin. I eat it in the cold.

I feel just like a kid.

"Doesn't our little Leprechaun look great?" my grampa says, toddling out of the store.

"Where's your coat?" I ask.

"Still on the sheep," my grampa asks. "I was born and raised in Michigan. March feels like June." He walks over and puts his arm around Noah. "Proud of you."

Noah ducks his green head. "Well, I'll never take over being Santa for you, but it's an honor that you're allowing me to take on the mantle of some of the bookstore's favorite costumed characters."

Even in the cold, I can feel my body warm. My grandfather and Noah could not be more different, and yet they could not be more the same.

Good books and great friends remind us we have more in common than separates us. We need to be reminded of that more than ever these days.

I usher my boys inside, and my body begins to thaw in the warmth of the bookstore.

"So, do we have our game plan set for the day?" I ask.

"I'm heading to the grade school in a few minutes to read to the kids, and then I'll host our St. Patrick's Day after-school party," Noah says.

"Your grandma and I are working with Sean O'Malley. His team will set up a test kitchen downstairs, and we should be ready to go at seven sharp with green beer and a demo of some of his favorite Irish recipes from his new cookbook, *Laughter Is Brightest Where Food Is Best*."

I nod. "Fabulous. I'll just head home for the day, then."

Their shocked faces turn quickly into smiling ones.

"Good one," my grampa says. "It's always crazy here around St. Patrick's."

It was a coup that I was one of the stops chosen for famed Food Channel host and chef Sean O'Malley, who became known for his reinvention of Irish classics and downhome food as well as his roguish good looks and mischievous behavior. His appearance is a ticketed event requiring an advance purchase of the book, and we sold out two hundred seats in less than twenty-four hours.

My heart flip-flops.

"And you've pulled all the permits so his demo is not an issue?"

"I did," Noah says. "And we already are approved for food and cooking since we have a small kitchen in the store and are on the list as an events space in the city."

"And we're sure we can cram everyone into the store?" I ask. "We've never gotten over a hundred and fifty downstairs before."

"What is this, Jeopardy? I'm sure, diva," Noah says. "I exchanged our old chairs for some new ones Fred found in the basement of Petoskey Scones. They're a slim line chair, so we could fit more of them into the rows. It'll be a tight squeeze, but it should work since customers will only be seated a short time."

"Speaking of squeezes," my grampa says, "how's your main squeeze?"

Noah's face suddenly turns as red as his beard.

"We've been talking and texting," he says. "And we have our double date with Susan and her new Single Kringle this

weekend. Fred's going to be in Chicago for a fitness training seminar. He's thinking of becoming manager of the local
gym, and eventually buying it and upgrading it."

My eyes widen. "That's amazing," I say.

"One day at a time," Noah says.

"Well, may the leprechauns dance over your bed and bring
you sweet dreams," my grampa says. He looks at us. "I've got
a million of 'em."

"I know," I say. "Noah's already shared about a hundred
of them."

They laugh.

"Time to get busy," I say.

There's nothing like a ton of green beer, a little leprechaun,
wonderful Irish food and great friends to make for a perfect
St. Patrick's Day.

I am tired and happily buzzed, warmed by the fire blazing
behind my back and the success of a wonderful event.

"Admiring what you've created?"

I take a bite of chocolate cake—whose batter was made
with stout—and shut my eyes.

"Back at'cha," I say to our guest of honor.

From a makeshift kitchen set up in the bookstore's basement, Sean O'Malley created a heavenly Irish feast: beer
cheese, corned beef and cabbage egg rolls, corned beef with
horseradish cream, and a spicy Guinness mustard and colcan-
non with garlic and leeks.

"Where did you learn to cook like this?" I say.

Sean laughs. "My mom and Nan's kitchen," he says. "My
family was working poor, and we cooked with what we had
on hand from recipe cards that had been passed down for generations. No Michelin-star chef will ever cook as well as our
grandmas, right?"

I nod, thinking of all the wonderful food my grandma makes and bakes.

"I'm just glad the fire department didn't shut us down," I say.

"Speaking of grandmas," Sean says. He lifts a mug of green beer into the air and gives an Irish cheers. "*Sláinte*, Betty!"

My grandmother laughs and takes a much too big slug of her beer. The foam turns her mouth green.

Sleigh By the Bay was not only at store capacity, but Sean's team had so many electrical cords snaking throughout the store that our basement resembled a herpetarium. The fire department showed up—I'm sure at the behest of a "concerned neighbor"—and they were ready to shut our show down until...

"They owed me," my grandma winks.

As a part-time process server, my grandma knows something about everyone in our little town. She holds more secrets than Pandora's box, and she rarely opens it to release them unless those she loves are threatened.

"I'm so sorry about all this hubbub, Joe," my grandma said to the assistant fire chief, who arrived—sirens blaring—about fifteen minutes before the event when Sean was set to begin. "We are at maximum capacity, not one person over, I promise you."

"Someone said the store lights were blinking," he replied. "Judging by the number of cars, I might have to shut this down."

"I completely understand," Grandma said. "Why don't we do this? I'll call Linda at the local paper and have her come report on this. I'd love to have a journalist on the scene, just to report the facts, you understand, especially since we haven't done a thing wrong." She stopped and, with great drama, placed her hand on her heart. "Oh, and while Linda's here, I do have those divorce papers for you in my car. What is this now? Number five? You've been a hard one to chase down,

Joe. I know you've been staying at the firehouse, and I was waiting for the right time so as not to embarrass you in front of your men. But now seems like a good time, doesn't it?"

Mic drop.

Joe gave the store a cursory glance. "Everything looks fine. All fine." He turned and waved his men back into the fire-truck before leaning into my grandma's ear and whispering, "I'm trying to work this out. Just give me a little time. Please."

My grandma nodded. "I understand, and I will," she said, patting his back. "I know how moody a twenty-one-year-old like your new girlfriend can be."

Mic pulverized.

Now, as the laughter dims, Sean turns his attention back to me.

"So, I've heard about this whole Single Kringle thing," he says. "I think the whole publishing world has."

"No, I think the whole world has."

Sean chuckles, and his face has the look of a mischievous child. He rubs his reddish five-o-clock shadow. "I have to tell you, this community loves you. Nearly every single person that had me autograph a book said they only wanted you to find love and happiness, just like your parents and grandparents had. It must be nice to have such support."

"It is, but it can be overwhelming when everyone not only knows your business but thinks they're your personal CEO." I take a sip of my beer. "It's difficult because I am happy."

"But?" Sean asks. "I hear a *but* in there."

"But," I say with a smile, "I feel like a piece of me is missing." I look around the table. "But I don't want to risk losing another piece of me either."

Sean nods. "Ah, life's ultimate puzzle."

I continue. "How do you do it?" I ask.

"Do what?"

"Your entire life is in the spotlight," I say. "Not only your career but also your entire love life."

"It's part of the celebrity game, unfortunately," he says. "And yet we all play the same game. People think I'm incapable of being hurt when there's a difficult breakup. People think it's easy for me to date. But I'm constantly thinking about what someone may want from me. Everyone sees me as the ultimate bachelor, but I'm really just a middle-aged man who's scared of being played for a fool. It doesn't matter whether you're a celebrity chef or a bookstore owner, a librarian in New Jersey or a policeman in Oregon. None of us wants to get our heart broken. But that's life, isn't it? Either we take the risk, or we don't."

I consider this man who has kept me company for decades of Saturday mornings on my television as if I'm seeing him for the very first time.

"And what if we don't?"

Sean smiles that famous smile. "I think you already know the answer to that."

I nod.

He continues. "Let me just say this. Our hearts are going to be broken whether we want them to or not. I miss my Nan every single day. It's why I make her food. It feels as if she's still with me in the kitchen. I can't ever get her back, but I can honor her memory with the food I make. I can honor her by meeting a woman with just as good a heart as she had. You do the same every day with your work here. You honor your family. And I'm confident that if you ever meet this mystery man—or someone else—he won't just be the man of your dreams, he'll be the man that mirrors the wonderful legacy your family has created."

"I'm so sorry," I say, wiping my eyes. "I'm emotional."

"No, you're drunk," my grampa says.

The table explodes in laughter.

"Everything old eventually comes back into style," my grandfather continues.

"Now you're saying I'm old, Grampa?"

"I'm saying so many of us seek new and better—be it food, jobs or people—but when it comes down to it, old is the best. And I'm not just saying that about myself." My grampa puts his hand on my arm. "We talk about love, and it sounds so old-fashioned, but it never goes out of style no matter whether we seek it in books or on all these new social media sites. You can *feel* the love at this table right now. I would not have become the man I did without your grandma's love. You would not be the woman you are without your parents' love. The only legacy we should leave in this world is the most old-fashioned—that we loved deeply and that we were loved deeply."

Sean extends his hand and shakes my grandfather's.

"*Sláinte*, St. Nick!"

Our St. Patrick's dinner goes late into the evening, until Noah's face paint smears and the edges of the room begin to fade into a soft vignette. The large poster of Sean's event still stands at the back of the bookstore: *Laughter Is Brightest Where Food Is Best.*

Through my office door, I can see the hearts from the Valentine's Day window still stacked against the wall in my office. Every few minutes, the heat from the vent moves across them, making them appear as if they are barely beating, just waiting to come back to life.

The words *St. Nick* float in the air and through my mind.

Jamie and I have FaceTimed nearly every weekend since our date. It's been nice getting to know him better.

He is truly a good guy.

And it's been amazing to watch Noah's love for himself grow as his relationship with Fred has developed.

My eyes drift from the hearts to an autographed book cover from Erma Bombeck.

Books.

Life.

Love.

Timing.

I smile.

Erma always had impeccable timing.

chapter 26

The Chicago River is neon green.

The skies have cleared over Chicago, and the sun sparkles on the river, making it resemble a Willy Wonka–esque candy-colored ribbon running smack-dab through the middle of the city.

"There is nothing like St. Patrick's Day in the city of Chicago," Holly says.

She is standing on the bridge wearing a bright green wig that matches the river, her face dotted with shamrocks, doing a live broadcast—part beauty tips, party city history—on social media.

"This unique tradition began in 1961 when Stephen Bailey, a business manager of the Chicago Journeymen Plumbers Local Union, witnessed a plumber who was wearing coveralls, which had originally been white, stained 'Irish' green from the fluorescent dye that was used to detect leaks in pipes and pollution in the river," Holly says. "Bailey thought it would be a great idea to dye the river green for St. Patrick's Day and so the tradition was born in 1962 when one hundred pounds of dye was poured in the river and the river remained green for a week. Over the next few years, they experimented with the amount and type of dye used before perfecting the process. Today the river is dyed with forty pounds of environmentally friendly dye, which, thankfully, keeps the river green only for a few hours so we Chicagoans aren't reminded of our post–St. Patrick's Day hangovers the next week."

Noah puts his arm around my back as Holly continues to broadcast.

"Nervous?"

He is wearing a green turtleneck that matches his eyes.

I nod. "You?"

"Yep," he says. "It's hard putting myself out there. I've never…"

He stops.

"Fallen in love?" I ask.

"No, I've fallen plenty of times." Noah stares out at the river. "No one's ever fallen back. I've never been loved."

"You are so loved," I argue.

"You know what I mean."

I look at the throng of revelers clogging downtown Chicago. A great many are out for the day looking to have fun and blow off some steam. But many are couples holding hands, laughing together, taking photos, holding on tightly to one another.

Everything fades so quickly, I think. *How do we make these memories last forever?*

I have a vivid memory of my father cutting the lawn in

Michigan, an emerald green swath. I was lying in a hammock strung between two sugar maples, the dappled sun warming me, and I remember how green the world was: the leaves, the grass, the bushes, the canopy of undergrowth in the woods. Michigan was green! My father spun the lawnmower at the end of the yard, scanning the lawn before him, ensuring he was following the lines and wouldn't leave a long strip of un-mown grass. His eyes matched the Michigan sky: as blue as the world around me. He saw me watching him and waved. I lifted my hand off the book I was reading and waved. I was just a little girl and it was just a tiny wave to my dad, and yet I remember I'd never felt safer in my whole life. In fact, that was one of the last moments I recall feeling so protected from the world's unrelenting winter.

As if reading my mind, Noah slips an arm around my waist, and I ease into the silhouette of his body and sigh.

Holly turns the camera on Noah and me.

"I'm out celebrating St. Patty's with my dear friends, Noah and Susan," she says. "Smile, guys!"

We turn and wave into the camera. The green river sparkles behind us.

"It's going to be a lucky day for these two," Holly continues. "You all know about Susan, the Single Kringle, right?"

"Gee, thanks for that great introduction," I say.

"Well, Noah is also going out on a date today with a possible beau, and I want you all to send the luck of the Irish to them as they get ready to find love."

"No pressure at all, diva," Noah says with a laugh.

"I'll bring you an update on their dates tomorrow," Holly says, "but for now, I'm sending you loads of four-leaf clovers, and we're off to drink a big, green beer!"

Holly blows kisses into her cell, ends her live feed, collapses her selfie stick, and touches me and Noah on our heads with it as if she's anointing us.

"The first thing we need to do is join all these lunatics by finding the closest green beer, dancing in an Irish bar and then getting you ready for your dates." Holly looks at me. "And I do mean that plural, though not necessarily in that order, especially considering that you both have dates today."

As if on cue, I feel my cell vibrate. I look at the screen and hold it up to Holly and Noah to show them the caller ID: Jamie.

"May the road rise up to meet ya!" Noah says.

I look at him.

"I didn't know what to say. Seemed fitting."

"Hi, Jamie. How are you?"

"I'm good. Happy St. Patty's Day."

"You, too."

"I just saw Holly's live feed. I know bachelor number two is lined up next, and I have to admit that I'm not sending you the luck of the Irish tonight."

I laugh.

"I was kind of hoping I might be able to see you, live and in-person again, maybe for coffee tomorrow."

I cover my cell and mouth, *He wants to have coffee tomorrow.* They both pantomime clap.

"Sure. Just text me where and when in the morning. I do have to get back to Petoskey by midafternoon, though."

"Sounds good," he says. "I miss you."

He misses me, I mouth.

He's the only one, Noah mouths back.

"See you tomorrow."

"Don't have fun tonight."

I laugh and hang up.

Holly taps me on the head again with her selfie stick.

"Queen!" Noah says.

We all hold hands and then head into a sea of green.

I wake with a start.

My cell is blurting that awful robotic alarm clock beep every second, the one that reminds you that you have to be at the airport at three thirty in the morning, or that, like now, you overslept and have only a short time to get ready for an important meeting.

I sit up, shut it off and then shake my head at my Pink Ladies.

In this case, we're more like the Three Stooges.

We all passed out in Holly's bed. Noah is in the middle, snoring, and Holly is on the far right, still in her green wig. She is drooling. I can't help myself. I take a video of them with my cell and then yell, "Wake up, sleepyheads!"

The two sit straight up in bed.

"Drool much?" I ask Holly.

She looks at her pillow.

"Delete it. Now."

I press Play.

"Snore much?" I ask Noah.

"Oh, my gosh," Holly says. "How could we sleep through that? It sounds like the world is being cut in half with a chainsaw."

"Diva," Noah says, his voice rising. "I think most people would rather date someone who snores rather than someone who might drown them in their sleep."

"Really, Rip van Winkle? Because you sound like you should be starring in *Jurassic Park*."

"A little social media payback," I say with a laugh. "We have about forty-five minutes to get ready. We overslept."

Holly yelps and leaps out of bed. "Why did we think we

could have a second green beer at eleven in the morning? We're not in our twenties anymore."

"Um, I am," Noah says.

"Shut up," Holly says with a laugh. She shakes her head to clear the cobwebs, reaches over and slugs the water sitting on her nightstand. "Let's roll, dream team."

We scurry around Holly's condo, a large, open loft featuring exposed brick walls and old wood beams. Much like my Victorian, Holly's condo is a mix of old and new: state-of-the-art stainless appliances, a coffee bar, custom bath, mammoth windows overlooking the city and yet her wood plank floors still have the original square nails.

A half hour, one shower and two big glasses of water later, I feel woozily better. The short turnaround has given me less time to fret.

"My hair is not cooperating!" I hear Noah yell from the bathroom.

I stop at the windows, knowing I have a few moments to gather myself, and look at the city of Chicago sparkling before me. There is a magic to the city—a beauty in the anonymity, the wealth of shops and restaurants—but I've always been a small town girl at heart. Holly loves to live as large as Lake Michigan, but I prefer to exist as a bay, tucking myself into the shores of my community.

"Remember our first apartment?"

Holly laughs.

"How could I forget?"

After graduating from college, Holly and I rented a garden apartment in the city. "Garden apartment" is a charming way to say renovated basement below grade. We had our lives all planned out: first, we would go into magazine publishing in Chicago, get some experience and then move to New York and go into book publishing. Our apartment was located a block from an L platform, and our tiny living room—big enough to hold a sofa that also served as our dining room—had a long, narrow window just above the sidewalk. All day and all night long, Holly and I would watch thousands of pairs of feet pass before our eyes. In fact, we became so obsessed with them that we began to make up stories about the people attached to the different shoes—vintage Converse, red-soled Louboutins, worn navy flats. In fact, when we would walk around the neighborhood, Holly and I would stare at the ground, searching shoes.

"Floral Doc Martens?" Holly suddenly asks.

"The girl who worked at Windy City Floral."

"Yes!" Holly says.

"Shiny black penny loafers?" I ask. "With shiny pennies in them?"

"The guy who ran the newspaper stand on LaSalle," Holly says. "Look how far we've come."

"It would be frightening if we saw shoes up here," I say. I turn and look at my friend. "It's like we've always seen, pardon the bad foot pun, into each other's souls. We've always been the perfect balance. I know I got mad at you—and the Pink Ladies, my grandparents, pretty much all of Chicago and Petoskey—but thank you for pushing me to do this...for pushing me out into the world again. After what happened to my grampa, I think I would have retreated again." I hesitate. "Maybe for the last time. I have no idea what's going to happen, but at least I—we—gave it a shot."

She opens her arms. We hug in the silence.

"And this place doesn't vibrate from the L going by every few minutes," I say into her shoulder. I hold her at arm's length. "So this is what it's like to date a lot."

"No, this is what it's like to date some quality men," she says. "There's a big difference."

"Do you ever get tired of serial dating?"

Her eyes are as soft as the evening clouds hovering over the city. "No, I actually enjoy it. I love meeting new people. I love the thought of falling in love. But, right now, I love my life, friends and family even more. My business is booming. I just want to sort of ride that wave. I made it. I made it in a field where few succeed, just like you. We're female entrepreneurs! I want to see how this part of my story unfolds first."

"My hair!" Noah yells again. "Help please!"

"I'll be right back," Holly says.

"Does this color make me look jaundiced?" Noah asks, hair crisis averted, as he stares into the doors of the elevator. "Or like I have scurvy?"

"I think you've had quite enough vitamin C this year," I say.

"Thank you, Grandma," Noah says to me, making fun of the fact that I am wearing a scarf pinned over my hair.

Noah is wearing a black turtleneck with a Burberry vintage check scarf and black peacoat.

"You look very dapper," Holly says. "Try to keep your nerves in check."

Noah looks at her with big eyes. "You're still wearing sweats and get to go home, eat a Giordano's deep dish pizza and watch *Legally Blonde*. Our lives are on the line here."

Holly stifles a smile as the elevator doors open.

We head onto the street.

"It's brisk," Holly says, zipping up her puffy coat and tossing the hood on her Bears sweatshirt out the back.

Brisk is the friendly word Chicagoans and Michiganians use when the windchill slaps you right in the face, pickpockets your internal organs and howls, "Who's your mama?"

They don't call Chicago the Windy City for nothing.

Although Chicago and Michigan are separated by a great

lake, many think the weather is largely the same, but there is a great divide. On the other side of the lake, Michigan receives much more snow, typically of the lake-effect kind. Since the frigid north wind travels southward over relatively warmer lake waters, Michigan's west and northern coasts are often on the receiving end of Mother Nature's snowblower. When it's not snowing, the days are typically overcast, albeit relatively mild due to the "banana belt" effect along the coastline, where the lake helps to keep the surrounding area a bit more temperate, especially when compared to Chicago.

Chicago, of course, receives its own fair share of snow, but there are more sunny days as well as many more frigid ones due to the wind that rotates off the lake. In the spring, fall and winter, I have chased down more hats here than I have cabs.

Noah stops in front of the window of a cute candle shop. His face registers complete horror when he sees his hair. His curly locks are blowing this way and that as if he's standing directly in front of an airplane that's about to take off.

"Why don't you call me grandma again now?" I ask.

Noah hunches over and puts his hands around his head, and races ahead of us, zipping left and right, trying to avoid pedestrians and the wind, as if that will do any good. From a distance, he resembles a malfunctioning Roomba.

"So, tell me about my date again just so I'm clear," I say.

"His name is Micah Harrison," Holly says as if she's a hostess on a dating show. "He's forty-one, a big runner—natch!—an attorney, he answered all the questions correctly, matches the physical stats of your Santa and said he talked to a Mrs. Claus before the race."

Thankfully, the restaurant Holly booked is only a couple of blocks from her condo. River North is jammed with restaurants and bars, but getting reservations to the hottest spots can take months. Holly, however, knows everyone in Chicago, and she's often invited to their soft and grand openings to spread the word in her inimitable way.

We stop in front of an old brownstone on a much quieter neighborhood street. An indiscreet sign reads Mi Madre.

"This is one of the newest, hippest spots in the area," Holly says. "It used to be a popular pop-up. The chef has taken favorites recipes from her childhood—ones her mother and grandmothers made in the US and Mexico—and updated them. You'll love the menu. It's not stuffy, and it's full of reinvented comfort foods. Jasmine is the hostess. She already knows you two will be across the restaurant from one another."

Noah gives me a hand signal, and I laugh.

"No, diva," he says. "I'm trying to take off that scarf. If you wear that inside and order potpie, not only will your date run, but I'll be forced to leave as well."

I remove my scarf and place it in my purse. My fingers touch the angel pin I've sneaked inside it.

"You have that look again," Holly says. "Just be yourself, the Susan everyone adores."

She turns to Noah.

"And the same goes for you, young man." Holly adjusts his scarf and then twirls his curls this way and that. "Remember, Fred already likes you. Don't try too hard."

"I'm nervous," Noah starts.

"Just be you," Holly says.

"All of me?" he asks.

"Yes, just let him see your inner light," Holly says. "It's bright enough to light the world."

"Thanks, Mom," Noah says, giving her a kiss on the cheek. "And thank you for walking us to our dates. Save a slice of pizza for me because I probably won't eat much. I don't want to bloat in the middle of this date."

Noah turns to me and points.

"And the bread basket is not your friend, got it?" he says.
Holly gives me a hug.

"Good luck," she says.

As we head up the stairs and into the restaurant, I can hear Holly say, "My little ones are growing up so fast."

"Hi, Jasmine?" I say to the hostess.

"Yes."

"We're Holly's friends," I say. "I'm Susan, and this is Noah, and we had reservations at seven."

"I've heard all about you!" Jasmine says in a husky whisper. "It's so sweet you're both looking for love. We're honored to be a part of that connection."

She takes our coats.

"Right this way."

Mi Madre has retained all of the beauty of the original brownstone, with the gorgeous moldings and flooring. A fireplace crackles in the center of the room. Plush booths in dark velvet fill the corners and line the walls of the restaurant, and tables dot the remaining space. The lower level has all been opened up, however, and only a long pony wall with a floating window separates the open kitchen.

"The chef loves for guests to watch her work," Jasmine explains. She leads us to a booth, but stops me as I begin to sit. "This is for Noah and his guest."

"Ooh, I love a booth," Noah says, sliding onto the seat.

"Enjoy," Jasmine says.

She takes me to a table in the very center of the room. I look around.

"Holly wanted you to be the center of attention tonight."

"Of course she did," I say with a smile and raised brow.

"You can see all the action from here," Jasmine says.

"Thank you. Um, Jasmine, could I ask you for a favor?"

She cocks her head, curious. "Of course."

I reach into my purse and hand her the angel pin. "Would you mind bringing this to my table when we're about to leave?"

Jasmine runs her hand over the pin. "It's beautiful."

"Thank you," I say. "It was my mother's. And it's a test. If my date knows what this is, then he's really the one."

"And if he doesn't?"

I shrug.

"I'll bring it over when I see the waiter bring the check."

"I really appreciate it."

Jasmine starts to walk away, but stops and turns back to me.

"You know," she says, "I was always a terrible test taker. Everything was geared for students who were able to memorize and regurgitate information. I was never that way. I was more of a visual learner. Sometimes a student fails a test not because they aren't capable or worthy of passing but because the test is flawed. One size does not always fit all."

Her not-so-subtle message flitters through my brain.

I take a seat and fidget with my napkin. A handsome man walks up to the hostess, and my heart leaps. Jasmine leads him into the restaurant, and as they get closer, I realize the man is Fred. I sit up. He is dressed in a dark suit, beautiful shoes and an emerald green turtleneck that fits his perfect body like a fitted glove. He looks like a movie star. He sees me and waves. At the booth, Noah stands and extends his hand. I can see it shaking from across the room. Fred cocks his head, opens his arms and gives Noah a big hug.

I watch the two settle into the booth next to one another and wait. After a few minutes, the waiter approaches and asks if I would like something to drink.

"I'll wait for my..." I stop. "Date."

Another server brings over a basket of bread, which smells just like the homemade bread my grandma makes.

"We have some honey butter as well as some herbed but-ter," he says.

As soon as I lift the napkin covering the bread, my cell trills.

NO, DIVA!

I look over, and Noah is giving me the shamey finger.

I dramatically re-cover the bread, and Noah sends me a gif of an audience giving a standing ovation. I am laughing when I hear, "Susan?"

I stand too quickly, my long legs hitting the table. Water cascades over the edge of my glass.

"You can call me Grace," I joke.

"Micah Harrison. I'm so, so sorry I'm late. I tried to find parking, which was impossible. The line for the valet was very long. And I'm out of excuses now."

"It's okay," I say. "Please. Have a seat."

Jasmine backs away, mouthing, *He's cute!*

My cell trills again.

He's cute!

He is.

Micah looks like an updated version of a *Mad Men* actor. He is wearing a suit, his black hair is slicked back, and his light-colored eyes resemble a snowy sky. He's tall, old-school hand-some, a black-and-white movie star sprung to life.

"This place has gotten loads of buzz," Micah says. "I can't believe you got reservations here. Thank you."

"It was all Holly," I say. "As you know, she's a force of na-ture."

He laughs. "She is. And I'm thankful for that because it brought us together." He stops. "Again. You look lovely."

"Thank you," I say. "How was your day?"

"I had to work, unfortunately," Micah says. "I'm a sports attorney, so there is no off-season for me."

"That sounds fascinating," I say. "Anyone I would know?"

"*Everyone* you would know," he says. "Seen a Bears, Cubs, Bulls or Blackhawks game? All of them."

I laugh. "You must work 24/7."

"I work a lot, but I've made an intention this year—not a resolution but an intention—to find a better balance." The waiter comes, goes over the wine and cocktail menu, and Micah asks if I like red wine. I nod, and he orders a bottle of Pinot Noir from Sonoma. "I can't believe they have it. It's wonderful. I hope you like it."

"I had a green beer before noon," I say. "*Anything* would be an improvement."

He laughs, hard. "You're..." He hesitates.

"Say it."

"...everything Holly said you would be. Natural. Real. Funny. Everything you seemed to be at the Santa Run. I'm not used to that."

This time, I laugh, even harder. "What are you used to, I'm scared to ask?"

"Mostly people—in both my work and personal life—who compensate for any insecurity or nervousness with attitude."

My heart feels as if it's taking flight. "I appreciate that. Especially your honesty."

Our wine comes. The waiter uncorks it, pours a taste for Micah. He swirls it, sniffs it, aerates it and, finally, sips. "Perfection."

The waiter pours two glasses.

"Cheers!" Micah says.

"Cheers!" I sip. "Wow, this is good."

"To good wine and a great date!"

"Well," I say. "You know an awful lot about me...like the world...tell me a little about yourself. Where you grew up? Why you dress as Santa? All that good stuff."

Micah smiles. "Ah, the world of social media," I say. "I tell my clients to watch every move when they're in public, and—irony of ironies—I end up meeting you this way. Well, where to start?"

Micah takes a sip of his wine and continues. "Probably the best place to start is that I was born and raised in Michigan."

"What? Really? Holly kept that a surprise. Where?"

"I was born and raised in Glenn. Know where that is?"

"I do."

I raise my hand, as all Michiganians do, and hold it out to Micah, palm forward. I point to the tip of my ring finger. "I live here, and you live here," I say, moving my finger down my hand to the outside of my palm. "I love to visit that area. Saugatuck and Douglas are so quaint."

"Exactly," Micah says. He reaches out and touches my palm with his finger. "Ironically, I grew up right where your love line ends."

My palm suddenly feels as if it's on fire, and I blush.

"Well, did you know that Glenn is known as 'The Pancake Town'?"

I shake my head. "No clue."

"It was back in the '30s, a massive blizzard hit Michigan, and hundreds of motorists were stranded in Glenn when the roads became impassable," Micah says. "Stranded motorists filled the town's restaurant, the schoolhouse, church, and then residents started taking cold travelers into their homes. There were so many visitors in need of food and shelter, Glenn's stores ran out of supplies. But, almost everyone had the ingredients necessary to make pancakes. For the next three days, the entire community rallied to feed stranded travelers griddlecakes for breakfast, lunch and dinner. That's how the town got its nickname, and we still hold pancake breakfasts and parades through the year to carry on the tradition."

"Is there a Pancake Queen?"

"Does Michigan love a festival?"

I laugh. "We celebrate everything, don't we? Blueberries, cherries, Yetis and pancakes." I stop. "So, you said 'we'...we still hold pancake breakfasts. Do you still have a connection there? How did your family come to Glenn? Do they still live there?"

"If you can believe it, my grandfather was one of the people stranded in Glenn," Micah says. "He was a truck driver, and he was hauling a mile-high load of Christmas trees from Michigan to Chicago. He so fell in love with the kindness of the community that he pulled the biggest tree from his truck and had the entire town gather to decorate it as a remembrance of how we can all pull together. A kid put a Santa cap on him. There's still an old photo of him by the tree with the community framed in one of the pancake restaurants. He moved my nana there, and that's where they started their family. My parents never left either."

"And you?"

"I love it there. My dad was the local attorney, but there wasn't, unfortunately, a lot of opportunity for me. But I still go back every holiday season, put on a Santa outfit with my dad and re-create the photo my papa took so long ago," Micah says. "Ironically, I was on my way to Glenn after the Santa Run in Chicago. The Pancake Festival was the next day. In the middle of the run, I got a call from a client demanding a trade. It was the front page of every sports page in America. That's why I never made it to O'Malley's. I called them, but..."

"It was a zoo," I finish. "A zoo of Santas."

Micah nods. "After we talked about our love of Christmas,

and the history of Mrs. Claus, I felt such a connection, almost a lightning strike, as if we were meant to meet. But I had no idea what your name was until that Single Kringle post went viral. It felt like lightning struck again."

My heart beats rapidly.

Is he the one? The Kris to my Kringle?

The waiter returns, and I order the lobster potpie, and Micah orders Mi Madre's Meatloaf. The food emits a feeling that you're sitting in your grandma's kitchen eating her home cooking...if grandma had gone to culinary school.

In the middle of our meal, the chef pops by our table to introduce herself.

"How are your dinners? I hope you like them."

"Like them?" I say. "If I could eat my plate, I would."

"Thank you," she says. "I just wanted to say hello. Holly informed me of how you two met, and I'm honored to be a part of your special evening."

For dessert, the chef sends over two pieces of Hoosier Sugar Cream Pie, a recipe the waiter says her grandmother learned at a church potluck, and a pie my own grandma still makes.

"My grandma calls this 'finger pie' because she mixes the ingredients in the crust with her finger," I say. I look at Micah. "That's how the Norcrosses roll."

"Well, this is delicious," he says. "And I know I'd be licking my fingers if I made it."

We finish our wine, and talk about Chicago, books, travel, and I'm so wrapped up in our conversation that I forget Noah and Fred are even here until they stop by our table. I introduce everyone.

"No need for hand signals tonight, huh?" Noah asks.

I shake my head, and spill the beans about our secret code to Micah. He laughs.

"Where are you two headed?" I ask.

"We're going to head to a little bar near here to continue our evening," Fred says. "Would you care to join us?"

"You boys take some time for yourselves tonight," I say. "Enjoy."

When they leave, I say, "He's like my son." I stop. "Like my sarcastic teenage son."

"We need good friends in our lives or we'd never make it."

"I couldn't agree more."

We chat until the restaurant clears and the waiter brings the check. I reach politely for my purse, but Micah stops me.

"It's the least I can do," he says. "I know this isn't the way anyone pictures a first date." Micah hands the waiter his credit card. "Features in the *Chicago Tribune*, interviews with *Extra*..."

"Just another typical blind date," I say.

We laugh.

"I had a wonderful time tonight," he says.

"Me, too." I take a breath. "I really did."

Micah looks into my eyes for the longest time, and—just like with Jamie—I feel very much at home with this man.

That's when I see Jasmine approaching.

"How was dinner?" she asks so innocently.

"Incredible," Micah says. "I've found a new favorite place in town. That is, if I can get reservations without Holly's help."

"You can call anytime," Jasmine says with a sweet smile. "Oh, Susan. Coat check found this on the ground. I noticed you were wearing it when you came in. It must have fallen off your coat."

"Oh, thank you," I say, flustered. "That means the world."

Jasmine leaves, and my instinct is to shove the pin into my purse, to hide it, to not know Micah's answer.

"What is that?" Micah asks.

The tables in the restaurant begin to spin, as if I'm on Mr. Toad's Wild Ride at Disneyland.

I place the pin on the white tablecloth. I take a deep breath, remaining quiet, so as not to sway the jury.

"What a beautiful pin," he says. "An angel. Wow, this is one of a kind. Did you wear it here for me to see?"

The tables stop spinning.

The one.

I nod.

"You wore it for me because of how we met, didn't you?"

I nod again.

"How sweet, Susan. I'm touched."

My heart is doing backflips.

"I've never seen anything like it before."

My heart sinks, and I begin to blink as rapidly as a lightning bug.

"Where did you get it? Did you buy it just for tonight?"

Micah looks at me. He is still talking, but I can only hear cicadas inside my head.

"Excuse me," is the only thing I can manage to say. "I need to head to the ladies' room. I'll be right back."

I leave him there, staring at a pin he's never seen before.

"Idiot!" I say once I reach the bathroom.

I stare in the mirror at myself for way too long, looking not just at my image but searching for an answer lurking underneath the surface. In fact, I am touching the mirror, trying to crawl inside of my head, when I hear the door open.

"He didn't pass the test, did he?"

I look at Jasmine in the mirror and shake my head.

"What are the odds that he would have a similar conversation with a random woman dressed as Mrs. Claus?" I ask her, my voice elevated. "It's like the world is playing some sort of cruel joke on me. It's not fair!"

"But do you like him?"

I nod.

"Then what does some test matter? What if all this—every moment of your life—was meant to lead you right here, right now? What if a single missed connection occurred on purpose so that your entire life could be rewired?"

"I keep asking myself the same thing," I sigh.

"But?"

"But there's another guy out there I met, too—a total stranger—who seemed to come into my life for a reason. He seemed not only to know me already but also to see right into my heart."

"That's amazing," Jasmine says. "But couldn't this man tonight do the same?"

"When it rains it pours," I say.

Jasmine opens her arms, I walk into them, and she hugs me.

"Holly told me all about your parents," she says. "I'm so, so sorry."

She lets go, and I look at her. "I know this is a lot coming from a total stranger, but I lost my younger brother when I was just a girl, and my heart is still an open wound. I see people waltz into this restaurant every night, and I can immediately tell which ones have been hurt in their lives because—even when they say hello—they look to the side or withhold a little touch of happiness in their voices as if they're just waiting for that pain to greet them again."

Jasmine continues. "I saw that in you when you walked in the restaurant tonight. Just remember we only get a short journey on this earth, and each day is not only a chance to heal but also to love with all your wounded heart."

Her words jolt me. "Thank you for sharing that, stranger."

"We're only strangers to one another if we choose not to connect."

She pulls a tissue off the holder on the bathroom counter and hands it to me.

"You should see me when I watch a dog food commercial," I say.

Jasmine laughs. "Good luck."

I take a moment to compose myself and return to Micah. He escorts me to the door, retrieves my coat and then pins the angel onto my collar. It is a sweet, simple gesture. Micah opens the door for me, places his hand on my back as I walk down the stairs.

"I don't want to push my luck," he says, "but I'd love to see you again."

"I'd like that," I say.

Would I?

Stop it, Susan.

"I'm usually back in Chicago every few weeks," I say. "Let me give you my number."

Micah puts my number into his cell. The wind whips down the street, and he takes me into his arms and holds me tight. Then he takes my face in his hands and kisses me. It is as lovely and old-fashioned as he is.

"Well," I say.

"The word that always means a date has come to an end."

"It's not the end," I say, surprising myself.

"I'll text you," Micah says.

"How Gen Z of you," I tease.

"No, that means I would make you follow me on TikTok. Do you want a ride? Or I can wait with you until your ride arrives."

"I'm staying with Holly. I'll just walk back. It'll be quicker than a car."

"Are you sure?" Micah asks. "It's night. I'm worried about your safety."

I smile at his concern. "Really, she lives just a couple of blocks away. Thank you, though. I'm a big girl. I'll be okay. I think the walk will do me good after that dinner. Sometimes, the fresh air helps me process things, too."

"I understand," he says. "Just promise me you will text me when you've made it home so I don't worry."

"I promise."

Micah gives me a big hug, and I watch him walk to the valet. As I turn to leave, I see Jasmine standing in the window. Her hands are formed in the shape of a heart. I laugh and wave goodbye and head down the street.

I turn at the corner, and the street bustles once again as Chicago continues its St. Patrick's party. The sidewalks and streets are filled with people dressed in green attempting to walk a straight line. I juke right and left to avoid being run into or spilled on, and beeline until my shoulder is directly against the storefronts so at least one side of me is protected.

I slow when I come upon a line of people waiting to get inside a bar. I look inside. Noah and Fred are standing in the window, slow dancing with one another, looking directly into each other's eyes as if the crazed world around them doesn't exist.

I am thrown back in time. I am slow dancing with Kyle Trimble at McDonald's and at my first Christmas formal before…

I scurry away from the window and, instead of heading back to Holly's, I head toward the river. I stop and look out at the water. It is still green, but the color is fading. It is returning to normal.

Am I injecting unreal color into my life right now? Will it fade?

In this vast crowd, I am the only one alone on the street. I turn and look into the windows of condos and apartment buildings all over the city.

I think of all those who are warm, safe, coupled.

I think of all those who are warm, safe, alone.

My phone hums. An endless stream of messages suddenly appears, as if I'd lost reception and now the entire world must know where I am.

Micah: I couldn't wait any longer. LMK you're okay. And, I had a REALLY good time. I can't wait to see you again.

Holly: How was it? Where are you? LMK!

Jamie: Can't wait to see you tomorrow!

I think of chucking my phone into the river, but I remember what Jasmine said and how blessed I am to have people in my life who love and care about me.

We're only strangers to one another if we choose not to connect.

I text everyone and then place my cell back into my purse and stand in the middle of Chicago on a brisk winter's night watching the river—illuminated by the stars and the city lights—wink at me with a green, knowing eye.

"Hello, life!" I yell at the river, my voice filled with every ounce of happiness I can muster.

"Go home, drunk!" someone calls from across the street.

chapter 27

"You're certainly not putting all your eggs in one basket, are you?"

"I thought the Easter Bunny wasn't supposed to talk?" I ask.

My grampa laughs. "Do you want chocolate or not?"

I reach into his basket and nab a foil-covered egg.

"Our little Susan has become—what do they call it—oh, yes, a man-eater," my grandma says in a deadpan.

I unwrap the chocolate and pop it in my mouth. "The candy sure is a lot sweeter than you two," I say.

"They're just pulling your rather long leg," Noah says.

My grandfather is dressed in an Easter Bunny costume. He resembles a very dapper Peter Cottontail, his white furry body dressed in an Easter blue jacket, a green-and-yellow-striped vest, and a floppy pink bow tie that matches his cute painted pink nose and the insides of his huge bunny ears, which rise like antennas over his blue eyes and buck teeth. He's carrying an old-fashioned Easter basket filled with fake grass, colored eggs and lots of candy.

Noah is dressed like a yellow chick bursting from an egg around his waist, while my grandmother is costumed like a daffodil sporting an Easter hat filled with live hyacinth, Easter lilies, crocus and tulips.

"*You're* all making fun of *me*?" I ask.

"The sacrifices we make for literature," my grandma says.

"The sacrifices I make for you," I add.

It is the weekend before Easter, about a month since St. Patrick's, and every year on this day Sleigh By the Bay holds our annual EGGS-Cited for Easter! party. My grampa hides eggs around the bookstore, filled with candy as well as half-off coupons for books, and we hold an Easter egg hunt for children and adults. We serve carrot cake, Peeps pretzels and deviled eggs, and Leah's Easter punch. It not only allows families to shop for last-minute Easter presents and basket gifts but also brings the community together after a long winter.

The sun streams through the windows.

And we have a perfect day.

It is a surprisingly balmy April day by Northern Michigan standards, meaning it's sunny and in the upper forties. The snowbanks are melting, and little rivers are running down the streets.

I am dating two men at the same time. Yes, you heard that right. Two. With a third date on the way. I feel a bit like one of those high school girls in a teen rom-com who is juggling the high school jock and the nerd but is secretly still in love with the guy she met at summer camp. After going on a first date with Micah and a second coffee date with Jamie, I continue to see both of them long-distance. We text and Face-

Time, and I have plans to see both in the coming weeks when I visit Holly in Chicago. I have begun marking our times to talk on my calendar in code (JM for Jamie Martin, MH for Micah Harrison), much like I do to distinguish between my publishing reps (SMP for St. Martin's Press, HC for Harper-Collins or PRH for PenguinRandomHouse).

"Here comes Peter Cottontail..."

Speaking of which...

Holly literally hops into the bookstore, singing.

"You look better than I do!" my grampa says.

She, too, is dressed as a rabbit. Jessica Rabbit, that is.

Think sexy Jessica Rabbit meets adorable bunny, complete with a little white bunny tail and a pink wig with adorable ears.

"Holly, this is a *children's* event," I say.

"*Who Framed Roger Rabbit* was for children," Holly says, blinking innocently at me.

"Diva, you actually look like Bugs Bunny's girlfriend, Lola," Noah says.

"See?" Holly protests. "Another cartoon."

She sniffs the air with her cute little twitching nose, which leads her to my grandma's Easter hat.

"You smell like heaven!" Holly turns to me. "Speaking of which..."

"Yes?"

"Your third and final date is coming up next week, and it's a heavenly one."

"Okay, stop with the puns," I say.

"No, keep talking," Grandma says. "She's been mum about the details of the third Santa."

"I asked Holly to remain quiet about it."

"Why?" Noah asks. "What's he like?"

Holly looks slowly and very dramatically around the group.

"He's a minister."

"Oh, my God, for real?" Noah asks. "Oh, I'm sorry. I didn't mean to say that."

"What religion?" my grampa asks.

"And this is exactly why I didn't want to discuss it," I say.

My grandma suddenly starts jumping up and down. Her hat looks like it's shaking in an earthquake.

"A man of God in our family!" she gushes. "It's a dream come true!"

"Okay, hold on to your petals, daffodil," I say. "We haven't even gone on a date yet. I know very little about him."

Holly hops onto a chair.

"Hear ye! Hear ye!" she starts. "Tristan Taylor is a forty-year-old United Church of Christ minister."

"UCC!" my grampa says triumphantly. "Keeping it in the family!"

Holly continues. "He used to be a school teacher before becoming a minister. He grew up in Traverse City, and he splits his time between Traverse City and Chicago, where his church has two sister branches. Susan will be attending a sunrise service in Traverse on Easter Sunday given by Tristan, and then going to brunch with him. And you gotta believe he's not lying about having met Susan at the race."

"Are you going to ask him what his favorite book is?" Noah says with a laugh. "I bet I know already. Authored by the true diva!"

The bell on the door tinkles, and a rush of families flock through the door promptly at one.

My grampa begins to hop around the store and offer kids chocolate.

"Nothing like getting them amped up to buy books."

I turn.

"Rita, what a nice surprise. What brings you in on a Saturday?"

"I wanted to look for some gifts for my great-nieces and -nephews," she says. Rita surveys the scene. "And I wanted to get some fresh air on this nice day."

Rita says this last sentence in a decidedly hopeful tone. She skews her eyes in my direction and then ducks her head.

I know her words are code for something deeper.

"Well, it's good to see you any day of the week."

"Thank you, Susan."

Winter is not for the fainthearted in Michigan. *Especially when you're alone.* I place my hand on her shoulder and give it a gentle rub.

The days exist in the dark, and—after a while—you cannot tell morning from night. It's as if you're sleepwalking. And when there is no one beside you to wake you from the months of cold and isolation, it can be hard to continue.

Rita and I are not that much different.

An electric blanket can warm us but cannot hold us tight in the middle of the night when we wake up shivering and scared. A fire can heat our homes but not our hearts. We make pots of soup and bake dozens of homemade cookies for one.

But Rita and I are united not only by memories and an undying love for my parents but also for what they built here: a love of books.

And that is what sustains us through winter.

Words are our sustenance, characters our companions, stories our escape, this store our warmth.

"I've heard about your dating life," Rita says.

I laugh. "Who hasn't? The groundhog didn't see his shadow this year. He saw mine as I was trying to crawl into his hole. Six more weeks of Susan!"

Rita chuckles. "Well, I hope it works out. I'm...this community is rooting for you. And I know how much your mother and father would have wanted you to meet someone. I know this has been a tough year for you. It has for me as well. Anniversaries can do that to a person. Life can't be all..."

Rita stops.

Funerals forever?

She doesn't finish her thought because Noah offers, "She's going out with a minister next Sunday!"

Rita's eyes widen.

"Go hatch somewhere else," I tell Noah.

But Rita smiles. "Your mother once said there would be no Christmas without Easter," Rita says.

"She was a wise woman," I say.

"So are you."

Winter can shatter your spirit and yet it can give you faith. I see the piles of snow melting in the window behind Rita, relenting, giving way to warmth, and I note its message to me.

Rita heads off into the chaos, and I watch the scene.

Bookstores, like winter, are not for the fainthearted either.

Did my grandparents believe they would start something that would not only unite but also change the lives of so many people in their community?

And yet they have battled small-minded people who have protested books—from Harry Potter to Jonathan Evison and Toni Morrison—without ever reading them. They have battled higher taxes, less parking, Amazon, supply chain issues, because they believed in the power of literature.

Which is why bookstores, like churches, are also places of faith.

Bookstores are the hearts of our communities, a place where it's okay to be yourself, to be unique, to be smart, to think critically, to find and use the singular voice God gave us that we too often and easily throw aside in order to fit into this hard world. Bookstores set a foundation for our children and our futures.

When I was a kid this bookstore saved my life. I was encouraged not only to read but to think beyond the small world in which I lived.

I look at all the children rushing around the store in search not only of an egg but also in search of themselves. I watch Noah entertaining them while dressed as a chick and think of how much he has grown over the years.

For those who never fit in at school, local bookstores and libraries served as their refuge. More than anything, books encourage us to dream, and I will tell you this, once that seed is planted, it immediately takes root in a child's soul. There is nothing bigger, or more special, than a dream.

And despite the stunning change in our world today—as well as in publishing—that core has remain unchanged. Reading changes lives. Books change lives. Bookstores change lives. And they will remain the centers of our communities and our lives. I can never restate the obvious enough: what I do changes lives. I know because it changed not only mine but those who I love most in the world.

I am the caretaker of dreams, and I take that job very seriously.

I am the keeper of a place where people find faith.

In community, in the world, in each other.

This is what has—and will always—give me strength and faith.

"Thinking about your date?" Holly asks, hopping by. "Keep the faith."

"Mind reader," I call to my friend who, for some reason, has stopped acting like a bunny and is now teaching kids how to do the chicken dance.

You gotta love Easter.

chapter 28

The sun rises shortly before seven in the morning. At its first light, rays splay across the bay. I cannot help but think the breathtaking beauty of the natural portrait before me resembles a biblical painting.

The sunrise service is being held in a park with spectacular views of Grand Traverse Bay. The world is dipped in frost, and it looks as if God Himself has draped His creations in glitter and gauze.

Father Tristan, as he is known at the UCC church, takes the podium. I got to meet him briefly while it was still dark, and I was still on my first cup of coffee, but now I see him—pardon the pun—in a whole new light. He is wearing a black clergy shirt and collar with a bright golden stole that mimics the sun emblazoned with crosses.

Tristan has salt-and-pepper hair—none of the men's real hair was visible under the Santa wig—round horn-rimmed glasses and a chiseled face. He resembles Clark Kent, if Clark had entered the clergy.

I look up at the sky.

Is it okay to think this way about a man of the cloth?

Tristan speaks: "For Christians, the reason for timing a service to coincide with the rising of the sun is simple. It was dawn when the first believers—in every gospel account, women—went to the tomb of Jesus, found the rock rolled away from the entrance and the body of Jesus gone. So it makes sense that, quite literally, this earth-shaking event would be celebrated as the sun comes up."

My eyes drift to the sun.

For decades, my family attended sunrise service on Easter. The first one after my parents died, I remember waking early—not excited to retrieve the basket of candy at the end of my bed or to await the Easter Bunny—but to head to sunrise service. As I stood holding my grandparents' hands while overlooking the bay on an early spring morning, I expected to see my parents again. I believed they would rise before my eyes and prove to me they existed, just like Susan wanted Santa to prove in *Miracle on 34th Street* that he could do anything.

"Lord, we lift our eyes to you."

Father Tristan is saying a prayer. I close my eyes.

"As the sun rises, may this moment stay with us, reminding us to look for the beautiful colors of promise in Your word. Lord, we lift our prayers to You. As the dew air falls, may we breathe this morning in and know that like the earth, You sustain us, keep us and work within us always."

I remember the cold Christmas morning—the first without my parents—when I got up, unable to sleep, and read *The Polar Express*. I needed to feel connected again somehow to my parents at Christmas. As I read, I could hear their voices in my head, as clearly as if they were snuggled beside in my bed reading to me.

"Seeing is believing, but sometimes the most real things in the world are the things we can't see."

That morning, I got dressed in my holiday finest—a pretty velvet dress I'd never worn—and marched into my grandparents' room and said, "We are going to church."

My grandmother wept.

Suddenly, I think of Jordan, who I have not seen since the holidays, and I shiver.

"Amen," I hear the parishioners say as one.

There is a hymn, and then the service is over. I wait as Tristan greets his parishioners as if they are old friends. He sees me and comes over.

"Let there be light!" he says with a laugh. "We can finally see one another."

I smile.

His eyes sparkle blue like the bay.

Check one.

"Not that I haven't already checked you out online," he continues. "Not that everyone hasn't checked you out online."

I laugh.

"So what should I call you?" I ask. "Tristan? Father Tristan?"

"Could there be anything less romantic than calling me Father Tristan?"

"Tristan, it is."

"I made brunch reservations at a little place just a few blocks away. You must be hungry after getting up so early and waiting for me to greet everyone. You up for a walk?"

We stroll into Traverse City, making small talk about the service. Tristan stops in front of a tiny coffee shop, packed with people. A line extends out the door. It is an old-fashioned joint, with guests seated at the counter, a cook slinging eggs and hash, and waitresses rushing around in aprons juggling coffee pots and platters of food.

"Now this is my kinda place," I say.

"I had a feeling you might like it," he says. "They make breakfast the way it should be." Tristan pauses. "With lots of bacon and even more butter."

Tristan heads to the hostess, and she greets him with a hug. He turns and motions toward me, and I cut the line with a feeling of complete embarrassment.

We are seated in a high-backed, red leather booth. We shrug off our coats.

"I could actually feel the Red Sea part," I say. I glance around. "It's like I'm with a celebrity."

"You are! Didn't you know?" he says with a chuckle. Tristan waves to a couple across the restaurant. "I actually made reservations weeks ago, so I'm not doing anything ungodly, don't worry. Besides, no one questions a minister getting a seat first. It's sort of like how passengers are relieved when they see a nun on their flight. Everyone feels very safe right now."

A waitress with a name tag reading Sally walks up.

"Coffee, Father?"

He nods.

"Coffee?" she asks me.

"I'm on a morning date with a minister," I say. "I need every advantage. Coffee, please."

Sally's eyebrows don't just rise over her eyes, they almost fly off her face.

"Well, this is a first," she remarks. "You better say a prayer your eggs aren't overcooked this morning with the size of this crowd, though."

She claps two menus down on the table before us and scoots

away. We pick them up and study the options for a moment. Sally returns.

"Ready?" she asks. "Sorry, but it's Easter Sunday. We gotta feed 'em and street 'em."

"Well, it's going to be the Skillet Scramble with bacon and biscuits and gravy on the side," we say at the same time.

We look up from our menus and stare at one another in complete surprise.

"Well, this was meant to be," Sally says. "As if the big man Himself had it planned." She smiles. "Sorry, I had to. But you two certainly seem like a good fit." Sally grabs the menus. "Like bacon and eggs." She smiles again. "Sorry, I had to again."

Sally sashays away, and I just look at Tristan.

"Speaking of bad jokes," I start. "I just have to ask what your favorite book is?"

He laughs.

"Asking for a friend," I say. "Actually, asking for myself as a bookseller."

"*Crime and Punishment*," he says.

"Seriously?" I gasp.

"No!" Tristan says with a laugh. "It was a crime and punishment to read in school. You know what it is," he says. "But *A Moveable Feast* is a close second."

"Seriously?" I repeat.

"This is Hemingway country," he says. "And I love Paris."

"I'm impressed. As do I."

Tristan pushes his glasses up his nose and studies me.

"Do you know how hard it is for a minster to date?" he asks. "You wouldn't believe who my parishioners try to set me up with—ninety-year-old great-great-grandmothers because they believe I only need 'companionship.' Oh, and the woman who has a sister who has a friend..."

I laugh. "Oh, I not only believe that, I've lived it."

Tristan continues. "Then there are the casseroles."

"The casseroles?"

"I receive about a half dozen casseroles a week from kindly women at the church," he says. "I filled my freezer and then the one in the garage. I started to fill the ones at the church when Father Bill pulled me aside and told me why the women were being so kind. Turns out they're known as The Casserole Queens. They're on the hunt for a good man. And I don't just mean a 'good' man, but they feel as if they were destined to meet a man of the cloth. I gained about fifteen pounds before I began to tell them all I had irritable bowel syndrome. If you think being a minister scares off some women, tell the rest you have stomach issues."

I nearly spew my coffee.

"So you're letting me know that being in my situation—social media's Single Kringle—really isn't as bad as your situation?"

"I'm saying that if anyone can understand what you're going through, it's me." He waits a beat and then asks, "I know you've been set up with a couple of other guys. How did that go?"

Do I tell a minister I'm dating two men long-distance? I mean, I try not to even think about that so God won't judge me. But if anyone could understand a long-distance relationship it would be a minister, right?

"Both are very nice men," I say. "But I'm not quite sure they're *the one*."

Tristan raises an arm and pumps his fist in the air.

"Yes!" he says.

His black shirt stretches across his chest and his arms, and muscles pop underneath.

My face immediately flushes, and I wince as if a lightning bolt might appear out of nowhere.

"Are you feeling okay?" he asks.

"Yes," I say. "It's my mind. Plays lots of tricks on me."

"Join the club," Tristan says.

Our breakfasts come, along with another round of coffee.

"This is good!" I say.

"Best breakfast in town," Tristan says, taking a big bite of his scramble. "So, I guess you want to know why a guy like me was at the Santa Run in the first place as well as why a minister would use a terrible pickup line?"

"It sorta crossed my mind."

"I'm not much of a runner actually," Tristan says. "I grew up in Traverse playing ice hockey. My legs are too big for running."

My mind whirls. I picture Hot Santa's legs in his running shorts.

"I started as a teacher at an inner-city school in Chicago, and I used sports as a way to bond with the boys in my class. Sometimes, kids in junior high wouldn't show up to class for days. I worried nonstop. I tried to start an after-school program as a way to keep the kids around and safe, but we didn't have the money, so I did everything I could think of to give some of these children a semblance of love, family and normalcy."

"That must have been a heart-wrenching job," I remark.

Tristan nods and continues.

"I re-created holidays for them, throwing parties at school where I'd dress as the Easter Bunny, or a pilgrim, or, of course, Santa, as an innocent way to give them food and gifts, as a way to let them celebrate a holiday they might otherwise not. There was a boy in my class, Jackson, a kid with the most infectious giggle and the most voracious reader. He didn't return to my class for a week. I went to his house and found out that he'd been shot. I sat with him in the hospital night after night, but Jackson didn't make it."

I put down my fork. "Oh, Tristan, I'm so sorry."

"It really forced me to recalibrate what I wanted to do with my life. I'd always felt a calling, and I thought it was to teach, but it was actually bigger than that to me," he says. "I ended up going to seminary school. I entered the Santa Run to raise funds for our church's shelters in Traverse and Chicago. I'm not the type of guy who uses pickup lines or just approaches women out of the blue, but I admired seeing a woman dressed as Mrs. Claus. I thought, 'Now here is a woman who knows herself, a woman who's comfortable with herself. She doesn't care what people think, or how she looks...'"

I laugh. "Gee, thanks."

"And you were smart when we talked," Tristan goes on. "I wanted to put myself out there for once. I feel as if my life is sort of just starting anew."

"Me, too," I say. "This whole thing has pushed me out of my comfort zone, and it's reminded me that there are good men out there in the world. Mostly because I think I already dated all the bad ones."

Tristan laughs.

"It's also renewed my faith, in people and myself. So you know I've got to ask the obvious question here. Is faith important to you?"

"It is," I say. I think of sunrise service. "Did you know I was named after the little girl in *Miracle on 34th Street*?"

Tristan shakes his head. "Love that movie."

"I was sort of the opposite of her growing up, though. I believed as a girl not only in God and Santa but all the good in the world. And then my parents died. I grew up UCC but stopped going to church after that. I didn't believe any longer. In anything. God was a fraud. Santa was a myth. Life was cruel. But I woke up the year after they died, the first Christmas without them, and felt a calling to read one of my parents' favorite books. I returned to church, but I never really fully let myself believe because I was so scared of being hurt again."

Tristan reaches out and takes my hand. His eyes are so understanding that I tell him about Jordan.

'For if you forgive other people when they sin against you, your heavenly Father will also forgive you,' Tristan says softly. "That's Matthew 6:14. From the King James Version. I didn't just make it up."

I lower my head and laugh, and he gives my hand a gentle, reassuring squeeze before releasing it.

"I'm trying," I say. "My grandma told me many years ago that it's easy to have faith when you've never been tested. True faith appears when you seem to have lost everything." I lift my eyes and look into Tristan's. "When I go to church now, I often find myself staring at the stained glass windows. I think of all the work that went into creating them… I think of how much work went into creating each of us."

I stop, my heart suddenly rising into my throat. "I feel now—at forty, after all I've been through in my life—as if my soul is a stained glass window dropped from heaven and then shoved back inside me, shards and all. They pierce me. And now I realize I would have it no other way for it makes me feel *everything*!—all the good, bad, dark, light, joy, pain— and I want to feel that. I *have* to feel that."

"Maybe you should go into the seminary," he says. "That was beautiful."

"I feel like Sleigh By the Bay is my and my community's adjunct church. We all come together at least once a week for something greater than all of us. We may bicker and fight, and differ on so many things, but faith and books give us a foundation from which to work."

I hesitate and continue. "Now I have to ask the obvious

VIOLA SHIPMAN

question. Why didn't you show up at O'Malley's after the race?"

Tristan's eyes widen and he shakes his head. "The ten-thousand-dollar question! I was running with a kid named Steph from the shelter who had never run before in his life. He was the one who goaded me to talk to you actually. Steph wanted to prove that he could do something he'd never done. He made it about a mile before he stopped, broke down and started bawling. It took me a half hour to convince him to go on, that he wasn't a quitter. We ended up walking—and by walking I mean shuffling—the last few miles of the race. It took us over three hours to finish. By that time, he was cold, and I had to get him home to his mom. I'm so sorry."

Sally returns and places a bill down before us. He picks it up.

"It's the least I can do for abandoning you," Tristan says.

"Just make sure to leave a good tip. The big guy's watchin'," Sally says. "Leave an even bigger tip if we helped make a love connection."

Do you know when you have those moments where you can see your future clear as a bell?

This is one.

As Tristan reaches for his wallet, I can actually envision myself with this good, kind, handsome man. I can see Sundays together. I can see navigating between Traverse, Chicago and Petoskey. I can see a world filled with stained glass windows and oodles of books, faith and forgiveness.

We stand, and Tristan helps me on with my coat.

We head outside, past the line of people waiting and walk back toward the park. Tristan takes my hand, and—despite the chill in the air—I warm immediately. When we reach the park, Tristan says, "Oh, my gosh, my mother has a pin just like that. She wears it every Christmas. Brings back such wonderful memories."

I had forgotten I was wearing it. I had forgotten I put it on my coat as "the test."

I am only slightly exaggerating when I say I swear I hear angels singing.

"It does. I wear it as connection and protection."

I want to give him a hint. I want to ask him, *Look familiar?* I want to make it easier for him.

For me.

"'And the angel said unto them, Fear not: for, behold, I bring you good tidings of great joy, which shall be to all people,'" Tristan says. "The angel Gabriel."

I hold my breath.

"Your pin is actually different than my mom's, though," Tristan continues. "The red and green bejeweled angel, cheeks puffed, blowing a golden trumpet. My mom's is simpler, a gold angel with diamond wings. It was her mom's. I've never seen one like this before. It must be so special."

The world around me seems to still. Everyone moves in slow motion.

Another nice man. Another good man. But yet another man who isn't the one I met at the run.

I search the bay beyond him for an answer.

Isn't the third time supposed to be a charm? I mean, c'mon, God, stop messing with me. Just how many women were dressed as Mrs. Claus at the race? And how many men hit on those women? The odds seem more insane than betting on a horse wearing sunglasses and rain boots to win the Kentucky Derby.

And yet here I stand, batting oh for three. I should be pulled from this lineup.

In the distance, a bell chimes, and I can't help but think of church and a line from *The Polar Express* about the boy listening for a sound he was afraid he'd never hear: the ringing bells of Santa's sleigh.

Will I ever hear the right bells?

My ears begin to ring, along with the bell, and the ringing in the cold air sings to me, *You will never find the one, but maybe you can be happy with one of these men.*

"I hope I can see you again," Tristan says.

"I'd like that," I say.

He leans in and kisses me. The kiss is better than I could have imagined, intense and filled with passion.

"Get a room, Father!" a kid on a bike yells as they whiz past.

We laugh and say our goodbyes.

As I drive home, I crank up the heat and roll down the windows. I need the sound of the bay to calm me, and the cold of the lake air to sober me.

My phone pings endlessly, everyone wanting to know how my date with Tristan went.

The ice on the bay is going through its early spring cycle of melting and refreezing, unsure of exactly what season it is.

"I understand," I say to the water as I drive.

chapter 29

MAY

Watch it, you idiot!

As a business owner in a resort town on Memorial Day, I can only think it, I cannot scream it.

But, man, am I screaming it inside.

What started as a peaceful run on a shockingly lovely Memorial Monday—which, in Northern Michigan, could mean anything from a surprise blizzard to a barbecue on the beach—has turned into survival.

How can I forget every single year that over the course of one weekend the town transforms from *Northern Exposure* to *Squid Game*?

I've almost been hit four times by cars in the street—drivers looking at their phones, or out-of-state visitors gawking at the cute shops—so I navigated to the sidewalk, which is even worse. Fudgies—which is what locals call the vacationers who visit during the summer wandering the town like zombies eating fudge—walk directly into me without looking.

I'm glad I'm on foot, though. I've always been worried I will hit a tourist when I'm lost in thought, or exhausted, and will have to haul their body into the back of my trunk and bury it somewhere.

I finally stop for a drink at the water fountain in the park not far from my home. There is a baseball field adjacent to it. A few bleachers sit behind home plate, and a small, chain-link fence encompasses the outfield. Overhead, the clouds bounce along the sky just like a grounder up the middle.

I walk over and put my hands to the fence and watch the kids play. School is still in session—and will be for a few more weeks due to the large number of snow days—but kids, like the tourists, are ready for the summer.

Some boys are playing catch in the infield, while some girls are kicking a soccer ball around in the outfield. Just off the third base line, a little boy stomps in a puddle.

I smile and lift my face to the sun, and I pull from the recesses of my memory banks an image of me doing the exact same thing as a girl. But I was in a dress, on the way to see my grandmother for our Memorial Day date, and I could hear my mother yell, *No, Susan! Don't!* when I was already in midair.

I open my eyes, and sun spots dance before me. I blink, and they disappear.

I think of being that girl.

Blink.

I think of my mother yelling at me.

Blink.

I think of never having children to play in this field.

Blink.

I think of my grandmother and how—somehow—another

year has passed, I am forty, and that it's time again for our standing date.

I blink and start jogging home.

I shower and put on a pretty summer dress. I grab a sweater in case it gets cool. I head out the front door with some scissors and snip some pretty pink peonies for my date.

My grandmother grew, and still does to this day, beautiful peonies—pink with white centers—in long rows outside her home. The blooms on the flowers grow so heavy and thick that the stem will just collapse, exhausted, like an old dog in the summer heat. I, like my mother, took starts of my grandma's peonies for our own gardens so the legacy—and the gifts—will never end.

I lift a peony to my nose, inhale and sigh.

Heaven.

If there were one word to describe the perfumed scent of these peonies, it would be heaven.

Heaven will smell just like this, my grandma always says.

My grandma hung her laundry line over the peonies so that when I'd stay with her the sheets would smell like heaven.

I stand and look at the flowers, petals soft as silk.

My mind whirs to Tristan and faith, Jamie and Micah, past and present.

I walk into the kitchen, my screen door banging shut, and begin wrapping the cut ends of the flowers in wet paper towels.

"Are you ready?" my grandma calls through the screen door. "God gave us a beautiful day for our Memorial Day visits."

"Coming." I head to the door. "You look nice."

My grandma is wearing a black dress and sensible shoes.

"Thank you," she says. "Can't break with tradition."

Our "visits" have taken place in the rain, snow, sunshine

and mud. And, over the years, our visits require more time, as more have gathered.

I lock the front door and follow her to her truck. Yes, she drives a truck. She loves it for hauling books and plants, for getting around the rain and snow, and to serve people.

"No one questions a granny in a truck," she says. "They either think she's crazy or toting a gun."

She pops the tailgate and opens the tonneau cover. I smile. "You're ready."

"Always."

The bed of the truck is filled with miniature American flags, peonies from my grandmothers' gardens—the ends smothered in wet paper towels—along with a cardboard box lined with sealed Ball jars filled with water. I add my peonies to the back, and she closes the cover again. When I get in the front seat, I have to move a box of Kleenex she has positioned in my seat.

"You're really ready," I say.

My grandmother turns on classical music and takes the side streets in town, avoiding the Memorial madhouse in Petoskey. I retrieve my buzzing cell, and begin to answer an endless stream of texts from the staff. This is one of the busiest days of the year for Sleigh By the Bay—the kickoff to the summer season—and I always take the afternoon off.

I fire replies, one after another, my fingers moving as quickly as Vivaldi.

Members of the Sleigh the Summer Book Club always get 20 percent off...no coupon necessary. They MUST show their book club card, though.

NO! Mary doesn't get two for one. She's been using this line for two decades. Give her a free bookmark. Makes her happy as a clam.

NO! Kids cannot use the staff bathroom, no matter how much their parents ask and how desperate they sound. We tried, AGAIN!, to make this work a few years ago, and our staff bathroom looked like it had been through a water-gun fight. Let them know there is a public bathroom available just down the block.

Maura Kendrick is twelve, but she looks twenty-one. She CANNOT buy books from the adult romance section. Her parents are attorneys, and they will kill me (if not sue me).

BUT! Chandler Moore CAN buy literary fiction. He's thirteen but attends a rural school and needs to be challenged.

My grandma glances over at my texts as she pulls into the cemetery.

"Some things never change, do they?"

No, they don't, I think.

The truck bumps along a gravel drive and underneath a metal gate, a sign reading Bayview Cemetery.

It is an oxymoron.

There is no view of the bay. Michigan cemeteries are not lush, lavish or large. They do not sit on breathtaking bluffs overlooking the waves of the lake. Graveyards, as we often simply call them, often rest on a rolling foothill or a quiet piece of country land next to a pastoral pasture or meandering stream. They are not filled with enormous marble headstones.

But Michigan cemeteries are plentiful. Families want to remain together. *Forever.*

My grandma parks the truck, we gather our goods and set out to visit our family.

Visiting these graveyards on Memorial Day with my mother and grandmother is how I got to know many of those family members I never had the chance to meet. Sometimes, during my childhood visits, my mom and grandma would laugh, sometimes they would cry—depending on the person and the length of time they had been gone—but they always ended with the same ritual: Mom and Grandma would kneel to say a prayer, pay their respects, and then place the peonies in a jar with water and plant American flags into the earth over the grave.

"See you next year," they would whisper, passing a kiss from their hands to the earth before standing again, interlocking arms, and slowly making their way to the next party guest.

When I was younger, after my parents had died, I hated coming here with my grandma. I just wanted to spend my Memorial Day with friends at the beach, or running around downtown greeting my "summer friends," kids I hadn't seen since the previous summer. I wanted to distance myself from death.

But my grandma refused to let me forget.

You let too much time pass, and you forget, she would say. *And you should never forget.*

We wend our way from grave to grave, stopping at an old headstone whose letters are weathered and worn.

"Your great-aunt Maude," my grandma says. "Remember her?"

I nod. "I remember all the weddings."

She laughs. "Married six times, not the norm for a woman of that era. She was one tough broad. Farm girl who worked her way through college, moved to Chicago and became one of the first women to hold a seat on the Chicago Mercantile Exchange. Maude never suffered a fool. Or a husband, for that matter." My grandma places some peonies in a container and sticks some flags in the earth. "Speaking of Maude, how are the many men in your life?"

"That is a terrible turn of phrase, Grandma."

"I thought it was well-timed. And…?"

"I'm still seeing all three men," I say.

"Did you hear that, Maude?" my grandma says, nudging the headstone with her elbow. "A gal after your own heart."

"Ha ha, Grandma. I really like them. They're all good guys."

"It sounds like there's a *but* in there."

"But I'm taking it slowly. I've seen Tristan in Traverse twice since our date, I've seen Jamie and Micah in Chicago a few times, and we all text and FaceTime a few times a month."

"We?"

"Not all of us together, Grandma. It's not an episode of *Sister Wives*."

"You mean husbands?"

"I can't keep up with you today," I say. "They're all wonderful men. Kind. Thoughtful. Handsome. Smart. Sweet."

"Sounds like another *but* in there."

"But I don't know anything yet."

"It must be hard to try and pick which one is *the* one. I mean all of them were at the race. Any of them could be your Santa. And I know you probably—despite what we've all said and promised—still feel a lot of pressure on you from everyone, including your friends, the town, me and your grampa, to make the right decision."

Do I tell her about the pin? I wonder. Or do I, like Maude's gravestone, share just the faintest of information?

"There is," I finally say. "I just want to take my time."

"You know I wasn't even looking to meet someone when I met your grandfather. Nor was your mother. We weren't searching for a Santa cap, or a handsome face, or big muscles, something just clicked. We knew." She snaps her fingers as she loves to do. "Just like that."

I feel like we already know each other, I can hear the mystery Santa say at the run. *Like we have a history, just like your pin.*

My grandma puts her arm around my waist.

"You'll figure it out, Susan." She gives me a squeeze and then whispers into my ear, "You'll know the exact moment, too, because your heart will glisten like the bay. Bells will ring, and you will hear Santa's sleigh."

"My poem, grandma. Really?"

"Really," she says.

She takes my hand, and we continue our visits until we finally reach my mother and father. There are plots of green earth surrounding them. Eight plots were purchased long ago, when death was just a distant thought: two for my grandparents, two for my parents, and four for me—one for me and my future husband as well as our children.

My heart pangs.

I have no idea who decided on eight plots, or how my future family had been so carefully considered, but my family had always been planners.

Will my life forever remain as empty as these plots?

My grandma wipes the gravestones clean and then stoops to clear some spring weeds. She places peonies in containers and plants some American flags into the earth.

She bows her head, says a prayer, stands and then turns to look at me.

"It would have been so much easier to run," she continues. "For all of us."

I look at her, cocking my head, not understanding.

"You know, we talked about it—your grandfather and I—after your parents died. Selling everything and leaving, going somewhere where we could start over, start fresh," Grandma says. "In a small town, we have all been defined by your parents' loss. *We* are the parents who lost a son and daughter-in-law. *You* are the girl who lost your parents. For many years, people were afraid to get too close as if our bad luck might rub onto them. And the hate so many had toward Jordan's parents, though they had nothing to do with it. I know it was hard on you because it was so hard on us. Everywhere we turn in town—the bookstore, the ice cream shop, in our gardens—we see your mom and dad. Their ghosts are real. But your grandfather asked what good running would ever do. 'The memories—good and bad—still live within us,' he said. He was right. We can never run far or fast enough. We can never disappear. You can't hide from life or outrun the past. You tried, but you came back."

She gestures around the cemetery, turning in a circle. "You know this community can drive me crazy sometimes. I mean, just look at Rita. I wanted to run from all these people as much as my memories. But who was there when we needed them most? They brought us food. They cared for us. I mean, Rita slept in our home for weeks helping me care for myself when I couldn't even get out of bed. She took you to school, covered shifts at Sleigh when Nicholas and I couldn't work. This community has saved our bookstore from going belly-up dozens of times. This community ended up saving my life."

My grandma holds up a peony and smells it.

"Our bookstore is like these flowers. It has taken root and grown into something beautiful, something heavenly, something that—long after we're gone—will still remain. And, call me old-fashioned, in this day and age where we can live anywhere in the world, there is something to be said for acknowledging the wonderful things we have right in our backyard. There is something to be said for having roots."

She holds her arms open, and we hug.

I kneel on the cool earth over the graves of my mother and father, plant a flag and say a prayer: a prayer that, long after I'm gone, someone takes the time to share my story, visit me on occasion and pass along my legacy.

The scent of the peonies fills my nose.

The scent smells like heaven.

chapter 30

JULY

The rooftop of Holly's condo is jammed, part MTV spring break party and part Hallmark Christmas movie.

"Oh, my gosh," Noah says. "I feel just like Connie Francis in *Where the Boys Are*."

He grabs Fred's hand and races toward the pool. "C'mon, George Hamilton."

Leah laughs. Suddenly, she sees Luka arrive and sprints across the rooftop to meet him, leaving me standing alone in the hot wind.

It is a scorching Chicago summer Saturday, where the concrete feels like a radiator, the air a rainforest and where—on my walk here—I saw a woman lose a heel into the melting asphalt.

A huge banner announcing the Annual Holly Jolly Christmas in July Party, undulates in the city breeze.

Holly is in the pool lounging on a reindeer float when she sees me.

"It's about time!" she yells over Mariah Carey Christmas music. "Did Rudolph get lost? Where have you been?"

"Traffic was a nightmare," I say. "And my grandparents were late getting to the store, which was a madhouse."

"Are you trying to guilt me?"

I look around. "Well, you did steal my idea a long time ago," I say. "So..."

"I *improved* your idea," Holly counters, gesturing at her bikini and the crowd on the rooftop. "And this is simply promotion for your idea."

She elegantly rolls out of the float with barely a splash in the pool and swims to the edge as gracefully as Esther Williams. Holly walks up the steps and emerges in a red, *Baywatch* bikini that reads Sleigh All Day across the bust in gold cursive. Her hair is slicked back, sunglasses atop her head, makeup intact.

"I would look like a drowned raccoon if I did that," I say.

"You would not! Stop it," she says. "You look..."

She stops and gives me a onceover.

"Very professional."

I look down at myself.

"I had an early morning meeting with an account rep from HarperCollins," I say. "I couldn't show up for it in a halter top. And I was in such a rush to leave, I forgot my overnight bag in the store."

"Well, we need to get you changed out of that blazer, honey," Holly says. "It's a hundred degrees. You look like you're here to sue summer."

She grabs my hand and escorts me toward the glass elevator. As we walk, I notice a table stacked with books and a Sleigh By the Bay banner across it, Leah and Noah perched behind it. I slow and look at Holly.

"People want to buy summer reads," Holly explains. "Beach reads. I brought the store to them today."

"You think of everything," I say.

It's then I notice that the entire crowd at the party seems to turn as one to watch me, cell phones in the air, the entire rooftop swaying to one side in slow motion like a field of Illinois corn in a windstorm.

"Is it my imagination, or is everyone staring at me?" I ask on the way to Holly's condo. "I haven't been judged this harshly since the first day of sorority rush when I wore sneakers."

"And I had to tell them you'd just had foot surgery," she says.

Holly ushers me inside her condo, and the cold from the air-conditioning whooshes over me. Holly leads me directly to her closet and starts shuffling through her clothes, hangers banging this way and that.

"I'm a good foot taller than you," I say. "Your clothes are like doll outfits on me."

She turns and inspects me, not seeming to hear me.

I grab her shoulders. "Okay, stop!" I say. "What's going on? You're acting stranger than normal."

"Promise you won't get mad."

I step back and take a seat in the chair adjacent from her bed. Whenever Holly asks me to promise not to get mad, it's bad. Like the time she didn't tell me she'd booked us in a hostel—not a hotel—until we'd arrived in Portugal, or when we were high over the ocean parasailing in Mexico and Holly said, *This turned out way better than I imagined considering I found these guys on a flyer in a bar.*

I don't answer.

She takes a seat on the end of the bed across from me.

"Jamie, Micah and Tristan are all here," she says.

"What?"

She jumps at the decibel level of my voice.

"Hear me out," Holly says. "You've been dating these three guys for a few months now, and keeping everyone—including not only them but also me and those who love you and helped make this happen—in the dark. *They* want to know—*we* all want to know—do you like one? Are any of them *the one*?"

"Perhaps I don't know," I say, looking down.

"And that's okay, Susan. But at least communicate your feelings to someone about what's going on. *Anyone*."

"I'm sorry," I say. "I really am trying to sort things out. It's been a long year between my fortieth-year funk, my grampa and all of this craziness."

"I know," Holly says. "They actually all reached out to me about coming. They wanted to meet each other, sort of like the guys did at the end of *The Dating Game*. I just felt like it might make everything less secretive. I thought maybe if you saw them all together it might help you put things into perspective and make a decision."

"Like kicking the tires at a used car lot?"

She laughs. "Good point. The timing just seemed right, especially considering the bookstore's annual Christmas in July party next week. Maybe seeing your Santas in the summer will be like seeing yourself in a changing room mirror."

"Horrifying?"

"Clarifying. It will lead you to make the right decision."

"This all just feels like too much pressure all of a sudden."

"Think about those three guys you've been seeing," Holly says. "They each know you're dating all of them. They post pictures on their social media, and then those are shared, and then people speculate." Holly jostles my knee anew. "They all like you, Susan. *Really* like you. You know why? Because you're an amazing, smart, resilient, fierce woman and friend. And if you don't want to be with any of them, so be it. You'll just be as fierce as you've always been, and we'll continue dancing to 'Single Ladies' whenever it comes on."

I smile.

Holly continues. "But I'm your best friend in the world, and I know there's something deeper going on with you. I don't know if you're just biding time, trying to make everyone happy, or if you really like all of them, or none of them, but I know that once Susan gets stuck in a routine, it can last forever, and that's often not healthy for you or for anyone."

My mind whirs to Jordan.

"So I'm sorry to push you, and I'm sorry I've made your life a social media spectacle, but when we became friends you signed up for this roller coaster ride, and I'm not ever letting you off." Holly looks into my eyes. "I love you, Susan. I only want the best for you."

"You have an odd way of showing it," I say.

She laughs.

"Let's get you dressed so you can chat with the Jonas Brothers, okay?"

We emerge on the rooftop a few minutes later, and the cell phones again fly into the Chicago sky. Holly has dressed me oh so subtly in an off-the-shoulder bandana-print romper, green top, red skirt, which feels uncomfortably short on my long legs, and tossed a Santa cap on top of my head.

Noah rushes over, applauding.

"Diva!" he says. "You look hot!"

"Holly already told me everything," I say. "Thank you for actually keeping a secret for the first time in your life."

He mimes that he's locking his lips with a key, which he then tosses into the pool. "Loose lips sink ships," Noah says. "And I'm Captain Stubing from *The Love Boat*."

I scan the crowd. Jamie is chatting with Leah and Luka,

Micah is in the pool, and Tristan is stationed in the corner talking to a few people.

"A woman walks into a bar," I say, "and takes a seat between a minister, an attorney and a financial planner." I look at my friends. "And—surprise—the punch line is me."

"You already got the joke wrong," Noah says, fixing my hair. "It's 'a very tall woman walks into a bar.'"

I laugh.

"You got this, boo," he says. "And your safe word today is *Maureen O'Hara*."

I think how I'd rather be at home right now watching *Miracle on 34th Street*.

My feet feel as if they're made of concrete until Noah gives me a big push, and I stumble across the rooftop.

"Go get 'em, girl!" he yells.

"Hi," I say when I reach Jamie. "Funny meeting you here."

He laughs and then leans in and gives me a kiss. "It's good to see you."

I turn to see if Micah and Tristan are watching. They are.

"You, too," I say.

"This is awkward," he says. "More so than our first date."

"I promise you I didn't plan for this to happen. I didn't even know you—all of you—were coming."

He smiles. "Well, Holly is full of surprises."

"That's a polite way of saying it." I stop and really look at him. He is so all-American handsome, standing here wearing a Cubs hat and tank top on a hot summer day, that my heart skips a beat.

"Hi! I'm Micah."

"I'm Tristan. Nice to meet you."

I turn, and the world moves in slow motion. Micah extends his hand to Jamie, and then Jamie extends his hand to Tristan. I am surrounded.

"It seemed silly to ignore one another any longer," Tristan shrugs. "It's the minister in me."

Tristan kisses my cheek, and then Micah does the same on my other cheek.

Tristan is wearing a very tight Christmas Vacation T-shirt with Chevy Chase's face on it that shows every muscle. And Micah is standing shirtless, gold drops of water running down his torso.

Every single person at the party now has their phones trained on the four of us. I see Noah racing over with a cocktail.

"Drink this, diva," he whispers. "Straight vodka with a whisper of cranberry."

I take a sip and wince at its strength. "Where's the whisper?"

"Don't judge, Judy. You need it. And smile. You look like a deer in the headlights. No! You actually look like the girl from the poster of *Jaws*, all innocent while a great white shark circles without her knowing. Except there's three sharks this time. Have fun!"

My three men are chatting now as if they're old friends. I'm amazed at how men can either be all testosterone-fueled rage or completely chill and at ease in a situation like this. They all recognize Micah from the sports pages, and Jamie and Tristan are quizzing him about his star clients.

"Man, that one-handed touchdown catch Booker made against the Packers was amazing!" Tristan says.

"He's a human highlight reel," Jamie adds. "How much the Bears gotta pay to keep him?"

I watch them talk, looking from one to the other. The three are so different, and yet so alike: they are kind men. Good men. They each look similar to the memory of the man I talked to at the race.

I should be doing cartwheels into the pool that, after years of worry about getting hurt again and years of horrible dates, my friends, family and community loved me enough to find three men who any woman would dream of meeting.

Micah.

Jamie.

Tristan.

My head pivots from one to another.

"Now that was a catch!" Tristan says.

"I agree. They need him on the team," Jamie says. "They're just not complete without him."

Not complete without him.

The humid Chicago air grips my body, and I suddenly feel claustrophobic and woozy. I take a sip of my cocktail and a step back from the three men to get some air and clarity. I take another sip and another step and then another…

It's too late to stop myself from falling backward into the pool.

I yelp, tossing my cocktail over my head, and make a monstrous splash. I can immediately feel the skin on my back burn from my reverse belly flop. The entire crowd yells, "Ooooh! Owww!"

When I come up, my Santa cap is draped around my face like a wet otter. I spew water and open my eyes. Everyone at the party is standing around the pool, capturing the moment on their phones.

As if on cue, "Grandma Got Run Over by a Reindeer" begins to play.

Jamie, Micah and Tristan are all leaning into the pool, trying to offer their assistance.

The lyrics to the song echo across the rooftop.

You can say there's no such thing as Santa
But as for me and Grandpa, we believe

The last thing I hear before I sink back underwater is Noah saying, "You didn't use your safe word!"

chapter 31

One of the first and most important things a true Northern Michigan native learns—not long after discovering the wonders of a fried smelt, the endless recipes you can make with a cherry and having the name of a reliable snow plow guy at the ready as soon as Halloween is over—is how to hunt for Petoskey stones.

I learned how to hunt for Michigan's state stone walking the beach alongside my father and grandfather.

It is just after 6 a.m., and I have come here at dawn not to run for once but to search.

July days in Michigan seem to last for weeks. Some sixteen hours of light bathe our bay in an ethereal glow from sunrise to spectacular sunset. It is a gift from God, this length of light, to brighten our days after months of winter.

Today, the sky is quite literally purple at sunrise. It is not quite morning, and it is not quite night. The day is in the process of becoming.

Like me.

The bay is calm, the water like glass, the waves still asleep, groggily lapping at the shoreline.

I can see my family in my reflection as clearly as I can hear their voices in the lullaby of the waves. I am a part of this land.

I have come to a little beach far off the beaten path this morning in search of stones as well as an answer.

This earth on which I stand has undergone seismic changes since the dawn of time. The pieces of fossilized coral that I have come here to find were deposited eons ago by glaciers. *We are all remnants of our past.*

The recent record high water levels in Michigan have made the Petoskeys easier to find as they are washed ashore. There was also a thunderstorm overnight, which I know only makes the chance of finding these elusive stones much easier.

People from all over the state and the country flock to our gorgeous shoreline every summer in search of sun, fun, stones and answers. By August, the beaches have nearly been picked clean of stones. I know time is of the essence.

You don't really need much to hunt for Petoskey stones, save for a good eye and something in which to gather them. I carry a bucket, the same one I carried when I was a child, a little pink pail—rusted just a bit, like me—featuring the image of a little girl in a red swimsuit standing in the lake, a lighthouse with a sun over it in the background.

This little beach is part sand and part rock. Quiet, rocky beaches are always the best place to search for Petoskeys. I walk the shoreline, hunched, scanning. I finally kick off my sandals, stick them into my bucket and step in the cool water.

Goose pimples cover my legs, and I giggle at the chill, as I do every time I step into these waters.

Petoskey stones are characterized by the hexagonal pattern that covers them. Each hexagon has a dark center radiating out to a white outline.

The waves sigh, and I can hear my father's voice explain the stones to me as I walk.

Petoskeys consist of tightly packed, six-sided corallites, which are the skeletons of the once-living coral polyps. The dark centers that look like eyes were actually the mouths of the coral, I can recall him telling me. *The lines surrounding the eyes were once tentacles which brought food into the mouth. The Petoskey stone, like the city, was named for the Ottawa Chief Pe-to-se-ga, meaning Rising Sun, because the stone's pattern resembles the rays of the sun.*

As if on cue, the world brightens. The sky turns from purple to deep blue. Clouds on the horizon turn from amber to gold, and they begin to form a tendril over the sky, a golden finger reaching from the heavens stopping directly over my head.

I look up and lift a finger to the sky.

"Hi, Dad," I say.

The waves lap, and I know my father is assisting me this morning in my search.

I look down into the water, and right before me, is a Petoskey stone, as big as my palm, gleaming in the water. I pick it up and place it in my bucket and continue searching the area, knowing if there is one, there will likely be others.

And there are! I find two smaller ones and another larger rock. Though they have such a distinctive pattern, like snowflakes no two are the same. They range greatly in size and color, from lighter to darker gray. I step out of the water and head from the sand to the rocks that have washed ashore. I step gingerly on the rocks. Out of the water, the Petoskey stones are much harder to find as they resemble ordinary limestone when they're dry, gray, dull, the hexagon pattern not as noticeable unless they are wet.

But my eyes have been trained from an early age to find what I'm seeking. I begin to pick up stones and carry them to the water. I dunk a lifeless rock into the bay and when I pull it out, I gasp at the beauty that has been revealed. I go back and forth between shore and water, rinsing and repeating, until my bucket is full, and its weight forces me to walk with a crooked gait and loud grunt.

Michigan state law states that one person cannot remove more than twenty-five pounds of rock or mineral from state land at any one time. A few years ago a man discovered a ninety-three-pound Petoskey stone. The news story went viral—even bigger than my own—and the state took the stone back after finding out about it. I would venture a guess—after hauling boxes of books my whole life—that I'm carrying about ten to twelve pounds of stones.

I stop to catch my breath.

An older woman with gray hair holding a cup of coffee walks the shore. She sees me and waves.

"Find anything good?" she calls.

I glance into my bucket. The stones are now dry and faded.

"I did! Lots of Petoskeys," I say. "Just up the beach a ways. You looking for anything in particular?"

She seems to consider my question. Her face is tan, her skin lined and etched from the sun. She lifts her face heavenward then looks at me.

"No," she finally says. "Most of the time, I just walk. People think I'm just an old woman wandering the beach at dawn or sunset, but I've learned to stop looking so hard. Sometimes, if you don't have an end goal in mind, the journey leads you to something you never dreamed you'd find, something even more spectacular. Happy hunting!"

I glance again into the bucket and watch the woman fade into the morning mist along the shore.

She is a living Petoskey, her soul filled with a million eyes, compartments of history. What the world too often glimpses on the surface will never capture the intricate beauty of what lies underwater.

I am akin to these stones.

We are all akin to these stones.

I pick up the bucket but turn one last time.

The sun is now in the sky, a million rays splintering across the water.

And a lone, long, golden finger of a cloud is pointing directly at the woman.

I finally have the answer to my search.

chapter 32

The shocking seasonal juxtaposition is not lost on me.

Although it is eighty degrees outside, a quick warmup since my morning rock hunt and revelation, and the streets are packed with tourists in shorts and swimsuits eating ice cream cones and chomping fudge, my grampa and grandma are perched in the window of the bookstore wearing their Santa and Mrs. Claus costumes as if it is snowing in December.

We have our same set from the holidays in one window, while the other is flocked in faux snow and stacked with summer titles underneath our Christmas in July banner.

This was my idea decades ago, after a particularly nightmarish summer season when we had a record rainfall and cold. In fact, it seemed to rain nearly every single day, and the temperature never moved out of the fifties, which you would think would be great for a bookstore. People have nothing better to do than read, right?

The problem was, no one came.

The town was desolate. Tourism dropped by nearly half.

People want warm, people want sun, no one wants to endure a real life *Wuthering Heights* on vacation.

So, out of desperation, sprang this idea. I thought that if locals flock to see my grandparents during the holidays, perhaps they would do the same in the summer.

It has now become one of the town's most beloved retail traditions.

I glance up at the rooftop of the building.

A sleigh sits atop Sleigh By the Bay, just like in the past.

A crowd begins to form in front of the bookstore. I take a few steps back, until I'm partially hidden behind a gaslight post. Within a few moments, a line is snaking down the block. I even see some media—including TV reporters and cameramen—spill from a couple of white vans.

My mind begins to put the pieces together:

Christmas in July. They think there might be a summer story here. A Santa scoop.

I pull the brim of my Santa cap down over my face and race through the alley to head into the back of the store.

It is packed. So packed, in fact, I have to navigate my way through the crowd with a sweet wave and polite 'Excuse me'.

I head upstairs.

"Ho! Ho! Ho!" I hear my grampa bellow to a little boy in a T-shirt and swim trunks. "What do you wish for Christmas in July?"

He leans down so the boy can whisper in his ear.

I can see my grampa mouth, *I'll have to ask your father if you have room for a giraffe.*

Holly comes rushing up all out of breath, a Santa cap atop her head, her lips coated in a glittery, glossy green lipstick.

"Where have you been?" she asks. "It's Christmas chaos."

Noah sidles up wearing red-striped leggings. "Diva, you are trending more than Dolly Parton right now, and no one outdoes the queen herself." He adjusts my Santa cap.

"By the looks and sounds of things, I think the media— and a lot of people—think there's going to be some sort of announcement," Holly says. "It feels like the finale of *The Bachelorette*." She looks at Noah. "I did sort of tease an announcement about an hour ago on social media."

"You did what?" I gasp.

"I just wanted to get a big crowd here to boost your summer sales. The Christmas in July posts coupled with the viral video of you literally falling head over heels into the pool with all three men trying to save you has stoked a lot of new attention and curiosity. And a lot of sales. I thought maybe you could just thank everyone for coming and thank the community for all the support."

"In boys and books," Noah says.

"It's all going to be okay," Holly says. "This will take a lot of pressure off you for sales if the weather turns early this winter."

I look around. My grandparents started this store because they loved literature. My parents joined because they believed in the power of books. I do, too.

How did I become the main character in this story? Or has the entire plotline of my life—my love of Christmas, the loss of my parents, being raised by my grandparents, having a cast of offbeat but well-meaning friends—led to this moment?

I think of my Petoskey stone hunt and the woman. I think of Holly's surprise announcement.

Did it all lead to this moment?

I can feel my heartbeat in my throat. Leah hands me a

glass of water as if reading my mind, and Noah massages my shoulders.

I look at them.

Or is my work already done?

They have their happy endings. They found their soul mates somehow, and both were wearing Santa hats.

Maybe writing that poem so long ago and believing in it despite everything was not meant for me but for them. Perhaps I'm just the conduit, the garland that pulls it all together.

Noah leans into my ear and whispers, "Your safe word today is *happiness*."

I turn, and he hugs me so tightly the world falls away for a moment.

"If everyone would gather outside, we're about ready for our big announcement," I hear Leah say over the intercom.

Big announcement? I mouth. *Really?*

She winks, walks over and whispers, "Just play along. Get 'em to buy books!"

Holly puts her hand on my back and guides me to the front door. I stop at the last second as the crowd filters outside, and, without thinking, rush over to my grampa and grandma still positioned in the window waving to the children outside.

I take a seat on Santa's lap.

"Susan?" he asks in his Edmund Gwenn voice.

"Are you okay, honey?" my grandma asks.

I look at my grampa and try to remember what Christmas was like before...before my childhood was ripped from me, before I lost faith, before I was scared to open my heart for fear I lose someone else I loved.

I try to remember what it was like to be Susan, the girl who still believed.

My grampa's eyes, so blue, twinkle in the bright sunlight behind his little glasses. He tilts his head, the pom-pom on the tip of the Santa cap swaying with him, leans in and whispers, "What do you wish for Christmas, Susan?"

I whisper into his ear, "All I want for Christmas is the way it used to be."

He grabs my face with his gloved hand and stares me right in the eye.

"I can't give that to you," he says, his voice barely audible. "If I could give any girl any gift in the world, I would grant you that wish. But I can't bring your parents back. No one can."

Santa's chin begins to tremble.

"What I can give to you, though, my beautiful girl," he continues, "is the hope that Christmas can be the way you want it to be. It can never be the same, but it can be filled with miracles and beauty and wishes you never dreamed or expected. But you already know Santa can't grant that to you. You know what you have to do. You've always known. You have to gift yourself forgiveness."

A tear runs down my grampa's face and into his beard, and I reach in and hug him with all my might. For a second, I am a girl again.

I am safe and loved.

The only thing any of us truly wishes for in this world.

And I realize I always have been.

I head outside and when I emerge, I have an idea of what it must be like to be a literary superstar. Cells flash, cameras go live, reporters yell questions.

"We are live from Petoskey, Michigan," a Detroit TV anchor I recognize whispers loudly into the camera. "We've been promised some sort of announcement today. Might we learn who Susan Norcross, Michigan's infamous Single Kringle—whose real-life story seems even more incredible than one of the novels in her popular bookstore, Sleigh By the Bay—has chosen? We are soon to find out. Stay tuned."

Holly steps behind the mic on the front steps.

"Welcome, everyone, to Sleigh By the Bay's Christmas in July celebration!"

People applaud.

"As you know, it's been quite a year here for our own Susan Norcross, owner of our beloved local bookstore, Sleigh By the Bay."

Many in the crowd hoot.

"And many of you already know her story. Susan's mother and grandmother both met their future husbands while each was dressed as Santa. Susan has always believed it was her destiny to meet a man the same way. In fact, when she was in grade school, she wrote an award-winning poem called 'The Single Kringle' about her family's history and established the 'Christmas criteria' the man she will eventually love must meet. However, the year after she wrote it, her parents were killed in a tragic drunk driving accident. Susan was taken in by her grandparents, who still dress as Mr. and Mrs. Claus every holiday season. Wave hello, Kringles!"

My grandparents wave in the window and then make their way to the front door.

"Susan's hope and belief in Santa and the future were shattered after the loss of her parents, but her friends and family—all of you gathered here today—buoyed her with your outpouring of love and support, personally and professionally."

Holly continues. "Last year, Susan and I signed up to race in Chicago's Santa Run. Susan, fittingly, came dressed as Mrs. Claus. At the start of the race, Susan met a man—who I'll call Hot Santa…"

The crowd titters.

"…and the two had an instant connection. The catch? They

never knew what the other looked like or found out one another's names. They were swept away when the race started, and Hot Santa yelled at Susan to meet him at a local bar. He never showed. That's where we came in! Her friends, grandparents and all of you—the local community—decided to try and find him so we set up a social media post seeking the Single Kringle that went viral. Why did I step in? Why do so many care so much?"

Holly scans the crowd and then turns toward me. "Susan is my best friend. I love her more than anyone in this world." Her voice breaks. "I've never met a more giving, caring person deserving of love. This has not been easy for her. And this has not been an easy year for her either. She turned forty, which is the same age her mother was when she died. As you can only imagine, she's scared of getting hurt once more, loving and losing all over again. And yet she has taken a chance. On love. On herself. She has put her heart on the line in hopes that maybe the man she wrote about so long ago isn't just in her imagination but that he is real, as real and as amazing a man as her grandfather is and her father was."

Holly pauses, and I hug her.

"Before we go any further, I just wanted to read the poem Susan wrote as a little girl, so we can remember the magic of this community and the magic of Christmas, even in July."

As Holly reads, I am a little girl again, sitting at my desk writing the stanzas in my notebook with a big, pink, glittery pen.

"Books haven't just been there for Susan, all of you have," Holly says after she's finished reading. "And so have three men—Jamie, Micah and Tristan—who we found on social media. I can say that my friend is happily dating right now, and perhaps one day one of them will be her forever Santa. Until then, she's enjoying the reindeer games."

The crowd laughs and applauds.

"Today, during—fittingly enough, Christmas in July—Susan just wanted to thank all of you for your support," Holly continues. "Susan?"

I move toward the microphone.

I am about to speak when I hear the TV anchor whisper too loudly into his lapel mic, "I don't think she's going to say anything about the guy she chose. Sorry, Marty. I had a hunch. Thought we had a scoop. Yeah, I know this sucks."

I scan the crowd. I look at Noah and Leah. I smile at my grandparents who have now moved onto the sidewalk and are surrounded by children. I look at the TV reporter.

"I had no idea how hard growing up would be. That I would lose my parents and then all hope. And turning forty... to be the same age my mother was when she died, has shaken me to my core this year. But, somehow, this crazy experiment has not only restored my faith that there are good men out there but also my faith in the world. I cannot thank you all enough for that."

People clap.

I see Noah's face. He mouths, *Happiness*, his safe word for me today.

The TV reporter and cameraman begin to exit, noisily jostling through the crowd. Another station watches, and follows suit.

"Wait!" I suddenly yell.

I step away from the mic and whisper into Holly's ear, "There's something I never told you. I was wearing my mother's angel pin when I met the mystery Santa. He commented on it. Jamie, Micah and Tristan had never seen it before."

Holly gasps.

The crowd titters.

"You mean...?" she starts.

"None of them are the guy I met at the race. I'm so sorry. I actually called them and told them after I had a moment of clarity hunting for Petoskey stones. They were upset, but all seemed to know my heart wasn't really in it, with any of them. I know how hard you've worked to make all of this happen. I didn't want to upset you. I didn't want to let anyone down."

She grabs my shoulders. "You aren't." Holly nods at the mic. "I think it's time you wrote the ending to your own story, don't you?"

I return to the mic, take a deep breath and continue. "I have been blessed—somehow, some way—to meet three of the most wonderful men in the world. They are good, kind men, and I can imagine having a blessed life with any of them. But when I wrote that poem, I had someone in mind, someone very specific. And at the Santa Run, I also had a secret. One that I've kept hidden until this very moment. One that I just shared with my friend."

The crowd murmurs at this turn of events. TV lights flash. Cameras are pointed at me.

I hold up my mother's angel pin, which I brought today as good luck.

"The day of the race, I was wearing this Christmas pin of my mother's, and the man who I connected with at the run somehow knew it was hers. He understood it had a history and was a part of me. Tristan, Micah and Jamie may have been at the run, but none of them were the Santa I spoke and connected with."

The crowd gasps.

"I've already talked to each of them and told them that. I also told them I'm sorry if I hurt them. It was never my intention. I think I just wanted a happy ending way too much. I'm sorry that I'm unable to give all of you the happy ending you want, too, but life is all about timing, and it's just not Christmas for me yet."

There is a long silence.

Finally, one person applauds, and then another, until there is a thunderous cheer, one that rolls all the way to the bay.

"But it is Christmas in July," Holly says, moving to the mic, "and Sleigh By the Bay is loaded with beach reads!"

chapter 33

There is nothing—not the beach, not a dip in the lake, not a Dreamsicle sunset nor chasing down the ice cream truck on a scorching day—that sums up summer more to me than the sound of a sprinkler.

The rhythmic chh-chh-chh has always spellbound me, as has the smell of the water on freshly mown grass in the summer heat. I stare into the water droplets—as gold as the sunshine—flying back and forth in the blue sky in front of an old-shingled cottage with an American flag flapping in the wind.

After my pronouncement and a long afternoon at the bookstore, I was told by my friends, employees and grandparents to "take a hike," quite literally.

"Enjoy this summer day," my grandma said. "You need it."

So, I have taken the circuitous route on foot back into town, avoiding my cell and keeping my head down, though I now realize the Santa cap I'm still wearing is akin to having a target on my back.

Out of nowhere, two kids, a boy and a girl, no more than six, race around from the back of the cottage and sprint—no holds barred—directly through the sprinkler. They giggle wildly, look at each other and then do it all over again.

They look up and see me, water dripping off their heads.

"Hi, Santa!" the little girl says with a big wave.

"That's not Santa, silly," the boy says. "That's a girl."

"It's Mrs. Claus, then," the girl says, voice indignant. "A girl can do anything a boy can do."

"And it's summer," the boy continues. "Santa is on vacation right now."

"Actually," I say, "Santa is downtown right now. He decided to visit Petoskey on vacation."

"No! Way!" the girl says. "C'mon!"

The girl races toward the cottage, yelling, "Mom! Dad!"

The boy starts to head inside but turns back at the last minute.

"If he was the real Santa, why did you run away from him?" the boy asks. "I'd never leave."

I smile.

"You're right," I say. "He wasn't the real one."

"I knew it!" the boy says. He looks at me. "But I'm still going to see him." He hesitates. "Just for my sister, you know."

He runs toward the cottage and takes the steps two at a time until he is standing on the wide front porch.

"You should do it!" he calls to me.

"Do what?"

"Run through the sprinkler," he says. "I know you want to. You have that look. My parents always do, but they never let themselves. Adults are so weird. They make all the easy stuff hard. Just do it. I promise it'll make you feel better."

The boy heads inside. I look left and then right.

I run into the sprinkler. The cold water hits me hard, right in the face, and it takes my breath away. I make it to the other side and race through the water again, screaming in glee like a kid.

My heart is racing and I do it one more time, eyes open. As I run, I am a girl racing through the hardware store sprinkler my dad rotated every few hours on our lawn, especially during a dry summer. I can see him in the window, laughing. I can still picture him setting up a Slip 'N Slide on the sloping hillside in our yard. The waterdrops fall around me, but suddenly, they are frozen in midair. It is snowing, the middle of winter, and I am racing outside the gym after being told my parents had been killed. I am standing alone, staring into the sky, screaming.

I still am.

When I step outside the sprinkler, dripping wet, my Santa cap plastered against my head, I feel remarkably sober.

A figure moves in the window. The little boy is standing there, giving me a big thumbs-up.

Why do adults make all the easy stuff hard?

I take off running.

This time, however, I know exactly where I must go.

I stop short, hearing a voice.

I tiptoe to the doorway, trying to keep my still-wet shoes from squeaking, and peek my head around the corner.

My heart jumps into my throat, and I shuffle my feet. My shoes squeak as if I just came to a screeching halt on a basketball court.

Rita turns like a corkscrew in her chair next to Jordan's bed. "What are you doing here?"

"What are *you* doing here?" I ask.

I step inside his room.

Nothing has changed and yet everything has changed.

"I've been coming here every summer since your parents were killed," Rita says, her voice soft.

It takes me a beat before I can ask, "Why?"

Rita turns back toward Jordan. "Do you remember the Christmas in July parties your parents used to have?"

I shake my head no at first, but it slowly turns into a nod.

"Barely," I say. "I was so young." Then I smile. "I think I had blocked them out."

"I thought they were the reason you started the event at the bookstore," Rita says, surprised.

Memories come flooding back.

"They probably were," I finally say. "I just never put two and two together."

"They were the highlight of my summer," Rita sighs. "I used to do so much of the planning and cooking because your parents were so busy with you and the store. I know I probably overstepped my boundaries, but it was a way I felt connected to Marilyn." There is silence for a moment. "She was my best friend in the world, Susan. She was my Holly, and I still miss her so much."

Rita continues. "I started coming here decades ago in July, searching for an answer. The first time I came was the day of your parents' annual party. I yelled at Jordan. I asked God to take him. I asked God how He could do something like this to you and your family. I am a woman of faith. It's not fair. How could God allow this young man to make such a terrible decision one night that could alter so many people's lives forever? I screamed, 'Why me?' so loudly that the nurses asked me to leave. And one July day, late at night, I snuck back and fell asleep in this very chair. I had a dream—so real and so vivid that I still don't believe it was a dream at all—that Jordan had woken up. His eyes were open, and he was saying, very clearly, 'Why not you?'"

My skin ripples with goose bumps.

"Over the years," Rita says, "I've spent July days here with Jordan. Sometimes I turn on the TV, and we watch Tigers games. Over time, I've come to believe that life is a lot like a baseball game. The tiny decisions we make from day to day, inning to inning, determine our lives. And sometimes, I've learned, it's just not your day. I've experienced a lot of loss in my life, Susan, just like you. That's made me so different than the fun, free-spirited woman I used to be. And I know I've not always been such a nice person, Susan. I can be overbearing. I can be cold. And I do that to protect myself. You've protected yourself, too, just in a different way. But I'm trying to change, and I know you are, too."

Rita pats the side of the bed, and I take a seat. Jordan's legs touch me.

"Now, why are you here?" she asks me.

"I've been coming every December seeking some sort of closure. He just keeps going."

"And so do you. But why are you really here?"

"I want to let it go," I say, suddenly exhausted. "I want to forgive him. I want to forgive myself. I just don't know how. If I had just gone with my parents to the hotel instead of making them take me to that stupid dance…"

"Stop!" Rita says, her voice ringing out in the quiet room. "It was not your fault. We cannot control the whys and the timing in life. It was a horrible accident that should never have happened. But it did. And I have to believe that God wants us to learn from it somehow. That's why we're all still here right now. Maybe that's what brought us all here to this very moment."

The machines beep. The facility is quiet. Everyone is out enjoying a beautiful summer day. Jordan's window is cracked open, and I can smell the bay on the wind.

"I could tell your heart wasn't invested in any of those men," Rita says. "I could tell you didn't hear bells ringing like you said you would in your poem."

"How did you know?" I ask.

"I know you better than you think," she says. "I helped raise you, Susan. Why do you think I come to the store every Monday? I want to see *you*. I *need* to see you. You were my family, the daughter I never had. I know we were never that close, but I still believe that maybe some of my toughness rubbed off on you and that's a reason you became the woman you did."

Rita suddenly smiles. "Who did you vote for?" she asks out of the blue.

"I'm sorry," I say. "I'm not following."

"Your fourth-grade teacher told me that you didn't vote for yourself when your poem won the contest. She told me at the awards ceremony she could tell by your cursive handwriting that you voted for another classmate."

Suddenly, the memory floods my mind, and my soul smiles. It's amazing what you choose to remember and what you choose to forget.

Rita smiles. "Ah, yes, I think I know," she says. "You've always been such a good person, Susan, just like your mom, but you've never let that someone special close enough to see that. You put everyone else first. It's time you make Susan the priority."

Rita takes my hand in hers.

"Forgive yourself Susan," she says. "Forgive God. Just let it go."

I start weeping, and Rita takes me in her arms. I have another flashback of Rita in bed beside me when I was a girl, holding me as I cried myself to sleep, whispering, *It's okay, it's okay, it's okay.*

"It's okay," Rita whispers.

I stand up and look down at Jordan.

I take off my Santa cap and place in on his head.

"I forgive me. I forgive God. I forgive."

"Now you'll be able to hear that bell clearly when it rings," Rita says after a few seconds. "It's probably been ringing your whole life, but you just couldn't hear it over the deafening sound of your grief."

In the distance, I hear the music from an ice cream truck.

chapter 34

In the blink of an eye, the season has switched from Halloween to Christmas, pumpkins to wreaths, falling leaves to decorated trees.

It is winter again.

I take a tiny box from a red Christmas tub and remove one of my mother's heirloom ornaments. It is a fragile beauty, pink as my home, "Merry Christmas!" written in white glitter.

I hang the ornament and reach for another, a beautiful, multicolored bulb with a gold star cut into its heart.

What good is keeping your heart in a box—protected, unseen—if you cannot share its beauty with others?

I secure it to a branch.

Of course, there's always the chance that it might break, be shattered into tiny shards, but I also know that it can be pieced back together again. As my grampa said, it may not be the same, but it can still be just as beautiful, albeit in a completely different way.

A few months ago, I wondered if it was the wrong men at the right time, or even the right men at the wrong time, but I've come to realize it's neither. It had to be the right Susan at the right time.

I'm a better, stronger, more giving soul after this year of Santa insanity. I am more whole than I've ever been. And that's a lovely place to be.

I don't need a man to complete me. I am not "single." I am coupled to community, to friends, to work, to passion, to books, to life.

Would it be nice to find someone someday to share my life with completely and without edit? Of course. But I no longer wallow in the fact that I'm alone, because I'm not. I'm loved, deeply. My family, my friends, my town—complete strangers—have proven that to me, and, if anything, I am even more proud of who and where I am.

A small town bookstore owner with a soul as bright as the bay on a winter's day.

The ice slowly dissolving.

Proudly displaying cracks for the world to see.

That's what I love most about the characters in my favorite books: women who have been knocked down by life, time and again, and yet get up and soldier on with faith, strength and resilience. I am fractured and forty. Sadly, there are too few books with protagonists like me. We should be celebrated. The broken are the most beautiful. And we are all broken. If we all would only just choose to share that with the world—not the faux perfection but all the times we've fallen backward into a pool—then the world would be a better place.

I finish decorating my tree, lit in the window, and smile. It may only be the first day of December, but I want to celebrate every single moment of the holidays this year.

I head back to the spare bedroom and take a deep breath before entering.

I open the closet and remove my parents' pillows. The scent of Old Spice and Shalimar overwhelm me. I give the pillows a hug and then reach for my parents' Santa caps. On the way out of the bedroom, I glance at the poem over the bed.

"It's time," I say.

I climb the stairs to the attic and place the pillows and caps in a green bin that I've already emptied.

"It's not goodbye," I say. "It's just time for some happy memories to nestle alongside the old ones."

I close the lid and turn off the lights.

I have a cup of soup and cocoa before the tree, watching the light fade outside and the tree lights glow, and then pull on my coat and boots. My early dinner hour is already over. It is snowing lightly, as it has been off and on since the town's Halloween parade, and the earth glistens. I exhale and watch my breath dance before my eyes. I head onto my sidewalk and turn to look at The Pink Lady all bedecked in garland and lights.

"Looks beautiful!" my neighbor, Charlie, calls. "You're among the first as usual."

"Among the first?" I call. "I thought I *was* the first."

"Ol' Bobby Brennan got his up over Thanksgiving," Charlie calls from across the street as he throws lights onto his bushes in the near dark. "Didn't you feel the power surge?"

I laugh.

"See you later, Charlie."

He waves and returns to work.

It is cold, but not frigid, and I feel exhilarated. I decide to walk to work, cutting by the Brennans to see Bobby's handiwork. I can see the lights a block away, casting the neighborhood in a glow. Bobby makes Clark Griswold look like an amateur. There is not a spare inch of roof, gutter, window, railing or lawn not covered by a bulb, wreath, garland, inflatable or candle. I stop and take a picture to show my grandparents.

Despite the chill in the air, a warmth covers my body as I enter downtown. It is already bedecked in Christmas, as it has been since the Thanksgiving parade, the gaslights wrapped in green boughs and adorned with wreaths. Every window in town is flocked and frosted, featuring Christmas displays ranging from partying penguins to the northern lights.

But the town knows Santa is ours.

I stop in front of Sleigh By the Bay and watch the happy scene in my front window.

The big sign on the front door reads: SANTA IS IN THE HO-HO-HOUSE!

The tiny paper plate clock that I made in grade school—red dots with the numbers written on them marking the time, popsicle sticks as the hands for the time—still hangs underneath the sign stating that Santa's here until 6:30 p.m.

And we are still here: not only my grandparents and me but also my parents, who live not only in us but will live in this bookstore forever.

I take a step back and can't help but smile. People are lined up out the door waiting to get their children's picture taken with Santa.

I watch my grandma take the hand of a little girl in a green velvet dress and lead her to Santa. She looks at the big, bearded man and then her parents, eyes wide, brimming with tears.

I move inside the door and cock my head to listen. I hear my grandma say, *"Don't be scared. It's just Santa. He loves all children."* The girl nods and Santa sweeps her into his arms with a hearty laugh.

Santa rocks her gently on his lap, and then I can see him ask her name. She looks at him, and I see her say, "Susan."

For a moment, my grampa is taken off guard. And then he sees me standing outside the window, and he smiles.

"Ho! Ho! Ho!" he says. "Such a beautiful name! Did you know that's my granddaughter's name?"

The girl shakes her head.

"It's a special name, meant only for the smartest, bravest little miracles in the world."

The girl smiles.

I realize Grampa is looking at me as he says this.

"What is your Christmas wish, Susan?"

Santa leans his ear toward her mouth—because it must remain a secret between child and Santa only—and Susan whispers her message.

Santa nods and gives the girl a kiss on top of her matching velvet bow. Then he turns and smiles for the camera.

The parents take a million shots.

I don't know how much time there is left for such scenes, how many more years I'll be blessed to witness this, so I simply stand here in our beloved bookstore for as long as I can and take a million mental pictures.

My cell rings. I rush to my office, shed my coat and wet boots and answer without looking.

"Happy December!"

Holly.

"Thank you," I say.

"How are the Clauses this first day of the holiday season?"

"Making magic," I say. "As usual. How are you? Sorry I haven't called since Thanksgiving. Been a whirlwind."

"I know," she says. "I'm actually calling for a reason."

My eyebrows lift. "I hate it when you call for a reason."

Holly laughs. "What is it?"

"Tristan called."

"Restraining order?"

Holly laughs, hard.

I continue. "I haven't spoken to him—or Micah or Jamie—much since July. I texted them a few times to say hi and ask how it's going, but I didn't want to be the ghost of their Christmas past."

"Perfect segue," Holly says. "Actually, I ran into him the other night at an event. Totally random. He told me he's organizing a fundraiser for Jackson, the little boy he said he told you about who was shot and killed in Chicago. Tristan wants to start the after-school program he always wanted, and he wondered if you might participate. I said I'd ask."

I close my eyes remembering Tristan's story.

"Of course," I say. "Is it an auction? How many books would he like to give away? Or perhaps I could get a big name author to speak or contribute."

"Actually," Holly says, "he wants you, Susan."

"What do you mean?"

"He's racing in the Santa Run again, and he's already enlisted Jamie and Micah to join as well as Leah, Luka, Noah and Fred." Holly hesitates. "And me."

"No," I say. "I can't go back to that."

"Just hear me out," Holly says, her voice surprisingly calm. "If you haven't noticed, social media is still clamoring about your missed connection, especially with the holidays approaching again. Everyone wonders, if it wasn't one of these three men, who was it? Who's the hot Santa? Who's the angel who understood your angel pin?"

"Okay, I get it, and I know you're actually brainstorming headlines and content for your site right now," I say. "Look, I'd love to help, but this seems so…"

"Random?" Holly asks. "That's why it's perfect. I actually believe it would serve as closure to you—closure on this forty-year funk, closure on finding Santa, closure on this run."

"New year, new me?"

"Exactly," she says. "To use a bookseller analogy, it's sort of like you cut out the cliffhanger from a Grisham novel. I think this might be a wonderful thing to do. For everyone. You could even talk about how tragedy changes us. I know Tristan wants to talk about Jackson's life, maybe this could give you a chance to talk about Jordan. These stories might resonate with folks, especially leading into the holidays." Holly stops for a moment. There is silence. "It's one day. What have you got to lose?"

"Seriously?" I ask. "Do you have no memory of what started a year ago."

I'm about to say no again and hang up when I hear Tristan's voice in my head.

'For if you forgive other people when they sin against you, your heavenly Father will also forgive you.'

A chance for total and full forgiveness. The final period at the end of my story.

"Okay, I'll do it."

Holly yelps and then just as quickly adds, "This is still Susan on the phone, right?"

chapter 35

"Can you hold my gloves for a second?"

"Of course," I say to a man dressed as Santa. "Are you okay?"

"I usually warm them by the fireplace, but you're way hotter."

I turn to my friends.

"Okay, I'm out!"

I start to walk away, but Noah grabs me on one side, and Holly grabs me on the other. They usher me away from the second consecutive Santa Claus to hit on me since we arrived at the Santa Run.

"I sort of thought the last pickup line was adorable," Noah admits. "If I was the Grinch, I wouldn't steal Christmas, I'd steal you."

Fred and Holly both say, "Awww!" at the same time, and I begin to second-guess the group of friends with which I've chosen to surround myself.

"Uh-huh," Holly says. "I know that look. Too late now."

Everyone is here. Noah and Fred, Leah and Luka, Holly and me.

Noah and Fred are holding hands, so are Leah and Luka. My heart smiles. Perhaps this was all meant to be: I was the conduit to two people I love finding the loves of their lives.

Both, of course, whom they first met while wearing Santa caps.

My work here is done.

Almost.

"Well, if it isn't the Peanuts gang!"

Three handsome Santas approach.

"And Mrs. Claus!"

Tristan, Micah and Jamie—all dressed as Santa—approach. They pull down their beards.

"*Now* you show me your faces!" I say.

They laugh.

Holly wanted our group to come as the Pink Ladies, but Luka and Fred both protested when they realized one of them would have to come as a Christmas Sandy in red leather pants, so Holly recalibrated and decided on a Peanuts Christmas. As a result, I'm surrounded by Luka as Charlie Brown, Fred as Linus—blanket in tow—Noah as Snoopy, Leah as Peppermint Patty and Holly as Lucy. Due to all the publicity, I had no choice but to return as Mrs. Claus.

"Thank you so much for doing this," Tristan says as he hugs me. "I can't tell you how much it means."

"It's an honor," I say. "I'm thrilled we could bring such awareness to your after-school program."

"We've raised over ten-thousand dollars thanks to you and Holly," he says. "And these guys."

"It's good to see you again," I say, hugging Micah and Jamie.

Three Santas surround me.

"I'm really sorry how things ended," I say. "I think all of you are incredible, but I just wasn't ready."

"And, let's be honest, we weren't the right guy," Tristan says. "But it actually…"

He stops short, and I notice Jamie and Micah both giving him a "stop talking" hand sign.

"What?" I ask. "What's going on?"

Jamie looks at them, and they nod. "We all actually met someone as a result of all this," he says.

"So many women reached out to us after what happened in July," Micah says. "And we each ended up meeting really wonderful women."

"Thank you," Tristan says. "You led us to the women of our dreams."

"Yeah," Jamie says, "you led us back to the women we met a year ago at this race who we thought were you, the ones dressed as Mrs. Claus who we hit on."

"The ones we felt we had an instant connection with," Micah adds.

I feel both simultaneously elated and upset by this news.

The Single Kringle conduit.

"I'm happy for you?"

My response comes out sounding like a question, and everyone laughs.

"Really, I am. That is just so amazing."

A bell rings, signaling the race will start in a few minutes.

I see three very pretty woman yell for Tristan, Micah and Jamie, and they walk over and begin to pose for pictures together. Holly is live on Instagram talking to the Peanuts gang.

I feel a flake on my nose. I look up. It is beginning to snow lightly, those dry snowflakes that seem to dance in the wind.

"You look just like my wife!"

I roll my eyes. Some poor girl getting the same line I got last year.

"Are you Christmas?"

I feel a tap on my shoulder. I turn.

"Because I want to Merry you."

Another Santa stands before me.

"I'm sorry," I say. "I can't do this. Mrs. Claus has had a long year."

He laughs. "Tell me about it."

This particular Santa is better dressed than the lot, and I do know my Santas. His costume looks vintage. The jacket is a rich, dark red velvet, and the white fur trim is not used sparingly: it runs the length and circumference of his jacket, rings his wrists and even outlines the top of his black boots. His white gloves are white, and not dingy, and his black belt—even from a distance—looks like real leather, not shiny plastic. He's wearing a red velvet cap that falls just-so over his white hair. His red lips are curled in a genuinely happy smile behind his long, curly beard. And, unlike so many of the surrounding Santas, I can tell that his bowl full of jelly is all stuffing because he's wearing running shorts and has legs made of marble.

And it's then I notice his eyes: they are the color of the sky behind him. Not just blue, the hue of a snow sky.

It begins to snow in earnest.

"I dialed this up to impress you," Santa says.

My heart stops.

His snowy eyes land on the Christmas pin I'm wearing on the fur lapel of my Mrs. Claus coat.

"That was your mother's, wasn't it? I knew it."

I touch my angel.

"I feel like we already know each other," Santa says. "Like we have a history, just like your pin."

"What's going on?" I ask. "Did Holly set you up? I'm super fragile right now. I can't take another joke."

"It's no joke," Santa says. He pulls down his beard. His handsome face is so familiar...the sky blue eyes, the dimples, the little scar on his chin from the time he fell off his bike delivering newspapers and the McCann's dog chased him, the white blonde hair and curled bang that still dive bombs his right eye, the boyishly handsome face.

And then I know.

"Kyle?" I gasp. "Kyle Trimble? What are you doing here?"

"Holly didn't send me. Rita did."

I feel as if I'm the figure standing inside a snow globe that someone has picked up and shaken. I have to grab Kyle's arm to steady myself.

"I was the Santa you met last year," he says. "I was the Santa you met so long ago. Remember our date at McDonald's?"

My mind flashes back to him wearing that Santa cap and telling me he was the one. I had forgotten that I was wearing my mother's pin for good luck. He remembered.

"I don't understand," I say.

"It was me, Susan. It's always been me. That's why we seemed so familiar to each other."

"But you didn't show up at the bar?"

"When the race started, I got a call from Doctors Without Borders. I'd signed up to volunteer, and Ukraine needed doctors immediately. I ran home to pack and then to the airport. I've been out of the country and off social media for a while now. I had no idea it was you until Rita reached out to me. Somehow, she found me. Somehow, she knew."

"Because I voted for you instead of myself in the 4th Grade Petoskey Christmas Poetry Contest," I say almost to myself. "She knew I voted for *you*."

Kyle looks at me curiously with those snow eyes.

"And because she was at McDonald's," I add. "That's how she knew. She always knew."

I shake my head and continue.

"But don't you have a girlfriend?"

"Oh, you mean the last time we texted?" he asks. "That was a long time ago, Susan, and it didn't work out." He hesitates. "I think I was meant to meet you again."

"You left Petoskey, though," I say. "You have a life in Chicago."

"I didn't run from Petoskey. That's my home. It will always be my home." He looks at me shyly. "I always thought you were too special for me."

"Me?"

"Yes, you. You've always been so strong, so smart, so independent. I thought you had it all figured out."

"Not until now," I say with a laugh. "It only took forty years."

"Then the next forty should be amazing," he says.

I hear sleigh bells jingle. A waving Santa in a sleigh pulled by a team of runners parts the crowd.

"Runners, take your positions!" a voice echoes.

A big bell chimes to start the race, echoing in the cold air. A crush of people pushes us forward, and Santa begins to be swept away. At the last minute, Kyle grabs my hand.

"You're not getting away this time!" he says, pulling me close.

"I like you, Susan," Kyle says. "If you'll let me, I'll be your Single Kringle." He grins. "Maybe forever."

The same words he said to me at McDonald's so long ago.

"You're the one," I say. "You've always been the one. I just know it now." Bells jingle again. "I can just hear it now."

Kyle takes off my Mrs. Claus glasses and kisses me, and the world stops.

We stand in the middle of the street, runners cheering and applauding as they race by us. When the crowd finally clears, I see Holly and the Peanuts gang, with Tristan, Micah and Jamie, watching us and shouting and jumping up and down. Holly has her cell trained on us.

"This story has a happy ending after all, folks," she says. "The Single Kringle has found her Santa!"

Kyle holds me close and whispers, "I can't believe I found you."

I look into his eyes and whisper, "Again."

And then he grabs my hand, and we begin to run toward our future.

epilogue

I lay out the paper for Rita, just as I've done every Monday for decades.

I fold the paper open to the obits. I run my finger over a photo.

She enters the bookstore and takes her usual seat by the fireplace.

It is a frigid February day, and I can hear the trees crack in the cold before the door shuts.

"Susan?"

I walk over to Rita.

"Are you okay?" she asks.

"Are you?"

Rita shrugs off her coat and then lifts the paper to her face.

"Goodbye, Jordan," she says to his picture.

Jordan passed away two weeks ago.

"We had our goodbyes, didn't we?" I ask Rita.

She nods.

"Let me know which funerals you'll be attending this week," I say. "I can pull some books for you."

I leave her to her paper and start to walk away.

"Susan?"

I turn back. "Is something wrong?"

"Actually, I'm thinking of starting a new tradition."

My eyes grow wide. "You? Really?"

She laughs. "Change is good," Rita says. "You taught me that."

"What's your new tradition?"

"I think I'll be coming every Friday now." She glances at me, and her eyes twinkle. "To see the wedding announcements."

I smile. "I love that idea."

"I can still buy them books, but in a totally new way, right?"

"Right."

"And when do you think I might see *your* announcement in the local paper?"

"Don't rush things," I say with a laugh.

"Your grandparents and I want to attend your wedding," she says. "We're not getting any younger."

"You're not that old, Rita."

"If I were milk, you'd sniff me."

I laugh, hard. "I promise that you will see me get married," I say. "This Santa was truly meant to be." I look at her. "I know I've already said it a million times, but thank you for reaching out to Kyle. You made this happen."

"No, *you* made this happen."

I lean down and hug her. When I start to let go, she holds on a few seconds longer.

"You better start thinking of a book, though," I say. "For yourself."

"Why?" she asks.

"You'll be doing a reading at the wedding."

Rita puts her hand on her heart. "Thank you."

"Speaking of which, I'm meeting Kyle for lunch and a special errand."

"Sounds intriguing."

"I'll see you…" I stop and smile. "Friday."

"Yes, Friday!"

I grab my coat and head out the door. My car struggles to turn over, the engine cursing the cold, and I drive to the park by the bay. Kyle is waiting for me on the pier.

I grab the picture frame from the passenger seat and scoot through the snow to meet him. He kisses me.

"Your lips are cold," I say.

"You think? Better warm them up again."

He kisses me, and I melt.

"Thank you for doing this," I say. "I'm glad you had a day off."

"Thank you for asking," he says. "It's an honor. I adored your parents."

We head out onto the frozen bay and stop in front of a hole cut in the ice. Light glows underwater on this dim day. I can see the crucifix below.

I kneel down onto the ice.

"I met my Santa," I say to the bay. "He was right there all along. Just like you said. You raised me to believe in fairy tales. You taught me to believe in Santa. I was raised on hope and Christmas miracles. Thank you."

I open the frame and pour my parents' ashes into the hole in the ice. They sink slowly down into the water and dance around the cross.

"I love you," I whisper. "I will always love you."

I stand, and Kyle hugs me.

"Let's say a prayer," he says.

We bow our heads.

"Wait, look!"

I open my eyes, and Kyle is pointing toward the horizon.

The sun is breaking out from behind the clouds, and the frozen ice shimmers. The glow from the hole in the ice meets the rays in the sky, and the entire bay is bathed in golden light.

"Make a wish," Kyle says.

I think of all the Santas in my life—from my dad and my grampa all the way back to Captain Santa—who believed in the goodness in the world, the kindness in others and the gift of hope. I think of how many times I've been asked to make a wish and how many times I wished for things that no one could ever give me.

Only I could gift myself hope.

"I already did," I say. "And it finally came true."

★ ★ ★ ★ ★

a personal
letter to readers

Growing up in the Ozarks, my parents and grandparents used
to take me to see Santa at a local department store in the near-
est "big" city. My brother and I had our pictures taken with
him nearly every year. I never realized the man in the costume wasn't really Santa until a boy in grade school told me
otherwise. "Grow up!" the kid told me. That was a small but
seminal moment in my life because it signaled a change from
childhood to adulthood.

   Why do we have to grow up? Especially when it comes to
those magical childhood moments and memories? What do
we too often "give up" as adults that we should hold on to?

   A Wish for Winter is a novel about believing and having faith in yourself and others. It's a novel about forgiveness, of yourself and others. It's a book about that critical moment when we go from child to adult, too often in the blink of an eye, and how that can change us forever.

Like so many of you, I'm sure, I used to make a Christmas list when I was a kid. It was often a long laundry list of every new toy and game. But my Grandma Shipman used to always ask me after we'd visit Santa what my wish was. "Not what you want," she'd say, "but what you wish for, more than anything in the world."

After my brother was killed in a tragic accident—much like Susan's parents are in the novel—my only wish was for my holidays and my life to be the way they used to be. "If I could give any child any gift in the world, I would grant you that wish," my grandma told me. "But I can't bring your brother back. No one can. What I can give to you, though, my beautiful boy," she continued, "is the hope that Christmas and life can be the way you want it to be. It can never be the same, but it can be filled with miracles and beauty and wishes you never dreamed or expected. But you have to gift that to yourself."

What do we wish for most in life? Not *things*, as my grandma taught me, but love, happiness, health, home, a passion for what we do. *A Wish for Winter* is about those simple wishes. It's about wanting to find love but fearing getting hurt again. It's about taking chances. It's about missed chances. It's also, I believe, my most unique novel to date. I mean, what if you felt it was your life's destiny to meet a man who had to be dressed as Santa Claus the first time you set eyes on him? The book is populated with a beautifully, kooky cast of characters, inspired by my own diverse, funny, loving family and friends.

A Wish for Winter is also a celebration of books. Susan, the owner of Sleigh By the Bay, is inspired by the real owners of McLean & Eakin Booksellers in gorgeous Petoskey, Michigan, where the novel is set. It's about how books save us, how bookstores are our heart, soul and community as well as how we too often are willing to believe in happy endings in books but not in our own lives.

My wish for you is that you know how much you are loved! I truly hope you love *A Wish for Winter*, and I cannot wait until June when my next summer novel (and it's a doozy!) will publish.

XOXO!
Viola

acknowledgments

First, I must thank all of you for making my wishes and dreams come true. I would not be able to write for a living without your continued love, friendship and support. You share as much of your lives and hearts with me as I do with you, and I am forever grateful and changed as a result.

To my agent, Wendy Sherman, who has been with me since my skin had elasticity. I can never express how much her fierce support and friendship has changed my life and career.

To my editor, Susan Swinwood: I feel as if we were forever destined to work together, and I am constantly grateful for your talent, support, belief, good heart and keen eye. I say it every time: Susan makes every book I write infinitely better with her guidance.

To my publicity team: Kathleen Carter, Heather Connor

and Leah Morse, thank you for working so, so hard and so, so tirelessly to make each book a success.

To Randy Chan: When you see one of my books in your local store, thank Randy.

To Pam Osti: Pam is a marketing maven, and I am forever grateful to her.

To all the indie booksellers across the US: You have become my friends and my heart, and I would not be here today without you. Thank you.

To Gary: My wish, like Susan's in the novel, was to find not just love but a love that would allow me to love myself again. Unconditional love. Love *without* conditions. You personify that. My life and the world is a better, brighter place because of your light.

To Michigan: The beauty of your shores and your people inspire me every day and every book. Your water flows in my veins.

To anyone reading this far: Pretend there is a cake before you, filled with lit candles. Now make a wish and blow!

A WISH FOR WINTER

VIOLA SHIPMAN

Reader's Guide

GRAYDON
HOUSE

1. A major theme of *A Wish for Winter* is loss. Have you ever experienced the loss of a loved one? Especially at an early age? How did that change your life and the life of your family? Did it alter the way you celebrated annual holidays? How?

2. Another significant theme is forgiveness. Have you ever been so angry at someone for hurting you that you found it difficult to forgive them? Conversely, have you ever hurt someone and found it hard to forgive yourself?

3. Does your family—like Susan's in the novel—have a legacy that defines it? What is it? Did that change your life? If so, how?

4. What is the one wish you had in childhood? Did it come true? Why or why not? What is the one wish you have as an adult? Are you working to make it come true?

5. *A Wish for Winter* covers a lot of favorite holidays. Do you have a favorite (Christmas, Valentine's Day, St. Patrick's, Easter, Fourth of July, Halloween, Thanksgiving)? Why? Which still makes you feel most like a kid?

6. I love to write about characters who are over forty and filled with life experience, who have experienced pain, are flawed and are not considered "perfect" by societal beauty standards (like me and Susan). Have you ever felt "less than" in our too exacting world? How did/does that make you feel? How has it affected your life?

7. My novels are meant as a tribute to our elders. Susan is raised by her grandparents; I grew up surrounded by mine and their impact still reverberates. How did your elders influence your life? How, in return, do you influence those in your life?

8. This is a novel about finding love...not just later-in-life romantic love but love of oneself. Have you found true love? Discuss your journey. Have you ever not loved yourself?

9. This is also a novel about not requiring the presence of a partner to be complete, fulfilled, worthy and happy. As I write, there is a difference between lonely and alone. Are you single? Discuss the pressure on women to be coupled in order to "be happy" in society.

10. Susan goes on some awful dates in the novel. What are some of the worst dates you've ever been on? What are the best? Did any lead to true love?

11. All three "Santas" that Susan dates are good, kind men at heart but not *the one*. Do you believe you must love yourself first to find true love? Have you felt you've ever let *the one* slip away?

12. Sleigh By the Bay is inspired by McLean & Eakin, a real-life independent bookseller in Petoskey, Michigan. What is

your favorite indie store? What do you love most about bookstores? (I love EVERYTHING about them!)

13. Do you have a favorite book, or a favorite holiday book? What is your favorite book to gift someone? Is there a poem that's impacted your life?

14. Faith plays a big part in this novel. I believe faith comes to call when you are truly tested in life. Is it important in your life?

15. Winter is as big a character as any of the novel's protagonists. The season actually impacts Susan greatly. Do you like winter? Why or why not?

A
Sugarplum
Christmas

"*[She] still had the wounded Nutcracker wrapped in her handkerchief, and she carried him in her arms. Now she placed him cautiously on the table, unwrapped him softly, softly, and tended to the injuries. Nutcracker was very pale, but he beamed so ruefully and amiably that his smile shot right through her heart.*"

— E.T.A. Hoffmann, *The Nutcracker*

prologue

THE NUTCRACKER BALLET

When I was five, my grandmother took me to see *The Nutcracker*. She drove me all the way to Chicago, prattling the entire time about how magical the experience was going to be. I was a tomboy, more prone to climbing trees than watching ballet. The entire drive, my grandma kept rapping me on the shoulder with her gloved hand.

"Stop fidgeting!" she'd admonish.

I was not used to wearing a pretty dress with a frilly collar, and I felt as if I were being choked.

I pulled on her hand, trying to break free, the entire time we climbed the steps to the ballet and then down the stairs to our seats. I simultaneously rocked in my seat and kicked the back of the one in front of me until a very snooty usher warned my grandma we would be asked to leave unless "the demon child began to exhibit some manners."

"Good!" I answered.

But when the lights went down and the ballet began, I was spellbound. I was no longer Debbie Hutchins. My grandma, wearing her dramatic red cape, was no longer my grandma. We were at a 1915 Christmas Eve party. I was Clara, the young girl given a magical nutcracker doll that came to life in her dreams, battled the evil King of the Mice, and took me to a Crystal Palace full of dancing.

On the ride home, I was the one who couldn't stop prattling on about the ballet. I not only wanted to dance, right that very moment, but also collect those magical nutcrackers.

That Christmas, my grandmother—as usual—packed gifts underneath her silver tree heavy with Shiny Brite ornaments. I had three big packages that I rattled for days as well as one envelope perched in a branch that I unsuccessfully tried to steam open with my grandmother's teapot. My parents, staunch Protestants, were not generous of emotion, gift or leisure time.

"Spare the rod, spoil the child," was my father's mantra.

My grandmother, however, didn't listen.

"Pshaw!" she would say. "Children deserve to be spoiled."

On Christmas Day, I ripped those packages open, tossing paper left and right. I received three German nutcrackers: a soldier, a king and—my favorite—a horseman on a real rocking horse.

I opened the envelope last, and my grandma's gift reduced this tomboy to tears.

"One year of ballet classes," my grandma announced to the room over my heaves.

I spun around the room clumsily, doing my best sugarplum fairy dance, kicking wrapping paper this way and that.

"Thank you, Grandma!" I said. "Thank you, thank you, thank you!"

The next few Christmases, I collected more and more nut-crackers, and more years of dance classes.

And then one holiday as my grandma was putting up her silver tree, there was a crash. She had a heart attack reaching to adjust the star, and we found her lying on top of the tree.

Just like that, she was gone, along with my dreams.

My mom and dad boxed up her belongings and beloved decorations—the silver tree, ornaments, appliqué tree skirts, snow globes—and sold them off at an auction as if she'd never existed, as if she were a fantasy, just like Clara and *The Nutcracker*.

I watched the crowd come like a swarm of locusts and ravage my grandmother's house until it was empty. I watched my parents count the cash on a calculator the size of a dinner plate.

Nothing was real anymore.

So I gathered my nutcrackers and sold them all that day to the highest bidder.

chapter 1

THE NUTCRACKER SOLDIER
DECEMBER 2022

Estate sales are like war. All the junkers arrive before first light, ready to pounce.

I am already late, thanks to the predawn line at Starbucks and the chatty woman in front of me in the drive-through, who acted like she'd never had a Pumpkin Spice Latte in her life. She nearly spilled her latte when I laid on the horn.

My tardiness has relegated me to a side street, a block over from the estate sale, on Heritage Hill, the historic district of stately old homes in Grand Rapids, Michigan.

The beautiful neighborhood, not far from downtown GR, is filled with a mix of some 1,300 historic homes—mansions to bungalows—featuring 60 different architectural styles dating from 1844. It is one of my favorite neighborhoods in the city. My grandma owned a beautiful Victorian, not too far down the block from a Frank Lloyd Wright craftsman—and its massive picture window was the perfect showcase for her Christmas tree.

My heart pangs, and I blame it on the caffeine.

I look at the old home, another Victorian in need of repair, and I already know this will be a good estate sale.

A family that wants to rid itself of its memories and its "junk" as quickly as possible.

The line of cars already parked in front of the house flicker with light from cell phones, cigarettes and radios, and it looks as if a horde of mammoth fireflies has come to life in December. I know many of the junkers by their cars alone. We've been running in the same circles for years. Some own antique malls—the nice ones in cities and lakeshore resort towns—while others run ratty shops on empty town squares in tiny towns across the middle of the Mitten. A few are interior designers, while a couple are home stagers or theatrical set designers. Too many are hoarders, their basements, attics, garages, pole barns and yards filled with anything they can get their hands on. And some, like me, have their own online shops.

Most come seeking very specific items. Top of the list is furniture. For many years, Grand Rapids was known as Furniture City of America, following the city's showcase of its wooden wares at the Philadelphia Centennial Exposition in 1876. Buyers from all over the world looked to Grand Rapids for its fine wood furniture. Many of the factories' workers lived within walking distance of them or close to streetcar lines, while the owners chose to live in large homes high on the bluffs overlooking downtown.

Heritage Hill.

Over time, other materials replaced wood, but nothing

could replace the city as Furniture City. Midcentury furniture soon took hold. Today, buyers at these sales hope to stumble across an overlooked hoop back armchair from the 1800s on which Grandma used to dry dish towels, or a Herman Miller Eames lounge chair hidden behind oil cans in the garage that Great Uncle Joe always thought was too ugly to be in the house.

But I am not here for furniture. I am here for the holiday decor. The boxes and bins filled with the decorations family forgot, or wants to forget, the memories too much to relive.

I seek the snaking strings of lights—the vintage, multicolored, big bulbs—no one can untangle, the dented plastic molds of Santa's jolly face and Rudolph's red nose, the manger scenes missing a Wise Man or a few sheep, leaky snow globes, bottlebrush trees that have lost their snow, heirloom glass ornaments.

And if none of what I buy is truly an heirloom, I can still make it all seem shiny to someone who wants to believe.

I turn around and glance at the house, waiting for the front door to open. Shadows shift in front of the window, and I suddenly see my grandfather—an accountant for a furniture company—and my grandmother, a high school English teacher—hugging in the front window by the Christmas tree.

"One day these memories will all be yours," I can hear my grandma say.

I take a sip of coffee, and again my heart pangs.

Memories. History.

People will believe anything you tell them.

Especially online.

Despite having the entire world of knowledge at their fingertips, they will swallow any story you toss out, hook, line and sinker.

We believe what we want to believe these days, what we

need to believe, and visit those virtual places that reaffirm those beliefs rather than challenge them. This, despite the fact that every fact is available with just a simple click.

Why have we become lemmings?

Why have I become a purveyor of holiday lies?

Online, I am known as *The Sugarplum Fairy*. I welcome buyers into my virtual holiday kingdom filled with antiques and heirlooms, where ripped festive table runners are made of "delicate French lace" and plastic candy canes become "rare vintage ornaments."

It is a kingdom of lies and junk.

A random snowflake appears in the streetlight, and it twirls down onto my windshield, and then instantly disappears.

I think of *The Nutcracker* ballet I watched so long ago with my grandma.

I am not The Sugarplum Fairy who is the ruler of the Land of Sweets; I am The Sugarplum Fairy who is the ruler of the Land of Sweet Memories. But we both have something in common: we live only in people's dreams.

I see a blur of movement and a flash of light, and I turn. The front door is open, and the junkers are on the move. I scurry from my car, locking it with my key fob as I run. The smell of mothballs and pine-scented cleaner overwhelms me as I hit the front door.

"Hi, Debbie!"

Elaine, who owns the estate sale company, greets me with a raised Styrofoam cup of coffee. I slow my jog and take a look around the living room, which seems as if it's been perfectly preserved from the 1970s: mauve shag carpet, a TV console as big as a Buick, orange crackle lamps.

"I'm surprised you're not first today," Elaine continues. "What next?" Elaine acts as if she's peeking out the front door. "No. The earth hasn't frozen over yet."

"Ha ha," I say. "If this estate sale was in Palm Springs, you'd make a fortune. Sorry about that."

"Oh, midcentury is hot again. Check out the prices."

I stop and look at a price tag on a lamp.

"Ouch," I say.

"One of a kind." Elaine eyes me, lifts a brow and takes a sip of coffee as if to keep her from saying what's on her mind: *The real deal. Unlike what you sell.*

Elaine's estate sales are well-respected, well-oiled machines. Items are marked with a selling price, and if a buyer does not want to pay the marked price, she will accept bids, but that means taking the chance that someone will pay the marked price before the sale ends. Everyone at Elaine's sales pays the marked price *or more.* That's because Elaine invites in her top clients first, before opening up the door at 9:00 a.m. when it becomes first come, first served. Elaine well knows, as we all do, that there are too many lookie-loos who will drain your day asking questions, eating the free cookies and bartering, offering a quarter for something marked fifty dollars.

I turn. A line is already forming at the door.

"Where is it?" I ask.

Elaine nods toward the staircase behind her. "All the way up. Don't stop till the top."

I grab the ornate wooden banister and climb three very steep floors, stopping at each landing to catch my breath, before emerging into a large room with a fireplace with a fancy mantel, ornate trim work, gilded wainscoting and a turret. This looks as if it might have been a parlor, a gentleman's office or perhaps even a child's bedroom. I pick a path through all the boxes and wend my way to the turret. There is fabric of muslin and dimity, heavy curtains layered over frilly white, held back by brass pulls. This room is unlike any on the other floors—it's stopped in the 1870s while the rest stopped in the 1970s.

I scan the room. That's when I finally notice the tiny closet, with the door flung open. Inside it, red and green tubs and stacked boxes. There is a sign over the door that reads: "Christmas Decorations."

I jump over a box of children's toys and beeline toward the closet.

Another sign on the side of a tub reads: ITEM #314-ALL DECO-$300.00

I peek inside the cardboard boxes on top: strands of lights with frayed wires, mangled elves, ornaments of pets' paw prints.

"Three hundred dollars!" I yelp. "For this?"

I hear footsteps.

"Oooh," a woman says. "Look at all the holiday decorations!"

"Mine!" I say, grabbing the tag. "I was here first!"

She throws up her hands and gives me a wild-eyed look. She turns to her friend and twirls her finger around her temple to indicate that I'm crazy. I stack boxes in my arms and begin to navigate the stairs. When I reach the bottom, Elaine looks at me and says, "I'm not going to negotiate the price. There's some nice stuff in there."

"Really? How much can I charge to electrocute someone?"

"Oh, I'm sure you'll make it all seem very special to your buyers."

My eyes narrow.

"Listen," Elaine says, sensing my tension. "I'll throw in these, too. I actually had my eye on them for you anyway."

I follow her eyes toward a dusty box of *Encyclopedia Britannica.*

"I know how much your grandmother loved to use them as a teacher."

I forget Grand Rapids is all Six Degrees of Kevin Bacon. Everybody knows someone who knows someone in your family, went to school with someone in your family, or—in my case—had my grandma as an English teacher.

"Thank you." My voice is soft. I pull out my cell and Venmo Elaine my payment. She motions for a mover to help carry my finds to my SUV. I lower the back seats, and soon the car is filled with boxes.

I start to lower the trunk, but stop, curiosity killing the cat. I begin to peek in bins and boxes. I glance at a green bin with a Magic Marker "NC" on its side.

"North Carolina?" I mumble. "Low Country deco? Maybe a gator in a Santa hat?"

I'm able to lift the top of the tub just enough to peek inside.

A nutcracker soldier stares back at me.

chapter 2

THE NUTCRACKER KING

I am alone in the loft of my condo overlooking the Grand River. Flurries fall, illuminated in the holiday lights along the riverfront, and I feel as if I have been catapulted back in time.

My estate sale boxes of holiday decorations are stacked in the loft, an open area above my living space that I use as my office. The lid remains shut on the nutcracker soldier. There are more in there. I have tried diligently over the years of junking to avoid buying nutcrackers, even going so far as to sell them before I've even left an estate sale. They're too painful to even look at.

The box is heavy.

As is my heart.

I've felt alone since the day my grandmother died. It was the day I learned that something you love more than anything can disappear in the blink of an eye and that memories can be just tossed aside as easily as junk.

Junk.

Such an odd word. I once looked it up to trace its origin, discovering that it likely started as a nautical term centuries ago. If I remember correctly, I think it meant "old cable or rope," which was extended from a ship to gather old refuse or any discarded items.

Old rope.

From the present to the past.

I take a deep breath and begin to create listings for my website.

Victorian Holiday Decorations!

New Finds from a Special Time!
Have a "Dickens" of a Christmas This Year!

Miniature Village
Tiny homes representing a Victorian neighborhood (eight total)
Only $199.99!

Delicate Glass Ornaments
Victorian Fruit-Shaped Works of Art (four total)
Only $99.99!

Embellishments
Lace and ribbon images of angels, fairies, birds and stars (20+ total/all sold together)
Only $149.99!

Sheet Music Ornaments
Crafted from Victorian sheet music and patterned paper

(10 total/all sold together)
Only $99.00!

I begin to upload the photos I've taken of the items. I have
spent a few days making them look as if they truly are vintage Victorian. They are not. The houses from the miniature
village are warped, molded and featured tags from Venture,
a discount department store no longer in business. The embellishments were purchased from Michael's, and the sheet
music ornaments were obviously made by children with little
hand-eye coordination.

But I've perched them under Christmas trees and on pine
branches along the river, and even made videos with holiday music.

Most buyers won't even notice the difference. Some will.
They will make my life miserable for a few days when they
ask for their money back. But most will not, or they'll realize it's not worth the fight. It's too much hassle to argue with
an invisible presence. And those who are enraged and go online to warn others with a one-star rating and toxic review
will simply be obliterated by the hundreds of fake accounts I
have created that ensure my rating always stays a solid 4-plus.

But Elaine was also right. There were some lovely finds
among the holiday bins that I purchased. I plan to post those
right before Christmas, when people are desperate for gifts or
holiday decorations for a party, or just feel lonely—and I can
ask the moon for them.

I skew my eyes away from my laptop and toward the bin
of nutcrackers.

And yet I know that if the majority of the decorations I purchased were less than "vintage," the nutcrackers must be, too.

I take another deep breath to steel myself for the next lie.

Heirloom Nutcracker Soldier from Germany
I collected nutcrackers as a child but must part with them
due to a move...looking for a good home for my memo-
ries and protectors...
LOTS more nutcrackers available soon!
Only $650.00!

The price, I know, is only a touch inflated were my find to
be a true vintage nutcracker soldier in good shape. Pristine-
condition nutcrackers can fetch nearly four figures.

I take a sip of my hearty Cab, and then another. It is my
second glass, and the wine—which packs more punch than a
carnival strongman—is already getting to me. I glance at the
box again, and I swear I can see it shake, the nutcrackers trying to break free.

I stand and pull my fleece robe even tighter around my
body. I walk over to the box, kneel on the carpet and lift the
lid.

A wooden soldier nutcracker with a rifle stares at me. I
reach in and pull him free.

My heart skips a beat. He is exquisite. He looks just like
the ones I had as a girl.

The nutcracker is roughly a foot tall, the rifle as big as his
body, and he is perched atop a little stand in black-and-white
boots. He is hand-painted in bold traditional colors. He wears
a top hat with a shiny emblem, a blue coat with red cuffs and
white pants. The soldier has sky blue eyes and a puff of white
hair flowing from the top hat that matches his long beard. A
painted white mustache sits atop eight perfect teeth—four on
the top and four on the bottom—disguising the spot where
the mouth opens.

I know a fake when I see one. This looks incredibly real.

Are my eyes, the wine and all the guilt and memories playing tricks on me? This couldn't be a vintage Erzgebirge nutcracker, could it?

I spin the nutcracker in my hands.

On the bottom is the original sticker: Original Erzgebirge hergestellt in der DDR.

My mind reels, and I take a seat on the floor. I stare at the soldier and then at the box. All of his fellow wooden countrymen are stacked upon one another. I can't help but feel sorry for the way they're carelessly packed.

I pick up another soldier, this one in bright red and white atop a green base, holding a saber. Beneath him is a king holding a scroll. Tumbled to his side is a horseman, much like one I had: a nutcracker riding a rocking horse.

Without thinking, I stand the nutcrackers in a semicircle around my body.

Immediately after my grandmother died, I did the same on the shag carpet in front of my bed. The horseman was set to ride off, the soldiers were lined up before their king, the entire wooden army facing my door, ready to protect me from the evils of the world.

But it was too late: my grandmother was already gone.

My protectors soon followed.

My walls collapsed.

My childhood kingdom faded.

I hear a ding from my laptop.

Someone already wants you.

I actually didn't lie.

I shut my eyes. I can hear my grandma say, "This nutcracker will always protect you, even after I'm gone."

All of a sudden, I stuff a king into one pocket of my robe and the horseman into the other. I throw open the sliding door to my tiny balcony overlooking the river, and the north wind smacks me hard in the face. But it doesn't sober or stop me. I step outside. I dangle the nutcracker soldier, upside down, feet heavenward, over the balcony.

"I hope you can fly," I say.

I can't let go of the past.

I can't let go of my sadness.

I can't let go of my anger.

But I can let go of this nutcracker, just like I did so long ago.

The cold numbs my fingers, and I begin to unclench my hand.

My grip loosens, and I am about to let go when I see the soldier's rifle flutter.

My eyes, tearing up in the wind, blurred from the cold and wine, are deceiving me, and I shake my head to clear it.

And that's when I see it: what looks like a scrap of paper, wrapped around the rifle, fluttering in the wind.

I tighten my hand around the nutcracker at the last second and head back inside. I wipe my eyes, take a seat at my desk and train my lamp on the nutcracker's arm.

It *is* a piece of paper, bound around the rifle and sealed, barely, with a piece of yellowed transparent tape. I stand, head down to my bathroom and grab a pair of tweezers. When I return, I begin to unhinge the tape with the tweezers, slowly and carefully, one millimeter at a time so as not to tear the old paper. Suddenly, the tape gives, and the paper comes to life, springing forth as if it has filled its lungs with oxygen after years of being suffocated.

I take the paper and unfold it. It looks as if it came from a small notepad, like the kind my grandma used to keep by her rotary phone to jot down a number. There is slanted handwriting, pretty cursive in ink now faded to the color of a bruise. The words are tiny, and I squint. I put on my readers

34

and hold the paper to my eyes by the lamp. The number *one*, in a circle, sits in the upper left hand of the page.

Dear Gabriel:
I doubt you will ever know me. Probably only as the great-grandma who died in her relic of a home surrounded by the things she loved. My mind is fading. I am old. You are a baby. I can only hope you will remember me. Remember family. Remember the history that made us who we are.

These nutcrackers are part of our history.

Our ancestors were born in the Erzgebirge region of East Germany. Mining was the way of life. When the ore was depleted, the Wagners had to seek a new way to feed their families. So, our people went into woodcarving. Our homeland became famous for our Christmas traditions, namely, the nutcracker.

The letter abruptly ends.
"No!" I say out loud.
I grab the king from my robe pocket. There is no paper. I take the horseman from my other pocket.
"Yes!"
A worn piece of paper is halved and tucked under the tiny black leather strap that serves as the horse's rein. I move the nutcracker's hand holding the rein just enough to get the tweezers in to grab the paper. I open it, my heart racing. There is a number *three* in a circle at the top left of the paper.
"No!" I say. "Where's two?"
I race to the nutcrackers I placed in a semicircle on the floor and begin grabbing one after another, searching their wooden bodies and accoutrements for any sign of paper.
Nothing.

I sit back and rock, just like the little horse sitting on my desk still is after my sudden departure. Returning to my desk, I pick up my wine, take a healthy sip and then grab the remaining letter number three.

"I might be missing a puzzle piece, but I still have you."

I know my random scroll of memories, or these nutcrackers, may never reach you...

I stop.
Scroll!
I grab the nutcracker king and gently pop off the top of the scroll he is holding.

"You are a crafty woman," I say to the king.

Inside is a piece of paper, rolled just like a scroll. I extract it with my tweezers and unroll it. It is a much bigger piece of paper, a slightly longer letter. A number *two* sits at the top.

Today, the nutcracker is probably the most famous legacy of Erzgebirge (besides you, my angel!). Its figures of kings, soldiers and gendarmes represented society of the time. According to German legend, nutcrackers are considered a symbol of good luck and bring protection to a family and its home. And, according to folklore, a puppet-maker created a doll with a mouth for a lever to crack nuts and won a nut-cracking contest.

These nutcrackers not only saved the place where our family started, but they saved me, too. When I was little, they were my protectors, my friends. When I grew up, I would set them on my mantel during the holidays. I not only felt protected and safe, I felt like I was home. I felt like my family surrounded me.

I knew Christmas was finally here.

If you receive these, my legacy will be fulfilled. I doubt you will, though. Maybe I'm just using this as a way to write my final memories, or play a game with my family to see if I really mattered. I will never know. Only you will. I doubt it. My kids were never one for embracing tradition. They want new. History could be thrown out like the bathwater.

Letter two ends, and I grab the third, starting where I'd left off:

I know my random scroll of memories, or these nutcrackers, may never reach you, and I know if you do receive my collection, you'll wonder what this has to do with you. But one day you will be my age, and you will reflect on your life. Will those around you even see you as human any longer, or just "old"? How we view people—and things—that have aged and survived defines us as souls and societies. Do they mean something? Or do we just toss them aside?

I can feel my heart rise into my throat.

I hope these end up in your hands. You continue our lineage. But that doesn't mean our family history survives. It requires effort. You have your whole life ahead. May these nutcrackers fill you with memories and bring you good luck. I love you, my angel Gabriel. And I will be with you forever through these nutcrackers, even if I'm not there. Merry Christmas. Gigi (Great Grandma Ingrid)

I pick up the rocking horse and hold it close to me. And then I bow my head and weep.

chapter 3

THE NUTCRACKER HORSEMAN

I wake up on the sofa in my loft. A line of nutcrackers sits before me, a line of protection.

There is a creak. The nutcracker horseman rocks gently in the heat blowing from the vent. The horseman sports a black mustache and regal hat, a bright blue jacket with gold embellishment, and an expression that looks deeply serious—as if he's about to deliver a note of grave importance to the king—but is lightened by delightfully rosy cheeks. The horse's mane is soft and gray as if it's been dusted in snow, but its rocking horse body is painted in bright, celebratory colors and whimsical design, almost as if it's a carousel come to life.

Questions circle in my head, as the horse rocks.

What is it about the face of a toy that makes you feel so safe and loved? Why can we remember a finite memory from decades ago and yet forget to put gas in our cars?

Is it the memory itself, or is it our desire to go back in time before we had been scarred by life? Is it the toy, or instinctual need to feel safe and loved again?

Do we rid ourselves of our heirlooms in order to declutter our lives, or do we rid ourselves of these memories to defend ourselves from more pain?

I stare at the nutcracker.

My second year in ballet, our class was invited to participate in a regional production of *The Nutcracker*. I was so excited that when my grandma came to pick me up from class, I sprinted to her with such velocity that I knocked her onto the ground.

"Part tomboy, part ballerina," she laughed, as two parents helped her up. "Let's focus on the ballerina part."

The youngest girls were picked to be dancing lambs, and my class was selected to be dancing flowers. We attended only the rehearsals that included us, and I couldn't sleep for weeks leading up to opening night. The night before my performance, my parents informed me they had to work.

"Work always takes priority over play," my father told me.

"I'm not playing," I said.

"It's all pretend," he remarked.

The disappointment nearly spoiled my performance.

"Drown out all the noise," my grandma told me before the show began. "*The Nutcracker* may be 'pretend,' but it makes us feel better. And there's much too little of that in the world."

I will never forget my first real show. My "stems" were shaking so hard, I didn't even know if I could spin. The lights were blinding, but somehow I still managed to locate my grandma's face in the crowd, beaming brighter than the spotlights. I couldn't help myself: I waved, and my grandma threw a gloved hand over her mouth to stifle her laughter.

I stood in the wings and watched the rest of the ballet, mesmerized. I was stunned when a real horse trotted out on stage.

"A horse!" I blurted, earning me a chorus of "Shhs" from the crew.

You can only imagine my reaction when the horse began to dance around to the music, as if it were a premier danseur. I didn't realize until the horse pranced offstage that it was actually two men in a very realistic costume.

By the end of my first performance of *The Nutcracker* I more fully understood the passion, the beauty, the music, the talent and the commitment.

Moreover, I understood the meaning and tradition of Christmas. It was meant to be magical. It was meant to remind us to slow down and appreciate the wonder and meaning of the season. It was meant to be spent with family.

I stare at the nutcracker horseman, still rocking.

You can rid yourself of everything in life but memories.

I am seated by the window at one of my favorite coffee shops in downtown Grand Rapids. I come here nearly every day for the coffee. I live for their holiday latte, which has a touch of eggnog and gingerbread. It is Christmas in a mug, without being cloyingly sweet.

But, mostly, I come here for the memories. The less painful ones, anyway.

They roast their own beans, and the entire place—even from a mile away—smells like coffee. They also bake their own goodies: glorious streusel-topped blueberry and caramel apple muffins, scones, breads and cookies.

The shop, located in a tight, two-story building that used to be a home, smells exactly like my grandparents' house did during the holidays: sugar, and spice and everything nice.

My laptop dings. My heart pings.

Nice.

I know the exact moment I stopped being nice. But why did I allow the pain to take root, then consciously water the tendrils and let them take over my soul?

A car honks, and I look up.

My seat faces an intersection, one that looks akin to a very complicated Venn diagram, streets zigzagging in four nonsensical directions from the center point in front of me. There is an accident here nearly every day.

When I look out, especially on a winter's day like this, I can still picture the time when horse-drawn carriages trotted up and down the streets, locals dressed to the nines on their way to grand holiday parties on Heritage Hill.

My mind whirs to the nutcrackers. I took pictures of them around town before I came here. I placed the king in front of the grand steps leading to the city's public library. Snow was gently falling, and the photo looks as if it had been taken two hundred years ago in some faraway land. The rocking horse I placed in front of the hobby farm at the local zoo, goat and sheep in the background. At the last minute, I found an acorn, and I placed it in the horseman's mouth, careful not to scrape his painted face. I want to show how incredibly constructed these works of art truly are and how well they've been maintained. I uploaded the images when I settled in at the coffee shop.

"Ma'am?"

I look up. A girl in an apron stands before me. She looks twelve. She is all dewy skin, sparkly eyes and no wrinkles.

I am a "ma'am" now. *When did that happen? But* I already know: it happened a long time ago, when I lost all hope. I am a "ma'am" to the younger generation: a nondescript woman of a certain age. I glance at my reflection in the window. I've let my hair go gray, and it's not that stunning silver so many women are blessed to have, but instead the dingy color of an old car bumper. My readers are as red as my too-round cheeks, I am not wearing makeup and I am sporting a nubby sweater that is incredibly comfortable but not what anybody might ever describe as attractive.

"Ma'am?"

I look up again. "Sorry."

"Would you like to try one of our Christmas cookies?"

"Oh, no, thank you," I say.

"They're free. A thank-you to our customers."

I finally look at the tray she is holding. It is filled with beautiful sugar cookies in shapes of bells, angels and trees, inch-thick frosting coating each one. They look like delicious works of art.

The room spins for a moment. I can picture my grandmother in her apron, hand atop mine, helping me press shapes into dough with her heirloom Christmas cookie cutters. Then we'd ice them a mile high and make the bells sparkle with sprinkles. I would always sneak a few cookies to my nutcrackers, too, as pretend sustenance.

"I'd better not," I say.

"Okay," she says. "Have a great day."

The girl turns, and then at the last second swivels toward me again.

"Why not?" she asks. "It's almost Christmas. Maybe this is just the thing that puts you in the holiday spirit and makes this day better than any other." She looks at me. "I've already had three."

Her name tag reads "Olivia," and she's drawn a happy face in the O and put little hearts over the i's.

How nice must it be to be this unscarred by life. To believe that life can be so simple: you eat a Christmas cookie and a sweet day comes to life. How nice to try to make a friend with a small gesture. To be brave enough to reach out in the first place.

Olivia decides for me, placing a Santa—beard thick with frosting—on a napkin beside my mug and laptop.

"My grandma says nothing can stop the holiday spirit. But that sometimes holiday spirit is like a dance, and somebody's gotta take the lead."

She walks away, and my laptop pings.

I have a full-price offer from a buyer for all three nutcrackers: The soldier, king and horseman. —nc59

I open the calculator on my laptop and add up my bounty.
And I have A LOT more! I type.
I want them ALL! nc59 types back.
It is going to be a great Christmas after all, I think.
I grab the cookie and take a celebratory bite. I shut my eyes.
It tastes like...home.
I open my eyes and type, DEAL!
I hover my finger over the return key, ready to accept the offer, when a little girl in a winter coat walks inside. She is wearing tights and ballet slippers.

Her mom follows, yelling, "Your shoes! Your shoes!"

The girl struts to the counter and opens her coat, revealing a glittery pink tutu. "One hot chocolate and one cookie that looks like Santa!" she says with all the confidence of an adult.

The room whirls again.

I see the cookie in front of me. I stare at the nutcracker on my screen. I see my reflection in the window.

And then I see what I must do as clearly as the little girl pirouetting with her cookie.

But can I do it?

I shut my laptop, wrap my cookie in a napkin and shove it in my coat pocket, rushing out of the coffeehouse.

chapter 4

THE NUTCRACKER DROSSELMEYER

Growing up, one of my favorite holiday activities was watching old Christmas cartoons with my grandma: *A Charlie Brown Christmas, Frosty the Snowman, How the Grinch Stole Christmas, Santa Claus Is Comin' to Town*.

But my favorite of all time might have been *Rudolph the Red-Nosed Reindeer*. I loved the way the stop-motion movie looked. It was magical, almost as if I were dreaming, and my entire life was a cartoon. Sometimes, I would fall asleep, and when I'd wake up, I'd be curled next to my grandma, a quilt over my body. If I'd wake up with a start, she would caress my hair and say, "It's okay. I'm right here. I'm right here. Everything's okay."

My grandma made me—this part tomboy, part dancer girl—feel special. My grandma made me feel loved.

That's really why I loved *Rudolph* so much: I often felt like I belonged on the Island of Misfit Toys. I felt cast away and unwanted by my own strict parents.

I felt for the Charlie-in-the-Box who wasn't Jack, the spotted elephant, the train with square wheels, the bird that swam, the boat that couldn't stay afloat, the cowboy who rode an ostrich and, especially, the two tin soldiers who wanted to be made of wood.

All we want as children is to feel safe and loved. Feeling like a misfit can arise for a host of reasons, none of which are in our control. Maybe we are born with red hair and freckles, maybe we have brown eyes instead of blue, maybe we like to climb trees and dance, or maybe we just want our mother and father to tell us they love us more than anything in the world, that we're the center of their universe and they will protect us no matter what.

Too often, feeling like a misfit leaves a scar that never heals.

You grow up feeling like a water pistol that squirts jelly.

I stare at the nutcrackers.

Or a tin soldier that wants to be made of wood.

I have come home with a mission. I have come home to test my misfit-ness.

I am curled up on the couch, just as I used to do with my grandma. I have a cup of hot chocolate, stacked with a mountain of marshmallows. On my TV, ready to play, is the classic 1977 version of *The Nutcracker* with Mikhail Baryshnikov and Gelsey Kirkland.

Will I be moved by the ballet as I was a child? Or is my Christmas spirit already as dead as Jacob Marley?

I hit Play.

At first, I watch, distanced. Slowly, my fingers begin to dance on my mug, and then my feet twirl. I realize after a while that I am sitting up, spine straight, mesmerized.

I watch Baryshnikov and Kirkland dance as one, and I can hear the young barista's voice echo in my head: "My grandma says nothing can stop the holiday spirit. But that sometimes holiday spirit is like a dance, and somebody's gotta take the lead."

When *The Nutcracker* is over, I realize I've had the story wrong my entire life. It's not about Clara, first love or even the eternal fantasy of Christmas come to full life. No, this is Drosselmeyer's story, the "sort of Santa" who makes everything happen. Drosselmeyer is the uncle of the nutcracker prince, who is then transformed into a wooden doll by the Mouse King. Every moment on stage is Drosselmeyer's attempt to break the spell of long ago and bring his nephew back to life.

I stand up suddenly.

"I am Drosselmeyer!"

My dramatic exclamation in the quiet of my condo stuns me and then emboldens me.

"Only I can break the spell! If not, I will continue on, as wooden as I've always been."

My laptop dings.

Do we have a deal? And how much for the other nutcrackers? I want them ALL! Please let me know ASAP! —nc59

Yet again, I do not respond.

Instead, I google *Ingrid Wagner obituary*.

Her death notice pops up. But, really, it's the story of her life, all our lives: A family that immigrated to America for a better life. A woman who worked and sacrificed her whole life for her family. A woman who gave back to the community. A woman who loved heirlooms.

A life summed up in 250 words.

I find what I'm looking for at the end.

She is survived by a grandson, Stephen Wagner of Grand Rapids, his wife, Beth, and a great-grandson, Gabriel.

"Bingo," I say.

I grab my cell and call Elaine.

"Merry Christmas," she says when she answers. "How are your online holiday sales going?"

"I need a favor," I say. "I need a phone number and an address."

"You know I can't do that, MacGyver," she says.

I explain, for the first time, my story, my life, my love and my loss.

Elaine is silent for the longest time. For a moment, I think she's hung up the phone.

"Do you have a pen?" she finally says.

I am sitting outside a stranger's home. In the mirror, I can see the faces of the nutcrackers staring at me as if I'm about to drop my kids off at a friend's home for a sleepover. They look excited, but a touch afraid.

"I feel you," I say.

I take a deep breath, step out of my car, grab the box and head to the front door.

It is a lovely home in Ada, a gorgeous suburb outside the city filled with large homes on expansive lawns. I stop before I ring the bell. It is so quiet out here that I can hear the whisper of the light snow as it falls.

"You must be Debbie?"

There is a whoosh of warm air when the door opens. The woman before me is as rosy-cheeked as the nutcrackers.

"Just put everything in the oven for dinner," she says. A man appears behind her. "Well, I can't take credit for it. Steve cooked tonight. We take turns, now that we both work from home."

They are both wearing jeans, black sweaters and wooly socks.

A Gap ad come to life, I think.

"Oh, I'm sorry. I'm Beth," she continues, extending her hand.

"Steve," he says. "It's nice to meet you. Come in. Please."

I stop on the entry rug. The home is beautiful, a new-construction farmhouse meant to look old but eye-poppingly perfect: gleaming dark wood floors lead to an open-concept living room with a towering stone fireplace and a mammoth kitchen with two counters, white shiplap contrasted against black window frames.

"Should I take off my shoes?"

"No," Beth says with a laugh. "We have a three-year-old. We wear socks to wipe up the messes as we go."

I smile.

"But you already know that," she continues. "Come, have a seat."

She takes my coat, and I follow them into the living room. Steve gestures to the couch, where the most adorable boy is seated, eyes transfixed on a holiday cartoon on the television. I know it instantly when I hear the deep voice of Burl Ives.

Rudolph the Red-Nosed Reindeer.

"Say hello to Mrs. Hutchins, Gabriel," Beth says.

His eyes skew in my direction. I can tell he doesn't like the intrusion.

"Hi," he says with a tiny wave.

But then Gabriel sees I am holding a box. When I set it on the coffee table and take a seat, he leans forward and glances inside.

"Toys!" he yells. "For me?"

"Gabriel," Steve says in his best dad voice. "Mrs. Hutchins is here for a very special reason. I'm going to turn off the TV for a bit so we can talk."

"No!" he says.

"It's okay," I say. "*Rudolph* is my favorite!"

Gabriel skews his eyes at me again. "Why?"

"Well, Rudolph saves the day for Santa. And I love all the misfit toys."

"Why?"

"Because they're all special like Rudolph." I nod at the box. "Like these nutcrackers."

"Would you like something to drink?" Beth asks.

I look at Gabriel. He's drinking hot chocolate topped with marshmallows.

"I'll have what he's having," I say.

Beth laughs. "*When Harry Met Sally.* Loved that movie. One cocoa coming up."

When we are all seated, we chat for a few minutes and watch the last few minutes of *Rudolph.* Then Steve turns off the TV.

"I can't tell you how surprised I was to receive your call," Steve finally starts. "I'd actually forgotten my grandmother had all these nutcrackers." He stares at the box. There is a long pause, before he looks up at me and says, "I had no say in the estate sale. I just want you to know that. I just..."

He stops. Beth leans over in the chair next to his and rubs his leg. "He has a lot of guilt over the way things went down."

"My parents just wanted everything gone," he says. "My grandmother was sick for a very long time. I think they just couldn't deal with the memories any longer, but it didn't sit well with me."

All of a sudden, everything around me—the fire, the candles, the lamps—seems to take on a new light. His words make me recalibrate my entire life.

Is that why my parents got rid of everything, because they couldn't deal with the painful memories?

Is that why I did, too?

"I come from a similar family," I finally say.

Steve reaches over and plucks the rocking horse nutcracker from the box. He holds it up and stares at it. Then, like a kid, he makes a whinnying sound, before placing the nutcracker on his lap and rocking it to and fro.

"Daddy," Gabriel giggles.

"I used to play with these all the time at Christmas when I was a kid," he says to his son. "Here."

He hands me the rocking horse, and I give it to Gabriel. He mimics his father's whinny and then rocks it back and forth on the couch. "Ride, horsey, ride."

Steve looks into the fire and then at me.

"My grandma used to tell me so many stories about the history of our family—and these nutcrackers—when I was a boy. She said these nutcrackers represented power and strength, and that they were like a watchdog guarding our family from evil and danger. That's why they bared their teeth. They were symbols and protectors of goodwill. What was the quote she used to say about nutcrackers? Something along the lines of, 'Don't be afraid, though my look is grim. I won't bite. My heart is filled with happiness.'"

He looks at his son rocking the horse.

"She told me that nutcrackers embodied the cycle of life. When a nut falls, it grows into a strong tree that lives for many years in order to nourish not only the land but also the legacy of our ancestral woodcrafters. In the spring, she would take me out to sit under the grand, old trees in her yard and make me listen to the rustle of the wind through their leaves. 'It's your history whispering,' she would say."

Steve is silent for the longest time. When I look at him, his chin is quivering.

"I loved that woman. I miss her so much."

"Are you okay, Daddy?" Gabriel asks.

Steve gathers himself. "I am, buddy. I'm good." He looks at me. "I'm sorry. It's the holidays, and I'm a little more emotional than usual this year. You said you had notes from her? May I see them?"

"Of course. I'm so sorry. That's why I'm here."

I reach into the box and retrieve a storage bag, where I've placed the notes, and hand it to Steve. He reads the notes, handing each one to his wife after he has finished. When he's done, he lifts his head and shuts his eyes, mouthing what seems like a silent prayer to himself.

Steve stands, picks up the box of nutcrackers and sits on the floor in front of the fireplace. "C'mere, buddy."

Gabriel toddles off the sofa and tumbles into his father's arms.

"These are from Gigi, your great-grandmother."

"Gigi?" Gabriel asks. He lifts his shoulders very dramatically, not understanding.

"She was *my* grandma, just like Grandma Sue and Grandma Loraine are to you. I used to play with these nutcrackers at Christmas when I was a boy your age. Gigi wanted you to have these."

"Me? Why?"

"Because she loved you, even though she hardly knew you."

"Why?"

"Because she was a part of you, and you were a part of her. These nutcrackers are part of our family. They represent tradition. They represent home. They represent Christmas." He stops. "They represent love. A love that never ends."

Steve looks at me from the floor.

"And this amazing woman knew that. She found these and found us because she knew Gigi wanted us to have them, so love and memories would always fill our home."

"Thank you," Gabriel says.

"You're welcome," I say. "I used to have nutcrackers when I was a little girl. My grandma gave them to me."

"What happened to them?" Beth asks.

"I…" I hesitate. "I lost them. But I know these little guys were meant to come here. They were meant to come home again."

A buzzer goes off in the kitchen.

"Well," I say, "I best let you have dinner. I'm sorry to have taken so much of your time, and I'm so grateful you allowed me to reach out to you and return these."

Steve and Beth stand, and they walk me to the door. I put on my coat. "Thank you again," I say.

"No," Steve says. "Thank *you*."

He opens his arms and hugs me tightly. Beth opens the door for me, and I'm about to step into the snow when I hear, "Wait!"

I turn.

Gabriel comes toddling toward me, all adorably off-kilter, holding something behind his back.

"You lost your…" He stops and looks at his dad.

"Nutcrackers," Steve says.

"Yeah! And you found ours. So you need one, too."

From behind his back, he produces the rocking horse. "It's…"

This time he looks at his mom. She reads his mind.

"Special," Beth says.

"Yeah! Like you."

The pure innocence of this child's gesture catches me completely off guard, and I am suddenly reduced to tears. I stand in these strangers' home shedding decades of guilt, sadness, loss and regret. I cry even harder when the entire family embraces me as one.

"Thank you," I say. "You will never know how much this has meant to me."

"We can say the exact same thing," Steve says.

On my drive home, the nutcracker horseman rocks back and forth, and back and forth, sitting on my dashboard. With the snow falling on the windshield, the nutcracker looks as if he's riding wildly through a winter storm trying desperately to make it home for Christmas.

epilogue

THE NUTCRACKER BALLET
DECEMBER 2023

The snow dances as the Rat Pack sings. Alexa is playing my grandparents' favorite holiday music: Dean Martin and Frank Sinatra. I smile at my reflection in the mirror and then give myself a little wave.

"I've missed you," I say.

I barely recognize myself, inside and out.

On the outside, I've certainly undergone a transformation: I am walking—and even jogging—again, along the riverfront, through Heritage Hill, even downtown. My hair has gone from gray to silver. I wanted to own my age, but I also wanted to be—as Olivia at the coffeehouse recently called me—a "silver fox."

I am wearing makeup again. Not a lot, but enough to bring

out my best features and also make me feel as if I'm not only celebrating the season but most importantly *me*.

I move to my little closet and scan the racks.

I am about to grab something warm and comfortable—another cute but nubby and well-worn holiday sweater—but instead pick out an all-black outfit: a tailored blouse and jacket, tapered pants and a pair of new, very high, black leather boots. I dress, tucking and lint-brushing as I go, and reach for my winter coat when "A Marshmallow World" by Frank and Dean begins to play. I smile and sing along.

I reach into the back of my closet and yank a garment bag loose, rattling hangers as I pull it free. I take it to my bed and unzip the bag.

My grandmother's Christmas cape—as red as Rudolph's nose—looks at me. This is the cape she wore when she took me to see *The Nutcracker*.

"Perfect," I say.

I toss it around my shoulders with all the drama of a flamenco dancer and then pin it with a beautiful holiday brooch in the shape of a Christmas tree.

I head to the kitchen and grab my car keys when my laptop pings with a message.

Are you still open?

My online store, The Sugarplum Fairy Shoppe, has a flashing banner that reads:

Temporarily Closed!
Opening again soon under new management.

I chuckle at my inside joke.

I am the "new" management, of course, except this time I

will do it right, offering true heirlooms at a fair price. And I will have a partner, just like Frank had with Dean.

Earlier this year, I went into business with Elaine. She actually reached out to me—fittingly—last Valentine's Day, and we met for coffee.

"You've always had such a great eye, and I've always known you had a great heart, too," she said, looking out at the drifts piled along the sidewalk. "It was just buried."

Elaine then pulled out her laptop along with a business plan. My name was listed at the top. Her idea: we merge our businesses. Her estate sale company was growing and needed additional power and funding.

"I'm losing a large percentage of every sale," Elaine explained. "The clients take a huge chunk, then I invite my favorite customers who buy the rest of the quality items at a good price, before the lookie-loos come to nickel-and-dime me. I thought, 'What if I were to take the best items from the estates and sell them online, where most people are shopping these days?' You've done such a great job at this, Debbie... It just hasn't always been the most, shall we say, ethical? What if we teamed up for an exclusive shop that listed heirlooms of only the highest quality? Furniture, holiday decorations, clothing, home goods? We could be unstoppable."

I am now very cash poor, but—for the first time in decades—emotionally rich.

Check back soon! I write. Prepare to have your mind blown!

I jump into my car and point it toward Ada.

"You're late," Beth says when she opens the door. "But I can see why. You look amazing."

I spin. Twice.

We hug, and I hear a squeal. Gabriel races toward me. I pick him up and twirl again. He giggles.

"You look very dapper," I say, touching his adorable little bow tie.

He looks at me curiously.

"Dapper means handsome," I say.

He looks at me again.

"I missed you!" I say.

"Me, too. C'mon!"

I look at Beth, and she shrugs. Gabriel grabs my hand, and I follow him into the living room, past all the guests the Wagners have invited to their holiday open house, waving at Steve as I go.

"Sit!" Gabriel tells me. "On the floor!"

I do as instructed.

"Shut your eyes!"

I hear rustling. "Okay! You can open them now."

A gift, wrapped only as it could be by a child, sits on my lap. The wrapping paper is already coming off, and a bow has been slapped onto the top. It couldn't be cuter.

I open it, and my face breaks into a huge smile.

"I got to make a Christmas present for someone in my family at school," he says excitedly. "So I made this for you!"

It's a drawing of a nutcracker, done in crayon, with lots of glitter and glue. Gabriel has glued nuts and acorns in the shape of a heart around the nutcracker.

Something about this simple gift and the words Gabriel has used—especially *family*—makes tears spring to my eyes.

"Are you sad?"

"No, I'm happy."

I hug him. When I look up, Beth and Steve are standing with their hands on their hearts.

"I will treasure this forever," I say.

For the last year, I've seen Gabriel and the Wagners every month or so. They've invited me to dinner, and I attended

Gabriel's preschool class's fall concert. We've gone to the zoo. We've, of course, gone junkin' for nutcrackers. I feel like I have a family again.

"You changed us," Steve told me last spring. "You made us remember who we are as a family and what matters most."

"No, you changed me," I told him. "Forever."

I stand, and Steve offers me a drink. I check my watch.

"I'd love to, but I have to go," I say.

"Where are you off to in such a hurry?" Beth asks.

"I have a ticket to *The Nutcracker*."

"Well, if that's an excuse to get out of here, it's the best one I've ever heard," Steve says.

I laugh and give them all big hugs. "Merry Christmas!" I call on my way out the door.

I listen to the ballet's music as I drive to the theater. My heart pounds with excitement as the lights flash and the crowd is seated. And then my seat begins to shake. I turn, and a little girl is kicking the back of my chair with her foot.

"I don't want to be here!" she says.

The little girl is fidgeting with the bow on her head.

"I'm so sorry," the mother mouths to me.

"It's okay," I say.

Because I've been there. Because I know.

"Did you know nutcrackers bring good luck?" I ask the little girl.

She gives me a look and crosses her arms with complete indignation.

"And that if you believe in the magic of Christmas, then all of your dreams will come true?"

She drops her arms. "Really?" she asks.

"Really," I say. "What's your name?"

"Molly."

"What a beautiful name." The lights dim. "Oh, it's about to start. Enjoy!"

The mother looks at me, and her face eases. "Thank you."

An usher standing guard in the aisle mouths the mother's words to me, too.

The lights go down and the ballet begins. After a few numbers, I turn as quietly as I can in my chair. The little girl's mouth is wide open. She is still. Her hand flutters like a butterfly to the music.

The magic of Christmas has come to life in front of her very eyes.

I turn back.

Mine, too.

★ ★ ★ ★ ★